TALK *Nerdy* TO ME

C.M. Owens

Chapter 1

BRITT

This is going well already. That's sarcasm, in case you're wondering. Using sarcasm proves to be simpler than detecting it.

"What are the odds that the manager, assistant manager, and backup assistant manager all get sick on the one weekend you're in charge?" Raya asks as she starts getting the bar ready.

I had to call in the favor she owed me because the usual bartender, on top of everything else, decided to move to New York to pursue modeling.

Today.

This morning, to be exact.

"There's not an exactitude on the odds, but I can show you the math I did on it earlier, if you're being literal," I state to Raya.

She blinks. "Of course you did the math."

I'm not sure if she wants to see it or not, but it'll have to wait until I finish. I'm struggling with all the things to do that I don't fully understand how to do. Since everyone else is busy watching the band warm up, I'm busy setting up the VIP booths on my own.

It's Under 21 weekend, I remind myself. I don't need to serve alcohol. I simply charge the same prices for the virgin alternatives, and don't let the club burn to the ground—Dane's parting words of guidance.

Virgin. I'm essentially running Virgin weekend. The irony is almost frustrating.

"I can wait tables, too." Raya smiles as though she feels she's successfully staved off my impending meltdown.

I look down, trying to figure out if we've done enough to recover from the abrupt, maddening issues.

In my head, this all worked out spectacularly. Harley and I even plotted out hypotheticals of every conflict that could arise and how I should handle it. Yet we didn't plan for this. We couldn't have seen these hurdles coming, due to the minute fraction of a chance something like this *could* happen.

As usual, the human element messed up the plans my head had.

"Hi," a smooth, male voice says from behind me, interrupting my conversation with Raya—who has already abandoned me, apparently.

How long was I inside my own head?

A throat clearing from behind me reminds me someone is beckoning for my attention. Remembering it's considered rude to simply ignore people, I turn to face whoever it is.

Before my eyes can even find my beckoner, I'm distracted by the burlesque dancers…who are stripping down to their lingerie to get ready for the stage.

They need their masks on! No one is supposed to get down to their lace without a mask. Dane specifically stated that rule to me five times, apparently forgetting I have an eidetic memory. It appears as if it's them he should have been repeating himself for.

"Hi," I say, though my attention is still focused on the maskless ladies, who are joining all the other rebels by skipping simple rules. "What do you want?"

He snickers as though something is funny, so I finally face him.

And I go a little…rigid.

It's rare the words in my mouth don't come out.

I'm just gawking and standing perfectly still, eyes wide as I take him in.

Base Masters. I'm not sure why I'm so surprised to see him, since he's one of the few allowed to be in here before hours.

I've never had to see him this close before, and now I'm getting this weird feeling in the pit of my stomach. And lower. Oh, yes—arousal. Now I recognize it.

Being aroused has never left my body unable to function, though. My mouth is still parted like it expects to expel more words, but…still…nothing. I'm just gaping in most every sense of the word.

What's wrong with me?

His dark hair is sticking up in short spikes that actually suit him. I think he has on eyeliner, but I could be wrong. He's a lot taller, so I'm still gaping with my head tilted back so that I can see him. I'm positive it's not a very attractive scene.

A black T-shirt that says "*The Fallen*" is fitted against his body like he wants to hint to the lean contours of definition it barely conceals.

I stare at that too. And his arms that have some ink peeking out from under the short sleeves, alluding to hidden tattoos.

He's smirking while my eyes move over him, idly wondering how long I can look before it becomes rude or imposing. Deciding it's been long enough, I yank my gaze back to the masquerade women.

"Actually, I think I know the answer to my question now," he says, looking me over as though he's amused.

Don't trust my judgment on assessing moods, though. For all I know, he could be constipated. I've mistaken the two before.

He shakes his head; however, I don't know why he does it. "That's a real shame," he says on a long sigh.

What?

"What question do you know the answer to? And what's a shame?" I ask as he turns away, the ability to speak returning with the loss of his attention, as though the two are linked.

A phenomenon I will definitely explore later.

He just laughs as he walks away, leaving me thoroughly confused, but I have more important things to worry about.

I have to keep my brother's club from falling apart for one night.

Chapter 2

BASE

"She's gay, and that means we can't compete with mostly naked women in sexy lingerie if she's gay. She was just too distracted to hear us playing. So we're good. Let's get ready. People are pouring in now," I tell the guys.

"Who's gay?" Sticks asks while adjusting the height on one of his cymbals.

"The girl who wasn't hypnotized by us," Taylor snorts, rolling his eyes at me.

"You're so fucking vain," Sticks says pointedly at me.

"A potential label is coming tonight. Just needed my head on right," I say unapologetically. "Stage performance is fifty/fifty on talent and mentality. Everything needs to be on."

"This is gonna be the one. I can feel it," Randy says, tense and likely to fuck up five or six times each song.

He's not great when he's on. He's terrible when he's tense. Which means we need to sound twice as good tonight to cover for his less than stellar performance.

Sticks gives me a look like he's thinking the same thing. But we're a band.

"You bitches just try not to mess anything up," Randy says as he winks at us. "I know how nervous you all get."

Groaning inwardly at how oblivious he is, I roll my eyes and ready myself for my introduction.

We always have a damn good turnout here. It's why we

wanted the label to see us in action in this element, when the crowd is fueling us.

The trance is always strongest here.

The doors have been opened, and the masses have flocked in, everyone is now packed inside.

Usually we don't play right at opening time, but since we're playing for a younger crowd, I don't mind it.

I see the redhead from earlier as she walks around the stage, attempting to wave the waitresses in gear, who have stopped waiting the now-full tables in anticipation of our set.

Little Red needs to go back to waiting tables and ogling the burlesque dancers. The more people lost in us, the better. We need that damn trance to be on point tonight.

I can barely see her when she disappears from the bit of the crowd I can see from this backstage angle.

"And Base Masters!" Sticks yells, cuing me to get my ass out on stage.

I head straight for the mic, offering my best panty-dropping smile to the girls who have gathered the closest.

It's all part of the game. All part of the show.

Work the crowd.

Fire everyone up.

Feed the trance.

Chapter 3

BASE

"I saw your ride leave without you. Do you need a lift?" Raya asks as she weirdly wipes down the bar.

Did something happen I don't know about? I thought she lived on a vineyard three hours from here and about to marry rich. Why the hell is she working here?

"If it wouldn't piss off your fiancé, yeah," I tell her as I lean against the bar and glance back over at Red.

It's like she's unaware there are even people around as she quickly flips through a thick binder.

"You don't really seem surprised they left you behind," Raya says as I just watch Red's finger slide down each page at a rapid pace.

She can't actually read that damn fast, can she?

"They're dicks. I'd be more surprised if they hung around this long after curtains," I tell her, smirking when Red snaps the book shut like she's found what she's been searching for and starts moving around the room like she's checking everything out.

"What's her deal?" I ask Raya, gesturing to Red.

She doesn't answer immediately, and when I turn my head, Raya's simply arching an eyebrow at me. Her eyes move to Red, then they dart back to mine.

"She's young, hot, and could probably use some friends her own age who aren't married with kids," she says like she's stating something surprising while she blinks a few rapid times.

"What?" I ask as she just continues to blink for a second or two longer.

"Hey, Britt, can you give Base a ride?" she calls out to Red.

Looks like I can stop calling her Red now. I finally have a name.

My lips spread in a smile when Britt's eyes widen and seem to freeze on me. Maybe she's bisexual?

Usually I don't care about someone's sexual orientation, but in this case, I'd seriously like to know. If she's straight, she really fucking doesn't like us at all, because she's paid zero attention to us all night. It seems like her focus has been specifically targeted on the large amount of women who work here.

"Um...to where?" Britt finally asks, seeming confused.

"My house. It's on the beach. Not too far, but too far to walk while carrying this," I say, motioning to my case that is carrying my new favorite baby.

"Oh...yeah. Sure," she says, sounding hella uncertain. "Just let me shut the lights off."

"You covering for the manager or something?" I ask, following behind her as everyone filters out.

Raya has vanished just that fast.

"Yes," she states flatly.

"Do you usually have to do this sort of thing?"

She shakes her head, and says, "No." That's all I get.

"Have you worked here long?"

"No," she says simply.

I can't tell if she hates talking in general or if she just hates talking to me…

She mutters something to herself when she stumbles into a barstool, and then she glares at it like the thing jumped out in front of her.

"Are you always this...odd?" I ask, trying my damnedest not to laugh as she makes her way to the large breaker box, struggling to walk in the heels she's wearing.

"Yes." Deadpan. She's not joking, is she?

Intrigued, I prop up as she flips the lights off one by one until we're shrouded by the darkness.

Chapter 4

BRITT

Why did I tell him I'd give him a ride? Bruce would have done it. Maybe he'll still be in the parking lot.

I should have told Raya my cognitive functions aren't properly performing around him.

As well as I'm doing so far, I'm worried I'll grow more socially awkward by the second. And Base is friends with most of my family, so that will likely cause discomfort within the group.

"You anti-conversation?" he asks almost randomly.

Am I not conversing? I've answered every question he's asked.

"No," I answer.

"Ah, so it's just me you don't want to talk to."

I turn and feel my forehead creasing as I try to see him in the dark to no true avail.

"I don't understand the reasoning that led to that conclusion," I confess.

He chuckles as though I've said something funny, but how can that be funny?

"Are *you* always this odd?" I muse, curious if he's just as weird as I am. Maybe that's why he's laughing at nothing.

He laughs more, which I find relieving. Good. He *is* weird. Just like me. Even though it's a different sort of weird than me, it still makes me relax a little.

"So, Britt, what's got you working tonight?" he asks as I start trying to find my way through the dark club, inwardly groaning when that same vicious barstool blocks my path again.

"I had to help," I answer.

A hand finds the small of my back, and my breath hitches in my throat. Why is he touching me? Is there a hidden meaning?

"I can navigate this club in the dark a little better than you," he says by way of explaining his welcome/unwelcome hand.

Now I get it.

His hand is almost burning my skin through the fabric of my dress as he guides me. It shouldn't be a literal sentence, but it feels like it is.

"Are you always this hot?" I ask, which seems to provoke his mysterious roar of laughter once again.

Is there anything he won't laugh at?

I'm almost tempted to form a list of non-humorous topics just to test the theory.

"Is that you're way of saying I'm you're type," he asks, sounding distinctly amused.

Type? I asked if he was always this hot. I didn't say anything about types—*oohhh.*

"I mean your hand. It's hot," I explain, quickly recovering.

I know you're not supposed to just blurt out a man is hot. I've been told that very directly by seven different women.

His chuckles continue, and I start to worry he's not just weird, but also making fun of me.

He asked me about Dane, so obviously he knows who I am. I find it hard to believe he'd make fun of me. Everyone says he's so nice.

People should come with manuals that explain their reactions.

His laughter tapers off when I just stare at him. "You're serious," he says like he's surprised. "My hand is a normal temperature. I'm actually surprised it's not cold. I've held about ten bottles of ice cold water since the last set ended."

Definitely not cold. I'm weird, not numb.

I type in the code to arm the alarm, while he turns his head away to avoid seeing. That's at least polite, but he's still touching me.

When we *finally* reach the outside, his guiding hand falls away from my back. Oddly enough, a pang of disappointment strikes, and a sliver of cold works its way into the vacant spot. I ignore it while I lock up from the outside.

"Masters," I murmur to myself, thinking of Base's cousin Tag as I begin my trek through the mostly empty parking lot.

Maybe that's why he laughs for no reason at all. Tag is an odd one. He constantly makes jokes I don't understand, even though everyone else seems to laugh. I've decided they're just being polite, so I try to laugh, too.

"Yes," he drawls, though I have no idea why he's saying *yes* or why he looks so amused.

I can't tell if I'm the one making this situation awkward all on my own or if he's intentionally piling on.

I unlock my car, and Base stops, letting his eyebrows cock up in surprise.

"That's a very expensive car," he says, stating something random and obvious, even seeming confused by it.

He is weird, see?

"Yes, it is," I say, uncertain why he found it necessary to bring it up at all. Since he's just staring, I try to guess the reason for his hesitation. "Is it somehow offending you?"

He gives me a look that I don't understand, and then he decides against whatever he was about to say as he climbs in. It's already after three in the morning now. I wish he'd stop dallying. I'm exhausted.

"How far are we going?" I ask him as I busy myself with all my pre-driving checks.

Again, his eyebrows cock up, and his eyes rake over my body.

Why am I blushing right now? I can feel my cheeks burning. I've seen guys look at me like that before.

That look is usually only involved when there's cleavage. I don't have cleavage today.

Focus, Britt. Admittedly, he's weird, but still has enough other qualities to make up for it. And girls don't seem to mind weird guys as much as guys mind weird girls.

It's one of those double-standards I find unreasonably unfair.

Reasons to avoid Base Masters start ticking off in my head like a checklist.

I don't need to set myself up for utter failure.

The rejections are starting to become redundant.

Tria calls Base the forbidden unicorn.

From what I gather, it's the guy no smart girl should try to catch because he's too pretty and he's a musician—her words. I don't understand the link between a pretty musician and fabled horned creatures.

"Don't I wish," he says on a breath to himself, confusing me. But then he brings his eyes back up to meet mine. "Take a right on Jordan, and follow the beach until you see a house with every light on."

I crank the car, mulling over his last bit about all the lights. "Are you scared of the dark?" I ask, delving into the depth of his weirdness.

He coughs on his laughter this time. He should get that seen about. That could be harmful. To laugh like that so often could possibly cause him to rupture something. For all he knows, they could be signs of repetitive seizures.

"No. My roommates don't believe in sleep. We're renting a place from Tag. He's my cousin, and he's the one who got me the audition for a regular gig at Silk a while back. How long have you worked there?"

Technically, this was my debut. I know everything about the

club, but I've never worked there before.

"One day."

"One day and you have the keys and a security code? You must have made one hell of an impression on Dane," he says distractedly as he types something on his phone.

From my peripheral, I can see him lift his eyes and start staring at me as I drive, even as I try to process what any of that is supposed to mean.

I decide he's just stating something rhetorical and doesn't need any rhetorical follow-up comments on the matter.

"Did you even listen to the set?" he asks when I stay quiet.

Should I tell him the music is too loud?

Probably not. I'm sure someone would probably tell me that's rude.

"It sounded well."

I hope they did well. People seemed to be enjoying themselves, so I assume they were either too intoxicated to know better, or they genuinely enjoyed the band. Since it was under twenty-one night, you'd think the crowd would be sober. I don't particularly think they were.

"We did *well*?" he asks like he can't believe I just used that word.

"You did... bad?" I ask, confused. Are musicians among the culture that uses bad as good?

"You didn't even listen to us, did you? How is that even possible?" he groans, but a smile plays on his lips. "You're so—"

"Weird," I say simply, filling in his void for the right word. "I know."

"I was going to say interesting. Not weird."

I glance over to see his very distracting smile. He needs to put that thing away. I might be *different*, but I'm still a girl with regular hormones and completely unsated needs, an inconveniently curious nature, and all thanks to my infuriating blockade called a hymen that particularly terrifies most men, I'm still a virgin.

"I think we're here," I say when I see a large house with lights glaring from every window.

A large group of people are hanging out on the raised side-deck beside the oceanfront pool. The girls have stripped down to their underwear, and they're diving into said pool. It actually looks a little fun.

Dane and his friends do stuff like this all the time, but I always feel like a tagalong because of the ever-expanding legion of couples. I usually just observe their interactions, wondering how people get that comfortable with such ease.

If I spontaneously stripped down to my underwear at one of their parties, five Sterlings would immediately be throwing blankets at me and yelling for me to cover up.

They do the same when I wear a bikini with no cover-up.

"You want to stay and party with us?" Base asks, drawing my attention back to him as he puts his hand on the door to get out.

"Um...no. It's fine."

I appreciate the polite gesture, but I'd stick out terribly in a setting where I know no one who could serve as a buffer.

"Have you got something pressing you have to do tomorrow morning? And by tomorrow morning, I mean when the sun rises in a few hours," he says, while I continue to stare ahead at all the fun.

"Nothing so early."

I smile when I see one of the guys scooping a girl over his shoulder and tossing her into the water.

"Then come on. We don't bite." He pauses. "On second thought, there has been some biting in the past. Regardless, it'll be fun," he says, teasing me. I think he's teasing, anyway.

I'm certainly not opposed to the prospect of fun, but I'm not fond of being bitten.

"Are you sure? You realize I'm not exactly the type of person people invite to a party," I state for clarification.

Anyone who knows the Sterlings are fully aware of my limited social graces. Though, I have improved a lot.

He frowns. I'm not sure if that's confusion or constipation—*really, though, too many expressions resemble constipation*. There should be a handbook.

"Then you should start coming to the parties you *are* invited to," he says, letting his expression change again as that smile he wears so well spreads across his lips.

I'll probably be laughed at even more than he's already laughed at me, but I nod in agreement and open the door to get out.

"Atta girl. You'll be pleased to know the guys always bring home an excess of women, and I'm sure some of them are switch-hitters…if that's your thing…"

I have absolutely no idea what he's talking about, but instead of asking, I do what I do with my group and just nod like it makes all the sense in the world. However, I do wish I had one of my people to play buffer right now.

"Cool," I say, sounding utterly ridiculous even to myself.

"Knew it," he says as he cracks his neck.

"Knew what?" I ask, moving closer to his side as we start up the steps.

"Nothing. You drink?"

Finally. Something I understand. "Yes, please. I'd love a cranberry juice. I kept seeing them all night but never had time to drink one."

"And vodka?" he asks, grinning.

Sigh. I thought I understood. "Never tried it."

"Then let's remedy that. I'll mix the drink while you meet everyone."

I'll only have a sip if it has alcohol. I'll wait until I get home to have just cranberry juice.

"So he did bring a girl," the drummer from the band says, smiling as we walk his way.

Base quickly runs through introductions, and I memorize each face with each name, smiling my practiced smile the entire time. Then the guys start introducing the girls, and the girls correct them when they get the names wrong.

Forgetting names is considered rude. It's one rude thing I manage to avoid doing.

"It's a lot of people, but you'll just need to learn my bandmates' names," Base whispers.

"I think I've got it. Sticks, drummer. Taylor, keyboardist. Ricky, bass guitarist." In quick succession, I point at each girl as I call out their names. "Trixie, Ginger, Mary, Misty, Cindy, Crystal, and Amber. Right?" I ask.

There. Now I've set the precedent that I'm not intentionally rude, and I can build onto the foundation from there.

It goes a little quiet. Everyone is staring at me like I have some explaining to do. I know that look really well.

"Seeing the faces while hearing the names is an easy recording mechanism. Recording things I read is actually easier."

Still…no one speaks.

"I'm Britt," I say when the silence stretches on.

"Why do I feel like I know you?" Sticks asks, pointing a drumstick at me as the intensity in his eyes doubles, presumably putting an effort into extracting a memory.

"We don't know each other," I assure him. "I don't forget encounters."

"You keep getting more interesting, Britt," Base says, smiling as he heads into the house, leaving me out here on my own.

Am I supposed to follow him? I'm his guest, right?

"You seriously look very familiar," Sticks says, tapping his chin like he's giving it thought.

"I was just at the club," I supply.

He flashes a grin at Taylor. "Too fucking sweet, man."

How does he know if I'm sweet or not? He's only just met me.

"So you work at Silk?" Taylor asks.

"Yes," I answer simply, not elaborating on the fact it's temporary or that I have an internship with Harley.

I'm not sure why he's giving me that look—the confused/constipated face. Base gave it to me earlier, but I'm answering their questions.

"O...kay. Nothing to add to that?" he asks unsurely.

"Outside of my circle, people seem to lose interest when I'm detailing information about topics that aren't interesting enough to be detailed—i.e. this topic isn't interesting enough to be detailed."

I'm definitely making it awkward. The more I talk, the worse I'll make it, so I just stand quietly as everyone shifts around on their feet like they don't know what to say now.

"Glad Base found a woman, because I'm not sharing," Taylor says, grabbing two girls by the waist and pulling them with him as he crashes into the pool.

It slightly breaks up the growing tension.

I'm curious about that comment, but I don't feel comfortable asking too many questions just yet.

Base walks back out, sans guitar case, and he's carrying a glass of red liquid in his hand.

"Your drink," he says, smiling down at me as he collapses to the chair across from me.

I take it and cautiously sip it, tasting nothing more than cranberry juice. Good. He decided not to add vodka. My next sip is generous, and he smiles.

"Like it?"

I smile and nod, and he takes a sip of what appears to be a dark soda.

"Cranberry juice and vodka?" Trixie says, turning her nose up. I guess that means it does have vodka, since Base nods.

I put the drink down after the second sip.

"I hate that stuff. I prefer Jack and Coke," she adds, glancing at his drink.

Base holds his drink up. "Same here, but you can't have mine." To me he says, "Very little vodka at all. Not even half a shot."

I just nod, even though I'm still finished with it.

Trixie rolls her eyes, and then she takes a seat next to Base—very close to Base. There's no rational reason why that bothers me or why I almost vocalize that it bothers me.

I swallow *all* the words very hard.

"It's a big deck," he says when her arm touches his in the chair as she slides almost right against him.

I swallow more words. It's completely wrong for me to say anything at all.

"I don't want to sit alone, and everyone else is in the pool," she tells him, turning her body in a way that suggests I'm now eavesdropping on their conversation instead of being included.

Several of the partiers climb free from the pool, and they slowly start to make their way toward our table as they laugh and talk about stuff I'm not very well versed with.

I'll have to read up on music if they decide to include me again. Next time I'll bring a buffer. My buffers make everything I say sound like part of my charming quirk, and people feel instantly more comfortable around me.

I've never been able to do that all by myself.

Chapter 5

BASE

"You can scoot over some," I groan.

I swear, every time there's an unwelcome hand snaking up the inside of my leg like I'm supposed to allow every girl to touch whatever she wants, I remember why I hate fucking parties.

"I have a sensitive nose. Can that drink be tossed out or walked away?" she asks Britt before turning back to me, already half wasted as she slurs the words.

"I'm trying hard not to be an ass right now, but you're getting on my nerves," I tell her in the nicest fucking way I can.

"That drink smells disgusting. I don't know how she's drinking it without gagging," she says instead of giving me any space.

People have no personal boundaries when they're drinking with us.

Britt swallows the sip in her mouth before brightly saying, "Oh. I don't have a gag reflex."

I almost strangle to death before the gulp lodged in my throat spews across the deck, and several of the guys cough on air. I'm sort of ashamed my dick just went completely hard in less than two seconds.

I really thought I was more evolved than that.

"Marry me," Taylor says as he starts walking on his knees toward Britt.

I realize then that Britt is dead serious and doesn't seem to have a clue what it means to have said that in front of four fucking perverted guys.

She slinks back like she's shrinking in confusion at the outburst she can't make sense of.

But…I get why the chicks are giving her the look that says they're calling bullshit on playing coy.

I watch it all play out, and then I immediately decide I want to know more about Britt. Starting with her last name and what Britt is short for.

I could really see myself hanging out with her, especially since there won't be any sex. Then I can find out why the hell she hates my music.

She sips her drink quietly, appearing timid, probably because she doesn't know why everyone is laughing. She's different. Not weird, but different.

"Let's swim," Sticks says to someone.

He picks someone up, ignoring her squealing cries of mock protest, and then he launches her into the pool. I only notice from my peripheral because I'm busy watching someone else.

Britt's eyes raise, and an amused, childlike grin spreads as she watches them.

I'm half curious if someone is watching me watch Britt to complete the circle of spectators.

Taylor grabs up another girl, and she giggles uncontrollably on their way to mimic the same action. Britt's eyes light up again with excitement, and I can't seem to look away. Until...

"Get your wet arm off me," I grumble to the girl I don't want touching me.

She rolls her eyes, annoyed, but she doesn't move. "You're normally more fun."

A sound draws my attention back to Britt, and my grin spreads when I realize that sound is her laugh. She's tuned everything else out as she watches the fun going on around her.

I stand up, going unnoticed by her as I finally see my

opportunity to escape. I walk around behind Britt, smirking as she remains unaware, and I scoop her up from the chair.

She makes a small sound of amusement, but there's no loud scream.

"What are you doing?" she chuckles, making my smile only grow.

"I've never been much of a spectator," I say before moving at a decent speed and leaping out to the center of the pool, keeping her strapped to me.

A slight squeal escapes her lips seconds before we slap the water.

Once submerged, her body wiggles free and tangles around me, making me almost groan when one of her legs comes to rest between both of mine, pressing against the unprovoked erection I have.

I really don't want to get slapped for something I seriously can't help right now.

I hold onto her and push against the bottom of the pool to launch us upward. The second we surface, I'm rewarded with the laugh again.

It's the first genuine smile I've seen from her.

She clings to my neck with one hand while wiping water out of her face with the other.

Ah, hell. Her dress is soaked, making life *harder*.

Wet's a good look on her. How fucking long has it been since I had sex? I really thought I was more evolved than this, damn it.

It takes more strength than I care to admit to remember she doesn't like guys. Though, technically, she hasn't stated it definitively.

"You okay?" she asks, drawing my eyes back up.

Nope. In deflection, I playfully dunk her, but her legs tighten around me, and I jerk her right back up, greeted by her laughter once more.

I have to stop. I won't be able to walk if I get any harder. Not to mention, this could get awkward real damn fast if she notices.

I start to separate, but her body presses against mine as though she doesn't want to be let go. Taylor's jackass self comes and rips her away from me, picking her up high over his head, and making her laugh a helluva lot louder.

Fucker.

He drops her into the water, and I hear the telltale sound of fabric ripping.

She quickly surfaces, still laughing, and I frown when I see the strap on her dress has been ripped.

"You ripped her dress," Sticks points out.

He shrugs. "I'll buy her a new one."

"It's fine. I have more," Britt says, still grinning.

Taylor grins, seeming a little too enamored by her. I glare at him until his eyes widen toward the girl I've looked away from. I cut my eyes back just in time to see Britt tossing her dress poolside.

Lace...so much sexy lace. Girls don't wear shit like that unless they're wearing it for someone.

Her bra is red lace with black trim, her panties are those that are just the right amount of material. Not a thong, but not fully covering her ass... fuck me.

Guess I'm hiding in the pool for a bit longer.

"She's gay," I murmur to Taylor, finding it necessary to shatter whatever delusional things he has going on in his head.

"I'll turn her," he says as though it's become his new life's mission.

"They always turn back, man," Randy says as though he's being entirely serious as he claps Taylor's shoulder.

"I was joking, you idiot," Taylor says as he gives Randy a disbelieving look.

Randy bristles. "Y-yeah. I know. I was doing the anti-PC

comedian thing too," Randy defends.

Rolling my eyes, I start to tell them they're both idiots, when I feel hands on my shoulders, feet pressing against the inside-bends of my knees, and I'm being dunked under the water. I shoot back up to choke down some air, and I'm met with that even louder laughter. Britt's hand is over her mouth as she tries to smother it, almost looking horrified when I cough a little water up.

"Sorry," she says when she manages to swallow the rest of her laughter.

"My turn," I say as I dive for her.

She yelps and starts trying to swim away, but I catch her quickly. She stops trying to get away and abruptly turns to wrap herself around me.

Annnnd…I'm less evolved once again.

She's trying to stop me from throwing her or dunking her, not realizing I'm an animal, apparently.

I can't help but want to groan when her pelvis just barely touches the embarrassingly hard—

"If I go, you're going with me," she says, still laughing as she breaks through my thoughts.

Everything she says gets turned dirty in my head right now. I've turned into Randy.

"Is that so?" I ask, trying to sound playful instead of turned on, not wanting to make her uncomfortable or freak her out.

"Mmmhmm," she says, still grinning.

This hurts. Physically hurts.

"I have to get out of this shirt," I mumble, looking for any excuse to put some space between us.

Before I have time to process what's going on, my shirt is being slid over my head. I raise my arms to make it easier for her, and a few catcalls reach my ears. If they only fucking knew…

"Happy?" she says, tossing the shirt outside the pool, and then she wraps herself back around me.

Surely she's fucking noticed it by now. She's fucking straddling me, and *it* can certainly feel her.

She's oblivious. Somehow.

I think.

"Sure," I mumble, but I start spinning her around in the water, distracting myself and trying to lift her higher on my body so *it* can't feel her anymore.

Her laughter bubbles free as she clings to me. Fortunately, the less intense position does help.

The second I stop spinning, she swings herself back up, hands going to my shoulders as her eyes fix to mine and she gives me that genuine smile again.

I finally do something stupid.

Chapter 6

BRITT

His head dips, and lips touch mine with no warning at all. Freezing up, I don't react at first, but then I slowly start moving with him, trying not to mess this up.

It's the wet lingerie, right? I was told to wear lingerie if I ever wanted to lose my virginity outside of the underwear-forgiveness parameters one can only establish through a more intimate relationship.

I've never had a physical reaction as strong as this, and my body is telling me all sorts of crazy things to do. Like cling to him half-dressed in a pool.

He groans slightly when his tongue slides between my parted lips, and my hands tangle in his hair as I pull him even closer. When my legs tighten against his waist, I immediately zero in on the fact it might have actually been me arousing him this entire time instead of inadvertent stimulation, and…panic consumes me.

Why am I panicking?

This is exactly what I've wanted forever, and I'm finally kissing a guy who could quite possibly be perfect for the removal of my hymen.

But the panic ensues. My heartbeat thrums in my ears, and I almost get a little queasy from the nervousness. It feels like a ball is physically manifesting in the pit of my stomach and somehow constricting my heart at the same time.

Tearing my lips away, I blurt out, "I can't do—"

He groans, interrupting me before I can even figure out how my sentence needs to end. "I know. Shit. Sorry. I just got caught up," he says on a shaky exhale.

Good. He understands. I think. I'm not even sure I understand, but I'm usually the last to catch on to things that take a better sense of emotional awareness. I'll have to dissect the minor panic attack later.

Distraction takes us both out of the awkward moment. A fight between Trixie and Cindy breaks out. Hair is pulled, threats are made, and high-pitch warrior cries are wailed during some heavy slapping sounds.

Base drops his hold on me, making me feel a little abandoned as he climbs out of the pool to go help. When I pulled his shirt off, I wasn't thinking about having such a strong physical reaction to his body.

All combined, I found it…overwhelming. Human nature is a demanding source of primal urges when faced with new experiences.

It's not like his is the first attractive male body I've seen. It's Sterling Shore.

There's an abundance of them.

Now I've just pushed away a viable candidate for no logical reason, after working so hard to find one.

And now I feel…awkward. Even more so than usual. I'm also extremely ready to leave and escape the awkwardness, which is new.

Base chuckles as he restrains Trixie, and Taylor laughs while holding back Cindy.

"Time to break up the party, ladies. If you're not sleeping in, you should be calling a cab," Sticks calls out. "Fights mean the nights over."

At least that's one excuse I can use to get out of here. My cheeks feel like they're on fire, and my entire body is humming with…something.

I swim to the edge, averting anyone's eyes as I heave myself out.

"Two cabs will be here in five minutes," Randy says to the group, and then he walks toward me. "You staying or do you need a cab?"

"I drove, and the alcohol I ingested was considerably below the legal amount," I tell him tightly, struggling to get my dress on.

It's a vain effort. A wet dress that was already made to be tight is never going back on.

"We've got towels over there," he says, motioning toward a rack.

"Can I borrow one to drive home in? I'll bring it back to the club," I tell him as I grab one and start quickly toweling off.

I don't mind being in underwear, but if I get pulled over, I might be arrested. Which means I'd have to call someone to bail me out.

And then I'll be the teenager and not the adult I'm trying to be while working toward partner. I could call Brin. Brin said she'd get me out of jail if I ever needed her to. The offer seemed pointless then…

"I'll loan you a shirt and boxers," Sticks says, grinning as he walks toward me.

"That would be great," I say in slight relief, though I'll still technically be in underwear.

At least it won't be *my* underwear.

I blame the confusing night for heeding Harley's advice for going bold. Maybe next time I'll be less *bold,* and not take off my dress.

Sticks disappears into the house as the cabs pull up to the back, waiting on the fighting girls to be escorted out. I glance over the railing as Base starts trying to put Trixie in the back seat of the cab.

She abruptly slings her arms around his neck and tugs him down for a somewhat painful-looking kiss.

That feeling from earlier is back. I think now I'm positive it's jealousy. It's not fun. It's also very inappropriate to feel after simply sharing one casual kiss with him.

This fresh conflict is extremely unexpected.

I never expected to be a jealous person.

He makes some sound as he starts pushing her back, but she jumps up and wraps her legs around his waist. I look away, unable to stomach that. I'm imposing at this point by continuing to stare.

I am really, *really* ready to go now.

"Here you go," Sticks says, startling me with a white t-shirt and a pair of boxers as I turn my back on the scene.

"Thanks," I mutter, gratefully accepting the clothes, and then I walk down the stairs, pulling the shirt on as I go.

Told you: the human element always messes up the plans my head had.

Chapter 7

BASE

"Dude, you're such a fuck up," Sticks says, making me turn away from my morning fridge perusal.

"Why's that?" I ask, resuming my task. I'm starving.

"The girl was sober, and you kissed another girl after kissing her? Have you completely lost your mind?" Randy asks around a mouthful. "You can only kiss two chicks if they're *both* cool with it."

I give a small shudder thinking back to the unwanted kiss of the evening. I can't be too pissed, since I'd also just fucking kissed someone—who was uninterested—without permission and made her immediately uncomfortable.

"First of all, she kissed me. Secondly, the 'kiss' was mostly just her sucking my nose. And it took for-fucking-ever to get her off me without hurting her. There was no *me* kissing *her*. Secondly, Britt is gay, and I'm pretty sure I pissed her off when *I* kissed *her* in the pool."

Randy groans from the table. "She's gay? Damn. I could have sworn she was into me after you fucked up your chance. We had this look pass between us."

I roll my eyes. He thinks everyone is into him.

"We need to rehearse before Monday. By the way, your date left her dress," Sticks says, grinning as he carries in the broken-strap dress that's been left at the pool all night.

"She wasn't my date. Long story," I murmur absently, frowning when my stomach grumbles and begs for food.

I can't talk when my body is trying to eat itself.

I pat my abs, trying to soothe my stomach, and I earn a few chuckles from the jerks around me.

I don't feel like talking about Britt, so I'm glad my stomach has interrupted the conversation. I'd rather talk to Britt about Britt.

Unfortunately, it'll have to wait, because I don't have her number, her last name, her address, or any other means that could help me locate her.

But I'm sure I'll see her at Silk the next time we play, so I'm putting a pin in it until then. I'll at least apologize.

Chapter 8

BRITT

My sexual behavior essay is due soon in psychology, and I'm two sentences in and stumped.

I'm not a writer either, so it's hard to simply wing it. *Writer. Of course*. I'll call Rain. She knows all about sex and writing. She's perfect.

"Britt?" Dane asks.

I pull my phone back, seeing I did indeed dial Rain. He's probably had more sex than Rain, statistically speaking.

"What's up?" he asks. "Rain's just getting out of the shower."

"It's fine. You may be able to help me. I need to know why people enjoy having sex so much, aside from the obvious. Also, I need if it's anything like animals in heat. And I need to know what circumstances propel you into those situations where you're suddenly carnal and desperate to have someone."

My mind immediately detours to the pool where Base kissed me, and I clear my throat.

"Never mind about that last one. Just answer the rest," I amend.

He coughs hard, over and over, as if he can't catch his breath. Did he swallow a fly or something? I always hate it when I accidentally swallow a bug.

"Dane?" I prompt. "I need you to explain sex so I can finish this."

"Finish *what*?" he asks in a strange, panicky octave.

"My paper, of course. What else? It's for Psych class."

I hear a heavy breath fall through his lips, and then there's some indistinguishable muttering that follows that.

"What did I tell you about invasive questions?" he asks seriously.

Hmm. His lectures have all been about not asking other people invasive questions. "You exempted yourself from that when you said I could come to you for anything," I clarify.

"I realize I said anything, but..." He groans, pausing and making some unusual sound. "Fine. Sex is...well, you feel...um...I don't...shit. Talk to Rain."

Rain chuckles as her voice comes over the phone. "Read those books I gave you," she says before I can even ask her the same question.

Considering Dane's reputation, I'm surprised he doesn't seem to know enough about sex to help me.

"Read *those* books?" I ask.

I thought they were romance, not erotica, but the lines in that category seem to be blurred these days.

"Yes. Read them. It'll give you a semi-realistic grasp of most things. Then grab some more stuff. The bookstore has plenty of things that will help you. Especially since you respond better with written words."

I don't want to tell her I've already read them and they made no sense at all.

At. All.

"Thank you. You were so much more helpful than Dane. He doesn't know much about sex, so maybe you should make him read those books. Perhaps he and I can discuss our own personal take-away in a book club sort of format."

There. Now I'll still find a way to get answers without admitting the books made no sense.

She starts laughing really loudly, and I hear Dane groan.

Apparently I'm on speaker.

He really should be educating himself. I've read the various statistics on the number of women who leave a man if they're not sexually satisfied. I never want Rain to leave him.

"I'll make sure he brushes up on some stuff," Rain assures me. "By the way, we're coming home early. The tour cancelled my last event due to a storm surge. We'll be home in the morning."

"Good," I say, since Silk is in decent condition and I can show them I'm perfectly capable of doing adult things.

They start whispering and snickering, letting me know they've forgotten me and now they're playing.

"I do better with show than tell," Dane says, confusing me.

I shake my head and hang up. They're weird too.

Chapter 9

BASE

What the actual fuck is going on in the park?

It looks like *Lord of the Rings* just exploded on a random Sunday evening. It's really hard to get some quiet writing time in when people are walking by in full-on renaissance gear and elf ears.

"Save the queen!" a bunch of people shout from the back entrance.

"Kill the queen!" is shouted from the group walking by in front of me.

What the…

Propping up my guitar, I lean forward, studying this random little gathering, as tents start popping up all over the park. I'm scratching my head at their words and interactions, trying to figure out if this is for real right now.

I've traveled a lot, and I don't know if I've ever seen so many men in tights. *Ever.*

My eyebrows almost hit my hairline when I spot a familiar face among the ever-growing gathering.

Dale Sterling.

In a leather tunic.

And…tights.

Dale Sterling picking a wedgie while in tights…

I look around, wondering if I've somehow landed in an alternate universe.

Since I'm clearly too distracted to try and write new music right now, I put my acoustic back in its case and jog over to Dale. His eyes flick toward me as I approach, then away, then back again, before they widen with a satisfying amount of horror.

He groans while pinching the bridge of his nose, and my smile spreads before I can stop it.

"Apparently I sat down in modern-day Sterling Shore, and woke up in medieval Camel-toe-lot," I tell him as he shakes his head, refusing to look at me again.

"She swore I wouldn't see anyone who wasn't a part of this," he mutters almost too low for me to hear.

"So...um...nice...*tights*," I say with a growing grin.

"They're leggings," he bites out. Then he groans and scrubs a hand over his face, before adding, "As if that makes it any better."

I'm trying not to smile mockingly. Really, I am. But that's a lot of man to squeeze into some small tights—I mean, *leggings*.

My grin only grows, regardless of my attempts to stow it.

Another familiar face comes into view—only she's wearing a *royal* gown and a crown to match...

"So what am I looking at?" I ask him.

"Currently, you're looking at my fiancée," he states, deadpan.

Five guys are standing on crates, making music with their mouths—only it's not very good. Another is rapping, but again, not...good at all.

"Yo, the queen rode in with all her merry men, and the last thing the elf prince said was I'll have you again..."

Cringing and looking away from the train wreck of loud spitting instead of beat-boxing, I look over at Dale and quirk an eyebrow.

"The park is closed off for this. How did you get in without dressing the damn part?" he asks.

"I've been here for hours trying to write music. Unsuccessfully, but still…" I gesture around to everyone. "Then this happens, so my focus is shot for good now."

"You should go. They don't like out-of-character people watching them because it makes them feel judged." He glares at me a little. "Now I get why. I'm with them, and the judgmental outsiders need to go."

He swings a finger out and puts a hand on his hip like he's an officer pointing out the exit to me. My lips twitch, but I force the grin back this time while clearing my throat several times.

He rolls his eyes.

"So your fiancée is queen of the nerds? Impressive."

Before he can say anything, I hear, "Base?"

I turn to face the direction the familiar voice just came from, and my eyes widen as a slow, confused grin takes over my face.

Britt.

In a very showy little leather outfit.

A bow is in her hand, a quiver is attached to her thigh—that is mostly exposed, due to the really short brown-leather skirt that looks like it was intentionally ripped and frayed.

Her red hair is plaited in numerous braids and pulled back from her face to reveal…pointed ears. Pointed ears that she did not have last night, but they look seriously real right now.

And weirdly hot.

Her pale midriff is exposed, her cleavage is bared, and she looks like the sexiest elven archer I've ever seen.

My mouth opens, and I try to find words, but I'm still…distracted.

"Britt? What the damn hell are you wearing?" Dale snaps, confusing the hell out of me.

Until a sinking realization hits me with a *"Duh, you motherfucking dumbass"* bitch slap from Stupid Hell.

Britt. As in Britt fucking Sterling. As in the youngest of the

Sterling crew who is constantly in the gossip columns.

I'm such a motherfucking idiot.

I should have put it together last night when she had the keys and security code to Silk, and when she was blunt and expressionless for most of the night. It's so obvious now.

A small groan bubbles out of me as I glance over her again, taking her in with a completely new eye.

"My new outfit that Harley made me," Britt answers, genuinely smiling as she innocently models it for him.

"I'm going to kill the queen," Dale grumbles beside me, still glaring at Britt. Then frowns. "Wait, you two know each other?" he asks.

I start to speak, but Britt beats me to it.

"Barely. We met yesterday. I should get going." Her eyes flick to me, then down at my wardrobe. In an unimpressed, flat tone, she adds, "The Game Master will ask you to leave if you're wearing that."

Then she walks right by me like last night never even happened.

Like she isn't wearing a wet-dream costume—apparently I'm a closet nerd, because I'm debating putting on tights just to stick around and see what she does.

About five guys stumble over themselves to chase after her, but she doesn't even notice as she walks with tunnel-vision toward the *queen*. Not surprising, since she's into women, not men.

That's something I didn't know about Britt Sterling. Then again, I don't read the socialite section—also known as the gossip columns—as often as most Sterling Shore peeps.

There's a guy being carried in on a throne with at least ten guys of all sizes shouldering the horizontal platform as he's brought alongside the queen. A man-powered carriage of sorts…

"Shouldn't you be the king?" I ask, trying to mask my amusement.

"I'm a human squire," he says on a sigh. "I have to work my way up to elven king. Please. Fucking. Go. Away. We'll discuss how you know Britt later."

"We can discuss it now. I met her last night at Silk, and I was into her until I found out she was gay."

He snorts, then chokes back a laugh. "Right. Very gay," he says, though he's smiling in a way that makes me suspicious.

When I just arch an eyebrow at him, making no move to leave, he makes a frustrated sound.

"I'm still confused about what's going on, and I'm not leaving until someone fills me in," I decide to say.

"Land of the Lost Lore," Dale answers, turning toward me. "It's the name of Harley's current biggest web-based game, and she just released the newest levels. She does these LARP sessions to get people excited, and because she likes wearing a crown and prosthetic ears and, you know, leading a lore cult. Now that you know what's going on, will you please fucking leave? In about five minutes, they're going to make us talk in certain ways, and certain words will be prohibited. I'd like for there to be as few witnesses to this as possible."

"Can't imagine why," I state dryly.

A guy who defies all nerd clichés walks by in an outfit similar to Dale's, normal ears and all. I'm not surprised when he goes straight toward Britt.

"What's Britt supposed to be dressed like?" I decide to ask. "And what's that guy talking to her?"

Why is she laughing? What's he saying that has her laughing like that?

Dale is already narrowing his eyes on the scene, which confuses me.

"Britt is a Valkyrie princess. You earn your spot based on your game level. The guy is a level-one, mortal squire, like me. Those are the guys who come here to hit on the hot nerd girls since being nerdy went mainstream."

He starts to walk away, but a short guy in a wild headdress and some weird, leather clothing stops in front of him, clipboard in hand and bugle hanging on his hip like a weapon or something.

"User name and level," the guy says without looking up.

"Squireboy-seven-four-two-three," Dale mutters, casting a glance toward me when I choke back a laugh. "Level one," he adds, turning his attention back toward the short guy.

The guy peers up, scanning Dale with an unimpressed expression. "Figures," the guy mutters before stepping in front of me.

He starts to speak, then his eyes narrow when he sees me.

"Out! This is for Land of Lost Lore participants only!"

Dale is the one choking back a laugh now when the hostile little man pulls up his bugle and blows it loudly. Right in front of me.

Fucking hell.

Cursing, I cover my ears, wincing when it wails again.

"Intruder! Intruder!"

Britt's eyes swing in my direction as I back away, grinning in disbelief. I have to drop my hands from my ears to grab my guitar case, and the evil dick pounces.

The bugle wails loudly again, and Britt seems to hide her smile as she turns and walks away.

"Intruder!" the man shouts again.

When five possible ogres start heading toward me, I turn and jog away, carrying my guitar out of the park that is now manned by security, who is halting anyone not dressed appropriately from entering.

Britt fucking Sterling.

Unbelievable.

My mind is too boggled to try writing, so I go home to the loud house where the party has already started.

Sticks practically greets me at the door with a huge smile on his face.

"We partied with a Sterling last night and didn't even know it," he groans.

"Just learned that myself," I say with a tight smile, deciding not to elaborate as I drop my guitar and start pulling up the gossip columns I know about.

I'm sinking low, but my head's still spinning.

"I knew she looked familiar," Taylor says from a seat in the kitchen as he mixes drinks.

Sure enough, Britt Sterling's picture is in the socialite section. It's showing her from last night, talking about how the virgin princess Sterling manned the city's infamous Silk…

Virgin princess?

"There's a better site that mentions her leaving with you and wondering if you were going to pop her cherry," Sticks says with a grin.

"I'm sorry, what?" I ask, confused as hell.

"Any publicity for us is good publicity," Sticks goes on, as if that's the confusing part.

"You said she was gay," Taylor tells me, sounding like he's accusing me of something.

"She's not?" I ask, a new smile forming on my lips.

"No, she's a virgin. A legit virgin, who is obsessed with popping her cherry. Man, I've been following that story, expecting the girl to be a complete clinger or batshit crazy. I'm struggling to understand now why she's a virgin, since she's working so hard not to be one," Sticks groans. "Why'd you have to see her first? Why is she one of those people who looks really different in real life than in a picture? I *knew* she looked familiar."

"I'm sorry, what?" I say again, my smile gone and replaced by confusion once more.

Seems to be the theme of the day.

"She's been trying for like two or more years, to pop her cherry," Taylor explains, waggling his eyebrows. "But so far, no reports of any takers."

Scratching my jaw, I shake my head. No way in hell am I taking her virginity. Surely she's not really a virgin. That's just some sort of PR spin or something for the Sterling family. Has to be.

It feels like cheating, but Britt Sterling is becoming a mythical creature right now, and not because of the elf ears. I feel like I need to know who the hell this girl really is.

I blame writer's block for all the creepy shit I'm about to do.

After feeling like I've thoroughly violated her privacy by reading the numerous gossip tidbits—*this town is obsessed with Britt Sterling and her obsession with losing her virginity, apparently*—I sit back.

All her friends seem to be friends of her brother's. She grew up with nothing, though there's very little on her background other than the fact she was essentially homeless when Dane found her.

Studying a picture of her from one event, all I see is a girl with a fake smile and sad eyes, as though she's trying her best to blend in instead of stand out.

Running my fingers through my hair, I can't help but wonder why she doesn't have any friends of her own. Why she's an unwilling virgin. And why she's smiling with sad eyes.

Then…for the first time in months, despite the loud party going on and the shrieks and squeals, I feel the stirrings of a song form with ease.

Which means I'm about to get really fucking creepy. I'm going to get punched by a Sterling before this is all over. Odds aren't in my favor.

Chapter 10

BRITT

"So, did he get your number or anything?" Harley asks me.

She volunteered to help me with my paper when I talked to her about it yesterday before the Lore Games. Then she mentioned seeing Base Masters in the park. And…I'm not sure why I told her about the random kiss or the party. But I did.

And I'm starting to regret that, because she's way too excited for no reason at all.

"No," I tell her on a sigh. "Can we stop talking about him?"

Her lips purse. "He was staring at you the majority of the time before the Game Master kicked him out."

Why does my stomach do weird fluttery things the second I hear that? Why do I squirm uncomfortably every time his name is mentioned now?

They've talked about Base for a while, and until meeting him, I had no physical reactions or involuntary curiosity.

I'm scared to ask Harley what's going on with me, because it's clearly as simple as having a crush. Which will make me…an idiot.

And everyone seems to think I'm smart just because I have a great memory and can recite facts. Never mind that the facts never aid in moving conversation along the way I intend for them to do.

"Earth to Britt," she groans. "Seriously, do you like him? Because I think he's into you. It's hard to get some guys to appreciate a girl with elf ears."

Again…the flutters.

Fortunately, my door swings open, interrupting this conversation. I'd like to talk about anything other than Base.

"So how do you know Base Masters?" Dale asks as he steps into my house without knocking.

And…here we go again.

I focus my attention on the outline of my new draft, since Harley is supposed to handle Dale.

"Hello to you too," Harley says from beside me. "And knock before you just walk into someone's house," she adds, smirking when he rolls his eyes.

"What're you working on?" Dale asks.

"Sex paper," Harley tells him seriously.

My phone chimes with a text, and I look at it as the two of them talk about 'what the hell a sex paper' is, and 'what the actual fuck it has to do with Base Masters.'

"The two aren't technically linked," I point out distractedly when I start reading my text from the unknown number.

I got an invite to a party that I've been wanting, but can't attend unless I bring Britt Sterling. So…I know this is weird, but do you want to go to a party with me tonight? Btw, this is Krysta.

I start to tell her *no,* because the last party I attended outside of my family's circle was great…until it wasn't. Not to mention, even though she's Ruby's sister, I still don't know her very well.

Then I also remember what Base said about attending the parties I am invited to. She could be a buffer…

ME: Why do I need to be there?

KRYSTA: Because you're a Sterling? IDK

ME: You're a Sterling by blood.

KRYSTA: You're the one with the name. ;)

Dale and Harley are starting to inch closer as they argue, which means soon the kissing will begin—because when these people get mad at each other, they also get aroused.

Which means soon they'll be leaving. And I'll be here alone. As usual.

Krysta never hangs out with the group. Maybe she has even fewer friends than me.

ME: I'll go.

KRYSTA: Great! I'll pick you up in twenty.

Leaving Dale to argue with Harley about the numerous '*appropriate* curriculums an Ivy League college has to offer a girl's mind,' I go to grab my things, checking myself in the mirror to see how much work I can do in twenty minutes.

In the span of time it took me to go to my bedroom, the arguing has ceased, and the telltale smacking sounds have begun.

I may not understand *why* they do the things they do, but I have learned to predict what they'll be doing.

Deciding not to change, I go outside to wait on Krysta, just as Harley calls out, "Bye, Britt! We'll work on your paper more tomorrow!"

"Okay," is my only response.

I'm getting good at this fewer words responding thing. Even though I know the both of them would listen to me regardless of how many words I had to say to relay my point.

It's still good practice.

Krysta shows up almost directly after they leave, and I decide not to point out that it's only been twelve minutes instead of twenty, like she said.

When I get in the car, she smiles over at me.

"Thanks for doing this. I know it's sort of last minute, but I've seriously been trying to get an invite to one of these parties for a while."

I just return her smile, hoping she can't tell I'm already uncomfortable. Her gaze flicks to my shorts, then up to my shirt, and she shakes her head with a small smile still on her lips.

She's dressed in leather pants and a hot pink crop top. I'm wearing a Suicide Squad t-shirt and frayed jean shorts with flip flops.

"Should I have dressed up more?" I decide to ask.

"Nope. I should have dressed down, but there's a boy."

I don't really know what to say to that.

After a few minutes of silence, Krysta asks, "Does it bother you? That people invite you places because of you're a Sterling?"

"No," I say with a shrug.

She laughs quietly. "That's all you're going to tell me? Just no?"

"My name before meant nothing. And when it was attached to me, it was a reminder that I had a name, but no family to go with it. Sterling was a name my brother was proud to give me, and when people want me to go somewhere because of that name, I try my best to show gratitude. Before Sterling, I might as well have been nameless. It's daunting at times, sure, but I still enjoy it."

When she smiles, I relax, seeing that I haven't blurted out too much.

"Corbin thinks I should get my name changed, even though my bio dad doesn't want to claim me. He says the name is as much his as it is our father's, but…I don't know. It makes me feel like I'd look desperate," she confesses.

"Why would it make you look desperate?"

She laughs again. "I just know people would talk, and that's what they'd be saying."

She doesn't really make any sense if she'd think about it logically. "People always have something bad to say about Sterlings, so you'd blend in."

She glances over at me as she grimaces.

"But people talk about you because they hate that you're living the fairytale. Long, lost, rich, incredibly doting brother comes to find you, saves you from poverty, and brings you home where you're immediately loved and part of their extremely wealthy inner circle. I'm the slightly unstable daughter of a deranged woman with fatal attraction symptoms whose bio dad didn't want anything to do with her. It's less fairytale and more Jeepers Creepers."

As we take a familiar turn, I pull out my phone and google *Fatal Attraction* and *Jeepers Creepers*.

Trying to piece together her pop culture references, I say, "Most all fairytales were derived from a more morbid, less shiny tale. The dark undertones are always overshadowed by the happily-ever-afters by the optimists."

After realizing what *Jeepers Creepers* is, I frown. I'm not sure how a man-eating, humanoid monster has anything to do with this, but I'm guessing she meant it abstractly.

Anything too abstract sails over my head.

When she pulls up to a very familiar house, my stomach twists in those horrible metaphoric knots.

"I suppose you're right," she says.

At the exact same time, I ask, "Why are we here?"

I'm not sure why my heart is hammering, but I suddenly feel like running. Fast. Why am I panicking? The potential for conflict is low, so there's no reason to panic.

She frowns as she looks over. "This is where the party is." She gestures to all the cars. "Something wrong?"

Yes!

"No," I blurt out, since this should be okay and I'm irrationally panicking.

"Great. Then let's go in," she says as she pushes open her door.

I take a few more seconds to breathe, which I'm having to think about. I'm a girl who can't forget anything, and yet I'm struggling to remember how to perform simple, typically unconscious, cognitive functions.

Shakily, I push open the door and try not to overthink it. Krysta is already walking toward the steps that lead up to the pool, but she turns to wait on me.

Just as she opens her mouth to speak, I hear, "The Sterling girls have arrived!"

Her eyes widen, almost as though she wasn't expecting anyone to call her that. I assume. She also doesn't look too happy about it.

My eyes dart up to see Taylor and Sticks grinning down at us, and Krysta offers them a tight smile as she starts making her way up the steps. I follow, my eyes darting around the second I can see the pool, searching for a face I can't find.

Sticks grabs my hand, pulling it into his, and then makes a dramatic show of kneeling in front of me. I'm not dressed like the Valkyrie princess and this isn't a LARP session, so I have no idea why he's kneeling.

That's the only time people ever kneel before me.

"We had a Sterling at our house, and we didn't even know it," he says, grinning broadly. "We most graciously apologize."

He kisses my hand, then winks as he stands. As he goes to drop his arm around Krysta's shoulders, he calls out. "Grab yourself a drink, Britt *Sterling*. Tonight we find out all your secrets."

"I don't have secrets," I tell Taylor, who is standing beside me and smiling.

"Good. Then you won't mind telling us how you came to be a Sterling. Nothing in the gossip columns about that."

That makes me bristle. I don't have secrets, but I see no point in talking about things before my happily-ever-after came to be. I'm an optimist these days, and I'd like to forget all my darker undertones.

Fortunately, I have needs to attend and a logical reason for deflection.

"Can I use your bathroom to freshen up?" I ask, remembering Tria's wording about these situations.

"Sure. The one inside the door has a sink, but the can is out-of-order—"

"Of course it is," a girl groans near us. "That one is always messed up."

"I'm actually—" I pause, remembering the words considered rude to use among strangers when referencing this issue: *menstruating, bleeding, having my period, raining red…* "—shedding the extra lining that went unused when my uterus didn't receive a fertilized egg," I tell him.

There's an immediate realization that I've used too many words because he has a fast reaction.

His eyes widen, and he clears his throat as his cheeks go red. "There are three inside. All of them are easy to find," he says as he darts away.

And that's why Tria told me to word it differently.

I've yet to discover a way that doesn't get me that same reaction with every male stranger with whom this topic has come up.

Walking inside, I try not to glance around, worried I'll see Base with another girl or hear him with one. But finding a bathroom is not as easy as Taylor said it would be.

I'm not sure why I care if Base is with another girl. I'm not looking for a boyfriend. I've learned from everyone around me how this needs to go in order to achieve optimal relationship bliss.

I finally push open one door, spotting a bathroom in the back corner, but I stumble to a halt when I see that I'm in a bedroom that is attached to that bathroom.

Judging by the deep, soulful voice permeating the air, and soft guitar music that I couldn't hear over the party music, I come to the conclusion I'm in Base's room.

It's also obvious because Base is shirtless and lying on his bed while strumming an acoustic guitar and singing.

If I'm rambling this bad in my head, I definitely should *not* open my mouth.

Just as I start to run or something—*my cognitive functions are suffering that glitch again*—his eyes land on me and widen in clear surprise.

A slow smile crawls over his lips, and his eyes relax as his gaze sweeps over me. When he sits up, I remain rooted to my spot. I feel physically frozen in place.

Idly, I find myself wondering if this is one of the things I can blame my menstrual cycle for.

"Sorry!" I finally blurt out with zero finesse.

I realize why people sometimes cringe around me.

I've never gotten embarrassed before, and there's no reason for me to be embarrassed right now. But my cheeks are hot, and I'm definitely cringing. It's the one expression I am well versed with.

"I've literally been looking for your number for half the day," he says, his voice normal and not squeaky and ridiculous like mine. "I'm glad you came by."

I'm trying to figure out if that means he told Krysta to bring me, or if he didn't know I was coming…

I really wish people would just state things the exact way they mean them.

Life would be simpler.

"Why?" I elect to ask, deciding that's the best course of action.

His grin only grows, and he gestures to a wall that has numerous gossip columns about me pinned there. Also, there are a *lot* of pictures with my face or eyes cut out.

I dart my gaze away, since I promised Dane I'd never read any of those columns. Then I frown as Krysta's mention about *Fatal Attraction* pops into my mind.

"Why are you—"

"Yeah, I know…it's totally creepy," he interrupts, laughing under his breath, "but when I get inspiration for a song, it's usually a person that strikes it. I've written my own story a thousand times. To keep the music fresh, I look at other people."

He puts the guitar aside, and stands, moving toward me with what I can only assume is well-deserved confidence. I don't even realize I've fully moved inside the room until he pushes the door shut behind me, bringing his body really close to mine as he stares down at me.

"It's the eyes every time," he says, moving impossibly closer as he tilts my chin up with the tip of his finger. "I always want to write the stories that could tell me why that look is in their eyes. A girl with sad eyes while wearing a practiced smile has definitely intrigued me. Music is all about emotion, and yours had the right emotion to draw me in."

He gestures to the wall again. "I only pinned up the ones with your picture, because I wanted to capture more emotions."

As he moves to study one picture, I shift uncomfortably.

"And there're so many emotions in all of them, sometimes just enough subtle difference to change the entire story like a ripple effect. I've been writing all afternoon, and I haven't written anything solid in months," he adds.

He walks back, still grinning as he props against a wall.

"So what's it going to take to get you to tell me more about your story? Because that always adds more emotion to the eyes."

The first thing that pops into my head is that…if he'll take my virginity and make it good, I'll tell him every sordid detail. Even I realize that *that* is not an acceptable thing to say.

Is it?

He has my pictures pinned up, which I don't think is a social normality, even though he seems confident that it is, given his easy explanation. He even makes it sound charming.

But…I still don't think I should proposition him so soon.

Never mind. I like Base. He seems nice, and according to Maverick, all attractive musicians have sex with girls all the time, which means he'd have plenty of experience in making this nice.

Definitely going to ask him. So long as he'll comply with the standard test for sexually transmitted infections.

The words just won't seem to come out, though.

"I need your bathroom to properly tend to my body as it sheds the lining that went unused when my uterus didn't receive a fertilized egg," I tell him as a substitute, when inane and unexpected panic wads up in my throat.

I should have stuck with *freshen up*. Or I should have asked him to break my hymen—though that's just a figure of speech. The hymen actually only stretches after sexual intercourse, though it's still referred to as "breaking it," since it's irreversibly changed after that.

Head ramble.

His grin doesn't falter as he gestures to it. "Definitely the most unique way I've heard it referenced," he says, not laughing at me and not looking at me like I'm from another planet.

Hesitating, since I feel like this is almost a trick, given Taylor's reaction earlier, I dart into the bathroom. Finally.

This lining has been extra annoying to shed.

By the time I finish up and wash my hands, I expect him to be gone. But he's on the bed again, lying on his back with his guitar on his stomach as he strums lazily, not really making music.

"So, do I get your story?" he asks with a conversational tone as his eyes stay on the ceiling.

"The whole story?" I ask.

Usually there's a sense of urgency inside of me to change the topic. But I think his overly relaxed attitude is relaxing me. Odd, since I was in a panic before I went into the bathroom.

Maybe all my reactions to him are a direct result of my menstrual cycle.

"No. Never the whole story. Then I wouldn't have anything new to figure out. Start with a secret," he answers.

He stops strumming and pats the bed beside him with smirk on his lips. He's not the first guy to do that in my lifetime. But he's the first guy to do it playfully and clearly not sexually.

Another oddity is how the only ones who've propositioned me for sex are usually the ones I'm not attracted to. Rain assures me it's okay to be shallow, since I'm not looking at long-term.

Rambling in my head again…

Climbing onto the bed, my eyes meet his as I move toward the back corner next to him. His eyes rake over me again as that smile of his grows.

"I don't have secrets," I say when I'm sitting cross-legged beside him.

His gaze lingers on my shorts for a minute before his eyes lift to meet mine. "A girl that claims no secrets? You're trying to write the songs for me now."

His consistent grin is starting to infect me. That's the only thing to explain why I can't stop my own smile from forming when I don't even know what I'm smiling about.

"You may have the most expressive eyes I've ever seen," he tells me, strumming the strings on the guitar idly.

You can barely hear the party music thudding in here.

"Why aren't you at your own party?" I ask.

"Because I'm in the zone, and I'm not coming out of here until it's dried up. I'd take getting high off the creative buzz over getting drunk on booze any day. Now that you've come to visit me, I might not be coming out for a while."

I still don't know if he's the one who made sure to get me here.

"Since you have no secrets, tell me something that most people don't know instead," he goes on, still so relaxed, as though he really is high.

Only he doesn't have that glazed look I've seen in high eyes.

It's more of a…content, easy look, as though the world is off his shoulders. Then again, he might be high and I'm just insinuating what I hope is going on. After all, he's a musician. Maverick assures me that all musicians are high, and that I should never give one of them my 'V-card' no matter how much the 'groupie-effect' makes me want to.

I'm still learning Maverick-speak most days.

"I've always been terrified of rats. We go to the pet store a lot when we're out as a group, because Sean and Angel like to buy things for their pets. I don't react when I see rats, because the guys torment each other with the insects, rodents, or reptiles they fear individually. It's one case where I don't want to feel like I'm included."

He laughs under his breath, a soft, gentle rumbling as he stops strumming.

"But you want to be included in other ways?" he asks, eyes intently focused on mine.

"Of course. They're the only people to ever make me feel included. Even when I say the wrong things, they seem to like me even more. My favorite days are the days when we're all together."

His eyes seem to lighten, and he scoots closer to me as he lifts an arm and puts it behind his head.

"Most everyone wants to be included, and the majority of all people don't want to be scared with things that scare them," he says, not sounding like he's mocking me. "So in all actuality, you're not really telling me anything someone not close to you wouldn't guess on their own."

He gestures around.

"For instance, most people either assume or know that Tag lets me rent this house. A house I'd never be able to afford otherwise, even with three other bandmates splitting the rent. It'd be easy to figure out. Something most people don't know is that in a little over two more years, if I'm still playing in bars and no closer to getting a contract, I'm out."

"Out?" I echo, parroting the word that confuses me.

"Out," he says again, smiling a little tighter. "My dad spent his life chasing the same dream. Left me and my mom at home, while he slept his way through random towns and drank, snorted, or shot up with little money he had. Which, compared to Tag's dad, I got the good one."

He shrugs, not sounding like he's bitter or anything, but I decide not to comment or ask.

"But I swore if I didn't make it by the time I was twenty-four, I was done. I'll get a regular job doing something I don't hate, and live a nine-to-five life without ever wondering 'what if' because I gave it everything I have."

"You're twenty-two?"

"Just turned twenty-two," he says, arching an eyebrow at me. "Why do you sound so surprised?"

"I've heard a lot of ages from the girls. I'm not surprised, just glad you clarified."

He laughs quietly. "The Sterling's inner circle of girls talks about me a lot?"

"Only when they see you play. Maverick calls it the groupie-effect. I'm not sure I understand what that means."

He shakes his head, working a little harder to smother his laughter.

"What about Tag?" I ask. "He knows Vince Jaggons. And he owns a—"

He waves me off, grinning as he interrupts. "That's a much bigger favor than you realize. Even if he could pull those strings, I don't want that sort of favor. I've sent three demos to that label, and asked my cousin *not* to call in a favor that substantial."

"You want to make it on your own," I surmise. "I can relate."

I did the same thing when I applied for my internship. It's the one time I hid the Sterling name.

"Well, I'm not *that* noble," he says, grinning larger. "When you get that favor called in, the label doesn't care about your sound.

They care about your name and what your name can do for them. You lose all integrity that very second. They try to repackage you, change your sound, strip out the soul of your music until you're just a shell and singing whatever song you're told to like the cookie-cutter cutout they know will sell. Those bands break up most all the time. Or they stick around for the money and forget about the music until the fad has ended and they're forgotten. And everyone, Randy included, agreed that wasn't the route we wanted to take."

I lean back, genuinely intrigued now.

"When I make it, I want it to be for real. I want to keep the love and not lose myself to the beast of the industry. If I have to sell my soul, I'll start to resent the music."

I like the way he just talks, not acting like there's a specific amount of information he can share, even though he doesn't really know me.

"I've passed on decent job offers. I've only done casual relationships since junior high. And though I love a good party, I'll pass all day every day when there's a gig to play or a song that wants to be written. I'm all in right now, so that I can be free of it later if I don't make it."

Deciding to get more comfortable, I lie on my side, facing him, and he adjusts his guitar so that I can move just a little closer.

"Most people do want to fit in, but I struggle with more effort," I tell him, almost as though I'm subtly defending my answer from earlier, which isn't something I usually do. "Everyone assumes it was foster care that made me so socially inept. In some ways, I suppose it didn't help, but it's not the main source. But I let people think that, and I even use it as an excuse when I feel it necessary to avoid the seemingly unacceptable truth by everyone else's standard. Sometimes, the truth gets passed over as not being a severe enough truth. The simple truth is that it's just how I'm wired. I can't read social cues. I struggle with expressions or knowing when someone is sincere. I enjoy good-natured ribbing, but it's sometimes hard to differentiate from cleverly disguised mocking, so I'm careful when selecting new people to introduce into my life on a more regular occasion."

He twists, putting his guitar on the ground, then turns to face me a little more.

"I'm not mocking you when I laugh, for the record. I just find you intriguing."

I feel my smile before I even decide what expression to use, and it's an…easy smile. One that happens on its own. My favorite kind that usually only happens when I'm really comfortable with someone—which is rare.

And again, very odd timing, since I'm not physically comfortable being around him. My body feels as though it's on riot, if I'm being completely candid.

"So," I go on, "when they include me, it's a bigger deal to me than to some people. Since Harley came to get revenge on Dale and decided to fall in love with him instead, I've started fitting in even more."

His brow wrinkles for a second before he laughs softly again.

"Because of the park games where you're a Valkyrie princess?" he muses.

"Partially. I have a script there. It makes interacting with people much simpler." His eyes never leave mine as I speak, and he doesn't seem impatient.

I find myself relaxing more and more.

"What's with the obsession with sex the gossip columns keep referencing?" he asks, and I frown.

"The gossip columns say I'm obsessed with sex?" For the first time ever, I'm tempted to read them and break my promise to Dane.

His eyes widen a little. "Sorry. I just assumed you read the things about yourself."

"Dane asked me not to because of something to do with 'haterade.'"

His grin grows. "You always do what your brother tells you to?"

"Asked. He *asked* me not to read them," I state in correction.

"Dane has done a lot for me, and he's asked for very little at all. So yes, I'm always quick to oblige when he directly asks for something."

His smile falters. "You feel like you owe him?"

"No. He's made it clear that I don't. But I still want to be able to give back on the very rare occasion he asks for anything."

When his smile returns, he blows out a heavy breath.

"So are you gay, and are you obsessed with sex?" he asks, arching an eyebrow.

Given the context, I don't think he's asking about my sexual preferences… I mean, we're discussing happiness, right?

"I like guys and I'm happy," I decide to say, covering both bases. He starts laughing, but I continue, since he still doesn't seem to be mocking me. "I'm not obsessed with sex," I go on. "Maybe fixated at the moment, since it's proven to be much more difficult than I expected."

"Really?" he muses, his eyes raking over me, down to my toes and up again until his gaze locks with mine. "Why?"

"Bringing up my virginity tends to stall things when they actually *are* progressing."

He bursts out laughing, turning to put his head into the pillow to smother the sound.

"Five Sterlings cause issues as well, whenever they're hovering."

"I can see that," he says, still laughing.

"Then of course there are the ones who ask too many questions about my family. Everyone has warned me about social ladder climbers using me and possibly hurting me or the family. I'm not sure if they mean emotionally or physically, but either way, if they're warning me away, then I listen. And I'm supposed to avoid 'cherry pickers,' though I'm still not sure how to discern who chases virgins just to be the breaker of the most hymens. Contrary to popular belief, women maintain a hymen; it just stretches or tears during the first session of intercourse. That's why pain scales vary. I have a normal hymen; the opening in it grows larger as I grow, but I'm finished growing, so it should hurt the least now."

His laughter doubles, and he moves even closer, causing his jean-clad knee to brush against my shin. I have no clue why I shiver, but I do, and tingles ghost over my body.

As his laughter tapers off, I decide it's safe to continue talking, since it doesn't seem like he's put off.

"Mostly, I'd just like to not be a virgin anymore, but I don't want someone who will hurt me physically. I have an eidetic memory, so forgetting things is an issue, and I've read some horror stories. I'm not worried about getting hurt emotionally."

His smile vanishes. "You need to be prepared, and—"

"I have plenty of lubricant and condoms, and I've been on birth control for years," I tell him, practically gloating over my preparation skills. "Rain assures me I'll want a lot of sex as long as the first time isn't terrible, so I've stocked three drawers."

He scrubs a hand over his face. "That's certainly prepared," he mutters under his breath just loud enough for me to hear. "Definitely get someone who knows what they're doing," he says quietly, his eyes dipping to my mouth before coming back up.

He groans for no reason I can discern as he flops over to his back and puts his arm across his face. Without looking at me, he adds, "And I read about your memory, Girl Genius."

I look down and start picking at a loose thread on his black bedspread.

"So if I asked you for the square root of any number, you'd know it immediately" he asks, lifting his arm so he can see me.

"Doubtful. I'd have to do the math, even if it was in my head."

"Terrible inconvenience," he says with that same small smile.

I just glance around his room, taking in the sparse decorations and plain furniture that is peeling at all the edges. He doesn't seem to care much for *things*. I like that.

"So tell me something real, Britt Sterling. Something very few know. You're getting closer to a revelation; I can feel it," he says, still grinning. "You can tell me why you're really obsessed with sex."

When I open my mouth to correct him, he beats me to it.

"Sorry. You can explain your *fixation* with sex. The *real* reason."

Bristling, I decide to keep that to myself.

Instead, my eyes slowly lift to meet his, and I say something I've never said aloud to anyone. "Everyone thinks I'm smart."

"Everyone thinks you're a *genius*," he says absently as he picks his guitar back up. "The smartest of the smart. That doesn't have any relevance to the topic, though."

"Just because someone tests to be a genius, it doesn't mean they're smart."

He frowns at that, and I work a little harder to play along with this muse game of his. "I'm actually not very smart at all," I go on.

"How are you not smart?" he asks, sounding confused…or constipated. One day, I'll learn the difference.

Before I can answer, there's a knock at the door, saving me from the confession.

Chapter 11

BASE

How have I not met Britt Sterling sooner? Were they deliberately hiding her from me?

Her fucking eyes dance with so much emotion she doesn't express in any other way, almost as though she doesn't know how to. I've been looking into people's eyes for years, and never once stumbled across this much closet emotion.

The only thing interrupting this is the persistent banging on my door. When I try to simply ignore it, it finally swings open, and I glare over as Sticks walks in, grimacing.

"Sorry to interrupt, but the other Sterling girl is sick wasted, and she wants to get out of here. I told her not to play a drinking game with Taylor, but she was persistent."

Britt hurries off the bed, and I stand, grabbing a shirt to pull on as well as my guitar. I'm not ready to give her up just yet, because the music is playing in my head with so much of a buzz that I can't even consider losing the muse.

At least that's what I'm telling myself, because I should *not* be following Britt Sterling around for any other reason. She's way out of my fucking league.

The virginal princess with an army of very powerful people who would gut me if I hurt her…then ruin my career…should also be a red flag.

I make it outside to see the drunk girl in question being propped up by Taylor, who nods toward us as he gives me a tight smile. "I would have taken her home, but she needs someone to stay with her until she's hydrated and sober. Figured she'd prefer a friend over a random guy at a party," he explains.

Britt blinks. "We're not friends. This is the first time I've gone anywhere with her. Should I call someone else if a stranger will make her uncomfortable?"

The uncertainty on her face has me shoving my guitar at Sticks. "Put this in the back of the car she drove. I'll take them both home."

Sticks glances between me and Britt warily, but I don't say anything as I scoop Krysta up, hoping like hell she doesn't spray puke in my face when she lets out a pitiful groan.

"Fuck's sake, Taylor. What was she drinking?" I ask as I carry her down the steps.

He follows close behind. "Just the vodka. But she said she hasn't done any drinking in a while. Sorry, man."

Sticks gets my guitar put in the trunk, as Taylor helps me put Krysta on her stomach in the back seat. Britt just follows, looking like she has no idea what to do.

"Britt, what's the best way to handle a drunk person?"

As if on autopilot, she answers robotically. "Continually monitor the drunk person. Check and monitor breathing. Make sure intoxicated person does not slip from a state of sleeping to unconsciousness by waking them often. Contrary to popular belief, 'sleeping it off' is not safe. Ensure drunk person sleeps on their side with a pillow—"

I tip her chin up with my fingertips, and her words cut off. "I'll help you. Come on."

Her entire body visibly relaxes, and she climbs into the front seat while I go the driver's side.

Krysta pukes on the floorboard the second I climb in, and I immediately roll down the windows while fighting my gag reflex. Britt doesn't even make a face.

"At least it's her car," I say as we start backing out.

Britt looks over at me, a blank expression on her face. "I should call Maverick. He can help. Or Corbin, since he's her half-brother."

"We can handle a drunk girl," I tell her. "Handled plenty of drunks in my time."

"Then why did you ask me to tell you how to care for—"

"Because I wanted you to know you could handle it too," I interrupt, smirking when she studies me.

"I hate vodka," Krysta groans from the back.

In the next second, she starts snoring.

"Did she pass out or is she just sleeping?" Britt asks, sounding a little too worried.

"Relax," I tell her. "If she's puking, she'll be getting most of it up. Trust me."

She relaxes again, and we ride the rest of the way in relative silence, sans the sounds Krysta makes when she vomits twice more…then begins snoring again.

"All you have to do is ask me to pull over," I remind Krysta.

She groans her disapproval.

"How are you not even making a face?" I ask Britt, practically hanging my head out the window to breathe.

Britt is doing something on her phone, as she seriously answers, "I've been around a lot of unpleasant bodily fluids in my life, and my sense of smell has been dulled against them."

This is why I'm *fixated* on her right now. She claims to have no secrets, but only gives you tidbits of information that have curious minds like mine screaming for more.

Just as we pull up to a semi-large home on the beach, a little bug pulls in as well, and my eyebrows go up as a familiar tatted girl steps out and jogs toward us.

"I had to text Ruby to get Krysta's address, but she said she'd meet us here instead," Britt explains. "Which is better. Ruby's her sister. She should be with someone who cares about her the most."

"She's drunk, Britt. Not dying," I say with small smile as I step out.

Ruby stumbles when she sees me, and her eyebrows hit her hairline. A slow smile spreads and her gaze darts between Britt and me, as Britt also climbs out.

"I'm so not telling Corbin about this," she says with that smile *still* growing.

Britt tilts her head. "About Krysta getting drunk?" she asks so obliviously.

My own grin spreads as I go to help get Krysta out of the back seat.

"Yeah. About that," Ruby says, patting Britt's arm as she comes to help me out, then she groans and gags. "Man, I hope she knows she's cleaning that shit up. Care if I take her inside and wash her up?"

Britt just blinks. "Do whatever she needs done."

Ruby's eyes soften. "It's okay, Britt. You did okay. Stop worrying."

Until this moment, I didn't realize how worried Britt actually was, but her entire body is strung tight.

I carry Krysta into the shower—fully clothed—and leave Ruby to deal with it. Ruby thanks me with a small smile on her lips as she turns on the spray of water that slaps Krysta directly in the face.

Krysta jackknifes to the seated position, sputtering and cursing, and Ruby laughs like she's amused.

Sisters…

Turning, I walk out, pulling my now disgusting shirt over my head carefully, while holding my breath.

Britt is standing wide-eyed in the living room, her eyes on my body as I grin over at her. "Care if I wash this shirt?"

She points at the room off to the side, and trails me as I head to the washer. I just put the shirt in without turning it on, since I'm sure Ruby will want to add Krysta's clothes in.

Jogging outside, I go to grab my guitar, and return to see Britt pacing in the living room.

"Everything okay?" I ask, causing her eyes to flick to my chest again.

"You arouse me a lot," she states, causing me to…I don't even know how to react.

What the hell do I say to that?

Her cheeks heat, and she exhales harshly. "What I mean is that I panic with you, but I still think you would be the best candidate for my hymen issue."

My grip slips, and my guitar case bangs the floor when I drop it entirely.

Her eyes stare at me expectantly while I clear my throat. Repeatedly.

My mouth opens and closes a couple of times, but I end up clearing my throat some more while rubbing the back of my neck. This is the first time in my life I've been rendered speechless. And I've had some unusual sexual propositions after performances.

Instead of speaking, though, I resume clearing my throat some more.

"You're going to run now, aren't you?" she asks seriously, frowning. "I thought you were different."

More vomiting sounds come from the bathroom down the hall, serenading this moment, and I quirk an eyebrow as an incredulous smile spreads over my face.

"Not running," I tell her, which causes her smile to grow. "But I'm not taking your virginity either, pretty girl," I quickly add with a little less enthusiasm.

Her smile falls.

"Oh."

With that one word uttered, she expressionlessly turns and walks away, moving toward the bathroom without saying anything else.

Lips twitching, I grab my guitar from the case and take a seat, playing a new melody as it essentially composes itself. The lyrics aren't there yet, but I can feel them trying to form.

After a while, Britt emerges, almost stumbling when her eyes land on me. "I thought you'd be gone," she says, frowning.

"You're going to have to ask me to leave if you want me gone," I tell her with a smile, my fingers pausing on the strings.

She hesitates, almost as though she's thinking about what words to use. I'd rather just hear things fly from her mouth, uncensored, if I'm being honest.

Then maybe I could get inside her head a little better.

"I didn't mean at this precise moment," she finally says. "About the hymen issue, I mean," she adds so seriously, as though she's decided this is the best route to take for this conversation.

My grin grows, since I've *never* had a conversation like this.

"We can wait for them to leave," she states, then looks at me expectantly, as though she's come to the conclusion she's clarified things enough for me.

Wiping away my grin so that she doesn't take it wrong and get insulted, I shake my head.

"I'm one hundred percent focused on my music right now. The best I can offer is friendship, so I think it'd be a dick move to take your virginity," I tell her, trying to be as collected and calm as possible, even though the v-word does scare the shit outta me.

Given her approach, I'm starting to see why she's struggling to find any takers. And I'm an ass for liking the fact she's struggling.

I think it's part of the reason she is who she is.

I'm not in any sort of hurry to see someone take that away from her.

She stares at me for a moment before finally asking, "Why did you kiss me?"

Now that I know she's *not* gay, I feel like a total dick for kissing her, then leaving to help get the drunk chicks out of the party before someone drowned or got hurt enough to sue us. Especially since one of those drunk girls sort of kissed me.

"It was in the moment," I decide to answer. "I like to think I'm a passionate guy because most artists are, and I tend to do whatever the moment calls for without thinking too much about it. It's cliché but true."

She studies me again, as though she's running the words through her head. She has to overthink things because she thinks differently, or so I'm learning.

"I'm not going to become emotionally invested," she states matter-of-factly.

"That's usually the messiest entanglement because emotions don't disappear just because you pretend they don't exist," I tell her, still battling that grin.

If only she wasn't a virgin…

My gaze dips down to those cupid lips that definitely stir memories. If she hadn't stopped me, I might have accidentally have taken her v-card.

"Maverick had an efficient arrangement with Chloe that never resulted in hurt feelings, and he easily cut her out of his life in support of Harley, who he had no sexual attachment to. It was never messy."

My eyebrows go up. "I don't know who Chloe is, but I do know Mav, and I don't think he's the best Sterling for you to model your love life off of."

She frowns. "Why not? He's always been happy, and now he's in a healthy, happy relationship. He had sex with numerous women without emotional attachments or messy breakups. Tria assures me that the double standard for men and women is steadily declining."

I scrub a hand over my face. "Killin' me, smalls," I groan.

"I'm too young and inexperienced to deal with those types of emotions, and I'm aware of that," she tells me flatly.

I peer over at her in confusion. "What?"

"Dane lost his virginity to Rain, and vice-versa, and they were messy because of emotions—also due to youth. Kode obsessed about the wrong Noles sister for so long that he almost missed out on Tria, all because of youthful emotions. Corbin nearly destroyed himself and Ruby because of youthful emotions. Dale was insecure and somewhat self-centered, hurting someone who now means a lot to him because of youthful emotions. Maverick is the only one who didn't suffer painful attachments or heartbreaks before he found Salem."

She blinks at me, as though she expects me to piece all that together and tell her the conclusion she assumes I'll draw.

Finally, she says, "I don't want to suffer heartbreaks. I don't want to love someone and lose them because of timing and maturity. I don't want to do this wrong. I don't want to feel rejected by someone I've allowed myself to care about that I shouldn't have. I want to skip the dark undertones this time, and head straight for the happily-ever-after. But I want to enjoy life while I wait, because I don't want to feel like I've missed out on anything now that I have the chance to be happy."

I lean back, putting my guitar down as she gives me a lighter, more genuine smile.

"That's something no one else knows about me," she tells me, her smile slipping. "Please don't tell anyone."

"I thought you didn't have secrets," I say quietly, running my index finger over my bottom lip as I struggle not to give in.

Everything about her is testing my resolve.

"I don't, but people feel sorry for me a lot of times when I tell the truth, and I don't like that at all," she explains.

Heaving out a breath, I shake my head. "I'll give you a tip," I tell her, smirking when her brow furrows. "Stop asking someone to simply do the deed like it's a chore. It sucks the romance out of the moment, and things like this need to happen naturally. It's just too much pressure on the guy when someone is forced to overthink it."

Her smile immediately blooms. "Naturally?" she echoes. "Like in the moment. The way you said the pool was."

"Exactly," I tell her, walking a very frayed and fragile rope.

She nods. "That's the first time a male has given me that advice. Maverick told me to make sure I brought up my hymen as much as possible. Corbin said to always be upfront with letting men know how much I was ready to be done with my virginity. Even press the issue. That way they don't overthink it."

I choke on air, then burst out laughing, my body shaking with the force.

"They sabotaged me, didn't they?" she asks as I try to speak through my guffaws.

"Yes," I manage to say, expecting her to be angry when I look up.

Instead, she's smiling thoughtfully. "They sabotage each other a lot," she says as she nods like it makes perfect sense.

"Any more tips?" she asks as she pulls out a notebook that seems to have one list after another on every page she turns.

"On how to get a guy in bed?" I ask incredulously.

"It doesn't necessarily have to be done in bed," she states dryly. "I'm open to suggestions."

I am…going to get punched by a Sterling.

Chapter 12

BRITT

"Base Masters has been staying at my house all week, has no interest in taking my virginity, and rarely wears a shirt, even though I've expressly told him he arouses me. A lot," I decide to tell Harley on Friday at lunch.

She chokes on her sandwich, then guzzles her drink like she's trying to force an oversized piece of food down her throat, as her wide eyes stay fixed on me. She stomps her foot. Stands and sits. Finally, she slams her hand down on her desk, tears springing to her eyes as she struggles to dislodge the food apparently stuck in her throat.

We're eating in her office today, so I'm the lone witness to the entire scene.

"Do you need the Heimlich?" I ask her very seriously.

She waves me off and shakes her head, so I decide it's safe to continue.

"I've barely been home, but when I am home, I smell him everywhere. *See* him everywhere. And he's filling up my guest room with his things," I go on, as she makes some sound of frustration, coughing now as she drinks more water. "Not that I mind, since he's nice, and usually he has food for us. But I'm confused about his motives, since he's clearly not interested in me sexually."

She makes a sound, something akin to a whine, I believe.

She twists her body toward me, gripping one edge of her desk and gripping my hand. "Base Masters is in your house!" she hisses. "And you came into work?!"

I frown. "Of course I came in. I've been coming in all week. He was even disappointed that I didn't come to his show on Monday at Silk, even though I explained Dane was back and better at handling the club. But again, he doesn't have a sexual interest in me. He states his intentions, but I'm still confused. And you said I could come to you when I'm confused."

"And he doesn't wear a shirt?" she asks, her eyes staring at me as if she's using her creative-dream-gaze.

"You're not helping me sort this out," I point out.

She shakes her head, but a grin continues to travel over her lips. "You're fired. Now go home to Base."

I just stare at her.

"I can't be fired. I have a lot of work to do, and you're supposed to be grooming me for partner."

She groans. "You're not really fired, Britt. But feel free to miss as much work as necessary when Base Masters is at your house. In fact, take a couple of weeks off. Or work from home. I've offered you remote access plenty of times."

I go over all her words carefully, but none of them are the answer to my question.

"Why is he there?" I ask her.

"Did you invite him to be there?" she asks me, seeming to focus a little now.

"No. He came to my house when Krysta got sick, and he's stayed there. I only see him for about an hour or so a day, but that's still confusing me. *He's* confusing me. He wants to know things about me others don't, and in return he'll tell me things. I've apparently only given him one thing so far that was what he was looking for."

She fans herself a little with one hand as she props up on her other.

"Momma always said the artists and musicians were the oddest. Daddy always said that they'd be considered weird under any other circumstances." She sighs. "I hate both my parents, so what do they know?" she adds, chirping the words as she grins.

Maybe I glare at her. I'm not sure. But I am feeling unusually irritated right now.

"What does he do in the guest room?" she asks, waggling her eyebrows.

"He writes lyrics and composes music there—mostly on the walls. He asked for permission first. His bandmates were pulling in as I pulled out."

I think she whimpers. "What'd I'd have done to look like you when I was a teenager…" She gets a serious expression. "How old is he?"

"Twenty-two, but what does that have to—"

"Hold on. I need to text that to the girls," she says distractedly as she pulls out her phone.

"Harley!" I shout, then blink as my eyes widen in the same surprise hers do. "I'm so sorry. I have no idea why I just raised my voice," I tell her, a little horrified.

"Of course you don't," she says, smiling at me for reasons I—unsurprisingly—can't discern. "That's one of the many reasons I love you."

Still irrationally irritated, I sit back.

"But seriously, work from home for a while. And go to his shows when he asks you to."

Blowing out a frustrated breath, I stand up, not feeling any less confused than when I came in. And Harley insisting I work from home just makes me confused about her.

"Don't worry, I won't tell Dale," she says primly.

"Will he have a problem with me working from home?" I ask, *still* confused.

Her smile grows so wide that it looks painful. "I really do freaking adore you, you know?"

"I know," I tell her, since she's said that a number of times, usually when I'm confused. Which makes no sense. I'm not confused about her adoration for me, and I'm never asking about it when she says it.

Leaving the room, I grab my things then head home, mostly going through the motions on autopilot.

Just as I pull up, Sticks is also pulling up. His eyes go a little wide when he sees me.

"Hey, I didn't realize you were going to be here. Base said you worked until late most nights."

"Should I go?" I ask, assuming he wants time alone with Base.

He visibly restrains a smile. "Uh…no. This is your house, and I'm really fucking sorry that Base has just insinuated himself into your life. Usually it's characters in a TV show he draws his muse inspiration. Not the actual people. He says the emotions they fake are more genuine than the emotions they display off camera. He's never had a real-world muse before, and believe it or not, his creative process is one of the least crazy I've come across in this business."

"Okay," I state warily, unsure how to proceed.

"Look, I know he's intense, and I know he's like a bull going ninety to nothing toward a red flag, but I do appreciate you letting him invade your space. When he writes like this, gold comes out. And he's our only chance of ever getting a headlining spot. However, if it gets to be too much, let me know. I'll reel him in."

He's apologizing for him. That's something people usually have to do for me when I've said or done something too inappropriate. When I smile, Sticks arches an eyebrow.

"He's weird, isn't he?" I ask, feeling excited by the prospect Base Masters is significantly weird. Just differently weird than me.

"He can be," he agrees, smiling tightly. "But he's also brilliant when it comes to music. By far the most brilliant I've ever encountered. Brilliant artists are usually considered weird."

"Geniuses" are considered weird as well.

"I'm glad he's weird," I tell him, relaxing a little about Base being in my house. "Are you going back in?"

"If that's cool with you. I'm not so musically brilliant in the creative aspect, so I'm respectful enough to wait on an invite before simply walking into someone's house. I was going to draw Base out here." He grins like he's made a joke, and I smile back in return, not getting the joke but not wanting to look stupid either.

"You off work?" he asks as I push the door open.

The loud wailing of a guitar has Sticks grimacing, as I answer, "Yes."

"Shit. Is he always playing this loud?"

I shake my head. "He doesn't play when I'm home unless it's just the acoustic."

"At least he has that much sanity left," he grumbles. "Is he even sleeping or eating?"

"He eats with me nightly," I answer, frowning when he relaxes.

"Should I worry that he won't eat?" I ask loudly to make my voice carry over the even louder guitar.

"We've been trying to get him out so I could check to see how far off the reservation he is, but he's too deep in the zone to get out. He's only gotten out once since coming here, and that was Monday night for our gig at Silk. Tomorrow we're playing three hours away. And today he didn't answer any of our calls, which means he's slightly losing touch with reality. It happens."

Now I'm worried. I didn't know he was this weird or had weird tendencies that could cause him not to eat or sleep, and I have no idea if he's been sleeping since I've hidden in my room.

"Damn, it's loud, but it sounds fucking amazing. He really is in the zone. No wonder he's avoiding our calls today," Sticks says, closing his eyes as a smile spreads over his lips. "Most people wouldn't be so cool with him doing this," he goes on, his eyes opening and seeming to regard me carefully as I lead him toward Base's room.

The music grows louder with each step we draw closer.

"I'm weird too," I tell him, causing his smile to return.

When we push open the door, there Base Masters is. The small silver hoop seems out of place on his bottom lip, since I've never seen him wearing it before. However, like every other detail of his lips, I have noticed the very small piercing holes.

My eyes are also raking over his tribal arm tattoos, because as usual, he's shirtless. His eyes are closed, and a smirk is on his lips as he plays, seemingly oblivious to our intrusion.

His hair is damp, and his skin has a hint of a shine to it, like he's been exhausting himself. All of his muscles are flexed as he makes the guitar scream or sing or whatever they call it.

"Holy…shit…" The words Sticks says are almost lost over the music, and I look over to see his eyes searching the walls that are full of musical notes, some of which I've recently started learning, via the internet.

Though the playing part is not quite so simplistic. My hand-eye coordination doesn't cooperate.

Several lines of random song lyrics are scattered amongst the walls, having no obvious order.

"Yo!" Sticks shouts just as Base lingers on what seems to be the last note.

Base's eyes fly open, and an easy grin forms when he sees me and winks. His gaze flicks back to Sticks.

"How long you been standing there?" he asks him, as he starts removing the guitar and twisting knobs on the amplifier.

"Long enough to see why you've holed up in this poor girl's guest room without warning, and started writing all over her walls like this is your place instead of hers."

Base just grins broader. "I told her she'd have to tell me when she wanted me gone, and I'll paint over all of it before I go." When his eyes find mine again, those weird little butterflies erupt, finally making me understand that concept after redundantly hearing the figure of speech. "She hasn't told me to leave."

Sticks just grunts a comment I miss as he moves farther into the room to read some of the lyrics. Base's eyes stay on me, which I notice from my peripheral, because I'm pretending not to be awkward as I strain to focus on Sticks.

"Living life without lies or regrets, comes at the price of having no secrets," Sticks says, grinning as he looks over his shoulder at Base. "I want to hear the rest of that with the music."

"Later. It's not finished," Base answers, finally looking away from me as he grabs a notebook and hands it to Sticks.

When Sticks eyes widen, he says, "That's ten songs. You're saying—"

"I'm saying I have enough already for a new album, and I have even more to write. I also haven't gotten out the more complex ones. So fuck off until I'm dried up or she finally realizes I'm a nutcase and kicks me out."

Sticks laughs under his breath, his eyes flicking to the walls full of candid shots Base has taken of me with his Polaroid during this past week when I've shared tidbits of thoughts with him.

Most of the images have been reduced down to only my eyes, but a lot of them have my full face.

"If she hasn't figured out you're insane by now, I think it's safe to say you're in the clear," Sticks tells him while clapping his shoulder, then grimaces before wiping his hand on his pants. "Dude, take a fucking shower. Then get dressed. You're getting out before you start really losing touch."

"I'm good," Base tells him, waving him off as he goes to scribble on the wall.

Sticks casts a look over to me, then gestures like he's prompting me to speak or something.

"You should shower," I tell him, even though he doesn't stink.

I'm tempted to take a picture of *him* for a change, because he possibly looks the sexiest he's looked yet. Or my hormones are simply raging. One or the other.

Sticks covers his mouth and turns as his shoulders shake. Base looks over his shoulder at me, eyebrows up as he grins.

"Fine. I'll take a shower. But I'm only going out if my muse does. I'm staying in the zone, so it's her space or her presence."

Sticks turns a clear, expectant look toward me. "What d'you say, Britt Sterling? Can you handle a Friday night out? And do you have a fake ID?"

"I have fake IDs," I tell him, finally grateful for those.

"Plural?" Base asks, turning as he drops his pen.

"People at college gift them to me all the time so they can say their fake ID was good enough for a Sterling," I explain. "Apparently it's good marketing, according to them. They tell me as much every time I try to refuse them, and they say it'd help them out. I like helping people."

Sticks cocks his head, then shakes it as he says, "Rich people."

"Get dressed," Base tells me. "Maybe I'll find out what you do that makes men too aggressive when they dance with you."

If I'm not mistaken, he looks amused as he says that. And out of context, it sounds entirely too ridiculous.

"It was the environment," I tell him. "Most were drinking despite the absence of alcohol, and there's a certain violent dancing method some men believe to arouse a woman."

"I'm missing something," Sticks says, looking between us.

Base wipes away his smile as he begins telling him too much.

"Britt tried to pick up guys in a bar, since she loves dancing, but every time she ended up with guys too aggressive. Her brother made her take a bodyguard when she went, since she flew solo at a lot of under twenty-one hot spots. Naturally, I'm curious. This was supposed to be something most people don't know."

"Ah, gotcha," Sticks says as though that makes all the sense in the world.

"See? Sticks gets me," Base says, reaching down to start undoing his jeans.

I whirl around, putting my back to him, then pretty much run out of the room. Maybe everyone is right about me not being ready for sex if I'm running *away* from a guy undressing. A guy who I asked to *devirginize* me.

Webster's should accept that as a valid word, because it's quite practical.

"For fuck's sake, dude, wait until she's out of the room to start undressing. Or are you trying to get murdered by a Sterling?" I hear Sticks asking, and I almost break my no-eavesdropping rule.

Instead, I hurry to my room and take an inordinate amount of time getting ready.

Because apparently I'm going dancing.

On a Friday night.

With people I barely know.

I distinctly remember telling them I had fake IDs. There was never a vocalized agreement that I'd go. Apparently I somehow said something to allude to going.

How did I get myself into this?

Chapter 13

BASE

I'm dressed and waiting in the living room with Sticks as we wait on the other guys to arrive, and for Britt to come out of her room.

"You're seriously walking a thin, very fine line of super creepy; just sayin'," Sticks says as I finish posting some pics to Instagram from Monday night's show.

"I'm perfectly aware that I've already crossed that line, but Britt has zero friends outside of her brother's circle. Even those role-playing people just know her as the Valkyrie princess and not as herself. I'm going to change that so it feels like I'm giving back."

"How generous," Sticks says dryly.

I flip him off, since he makes me sound like a dick.

"That's not what I mean and you know it," I tell him distractedly.

Before he can fuck with me any more, Britt emerges, and I forget all the words. And all the music. For a solid fifteen seconds...

My eyes rake over her very fucking tight, strapless, black dress and stilettos. I quickly forget we're not in the room alone.

Sticks clears his throat and mutters, "You'd better be a motherfucking saint, you stupid bastard."

Her long, silky, red hair looks even brighter against the black as she stares at us, blinking. Expressionless. Though I can tell in her eyes she looks uneasy.

"Am I not dressed right?" she finally asks.

"Oh, you're dressed like a Sterling girl, that's for damn sure.

Forgot why the girls of that circle were so out of our league until right this second," Sticks goes on as he tugs at his collar. "But the place we're going is out of town, and less Fifth Avenue, more Second Street beside the tracks."

Her lips purse.

"He means jeans would make you blend easier, but you're more than welcome to wear that dress," I tell her, watching as her eyes relax.

"I'll change," she says, her smile returning as she turns and ducks back inside her bedroom.

I slap Sticks on the back of the head. "Don't speak in euphemisms."

"Sheesh, sorry. Didn't realize that was an issue," Sticks says, though there's a mocking grin on his lips.

I'm tempted to slap the shit out of him for it.

I hear the roar of Taylor's hideous Scooby van—yes, he has a fucking Mystery Van, fully replicated. It takes a lot of fucking confidence to roll up at gigs in that damn van.

Just sayin'.

Laughter and doors shutting sounds just as Britt walks back out, a pair of jeans that will also be testing my restraint, but not nearly as bad as the dress. I wish there was more *shirt* to her *shirt*—that would be a lot of help.

"Motherfucking saint," Sticks mutters again.

"Killin' me," I tell her, drawing a confused expression from her.

"Still not right?" she asks seriously.

"Can we keep her?" Sticks says. "Like even if your shit dries up tomorrow?"

Her shoulders slightly ease down, and she lowers back to her heels, her body visibly relaxing.

"Seriously, you look perfect, Red," Sticks says to her. "Let's roll before they bust up in here and wreck your house. I think Base has invaded your home enough for all of us."

I shove at him as I go to drop my arm around Britt's shoulders and begin steering her toward the door. She's strung so tight that I'm worried she's going to snap if I turn her too abruptly.

"Relax," I tell her, smirking when she presses up closer to me, while Sticks opens the door to two rowdy pricks.

"So he's actually getting out. How bad has he lost touch?" Taylor asks while doing zombie arms and staring blankly in front of him.

"Surprisingly, not as bad as we thought. We'll talk about it later. Let's get gone before he thinks of a tune he *has* to get out before we go," Sticks prompts, shoving at them to go back to the Scooby van.

"You're riding in style tonight, Sterling girl," Taylor says, opening the back doors to the Mystery Van.

Britt stares at it for a second, but doesn't bat an eye before climbing in.

Taylor just grins over at me, since she does it without complaining and takes a less-than-safe seat on his homemade, self-upholstered bench seat.

I slide in beside her, putting my arm back around her shoulders, hoping she relaxes a little so she can at least enjoy a night out.

Everyone loads up, with Randy taking shotgun and Sticks sitting on the opposite side of us. Britt stays quiet as everyone talks around her.

When the guys and I try to include her in the conversation by deliberately asking her questions, she pauses to think for a fraction of a second, barely noticeable, and commits to the smallest answer she can manage, as though there's a maximum word count she's sticking to. Five being that maximum.

Sticks casts a look at me, since he saw like I did that she was looser in her own house when it was just the two of us. I've essentially been in her personal space for days and she's still not completely comfortable with me.

But she's trooper enough to mask her discomfort with soft smiles and polite nods. As though she's been training the hell out of herself to blend in without drawing attention.

When the guys cut the music up and start singing obnoxiously loud to Metallica, I lean over, ignoring her sweet little shiver when my lips graze her ear.

"Do the Sterlings make you limit your word count or something?"

She frowns as she turns to face me. "Why do you want to vilify them? You keep asking antagonistic questions like that."

My lips twitch at the fact she's definitely saying more than five words when it's just with me.

"You're trying really hard to overthink things. Just making sure they haven't tried to filter you."

"I've asked for their advice on conversation material that won't get me gawked at when I speak to people. I say what I want to when I'm around them or when they bring people around me, because I can relax. They find my nature to be charming, but they're in a minority."

Twirling some of her unnaturally soft hair around the tip of my finger, I smile down at her.

"Sorry. I won't assume that again," I tell her, watching as the subtle bit of ire flees from her eyes immediately.

So fucking expressive, even when none of her other facial features give anything away.

"But don't filter yourself around them." I gesture to the guys. She opens her mouth to say something, when I add, "I'm serious."

She heaves out a breath, still looking uncomfortable, but doubling her efforts to *appear* comfortable. It's cute as much as it is frustrating, and it's a revelation as to what life is like from her eyes.

I stopped giving a shit about what people thought about me a long damn time ago. She honestly doesn't give a shit what people think either, but she cares if it causes her protective family issues.

I think. To be perfectly honest, I'm still working out how she thinks. It's not easy. At all.

As soon as we get to the club, which seems to take longer than an hour when you're stuck in the car with Randy, who is belting out off-key lyrics to every fucking song on the radio, I pull Britt's hand into mine.

Her fingers thread with mine, as I pull her toward the door. Taylor lifts his eyebrows and not-so-subtly looks between us several times before he goes still and simply stares expectantly.

I don't answer the unspoken question, since I've answered it a hundred times since I moved myself right the fuck into her spare room and started composing some of my best work to date.

We're not even halfway in when we're bombarded by a very small, familiar group of girls. Taylor throws his arms around two, dragging them toward the dance floor. Randy is vying for one's attention, who is trying to get mine.

Britt tries to escape, but I pull her closer.

Groaning, I turn to look at Sticks. "Who posted where we were going?"

"Who do you think?" he asks, eyes flicking to Randy.

"I fucking hate him some nights," I say too low for anyone to hear over the steady *thump* of the loud music.

"It'd be different if it was a squad of *different* girls all over the place throwing themselves at us. But when it's the same five every time, it makes it look like we can't get anyone else to stalk us."

"That's not at all what I meant," I point out dryly.

He just grins, but Britt distracts us by literally yelling. "I need to urinate!"

I release her hand, stifling a laugh, then nod as she warily looks through the throngs of people.

"I'll grab us some drinks," I call after her.

She waves a hand behind her, letting me know she heard, as she starts needling her way through the crowd.

Taylor is almost immediately back, sans the girls he helped to drag away, and yells, "I bought us just enough time for you to tell me what's going on between you and the Sterling girl, so I can know what sort of moves I'm allowed to make."

I turn an incredulous look on him.

"You better be joking, and we're just friends. Well, that last part is in progress."

She seems more at ease with letting me use her house as my crash pad while the muse is active, even though we just met. She's perfectly cool with me splashing her face on the walls, even though I admit that makes me sound like a creep. But she struggles with the concept of being friends?

Every time I think I have some idea of how she ticks, I'm left reeling again.

"Right. Friends. Always works out well when you want to fuck friends," he says in mock agreement.

"She's a virgin," Sticks says a little too fucking loud.

Taylor groans, then shakes his head. "Damn. I really thought that was all bullshit. You're an ass if you do anything then. Got it." As I move to the nearest bar to order some drinks, Taylor adds, "Do us all a favor and don't piss off the Sterlings while we're living in Sterling Shore."

I say nothing as I sip my beer, staring over the rim of it as I search the crowd, wondering when she's coming back.

Sticks and Taylor start talking about the music I've been writing, Sticks mostly relaying what little I've shared with him.

When I catch a flash of red hair, my beer pauses at my lips, and I slowly lower it as I stare at Britt. Drinking is probably a terrible idea. Even sober, I'm actively having to remind myself in mantra that she's a motherfucking virgin.

She's girl who is naïve enough to believe she can lose her virginity and have no emotions.

A girl who literally asked me to help with her 'hymen issue.'

"Motherfucking saint," I mutter to myself as she dances with the same confidence she walks with.

"You only have a small shot with her because the amount of rejection she's faced has substantially lowered her self-esteem," Sticks tells me like it's his duty to inform me of such.

"You're a better man than me," Taylor says when his eyes follow mine.

"He's really not. He's just telling himself that," Sticks says, the fucker sounding much too amused. "Guess urinating freed her bladder up for all that dropping low. Imagine if she had kept on the dress."

I really don't like either of them imagining that. At all.

The bottle almost slips from my hand, and I barely catch it, as an image I really don't need right now creeps into my own mind.

"This evening should be entertaining," Sticks adds while literally rubbing his hands together like the evil villain after his *mwahahahaha* laugh.

"I think life was easier when he thought she was gay. Hell, he kissed her like he was on a desperate mission to actually try to change her world," Taylor snorts, earning a glare from me.

When my eyes go back, the bottle does slip from my hand, shattering to the ground and causing Taylor and Sticks to leap back.

A familiar fucker is dancing with Britt, and she's smiling and laughing as she dances with him like they're friends. At least I hope it's a friendly dance.

She has had zero friends come over. She has also mentioned zero friends.

Then I realize why the dick is familiar.

"Oh, that tights-wearing, level-one, squire douche, nerd-girl-chasing son of a bitch," I say as I start stalking forward.

"What the hell kind of insult was that?" I hear Sticks asking as I start working my way through the crowd.

I crack my neck to the side when Britt decides to turn into a damn vixen and shakes her ass in a way a virgin shouldn't be allowed to move. It's simply not fucking fair to those of us trying not to be a total douchebag.

I decide Level-One Tights-Wearing Squire Boy is officially my least favorite person when he grabs her hips and drags her ass toward his crotch.

Probably not a good sign that I'm getting disconcertingly murderous just because some other guy is touching *my friend.*

Chapter 14

BRITT

Carefully, I try to extract myself from Tommy when he touches my waist and tries to dance behind me. *Tries to dance* being the operative phrase, since *failing* is sadly more accurate.

I'm always jarred and ready to run away when guys do that bizarre dance move that is nothing more than them violently bucking behind you. They do it so hard that it almost sends you tumbling to the floor, or at least stumbling around. It's not fun.

If they're that bad at dancing, they shouldn't dance. I don't ride horses right next to someone because I'm not good at it and someone could get hurt.

Finally managing to get turned around so I can face him, I try to keep my irrational annoyance out of my expressions. It's not like this song won't come on again, but I really just wanted to dance to it and enjoy it.

However, it's unimportant and unprepared-for conflict I have no choice but to avoid.

Just as he starts to move in closer, he frowns and pauses. Two other arms come around me much more invasively than Tommy's just were, fully wrapping around my middle.

More of those butterflies instead of uncomfortable tingles tells me it's the guy who confuses my body like no one else. And my mind. He definitely confuses my mind.

My hands seem to have a confused mind of their own when they come up and rest against his, as he starts moving behind me, dancing easily against me, and not bucking like he's trying to use one section of his body to see if he can knock me over. His body moves with mine instead of against it, and it becomes fun just that quickly.

Which shouldn't be surprising. Base seems to make everything different. Easy. As though he knows what someone needs in order for him to be so personal and invasive, yet make it charming and wanted. Almost like his presence is necessary after you've felt it, which is clearly not at all rational.

He turns me in his arms, and my eyes move up to his for a brief second before they bounce down to his lips that are pulled up at one corner of his mouth.

"I was on my way back, but—"

"But you really like this song?" he guesses, his grin forming.

How did he know that?

My grin grows, and I nod as he pulls me even closer, his hand going into my hair, as his other hand slides down to my hip. We're still dancing even when the song changes. Then…for a girl who can't forget, I quickly realize I misplaced the fact Tommy was still standing out here, only now he's tapping my shoulder.

His eyebrows are drawn down disapprovingly—*that expression I've seen on a variety of strangers and have figured it out*—as his gaze flicks to Base, whose grip is pulling me impossibly closer.

"Sorry! We'll dance some other time," I yell to him over the music, not even believing how relieved I am to be away from Tommy. Which is weird. I like Tommy usually. "This is Base. I came with him."

Tommy's eyes flick to Base incredulously, and Base seems to be smirking as he barely glances over at him. Wordlessly, Tommy leaves, presumably going back to his table of friends near the bathroom, as Base continues to dance with me.

"Who's he?" Base asks, not sounding overly interested.

"He's my squire a lot in the virtual world of *Land of the Lost Lore*. Recently, he was my physical squire in the park."

But it's almost like my words are getting lost in the music, because he just smiles and nods, almost as though he can't hear me or he's amused. Or maybe it's a sinister smile?

Sean is excellent at teaching me what a sinister smile looks like.

After a lot of dancing, my heartbeat is racing faster than usual. And I also keep pressing closer and closer to Base, until our fronts are so solidly touching that it becomes a little…uncomfortable for new reasons.

That arousal is definitely at an all-time high, and I've spent five minutes debating straddling his leg, and reminding myself he has already rejected me.

I think we're friends. Or I think that's his goal…to make us friends.

And I specifically remember Bella saying *friends don't straddle other friends' legs* at some point, though I never heard the context that comment was used in, since I merely overheard that line.

It seemed a bit odd at the time, since I had no idea why someone would *want* to straddle a leg. It unfortunately makes sense now.

Deciding to dull some of the ache, I turn, giving him my back, and start dancing on him that way. Unlike Tommy, he's not bucking away back there. His front grazes my back, and I arch into him, feeling the movements flowing so effortlessly between us.

His hand on my hip tightens, and he groans against my ear as one of his arms comes around my waist.

"Motherfucking saint," he says just barely loud enough for me to hear.

I turn my head to ask him what that means, and suck in a breath when my lips brush his on accident, because he's still leaned over and his face is significantly closer to mine than I was anticipating.

Just that barely-there ghost of a touch has my entire body responding. Even the slightest feel of the warm steel on his lip ring has me wondering what it'd be like to kiss him with it in.

His eyes flick over mine, lips still barely just parted, and his hand comes up, gently cupping the side of my face. I'm certain he's going to kiss me, until Randy suddenly bumps into us.

Base drops his hand on my cheek to steady me, and turns a glare on Randy, who is laughing really loud if I can hear him that easily over the steadily blaring music.

"We're ready to get out of here. Girls all around!" he shouts, and I bristle.

I forgot all about the girls who were here to gather with them. Which is weird, because I can't actually forget things. Maybe the memories just get suspended when Base's body is frustrating mine, and pushing all other thoughts to the back of my mind.

"I thought this was just a night out to have some fun," Base says, not sounding overly enthused.

"It is! Now that we're finished with the night-out portion of the evening, we're ready to have some fun!"

The girls crow with him, cheering and sloshing their drinks when they thrust them into the air in a toasting gesture. However, they seem pleasant enough.

Base mutters something as we start heading toward the front, but I remember it took exactly sixty-four minutes to come here, and that was without stopping for gas.

"I need to—" I pause, wondering if I should mention urinating again or if that would make me appear redundant. "—discharge urine," I decide to say.

His lips lift in a grin on one corner, and he goes with me to the bathrooms this time, for some reason.

"I'll wait right here," he says, pointing to his spot before pocketing his hands. "Just in case your song plays again."

I'm not sure why I grin, but I do. Idly, I notice him flick a definite smirk toward Tommy's table. I wave at Tommy, smiling at him, and he gives me a tight smile before returning his gaze to Base and clutching his beer bottle tighter.

My phone buzzes in my pocket, and I pull it out, seeing a text from Rain.

RAIN: I might have heard you have a certain shirtless Masters invading your house. Before I ask a favor, I need to know if he's in any way unwelcome. I can have him easily extracted without ever letting your brother know there was a problem.

I wish he was unwelcome. It would make this thickening layer of confusion much less of an issue.

ME: I don't want him to leave. I don't know why he's staying. He rejected my proposal.

I leave it at that.

RAIN: He's staying there, calling you his muse, and playing music shirtless?

ME: Harley told you, didn't she?

RAIN: WHY DIDN'T YOU TELL ME????????

RAIN: Don't worry. I won't tell your brother.

What does my brother have to do with anything? I told her Base rejected me, so that's not what she's referring to.

RAIN: We'll discuss this later, since I'm assuming you're out with him. Since…you're not at home. Tria and I were going to drop off some nice new clothes we bought you, maybe peek inside the house for a second…

ME: I'm confused. Is the favor me coming home so you can give me clothes and peek inside?

RAIN: No. The favor is we want you to bring Base to karaoke night. Don't worry, we're all happily married or in love. But Base

Masters at karaoke night…

Why does inviting Base to karaoke night feel like another rejection coming on?

Or worse, he'll go out of obligation, and I certainly can't tell obligatory expressions from constipation.

Still, I send her back an, *I'll ask.*

RAIN: Harley said you haven't seen him perform yet. How is that possible?

ME: I've been busy. I've heard him sing a little with really loud music, but he doesn't do it much when I'm in the house. He just asks me questions and tries to talk to me.

RAIN: But you haven't seen him PERFORM?

People call those 'shouty' caps, so why is she shouting at me so much?

ME: No.

RAIN: Then don't watch him perform until karaoke night. We want to see the magic happen.

ME: What magic?

RAIN: You'll see. ;)

Chapter 15

BASE

"I hate Randy. Let's kick him out of the band," Sticks says as he drops beside me on the wall.

"I would, but there was that blood offering, the chalice, a fire, and his Mom's terrifying grimoire all involved in that band pact we made," I tell him distractedly as I glance over some of my messages.

Without missing a beat, he says, "I voted for a simple pinky swear."

I snort out a laugh, not looking up from my phone as I swap over to emails.

"Why is the guy you made that weird insult about staring at us?" Sticks asks as he leans toward me just a little.

"Because he'd like to see me dead, most likely," I say with a shrug, lips twitching with the grin I manage to restrain.

I'm a cock-blocking motherfucker, and I doubt it'll be the last time I act like I have a right to block any *'candidates for her hymen issue.'*

Britt emerges, moving right up against my side, and I thread her fingers with mine as I start guiding her through people. Sticks falls in behind her, and we manage to weave all the way out of the building to where the van is getting loaded.

"Britt can sit in the floor with me. You still sober?" I ask Taylor as he walks toward us.

"Never drank a drop," he sighs.

Britt hesitates, her eyes on the girls.

"They're not vipers, Red," Sticks tells her, nudging her with his shoulder.

Why the hell does it bother me when *Sticks* touches her? This is *not* being friendly.

She gives a tight smile. "Why would you make that comment?" she asks like she needs more context.

It makes my smile start to spread.

"You were looking at them like you're worried," Taylor says quietly, almost as though he's working damn hard to reassure her that this won't be too bad.

Her face relaxes, and her smile spreads easily. "I'm capable of handling all types of people. I have word counts now to help ease the awkward conversations."

Sticks and Taylor exchange a confused look.

"I'm worried about the amount of semen possibly staining the shag carpeting, now that we'll be in the floor. On the ride over, you boasted how many girls you've had back there. I've never read about how many sexually transmitted infections can be transferred without actual sexual contact."

Taylor's eyebrows go up in surprise about the time Sticks and I both burst into laughter. I'm doubled over, losing my grip on her hand as my sides start to ache.

"We're clean," Taylor says, even as he fights his own laughter.

"The carpet is clean?" she asks, confused.

"No. I mean we all get tested fairly regularly after some questionable life choices," he tells her, working harder not to grin now.

"He means you're not going to catch something from the shag carpeting," Sticks tells her bluntly, and she exhales heavily while relaxing.

She barely gets inside before sticking out her hand and introducing herself to the girls. "Hi, I'm Britt Sterling."

One of the girls scoots over and pats the seat beside her. "You can sit here. Make the guys sit on the semen shag."

Britt immediately takes her up on it without even glancing in our direction.

I scrub a hand over the back of my neck. "You dicks should probably act at least a *little* classier. Just sayin'," Randy says on his way by as he scratches his balls.

"Fine. I'll wash the fucking van first thing tomorrow," Taylor grumbles as he climbs in and slams the door.

Sticks shakes with silent laughter, and I run a hand over my jaw, smiling a little at Britt as she eases into conversation this time with a more relaxed smile.

"You can stare at her from inside the van, man. Let's roll," Randy says in a dry, unimpressed tone as the fucker calls me out.

Britt's eyes immediately dart to mine, and she battles a smile as I climb in and drop to the floor next to her legs.

"So are you two a thing?" the chick next to her asks.

Just as I open my mouth to answer, Britt answers with zero hesitation or emotion, "No."

Randy snorts, and Sticks covers his mouth as his body starts shaking with suppressed laughter. .

"*Damn.* Just like that?" the chick asks Britt while snapping her fingers. "Not even an 'it's *complicated*' sort of thing?"

I get a few pitying looks like I'm a kicked puppy or some shit, and my lips twitch as I just arch an eyebrow at Britt.

"In all seriousness, she's out of his league. I mean, she's Sterling rich, and despite the fact she's still in college, she's also on the fast track to make partner at a major gaming corporation. She's barely even breaking a sweat while doing *all* of that…in her pajamas…most days. She's slumming just by being friends with us," Sticks says, his eyes laughing at me as I subtly flip him off.

Britt's eyes widen before she opens her mouth…then shuts it…then opens it again for few stuttered sounds.

Abruptly, she turns to me and blinks. "I said just *one* word and made it *this* bad. Now I can't think of any response that won't make this situation worse."

"Sticks thinks he's funny. All good, Britt," I tell her.

I drag her hand down to my mouth and kiss it, only confusing everyone in the van even more. I'm not sure why I find it so amusing.

Britt leans down, and I almost turn my head, but she speaks before I can. "Can you go to karaoke on Thursday?" she asks randomly.

My right eyebrow lifts as I turn to face her, our noses brushing. She doesn't pull back, and her eyes just stay fixed on mine like she's simply awaiting an answer.

My gaze darts to her lips as a slow grin tugs at my lips. "Sure."

Without even dallying for a split second, she pulls back and starts texting someone. My smile slips as I start getting confused.

"I'll let them know in the group message so they'll stop texting me in two-to-five minute increments," she says as though that's supposed to make sense.

I didn't realize this was going to be a group thing…

Her phone goes off again and she frowns as it continues buzzing more and more and more.

"Apparently, I just made that worse too," she sighs.

Sticks just rolls his eyes at me as I grin. The girls like me. At least I have them in my corner.

Chapter 16

BRITT

I can hear Base playing in his room when I get home Monday afternoon. Tempting as it is to go in there, I decide to sit down in the living room, bringing my email up on the TV so I can watch the links Harley sent me.

When he pauses and starts, I know it's likely he's scribbling notes or words, and I find myself smiling for no obvious reason. Maybe it's because the house doesn't have that eerie silence anymore when I get home.

I'm not investigating each sound to pinpoint what it is. I don't hear phantom footsteps when I'm in the shower anymore.

I, unfortunately, fell asleep on the way back from the club Saturday, and spent most of the day yesterday at the library while trying to complete my paper with Brin's unhelpful help. She wanted to know what I was doing at the library when Base Masters 'was shirtless in my house.'

I'm not sure why everyone keeps bringing that up. I've explained the rejection, and the fact he has no sexual interest in me.

The music stops again, as I finish up one of the videos and move onto the next. But I barely swallow back what is surely a painful screech, when Base is suddenly landing on the couch beside me, having leapt over the back.

"You're not at work," he tells me distractedly.

He's shirtless once again. Maybe shirts irritate his skin. If so, I'm sure I could find him some without abrasive material. I could make a list of quality material, as a matter of fact.

He props his feet up on the coffee table and stretches out his arm on the back of the couch behind my head.

"Harley became willfully uncompromising and told me to work from home, even though she refuses to explain why," I tell him absently, my eyes dipping to his chest as though gravity compels them.

They run down the line in the center of his abs, only getting distracted by the actual abs for a brief second, before dipping to his waistband where there are definitely muscles toned to a "V" shape.

I stop there instead of looking at his lap, and snap my eyes to the screen, wondering when I'll once again be in control of all my cognitive functions.

This is really getting ridiculous. I've given up trying to rationalize my inability to stop being attracted to him.

He nudges me with his shoulder.

"I figure I'll be ready to start rehearsing with them in a couple of weeks. You cool with me sticking around that much longer?" he asks as he messages someone on his phone.

I'm not even going to try and figure out why there's a distinct pang of disappointment in my chest. If I can't have him, then he might as well be gone so I can stop fantasizing.

I apparently like the frustration, because I really don't want him to leave.

"Stay as long as you need," I state quietly, my eyes staring at the screen I have paused.

"What're you watching?" he asks, putting his phone away. "Wait. I see men in tights. Is this LARPing caught on film?"

"It's segments of the trials. These are from Land of Lore. Land of *Lost* Lore has more creatures, more status, and a lot more world building."

His eyes flick to my ears as his grin grows. "Those elf ears should be on when watching, though, right?"

Frowning, I shake my head. "Why? I'm not role playing right now?"

His smile slips, and he mutters something about role-playing and being a saint that I don't catch the full context of.

"Is your name Base because Tagland is shortened to Tag?" I ask him. "Like a 'tag base' play on words?"

His eyebrows raise, and he peers over at me as he shakes his head slowly. "Nah. My mom likes to call me her anchor, and after a while she started calling me her base because I was her 'new foundation'. Then soon, she just called me Base as sort of a term of endearment. I was three when it stuck, and by fifteen, when I hurried to make sure the teacher called out *Base Masters* instead of my real name, I was thankful it stuck."

I'm smiling before I can stop myself. "What's your real name?"

"It's something very few people know," he says, as though he's letting me know this is a secret.

"Okay…"

"Eugene Cornelius Masters is my full name," he tells me, staring at me with what I think is supposed to be stern eyes, even as he seems to battle a smile. "Base was the clear choice. It sounded much more badass."

When I laugh, he winks, leaning back.

"What was your last name before Sterling?" he asks absently, as though he sees it to be no big deal.

"It's a name I won't say again," I state quietly.

"Why?" he asks, turning toward me again.

"Because it no longer has anything to do with the person I am. It's not a name that deserves recognition for the person I'm trying to become. And it's not a name attached to fond memories."

"But it's your name. Your past is still a part of you," he argues.

"It was my name," I agree. "And my past is a part of me. It can be a part of me without it getting any attention from the people who didn't know me when I had that name."

He wants to argue. It's his nature. He always wants people to see things from his eyes, and he passionately expresses that in a way that could cause someone to get caught up in his path.

But he also knows I won't engage in spontaneous conflict.

"I'd rather my past be left out of most questions."

"That's...complicated," he says, frowning, seeming as though he's fighting with his instinct to argue.

"It's part of the dark undertones that don't matter after the happily-ever-after," I remind him.

Blowing out a breath, he sinks down on the couch, getting comfortable as his arm brushes against mine.

"Compared to you, my story sounds fucking peachy," he says softly, tugging me even closer.

"If you start to pity me, I'll stop sharing things."

He laughs under his breath. "Pity is only there in the absence of admiration," he says, then gestures to the screen as his eyes return to it. "I'll spend my pity on these guys in tights who have to be embarrassed by the short tunics when it looks like there's a deer knuckle in the front of their pants."

My mind tries to process what he's saying, until I finally see the less-than-abstract comparison. There's an eye-widening sort of realization.

It's rare that I ever burst out into an actual fit of laughter. So rare that it startles me when I make some hideous noise and bray the rest of my laughter through pained and starved lungs.

He...snaps a picture of me. I can only hear it instead of seeing it since my eyes have been forced to screw shut with the painful hilarity.

I resent the joke by this point and don't find it funny anymore, but he'll snort, and I'll do that terrible braying thing all over again.

Never again will I be able to keep a straight face during those very serious moments on the battlefield.

My eyes open as I try to stifle the rest of my laughter. "What good will that picture do when your central focus is the eyes?" I ask, gesturing to the picture that hasn't started appearing yet.

He smirks as he shrugs, fanning the picture—which is actually not a good thing to do. "That one's just for me."

The remaining tendrils of laughter taper out, fading into the abruptly silent room. He walks the picture back toward his room, his eyes on it like he's waiting on it to develop.

At the very least, it was a picture he took for a non-muse reason. It's really, *really* unnecessary to be feeling the urge to blurt out something that will likely make him very uncomfortable.

I keep my mouth shut and try to remain as self-aware as humanly possible.

When he returns, he gestures back at the TV, and I hit *play.*

"So what's the point of these trials?" he asks.

"Unity. The community is expanding, and it's easy for that love to get spread too thin. Harley says she enjoys her girly touch on things, and she adds in the romance with these—"

"I never see you play the games," he points out, gesturing to my neatly tucked away gaming console.

"I mostly play on my laptop in my room or at the office," I explain. "Anyway, you get certain advantages in the gift of knowledge. In this particular game," I tell him, gesturing to the screen at Harley as she slinks around through a deserted part of the park, heading toward the throne in the center of the field, "the goal is to capture the queen."

"Then why is no one trying to capture—" His words cut off, because as soon as Harley gets on the throne, the screen goes to a group of men and women who are all hiding in various places to strategically ambush her.

"Their scrolls told them the objective was to capture the queen," I say as the film speeds up on its own, the hours in the top right hand dwindling on, as the people move in fast-forward speed, idling, killing time as they wait.

"It said if the queen touched the statue of the crowned lore, she was safe. Her advantage, however, was that the game was *over* if she reached the throne. The throne is on the other side of the park."

His lips part. "So the game is already over after just a few minutes, but no one knows that but the queen."

It stops on a spot where Harley is having to explain to some guys who've stumbled across her they haven't captured her; the game is, in fact, already over.

"Everyone assumes the queen *has* to go to that statue, when in reality—"

"The queen had too much of an advantage from the very beginning, and she wasn't playing the game. Everyone else was playing *her* game," he says, eyes going a little wide as a slow grin curves his lips. "You're going to have to talk nerdy to me more often, Britt," he adds, standing abruptly and bending over to press a hard kiss to my forehead.

Then he's gone, already jogging toward the guest room, while I try to remind myself that forehead kisses are completely platonic. I half wonder if he's installed a strobe light when the room flashes before I realize it's just me blinking uncontrollably.

People truly will believe I'm a robot if I continue to glitch like one. Robots are only sexy to a small demographic.

Base isn't in that demographic.

I've finished up the rest of the short clips by the time he walks back out, a shirt in his hand. My phone vibrating tries to help distract me from all the very eye-catching things.

"Please tell me you're hungry, because I'm starving, and I want to buy you dinner. It's my pathetic way of making up for all my crazy," he says, grabbing his own phone.

I look down, reading the message from Harley.

HARLEY: Taking in the sights? Figured out why I'm the world's best boss and most awesome friend yet?

Confused, I glance up to answer Base, only to get distracted immediately while he pulls on his shirt, his attention still on his phone. It's harder to look away when he doesn't know I'm looking.

Physically harder.

It's getting out of sorts.

I thought *taking off* of clothing was supposed to be the sexy part. Not the *putting on* of clothing.

My eyes flick down to my phone, then back up to Base, then back down again, and I have an *ooohhh* moment.

In the very next second, I want to do her physical harm.

ME: I told you he rejected me, or have you forgotten? How can this be anything other than cruel?

HARLEY: Did you mention your hymen before said rejection?

I blink.

ME: Yes.

HARLEY: Then there's still hope. Besides, no guy calls a girl his muse, takes photos of her all the time, and has zero attraction to her.

ME: You're supposed to help me be less confused. Not more confused.

HARLEY: I'm the world's best boss, and one day you'll buy me the appropriate mug. When that day comes, I'll know it's because you mean it and not because you're sucking up.

Following that, she sends me a picture of a mug with the requested captioning, *World's Best Boss.*

They genuinely find me to be random, but their collective train of thought eludes me the vast majority of the time when they're being purposely vague.

Putting my phone away, I notice Base grinning at me. "Why do you look frustrated?"

"Because Harley…doesn't always make sense…even though she's usually the one I understand the most."

Now it seems more and more like he's the one I understand the most. Then sometimes, I simply don't understand him, not even a little bit, not even at all.

"What'd she do that you don't understand?" he asks, that trademark smile of his inching across his face. "Maybe I can help translate."

"When I told her you were here and shirtless a lot—"

"You mentioned the fact I'm shirtless a lot?" he interrupts, his grin turning lopsided as he arches an eyebrow at me.

"It came up," I say with a shrug. "Anyway, she thinks she's 'the world's best boss' and an 'awesome friend' because she's making me work at home so I can see you shirtless."

His head drops back as his body shakes with evident silent laughter he keeps tucked away behind firmly pressed lips.

"After I specifically told her you rejected me," I go on, getting to the tedious part, since he asked. His silent laughter stops, judging by how his body goes still. "So I don't understand her current thought process."

He clears his throat, looking over at me with an expression I can't possibly decipher. Incredulity, maybe?

"I didn't reject you, Britt. I rejected taking something that personal from you, because it'd be a dick move. I'm still on the path to sainthood."

I have no idea what sainthood has to do with anything. I could point out the only thing I've deliberately offered was the one thing he rejected, therefore meaning he rejected me—but I don't.

Instead, I stand, grab my purse and slide on my sandals without commenting.

"Are you mad at me?" he asks, causing me to frown as I look over my shoulder.

"Why would I be mad at you?"

His lips twitch, and he exhales harshly.

"I told you my priorities right now are music. In two more years, if you're still up for grabs, I'll be the first person asking for a second chance," he says with an easy grin, one that reminds me of Maverick when he's being charming…and saying things just to be nice to people.

"Okay," is the only safe word I can find when I remain undecided on how sincere that comment is.

He's the type to spare feelings, so I can imagine him being artificially charming to cushion the sting of rejection.

I shouldn't have brought it up.

"And I'm back to getting one word answers," he mutters, pinching the bridge of his nose.

"I thought we were going to eat, because I'm actually hungry," I state in overt deflection.

Sensing the subtle tension from this really unexpected conflict, I turn and walk toward the door, hearing him laughing in a way that doesn't really sound like he's amused.

I would try to fix it, but the more I talk, the worse things usually get, especially without a buffer. I don't want to risk saying the wrong thing and accidentally escalating the situation until it spirals out of control.

I scrub a hand over the back of my neck. Avoiding all conflict is a lot harder when you spend more time together.

Chapter 17

BASE

"Tell me something no one else knows," I say to her as I drive *her* car.

I've decided to leave my truck at my place until the Sterling men organically learn how outrageously and inappropriately I've inserted myself into her life.

Not that I'm scared of the Sterlings, but…I'd like to delay being punched by a Sterling for as long as humanly possible.

"I used to eat crickets," she deadpans in answer to the question I forgot I asked. "I only stopped because people found it disgusting."

I miraculously choke back any sound. "If people thought it was disgusting, then clearly someone else knows that."

She taps her chin as though she's thinking. "Dane didn't blink."

"What?" I ask, confused.

She shrugs as she props up on the console, bringing herself closer to me as she stares ahead and speaks.

"When he found me, I was…far more socially inept than you know me now—"

"I wish I had known you then," I interrupt, keeping one hand on the wheel as I tug a strand of her hair with my other.

"Not really. It was sometimes hard to focus on a person and think, while also…appropriately communicating with said person unless I was simply reciting rehearsed conversation. I spent an unfortunate amount of time vocalizing arguments that should have been kept internalized, as well," she says, eyes distant like she's thinking back.

"It didn't take him long to start sorting me, when no one else had managed to do it for so many years."

I don't say anything much before brushing her hair out of her face and to the side.

"I still try to avoid conflict unless resolution is necessary to move forward," she adds as her eyes move back to mine. "I have a favor to ask."

My thumb strokes down her cheek.

"Name it," I say quietly, feeling the intense air around us.

"I don't like revisiting my past on command," she says very timidly.

My thumb freezes and my eyes go to hers.

"I realize it's a respectable rudimentary bonding mechanism to share one's life story within a friendship, but I will never do that. I say that with full certainty. I never actively think about it," she goes on. "I'll share small pieces at my own pace when I find it relevant to a situation at hand. But I'll simply continue to be vague and intentionally elusive about it. I don't like the sense of loneliness that accompanies those memories."

We just sit still in the parking lot for a few seconds while I toy with the ends of her hair.

"I'm telling you this because I see it as a probable future point of conflict I'd like to avoid," she adds when I just study her, my gaze raking over her face.

"That's perfectly fair," I tell her, my eyes dropping to her lips.

She gives a nod and turns to push her door open before stepping out of the car. I take an extra second or two to follow suit.

I hurry to open the door to the restaurant for her, but two girls walk out and pause when they see us…as though they're frozen in surprise.

"Britt!" one of them says very loudly…but I don't have Britt's memory, so I can't recall her name or how I know her.

"What are you two doing here?" the other one asks, her brows drawn tight as she looks between us like she's confused.

"We're hungry," Britt states as though it should be obvious, and I bite back a grin.

The other chick also restrains a smile.

"I meant together," she goes on. "And don't worry, I won't tell Wren," she adds.

"Nor will I tell Ethan," the other says as she mimes crossing her heart. "This is the first time in the hour I've been out of the house, that I'm finally okay with being away from Isa for a few minutes."

My smile only grows, because now I realize this is Bella and Allie. She's been in my environment so much but I've barely seen her in hers.

"You won't tell them I'm hungry?" Britt asks, confused.

"We won't tell them you were here with Base Masters," Bella dutifully explains between loud slurps of her straw.

"Oh, that doesn't matter. He's not a potential suitor because he already rejected me. We're trying to be friends now," Britt states matter-of-factly.

Bella sputters her milkshake. Allie chokes back a sound of surprise. I groan while scrubbing a hand over my face for the third or fourth time tonight.

"I didn't reject you," I quickly point out. Again.

"Sorry. He rejected taking my virginity because he feels it'd be a 'dick move,'" she continues, simply quoting me as though this is a perfectly natural conversation to have with two women I don't know, and with the door still open to the nosy burger joint.

Her honesty is usually my favorite part about her. However, I'd really like to have this conversation in private.

I'm starting to realize the drastic difference in her comfort level with them compared to other people.

Bella sighs, looking over at me like she's disappointed for reasons unbeknownst to me, before shaking her head.

"I promise they don't all suck," she says, patting Britt's hand.

"I don't think I suck," I feel the need to point out. Not sure why exactly I'm having to defend this, since it's technically the *right* thing. "I'm on the path to sainthood."

"Says the guy whose band is called *The Fallen,*" Bella, apparently too quick-witted, is fast to retort. "False advertisement, bro," she adds, doing this head weave thing as she snaps her fingers in a "Z" formation.

I don't know what to do with that, so I just stare…

"I'm tired," Bella says after a beat of silence. "Ignore me."

"I'm going to go order for us," I tell Britt, clutching her side to bring her attention to me. "Stop telling people I rejected you."

As I walk off, I just barely hear her quietly telling them, "I considered reciting the definition of rejection to him, but most people say it comes off as passive aggressive when I do that."

How the hell did sainthood suddenly turn me into the damn devil?

After getting the burgers ordered, I go back, hoping like hell those two are gone so I can once again explain to Britt that I did *not* reject her.

Unfortunately, they're not gone, and I catch the tail end of Britt saying, "No. I'm bringing Tommy. I made plans with him at the park during LARP, so we're changing plans instead of cancelling them. Now I have to find something else to wear."

"I'll come over and—"

"Say what now?" I cut in, quickly joining them outside, and *shutting* the door as I usher them off to the side.

Bella looks like she has the devil in her eyes when she answers me. "Britt's bringing a date to tomorrow's cookout at Dane's house. We were discussing what we're wearing."

"Tommy and I are friends," Britt states, confused.

"You're taking Tommy as your date somewhere?" I ask Britt, not missing the way Bella fucking grins.

Now that I remember who she is, I've decided I liked her better when she was on the front row and just dancing to the songs I was singing instead of making my life hell.

Allie elbows Bella, but I think she's just doing better at hiding her smile, because she definitely has humor dancing in her eyes when I glance at her.

"It's not a date," Britt says very dryly once again. "We were going to go to a town that has various cos play costumes to see if we could salvage anything to recycle and reuse as our own."

"He's a level one," I remind her.

She frowns. "So? Everyone is level-one at some point, and it's the responsibility of the upper levels to take on squires and train them. It's rare to have a chance to interact in the real world, unless you already know each other."

I don't have any idea what to say to any of that without making myself sound like a jealous dick right now.

"I have no idea what any of that means," Allie states flatly.

"Me neither, but now Tommy doesn't sound as sexy as I was hoping," Bella adds.

"I'll go with you tomorrow. Level-One Squire Boy can sit at home and work on getting to level two," I tell Britt, noticing the way she lifts her eyebrows like she's confused.

"Any of this make sense to you?" Bella stage whispers to Allie.

"Still nada," Allie quips.

"I can't change my plans now," Britt tells me, frowning. "Tria assured me it's rude to give less than twenty-four hours' notice before canceling."

"It's not rude. Just cancel," I argue, at the same time Bella says, "Totally rude. You have to bring Tommy now."

Why is this woman out to make my life hell?! When I glare over at her, she gives me a smartass grin.

"What the hell have I ever done to you?" I ask her very seriously.

"It's what you've *not* done for Britt while getting your muse—" Allie's hand abruptly clamps over Bella's mouth, and she starts dragging Bella away.

"See you tomorrow, Britt!" Allie calls, then wrangles Bella back and gets her hand over her mouth again before she can get something of her own—probably the last word—out.

There's actually a little bit of a struggle, before Bella finally shouts, "Not the nipples, you evil woman!"

Bella gets shoved into the car before adding, "Sheesh! You're freakishly strong these days when you're bullying a woman who is still recuperating from her body being put through hell!"

Motherfucking crazy rich people.

First, they have me questioning my resolve by flipping it to be a bad thing, making a motherfucking saint feel like the snake in Eden's tall grass. Now they're reveling in the fact Britt has a date, and I'm not so subtle with the whole jealousy thing.

But Britt, fortunately, doesn't seem to deduce that as easily as they clearly did.

Grabbing her hand, I drag her inside the restaurant and change our order so that it's to-go.

"Why are we leaving?" she asks as they finish bagging our stuff.

"No seats," I tell her as I use my free hand to grab the bags, leaving the drinks behind, and start dragging her back to the car.

"But it's mostly empty," she argues.

I really regret taking her out in public now. I like it better when I have her just to myself.

Chapter 18

BRITT

Okay, so I've established the fact Base is weird, but he's being weirder than usual. And much quieter.

He said nothing on the way home, and now that we've eaten—in complete silence—he's gone to his room to work on music. Something…he doesn't usually do if I'm here.

Now where exactly did this conflict come from? It's springing up like weeds around us tonight.

Tonight, instead of playing music, he's just listening to it. Loudly.

I'm curled up on my bed, watching a movie I have no interest in. I showered, brushed my teeth, shaved my legs…essentially anything to kill time, since I'm not used to having so much of it.

My paper is staring at me from across the room—the unfinished first draft. But I'm not in the mood to write about sex. It's becoming ever-so-clear that I might remain a virgin.

I'm way ahead on my job, per the latest usual, so I'm metaphorically twiddling my fingers as I await the next task.

Restless, I finally throw the covers back, needing answers to why he's being like this.

Since the music is still playing, I decide I'm not interrupting anything and open the door.

I realize too late I should have knocked, because this is his private space I've just thoughtlessly invaded.

My entire body freezes again. He's only in his boxers, eyes closed as he lies on his bed with his hands behind his head. Words get forgotten, along with my reason for bursting in without knocking, as I stare like an idiot.

"Hey," he says, causing my eyes to snap up as he leans over and cuts the music off, using his phone. "Everything okay?" he asks.

Oh, yeah. That's why I'm in here.

Shaking my head, I take a deep breath and prepare to ease into the gentle confrontation necessary to move forward. "You're mad at me about something," I state cautiously. "But I don't know what I did wrong, and—"

"I'm not even a little bit mad at you, Britt," he interrupts, gaze hesitating on my legs.

Feeling slightly less certain that he's angry now, my thoughts abruptly jump back to the fact he's only wearing his boxers.

"I am, however, irritated at myself, because I'm making a simple situation very messy without any benefits," he goes on…but I don't comprehend his meaning. At all.

He's being purposely vague.

He steps directly in front of me, and his arms move to the wall as he slowly and casually cages me in. My head falls back so I can meet his eyes as he stares down at me with a look I can't decipher.

"Ask me for something else," he says softly, confusing me as he presses his body even closer.

My gaze lingers on his lips. My attention is once again snagged by that hoop in his lip, even as I try to focus on the situation at hand.

"I don't understand you're meaning," I tell him very distractedly, still staring at his lips.

He smirks. "Ask for something else. I can't be the asshole who took your virginity and gave you nothing else in return. But I also don't want it in your head that I rejected you based on your standard of rejection."

Blinking, I look up, confused. Maybe it's the phrasing he's

taking personally.

Just as I open my mouth, he says, "So help me, Britt, if you start pointing out that it was a rejection, I'm going to make a really big mistake. So ask for something else. I swear I won't reject it."

I heave out a very frustrated breath. Surely he'd be confusing to anyone and not just me.

My eyes flick to his lips again, and I consider it. In all actuality, I only have one goal. But…

"I want to know what it feels like to kiss you when you're wearing that," I say before I can think about it too much, my finger lifting to run across the hoop.

A groan sounds in the back of his throat, and that's all the warning I get before his lips are suddenly on mine. It's so startling that I don't even close my eyes for the first second of it.

By second number two, my eyes are closed and the 'mush' term finally makes sense.

My entire body feels like it's trying to go limp.

His arms come around me as his tongue teases the seam of my lips before delicately destroying the rest of my ability to think.

Why am I moaning? It's too soon for moaning. And uniquely embarrassing.

My entire body feels like it needs to be closer, so I practically start climbing him, kissing him harder as control seems to flee from my grasp. His hands slide up, moving under my shirt, but not too far.

Another groan comes from him, and I know I whimper when he breaks the kiss that I wasn't ready to end this time.

"Fuck, *why* are you wearing pants?" he asks on a strained sound.

"Why *aren't* you?" I volley, just as his lips come back down on mine, swallowing the sounds that follow.

His grip on me tightens, and he turns me, backing me up until I feel the bed behind me. My fingers thread through his hair, and I can't stop myself from trying to pull him closer once again, even though I don't know how much closer we could possibly get.

He puts me down and immediately opens the button of my jeans. I don't stop him from pushing them down. In fact, I help him out, wiggling, kicking, and doing all I can to get free.

As soon as I kick them aside, he lifts me again, and we crash to the bed. Immediately settling himself between my thighs with no preamble, and kissing me as his thin boxers compete with my indecently thin panties.

There's a familiar pressure building as his body rocks against mine, and I try to catch my breath and kiss him harder all at the same time.

My mouth opens in a gasp, because it's like a tiny ripple of explosions flutter across my body with phantom butterfly wings. My hips arch in response, rubbing against him, finding such a more satisfying friction than anything I've ever manufactured.

It takes me a long moment to blink out of the surprise at what just happened.

He groans into my mouth, his hips thrusting with just the right amount of pressure. It causes me to break the kiss so I can suck in some much needed air. All the sensations are almost too much, because I've kissed before…but never quite so…insatiably.

My hands are all over him, greedily raking in even more sensations when he makes another sound that seems to just excite my entire body all over again.

I ignore the nicety about friends not straddling other friends' legs, because I'm desperate for more friction. His hands move up, jerking my underwear down hard on one side. He moves to mirror the action on the other side, and I freeze as I push against his chest.

The room goes silent, aside from both of our heavy breaths.

His hand stilled the second I panicked, and he remains bent over me. We both stay silent for a minute, calming, even as I try to wrap my head around the fact I just stopped for *no* reason at all.

And I can't make myself continue this very second, even

though I really, *really* want to. I wish he'd just work me through it instead of stopping just as abruptly.

His lips brush up the column of my throat as he slowly tugs my underwear back up with a gentler touch than he jerked them down.

"You see, Valkyrie Princess," he says softly next to my ear, "you think you're ready, but I know you're not. I've known it since the first night you stopped me—well, I've known it since I learned you're not gay."

I huff out a sound, even as I try to suck in air and not feel irrationally embarrassed about the current situation at hand.

His lips brush over my throat again, and I shiver, but still can't seem to get my body to cooperate with what I *know* I want to do.

"You think you want something cold and detached," he goes on softly. "Something easy and painless, because you're determined to avoid pain for the rest of your life."

Cutting my eyes away, I stare at his shoulder, idly wishing the answers to this puzzle were inked on his skin instead of the tribal signs.

"But trusting someone with something you're scared about, something that is now so built up so much in your head from the suspense that you're terrified it's going to be much worse than it really is? That takes emotion. Trust doesn't come easily. Or emotionlessly."

He leans up, using my chin to turn my face back to face his. In this moment, despite all my reading and preparation, I feel naïve.

"If you really didn't want to be a virgin, you wouldn't still be a virgin," he adds, as though he's summing everything up for me.

Feeling heat rise up my neck, I confess, "I'm scared."

I feel him grinning against my cheek when he bends to press a kiss there—a chaste kiss, unlike the more consuming one we shared earlier.

"It's okay to be scared," he tells me.

I feel coached. I feel doubly like a novice. Worst of all, in this moment, I feel utterly inferior.

And if I'm being completely honest, I sort of hate it.

"It's an irrational, unfounded fear that is preventing me from doing what I want, so it's *not* okay to be scared," I tell him as I gently shove at his chest, prompting him to move, as I continue to avert his eyes.

He mutters something under his breath, but moves, allowing me to stand up. Jerking my shirt down so that it hits mid-thigh the way it's supposed to, I quickly exit his room and head toward mine.

That's not exactly the conversation I was planning to have.

Maybe it was being caught off guard that led to my panic. Or maybe it's just Base who makes me panic.

Or maybe my hymen is doomed to stay frozen in its current state.

Dildo penetration for hymen breaking is really controversial on the message boards, and too many horror stories have been relayed.

I suppose I could take on water sports. Girls have altered their hymen on accident that way. It's not ideal, and I could end up—

"Britt," Base groans from behind me, jogging to catch up.

Gently, he tugs at my elbow, and with more reluctance than I care to question, I turn to face him, staring at his…chest.

Nope. Can't look him in the eyes. It feels like a physical impossibility. Embarrassment can have a crippling effect.

Idly, I notice he took the time to pull on some track pants. I almost want to thank him.

"Let's not make it weird, okay?" he asks, his tone seemingly amused.

I'm not amused, so I really hope I'm reading that tone wrong. Which is a high probability.

His finger comes under my chin, forcing my head up, as he grins down at me. He definitely looks amused.

"How about you show me your game that you're so into," he

suggests.

And people call me random.

"Okay," is all I say as I do a quick about-face and march into my room.

He follows me, and I pull up *Land of the Lost Lore* on my laptop just to give him a quick virtual tour for *no freaking reason.*

Getting settled onto the bed, I deliberately place the laptop between us, giving the game my complete focus as I start showing him around the world.

"This is Valhalla," I explain. "Only those with Valkyrie status can enter, unless a princess or queen allows you limited visitation."

"What's over there?" he asks, gesturing to a dark forest on the corner.

"It's Eden. I need to climb three more levels before I can enter," I tell him. "Taking on quests and new squires helps me achieve more level points."

As if summoned, a message box pops up from an unknown squire, since I'm not wearing my headset and have the audio feed disabled for this showing.

Quickly, I respond that I already have three squires, and another message appears.

"Oh," I say to myself when THEmanintraining explains he's actually Sean—Maverick's stepbrother. So I add him to my registry of squires.

"Who is Sean Young?" Base asks, leaning over me like he can learn more if he's closer to the screen.

Before I can answer, another message box pops up, but this squire is one I know immediately.

We still on for tomorrow? I forgot I still don't have your number.

Quickly, I type in my number on the message box, and reply with, *yes to tomorrow.*

"Is that Level-One?" Base growls.

"It shows you he's a squire right beside the user name," I point out, literally. My index finger almost touches the screen as I point to the squire box. "All squires are on level one."

He scrubs a hand over his face before exhaling harshly.

"You're still going with him tomorrow?" he asks incredulously.

"Why wouldn't I?" I ask, sincerely confused by how irritated he seems.

"We just kissed," he says as though it's obvious.

I bristle, certain he's not implying what I think he is.

"Tommy and I are friends," I remind him. "And I'm not sure what a kiss has to do with anything, considering you kissed another girl right after you kissed me the last time."

Oh. So this is why people insist on being petty. It's sort of…empowering, in a very immature, brash sort of way.

But for the first time since I admitted I was scared, I meet his eyes on my own, and he's unquestionably glaring at me.

"*She* sucked on my fucking nose. I did *not* kiss her. But you're willingly going on a date tomorrow, after we just had a very intense, intimate moment, and without a doubt he's going to be all over you," he says, his voice getting a little louder.

"Not that it should matter, but I have no intentions of kissing Tommy. As I stated, we're just friends."

He points between us. "So are we, and we still kissed," he says, then darts to his feet, and storms out like he's genuinely angry.

At me.

Like I've somehow betrayed him.

Which makes no sense, since Base has assured me we can't be together, and has now proven I'm not even as ready as I thought I was.

Closing my laptop, I go after him, feeling my own ire steadily rising with each step of progress I make. By the time I reach his door, I'm reeling in my own emotions that could just cause this situation to escalate.

I open my mouth to say something practical, smart, and logical, but he's already back down to his boxers and staring at his ceiling while lying on his bed. Why is his body so distracting?

His eyes dart to mine, narrowing on me.

"We're not friends! Friends don't straddle other friends' legs!" I shout, having no idea why that's the particular line that shoots through my lips like a poisonous dart.

At his confused expression, I turn and dart out.

This time, he doesn't follow.

Chapter 19

BRITT

"So your cousins and brother are like really rich, I assume," Tommy murmurs as he steps out of the car with me, his eyes taking in Dane's massive home.

I've let him do most of the talking, while I silently prepared a series of questions that have been driving me insane. I need the women.

"Yes," I state flatly as we walk around the side, heading to the back yard.

"I guess there will be fancy champagne and stuff then, right?" he asks, putting his hand at the small of my back.

I have no idea why that seems too personal and invasive, but I still wriggle away from his touch.

"No champagne," I tell him distractedly. "There's a two-beer maximum today since all the kids will be here."

"Kids?" he groans.

Relief fills me when I see Harley. Before we can reach her, we're intercepted by Dane, Maverick, and Corbin.

"Who's this?" Corbin asks, seeming genuinely intrigued.

Forcing a smile to hide my impatience, I gesture to Tommy. "Tommy is a squire."

All their eyebrows go up.

"In real life, I work at a surfboard shop and play a little guitar," he tells them with a smile, putting his hand out to shake theirs.

But the word *guitar* has me back to struggling with my

impatience to get to Harley.

"Guitar?" Maverick asks, sounding impressed. "Girls dig the guitar players."

Tommy just grins.

I stand here impatiently.

Dane offers Tommy a beer that Tommy takes.

"Did you drive here?" Dane asks Tommy as he sips the beer.

Tommy nods, making an *ahhh* sound as he lowers the beer.

It's all rather dull at the moment, and I'm tapping my foot as I try to remain in place.

"So how do you know Britt?" Maverick asks him, eyeing Tommy's beer in his hand.

"I told you; he's a squire," I remind them.

"Squire?" Dane asks, sounding so confused.

"Land of the Lost Lore," Tommy says, clearing his throat as he looks around.

I'm sure he's constipated, but it almost looks like shame is what he's hiding.

I have no idea what he has to be ashamed of. So that means his bowels must be blocked.

"Oh, you're referring to the game Britt and Harley love," Corbin finally surmises, even as his grin grows and his eyes narrow on Tommy. "Gotcha."

"It's just for fun. I don't take it as seriously as some people do," Tommy goes on.

I frown at him, my impatience forgotten. "It's a community of like-minded individuals who role play in escapism. It's okay to take it seriously. I made it to Valkyrie princess in record time, and I'm learning to make my own costumes."

He clears his throat again, shrugging as he gives the guys a smile. "Like I said, I don't take it as seriously as some people do."

Corbin pats my shoulder. "If Britt takes it seriously, then so do we. Maybe we should check it out and see if we can get involved."

They continue to stare at Tommy.

"Oh, I mean I could take it seriously, if I had more time," Tommy says, confusing me.

I'm quite confused enough at the moment. I don't need this added to it.

I start tapping my foot again.

"Need to be somewhere, Britt?" Maverick asks, his eyes on my quick-tapping foot.

"I need to talk to Harley."

"Then go on," Dane says, winking at me. "We'll show Tommy around. See what he thinks of the house and stuff."

Relieved that I can have some privacy, I thank him, and leave Tommy behind as I hurry to Harley, who is fortunately in the middle of most of the other girls.

Surely one of them can explain Base Masters to me. And my predicament.

"Twenty minutes," Rain is saying as she puts a twenty on the table.

"Thirty minutes. He looks like a trier," Ruby says as she throws a twenty down as well.

"He looks clueless enough to make it thirty-five minutes at least," Harley says, putting her own money onto the pile.

"Nope," Ash says, holding her daughter to her as she puts money in. "Twenty-three minutes and not a minute longer."

"I think you're all overestimating him. I say fifteen minutes. Tops. Maverick had that look in his eye…" Salem lets her sentence trail off as she tosses her own money down.

I've seen them do this before, and have wondered why, but I'm still reluctant to ask before I've drawn my own conclusions just to see how close I am. However, this is the first time I've been close to the growing money pile.

Just because I don't want to seem rude, I also lay down a twenty, even though I still haven't formed an educated guess as to what's going on.

Harley just grins at me. "How long?" she asks.

"How long until what?"

"Until Tommy leaves?" Tria asks as she walks up and puts money in, somehow knowing what the conversation is without having been over here prior. "I'm going with forty minutes. The guy isn't from Sterling Shore. Just overheard him telling the guys that. He's gonna be a long-hauler."

"Dammit. Maybe I should change mine," Rain says.

"I'm standing firm at fifteen," Salem interjects. "He's way too gullible and far too mousy, even though he looks like a jock. Look the look, but can't walk the walk."

"You're taking bets on how long Tommy lasts here?" I ask, looking behind me.

Tommy is smiling brightly as Dane shows him one of his many cars inside his garage. I can barely see them as they disappear inside, with Kode smirking as he jogs to catch up.

"He's not a date," I decide to say. "So he should make it the entire time. The guys were being really nice."

"Of course they were. You were standing there," Rain tells me, blinking. "They still think you're clueless about their sabotage attempts."

"Tommy isn't a date, so I say he lasts the entire party," I tell them, going on before they can argue. "By the way, they've sabotaged me more than I realized. Base assured me that men don't enjoy the constant mention of a hymen."

They all groan, but Harley quickly looks around. "Hurry and tell us about Base before they get back."

Ash sighs heavily. "Tag is going to cash in like crazy when he finds out I've kept this from him."

I'm going to have to assume *cash in* is now the new metaphor for *kill me,* given the context. They always say the guys are going to *kill them* when they've done something that will directly spark a feud. Obviously it's a metaphor, since no bodily harm ever comes to them.

"Again, they won't care about Base either," I dutifully point out. "He doesn't want my virginity, and he kissed me last night to show me that I wasn't ready yet."

"That makes…zero sense," Tria says, and I sag in relief as I take a seat, no longer feeling like a complete idiot.

"He proved I was scared, and—"

"Of course you're scared," Rain says softly. "Any girl who says she wasn't scared that first time was either really drunk or very disillusioned."

Already, I'm relaxing. I thought this was going to be an issue only I had, since I seem to have so many of those.

"This is why we've insisted on you waiting for someone who would give a damn and help you ease into this without—"

Something loud *cracks,* and then the distinct sound of shattering follows. We all jerk our attention to the garage.

"You don't think they'd actually kill him, do you?" Ash asks, leaning up as silence continues.

Tag starts quickly making his way toward the garage, his son trailing behind him as he skips.

In a few suspended breaths, riotous laughter starts wailing from the guys, and I relax again, even as all the other girls seem to tense.

"Everything okay, Dane?" Rain calls loudly.

"Fine. That was all Tommy. Not us."

"Sorry!" Tommy yells.

The girls all finally relax and turn their attention back to me.

"So last night he kissed you again?" Harley asks me.

Rolling my eyes, I answer, "Yes. And the kiss was more…intense. We ended up progressing when we went to the bed. And I tensed when he started pulling off my underwear—"

"Oh sweet heavens, they're going to kill him dead," Ash quietly murmurs, covering her face with her free hand and covering her daughter's ear that is facing me with her other hand.

The child coos, easily balanced in Ash's lap, unable to truly understand the inappropriate conversation. I'm not sure I understand why she covers the one ear.

Shaking out of the distraction, I carry on, "But when I tensed, he stopped and gave me a very embarrassing lecture about how I wasn't really ready."

"Oh, he's one of those," Tria says on a sigh. "The ones with just enough experience to forget they used to be virgins."

"It's sad, though, since Base would be perfect. He's not blowing through girls left and right, but he still gets his without being obnoxious about it," Harley says, as though she knows him, even though she doesn't.

"He's a good guy. A really good guy who defied the odds by having a good head on his shoulders, despite his father and the stereotype that plagues musicians," Ash says. "So I'm happy that he'll be living for another day, but he really would have been someone I trusted with you."

"So…he doesn't want me at all?" I surmise, expecting relief for having the confusion cleared up, but experiencing a pang of disappointment instead.

"Oh, he definitely wants you," Salem says.

The disappointment begins to war with hope, and I'm back to being really confused.

"But—"

Before I can finish that, I hear the sound of a car revving, even though it doesn't sound like the owner should be revving it, given the *whine* it emits instead of the *roar* I'm accustomed to hearing.

The guys emerge with large grins, exiting the garage—all five

Sterling men with Tag Masters. I never even spotted Dale before now.

"Damn. Fifteen minutes. Salem wins. Again," Rain groans.

"At least all the information my mother shoved into my head about reading men wasn't a complete waste," Salem is saying as I turn around, frowning as she rakes in all the money.

"That was Tommy leaving," I state, catching up a little slower, but still dumbfounded. "But he wasn't a date."

Ash lets Tria take the content little girl from her lap, as she pulls up her phone, distracting me momentarily.

"Okay, the guys are stopped far enough away for you to tell us more about Base."

Sitting back, I meet Harley's eyes, since she's the one who said that.

"I'm afraid I'm going to need everything explained in detail, because I'm really confused."

Chapter 20

BASE

"Fuck, I love this new sound," Sticks says through a very exaggerated moan as he stills his cymbal after the final note.

It's just me and him going over some of the music, since Randy and Taylor are off doing their part-time jobs.

"She's damn good for the music if that was just a sample," Sticks goes on.

I say nothing.

My head is in all the wrong places.

"Dude, either you tell me what has you pissed, or I'm going to crack you in the head with a drumstick." He wiggles the purported weapon. "Now."

Cursing, I put aside my guitar, and run a hand through my hair.

"Oh, so this *is* about her. Or about her being out with that 'Level-One motherfucker' you mentioned," he easily guesses, fucking grinning at me like the prick he is. "Please tell me we're about to do girl talk. I'll need to remember this moment for the rest of my life."

"I fucking hate you," I say as I stand and walk out, ignoring his mocking laughter as he tries to catch up.

Just as I reach the fridge, he says, "So let me guess…she brought up the virginity thing again, and you're still trying not to be a dick by not sticking *your* dick in a girl who deserves a lot better, right?"

I just glare over my shoulder, then reach down and snag a bottle of water, letting the fridge door close as I start moving through the house.

"Well, just hear me out. I think you're actually being a much bigger dick for the sake of not being a dick," he says, causing me to look over at him as I crash to the couch and prop my feet up.

"That doesn't make a damn bit of sense," I point out dryly, drinking the water as I shift my attention to the TV.

"It's obvious you like the girl. Hell, it'd be hard not to, as long as you can appreciate the fact she's a little different."

I cut my gaze toward him.

"Drop it."

He grins broader, clearly not ready to drop it. "She asked for one thing. One. Thing. With no strings attached. And instead, you've been giving her the boyfriend experience without the one thing she requested, so that, you know, she doesn't get attached or anything. Makes perfect sense."

Pinching my fingers together and lifting them in front of me, I tell him, "You're this close to getting punched."

"Look, I'm saying we have a few months before we go on tour for a solid year. A relationship with a deadline should be doable. You're living in her house, after making the dick move to insert yourself into her life and snap pictures of her all the time. *And she's been cool as shit about it*. As long as you both know the deadline, no worries. Get it out of your system. Get it out of hers. Otherwise, you're just going to want it more than you really do, and so will she. It's psychology, dude. Like one-oh-one or some shit."

After giving him a glare for a little longer, I turn my attention back to the TV, even though my mind is actually nowhere in the vicinity.

He's not telling me anything I haven't already thought of a thousand times since last night. I keep fucking with her head and mine, and I can't seem to stop myself.

"And you really think that's what she deserves?" I ask him

tightly.

He bats a dismissive hand. "She's asking for less."

"She doesn't really know what she wants. She just thinks she does."

"And you know her so well after just a couple short weeks," he deadpans. "You're even more arrogant than I thought. And that's saying something."

Groaning, I scrub a hand over my face, feeling my phone buzz in my pocket.

He continues on, pointing out the various ways I'm an arrogant dick, as though he's been making a list, while I read my text from Ash.

ASH: Britt's date made it fifteen minutes, and she'll need a ride home. Don't show up if you're just playing with her head. And get out of her house if that's the case.

Rapping my fingers, I stare at the screen, tempted to tell her I'm just friends with Britt. But even Britt knows that's an obvious lie.

I'm not sure what the hell we are, but friendship isn't in the cards for us on a platonic level.

"Since you're not even listening to me, how about you tell me what you've decided," Sticks drones on.

"I haven't decided anything, because it's not my decision to make," I grumble as I stand, ready to grab my keys and head out.

Walking past a mirror, I barely glance at it, moving on by. Then abruptly back up and take in the fact I'm overdue for a haircut, and because of this frustrating damn girl, I've managed to run my hands through my hair a thousand times, causing the shit to stick up everywhere.

After snagging a random hat from the floor, I pull it on backwards and grab my keys.

"Where're you going?" he calls out.

"To fuck with my head some more," I say just loud enough for me to hear.

Chapter 21

BASE

A lot of cars are here, and since there's a little music in the backyard, I assume that's where to go. I'm half surprised there isn't a valet service, even if it is just one of their casual outdoor gatherings.

The Sterlings have more money than they know what to do with.

It's one of the many reasons I've never gone to any of their private parties when Tag has invited me. I don't even know how to act around that much money.

Bristling, I walk through the back gate, and Maverick Sterling almost collides with me. There's a small girl on his shoulders who grabs his hair like a horse's reins and yanks him back.

With a yelp, he promptly lifts the kid and deposits her to the ground, telling her to go play, as he gives me an incredulous expression.

"I was beginning to think you were too cool to hang with us," he states flatly, smirking. "How many times has Tag invited you now?"

I don't correct him about who invited me this time. "A few."

"Look who the hell just showed up," he says, and my eyes land on the very laidback party that has most of their inner circle in attendance. Fortunately, I don't spot Bella.

Tag stumbles, his eyes widening when he sees me. Well, I guess that means he knows why I'm really here.

A few of the guys wave me over, since the party seems to have mostly split into three groups—guys, girls, and kids.

My gaze flicks over the girls' faces until I land on one stunned redhead, who is staring at me as though she's shocked to see me. Clearly Ash didn't tell her she sent me a text.

Why am I here?

Taking a seat with the guys, I idly listen as they carry on with a conversation about some dude who managed to bust a window on Dane's new Jag today.

My attention only turns to them when I realize they're talking about Tommy, telling Rye Clanton this information.

"He legit ran out of here," Maverick says, laughing under his breath as he joins in on the conversation.

"As soon as Dane said, '*You can write me a check or just go now and never speak to my sister again. Either way, we'll call it even,*'" Corbin drawls, his own sinister grin in place.

"Who won the pool?" one of them asks, confusing me.

"Salem. Of course," Maverick snorts, causing all of them to laugh like there's an inside joke.

All this *insider* chatter is annoying as hell. Is this how Britt felt on the ride out to the club?

At least I know how they got rid of Tommy.

Definitely more creative than I was expecting.

My eyes move back to Britt, noticing how all the girls are looking from me to her. When my lips twitch, Britt jerks her gaze away, and Rain grins at her as she says something.

"So how'd Tag convince you to come out here?" Corbin asks me as Rain weirdly puts money on the table they're sitting around.

Tria says something to Britt that I can't hear before she also puts down money. It's an annoying thing that I'm unable to read lips right now.

Britt shakes her head, putting her money down as though she's stating something important. I think I make out, '*he's not a date,*' but

I can't be sure.

"He didn't. Ash did," I tell Corbin, even as my eyes stay on Britt as she continues to animatedly argue something, while the money continues to collect on the table.

Before I have to answer more, Wren walks in with his daughter and…girlfriend? Wife? Fiancée? It's hard to keep up with these things. But Allie's eyes widen when she sees me, and she darts away from Wren to join the girls, digging money out of her purse as she goes as though she's in a hurry to join in on before all bets are closed.

"What the hell is going on over there?" I ask Tag as the guys start filling Wren in on what he's missed—mostly the garage story again.

Only this time, they're calling Tommy *Timmy* because they've already forgotten his name. Fucking rich people.

"What are you doing here?" Tag whisper yells at me, trying to keep from being overheard.

"That's yet to be decided," I answer absently.

"I saw in the socialite section that you'd been spending time with Britt, but since none of the guys mentioned it, I thought it was bullshit."

"Apparently they don't read the gossip columns," I answer distractedly as Ash gives me an apologetic smile and mouths something that suspiciously looks like *twenty-five,* while tossing some money down.

"But seriously, what are they doing?" I ask again.

He groans. "They're making bets on how long you last before the Sterlings manage to run you out."

"And twenty-five minutes is the amount of time Ash is giving me?" I ask incredulously. "She's the one who invited me."

"She really invited you? That wasn't just something you told them?" His eyebrows go up in surprise, then his eyes narrow when I nod. "Oh, I am so getting pancakes every morning for a week, two nights off from night duty, and some incredibly hot sex when I confront her with this."

"So glad I could be of assistance," I state dryly.

He grins, his eyes on Ash now, and she battles her own grin, like she knows what he's thinking. Unreal.

"You should probably go soon. Ash always guesses too long. The guys will be eager to get rid of you before you can weave your *groupie-effect* spell on Britt."

"You realize this sounds ridiculous, don't you?" I ask him as he stands.

"Completely ridiculous," he agrees without an ounce of humor in his tone as he goes to scoop up his son and mouths something at Ash.

My attention goes back to Britt, as she stares at me like she's expecting me to vanish at any moment because she thinks she made me up.

"Why are the girls collecting money?" I hear Maverick asking.

As one, four Sterlings turn an abrupt glare on me as though it's clicked in unison. Rye Clanton and Wren Prize just start grinning.

"I take it this is a common thing?" I muse, lips once again twitching as they stare at me like they want me dead. "What's the minimum bet?" I add.

Dale Sterling walks up late, spotting me for the first time, and he points at me. "Why is he here? He wasn't here when I went inside."

"Found out Britt isn't really gay," I tell him with a growing grin. "Though some dude in tights tried to convince me otherwise."

"They were leggings," he growls.

"Okay, so we're discussing *that* later," Maverick says in a way that makes it sound like he's annoyed he has to wait to probe. "And by later I mean as soon as this very bad nightmare ends."

"I'm a nightmare?" I ask with a grin, leaning back in my chair as I put my hands behind my neck.

"I'm stuck on the part where you said you *found out* Britt isn't gay. How exactly did you *find out?*" Kode asks me, eyes narrowing.

"I asked," I say simply, keeping my smile in place.

"Want to see my garage?" Dane asks me seriously.

"I think I'll pass," I say with a growing smile. "Windows or windshields or whatever are usually much harder to break than simply bumping into them. Something tells me there's not a fair chance in there to walk away without doing *priceless* damage that you, of course, know I can't possibly afford."

"Let's take a ride," Kode says with a cold smile.

"Again, I'll pass." My eyes flick to the girls, who are all watching like they're expecting me to dart away at any moment. I'm rather underwhelmed with their methods so far. "Just curious, what's the longest anyone has made it?"

"Anyone who came here to use Britt, take advantage of Britt, or probably hurt Britt has left before the forty-five minute mark," Dale points out with a very non-friendly smile of his own.

"I'm assuming *no* guy has made it past that mark then," I say, still meeting their angry glares with my nicest nice-guy smile I have. Mostly to be a dick.

People hate it when you smile at them while they plot your death.

However, these aren't thugs or mafia guys. They're not going to drag me to a dungeon and pop my bones out of place. They're also not merciless bastards. They're just average guys who have been pampered their entire lives.

"I know two label heads very personally who owe me favors," Kode says seriously, throwing down that monetary gauntlet I've been anticipating.

Sitting up, I place my elbows on the table. "So does Tag. I turned down his offer, and it didn't even have strings attached," I tell him.

"I bet you'd love a new guitar to make music on. Maybe even studio time to lay down tracks—"

I pause Corbin's monetary gauntlet with a hand up. "Lay down tracks? How old are you?"

He glares at me.

"Studio time is expensive," Maverick goes on, picking up where Corbin left off.

"Good thing I have a tab with Tag. Any money he puts into my career, I pay back—with interest—in installments," I tell them, watching as they all swing an accusatory glare toward Tag. "He went to my fucking mother and she made me do this."

Looking over my shoulder, I see Tag trying not to smirk as he pretends he doesn't notice them glowering his way.

"But you admit this would be an easy choice if you didn't have Tag backing you," Maverick says, bringing his eyes back to mine.

"I wouldn't have bothered driving over here if I thought I was the kind of guy to take a bribe and walk away from a friend so I could cash in," I tell them.

"Friend," Dale scoffs. "You already admitted to me you were interested."

"And you didn't tell us?" Kode snaps.

"I let him think she was gay," Dale defends. "How was I supposed to know he's *this* persistent? I thought he'd be like Maverick and move on in the next breath. Guys like him aren't supposed to have attention spans this big."

"Hey," Maverick says, throwing a hand up like he's been insulted.

"Sorry. Like Maverick *used* to be," Dale amends, much to my amusement.

"Still offended, because it had nothing to do with my attention span," Maverick decides to argue.

"I think we're losing touch with the real issue at hand," Corbin says, gesturing toward me.

It's like a little sitcom I've been missing out on. I assumed there'd be champagne flutes, penguin suits, and sticks shoved up asses. I've never seen the Sterlings this relaxed and…semi-normal.

What's normal really?

"I'm that issue," I state, as though everyone needs a reminder. "And there's not really any way to deal with me."

"Siri, where's the best place near me to hide a body?" Maverick asks his phone.

"Very funny," Siri replies, while I give him an incredulous look.

"I'll see if Alexa is more helpful," Corbin says, turning and walking toward the house.

"He's kidding, right?" I ask, lifting an eyebrow and wondering just how crazy they really are.

They all just stare at me, unblinking. They're full of shit.

Back to grinning, I shake my head.

"Given the fact no guy has made it through these tactics, I'm no longer surprised Britt's still a virgin. Apparently, you're keeping her isolated to the dickbag circles."

"Oh, for fuck's sake," Rye says under his breath, scrubbing a hand over his face. "The guy really does want to die."

"He's saying we suck at intimidation," Maverick states flatly, eyes passing over me like he wants the miracle solution to making me vanish.

"And bribery. You suck at that too," I remind him as I stand up, peering over at Britt again.

Her back is to me now, and some of the girls have dispersed.

Some kid eyes me up and down as I pass him, appearing as though he's sizing me up for whatever reason. Weird.

Britt stands and immediately comes toward me, as the girls—who are *subtly* inching closer—pretend they're not trying to listen in.

"Why are you here?" she asks me seriously. "And later will you tell me what they say to the guys? They don't know I know."

Never does she say anything I expect her to, and my grin starts before I can stop it. A chorus of audible feminine *awwwws,* has me lifting my eyes. At least five heads snap away, hair of all colors flying as they all go back to pretending they're not listening.

"You're over here betting on them making the guys leave; I saw you throw money in. Yet they don't know you're betting?"

"To be fair, the betting just started happening at the past two gatherings, and she didn't join in until today," Rain says, then clears her throat, *whistles,* and goes back to pretending she's not listening.

"Things usually happen around me that I don't bother asking someone to explain," Britt tells me, as though it should be obvious. "So me betting just means I'm joining in. It doesn't mean I know why."

"Why wouldn't you ask why?" I volley, unable to stop myself from smiling more.

"Because sometimes it's more fun to pretend you know why and try to guess the real reason why when people discuss it in the vague abstract around you."

My hand comes up, and my finger runs down the column of her throat as I study her eyes, full of curiosity and intrigue, brimming with more awareness than she credits herself for having.

"I'll tell you what they said as long as you promise no more dates while I'm around."

I expect more *awws,* but I look up to see some incredulous eyes on me, as though I've said the *wrong* thing. Do they really need me to prove I'm stupidly jealous?

I have bartering options, and I'm not above using them.

Britt starts to speak, when Rain says, "I'm sorry, did you just ask her not to date while you try to decide how you feel?"

"No?" I say, though for some stupid reason it feels like a question.

Ash even looks pissed at me. She never looks pissed at me. Hell, she fucking adores me. Drives Tag insane from time to time.

"Are you going to be dating anyone, kissing random girls, or flirting with anyone else while you're *hanging out* with Britt?" Tria asks, not seeming as *sweet* as usual.

Five angry Sterling men did nothing but amuse me.

Fucking women here are understatedly vicious. You can sense it rather than see it. It's like they want you to hear what an idiot you sound like, so that you know why they're glaring.

Yet they're not actually being truly abrasive. It's the subtlety that makes you feel like taking a step or two back.

"No," I say with decidedly infinite confidence that it's the right answer, as well as the truthful one.

They study me for a minute, then look away, resuming the courtesy of pretending not to listen.

Relaxing a little, I look back to find Britt just staring at me, waiting her turn to interject on the matter. "Only if you agree not to play with my head." She says this as though she's been coached.

"I swear to you, I'm not trying to play with your head."

"Damn it," Maverick's girlfriend—*um…Salem?*—says as she glances at her phone. Then Salem straightens, blinking rapidly. "Actually, I guess that's a good thing."

"Salem finally lost one, so there's hope," Harley says idly.

"Any chance we can talk somewhere more private?" I ask Britt, even as one side of my lips tug in a reluctant smile.

How can I not somewhat laugh at this? You don't picture the Sterlings being this way.

You expect pompous, arrogant, pretentious, snobby rich people.

I almost wish I had come over all those times Tag invited me now. Maybe then I could understand half of what they're saying.

She walks off to the side with me, and I lean up against the privacy fence as she stops very close, unknowingly showing them all how comfortable she is with me. Dane starts toward us and stops at least three times, but I barely notice him from my peripheral.

"I'm sorry about last night. Things got out of hand, and I tried to play it off—and came off like a bit of a dick without realizing it. But I'd already lost control by the time we hit the bed," I tell her, giving her back some of that honesty she shares so freely.

She just stares at me for a minute. "Why'd you come today?"

"I honestly don't know," I tell her on a long breath, hesitating. "In a few months, I have to go on tour. We'll be on the road for eight months to a year, depending on if we get to open at the larger events near the end. Sometimes you lose your spot at the really big ones because of someone else's pull."

"I know you're leaving. Ash told me tonight," she states, frowning. "Why are both of you telling me in the same night?"

This is one of those times where I wish I didn't have to be direct. I'd like to skate around the topic, so it doesn't sound as dickish as it really is.

In other words, Britt, I can be all yours for exactly three months before I go back to my one true love – music. I'll also be seeing you in between other musical interruptions. But you can totally be a mistress until I leave, as long as you can work around my schedule.

"So, what about Tommy leaving?" I ask in deflection. "You want to know how they got rid of him?"

She grins. "None of the girls know how. They thought it was threats, but it has to be more."

"I'll tell you all about it when they're not glaring at me from across the yard, deciding if they can get away with just a little bodily harm or not," I deadpan.

She looks over at them and back to me.

"They're having a difficult time distinguishing what a date is tonight. I feel I should warn you that I think they intend to sabotage you."

My grin grows again, and this time I get some *awwwwws*. Which means…

My eyes lift to see at least five of the women have moved in closer, even though they're *still* pretending not to listen.

Unbelievable.

They're nosier than Sticks and Taylor.

"You really have some weird timing on the *awws,*" I state flatly.

"So it's not just weird to me?" Britt muses, looking around.

Rain stifles a grin, and Harley does as well.

Apparently we're both on the outside of this inside joke.

"Britt!" Dane finally calls.

She looks over, and he gestures for her to join him.

"This is the part where they separate me from you and then you mysteriously go missing," she tells me. "Remember that I'm not supposed to know," she adds with a small grin, as though I'm now in on the conspiracy.

"At some point, you should probably get them back."

"I do. They just don't know it," she states with a larger smile.

"What do you do?"

"When I run into them at stores, I make sure to buy condoms and lubrication," she tells me proudly, even though it's spoken in a conspiratorial whisper. "Then I start talking about my plans for the items mentioned until they beg me to stop talking."

I choke back a laugh, tilting my head. "Every time?" I ask her.

"The first few times were done unwittingly, but now it's done on purpose. That's why I have three drawers full. I find it weird they haven't questioned it by now."

Tria snorts, turning so her body shakes with silent laughter. A few more women are doing the same.

"Oh, that's priceless. Why am I just finding out?" Salem asks, struggling not to laugh.

"This is actually the first time I've heard of that too," Harley says, her mouth gaping even as she smiles.

"Maybe you should have been applying your eavesdropping skills sooner," I quip.

Salem works harder not to laugh, and Harley just shakes her head. Salem finally gives up and heads over to that weird kid, who is…still sizing me up. I swear I'm not making that up.

"Britt!" Dane says louder, fortunately too far away to know what's going on.

"Let them divide and conquer. I'll find you when round two is over," I tell her.

She hesitates, her eyes flicking to me as though she has something else she wants to say.

"What?" I prompt.

"They've often had to apologize for me when I use inappropriate conversation to an offensive degree—for lack of social refinement that I'm still adapting to," she says, confusing me.

"What does that have to do with anything?"

She glances around. "This is the first time I've felt the urge to apologize for them. I'm not sure really what to say, other than I'm certain they won't actually cause you physical harm. And I'm sorry."

I wipe away my smile, trying to keep a straight face.

"Not the first time I've dealt with big brothers."

"I technically only have one brother," she points out.

I pat her hand, winking at her. "I'm aware."

She hesitates again, then finally walks off. Reluctantly.

Ash is immediately at my side. "Please be careful with her," she cautions.

"I told her I have three months until I leave for tour. I stopped, because it suddenly sounded like a cheesy line used in cheesy sailor films before they headed out to sea for months."

She stifles whatever sound she makes—definitely a laugh.

"Just do me a favor."

"Only if that favor has nothing to do with the bet," I tell her, causing her to suck in an indignant breath.

I glance over at her, and she drops the act, shrugging unapologetically. "I never win anything. I don't want you to run off, but if you decide you'd like to run off, do it in the next five minutes or not at all."

She walks away, and I turn just as Maverick Sterling approaches, a smirk on his lips as he guides the weird kid toward me.

"I'd like you to meet Sean. Sean is in your life more than anyone would ever realize. Remember that. For now, Sean needs to borrow your phone so he can use it to find his," Maverick says very seriously, as though he's delivering devastating news.

My eyes flick to Sean, who looks exasperated, then to Maverick, who looks expectant. "I think I'll pass," I state, arching an eyebrow at him.

"This is Maverick," the kid says, lazily gesturing to said Sterling, as he rolls his head so that his eyes can meet Mav's. "Maverick's an idiot."

I…just stare at them for a second, unsure if I'm allowed to have a reaction until someone else does.

Rain snorts, then coughs over a laugh, then snorts again. Kode turns away, his entire body shaking with laughter. Sean meant to say that as loudly as he could, I think.

Dane even struggles to hold a straight face, which he is apparently determined to attempt.

"Just this once, could you be on my side?" Maverick bites out.

The kid smirks. "You make it too easy."

Then the kid looks at me, rakes his eyes over me from head to toe with an unimpressed expression, and finally meets my gaze.

"You're here with Britt?" he asks me.

"Are you the new squire?" I ask him instead of answering, when his name rattles around in my head. At least I can find some common ground with him, maybe.

He smirks. "Yeah."

The way he says it is…no. I'm wrong. Have to be.

"What are you a squire for?" Maverick asks, confused.

"For the fire-hot Valkyrie Princess with the flaming red hair. She's legendary on the boards. Her avatar has brighter red hair than she does, but most everything else is accurate, including her cleavage, and she's the most coveted princess on the games," the kid says, causing me to work real damn hard not to…react at all. "And I'm establishing a pivotal, bonding memory to set up camp in times where she was younger and happier. It's called groundwork."

Maverick and I exchange a confused glance, before returning our attention to the cocky, pre-pubescent kid.

"So in six years, when we *happen* to bump into each other somewhere neutral, I won't be Sean, Maverick's little stepbrother. I'll be Sean; the guy who makes her think of a great time in her life, when she was at the highlight of her gaming presence. Sean—the short kid who grew into an irresistible man. Sean—the constant, subtle, *dependable* presence in her life."

I have no clue how to react. Still. Like not even a little bit.

"I really hope I'm not hearing you right," Maverick tells him, disbelief mixing in with adequate horror.

"Why six years?" I decide to ask, when Sean just smirks unapologetically at Maverick.

The kid levels me with a smug look. "Because I'll be legal. Duh. Then she's mine."

This kid is twelve?!

"You know she's like my sister, right? So it's crossing a line to talk about her like this," Maverick growls, eyes solely on Sean now.

Sean arches an eyebrow. "You're currently banging *my* sister, so you can't really use that argument."

By some miracle, I swallow my laugh before it escapes.

"No," Maverick bites out. "I'm *currently* wondering how well I'll fare in prison after I smother you in your sleep."

Sean glances at him from head to toe before seriously

answering, "Not too well. You're too pretty."

"You're—" I glance around, remembering there are kids out here, briefly forgetting a *kid* is in on this conversation as I word it semi-cautiously. "—hooking up with your stepsister?" I decide to ask, doing the math on that now.

Maverick points a finger at me. "Past the point of heckles, singer boy. She and I met *before* that revelation came to light. This is *not* about me." Then he glares at Sean. "Go. Away. I don't like you right now."

Sean just smirks as he looks back over at me.

"You're small for twelve," I say without thinking, and the kid's smirk falls as a flat expression steals his features.

"It's always the ones they underestimated that they forgot were coming at all," he says, the veiled threat not even subtle. "Remember I gave you six years. I'm charitable like that."

"Thanks." I can't help it. I grin. How can I take this kid serious?

He shrugs. "Just don't get jealous when I'm hitting her up on the game. I do my best work when girls forget I'm a kid."

I'm not so sure he is a kid at this point. I think it's an optical illusion.

"I'll try to contain my jealousy."

"Keep underestimating me," the kid fires back, smirk on his lips once again. "I'm taking an interest in her interests. Can you say the same? Even Dale is pulling on tights to be closer to his woman. You just expect to play your guitar and make her swoon. I bet you put forth zero effort."

"I really need more information about these damn tights," Maverick says under his breath, glancing toward Dale like he's desperate to learn now.

"Maverick misses the days when he used to wear tights for ballet," Sean supplies.

"I'm going to kill you," Maverick tells the wicked little spawn, his tone even.

Sean just grins up at me before winking. "Six years, rock star. Until you're past your prime, a total wash up, and looking desperately pathetic while carrying around your guitar from club to club," the kid goes on. "Enjoy it while it lasts."

Maverick stands beside me, both of us staring at the psychotic kid as he walks away. Sean winks at Britt, who waves absently at him as he passes her.

Britt is still talking to Dane, and he's smiling at her as he keeps her "distracted." I think Maverick failed at his task, due to the unpredictable, untamed serpent he tried to use.

To be fair, that kid is entirely too bizarre.

"Does it make me a horrible person to hate a kid?" I ask Maverick.

"No," he says immediately. "But he does fucking grow on you."

"Fungus can grow on you too," I decide to point out. "Doesn't mean you enjoy it."

He snorts out a laugh, then clears his throat, narrowing his eyes as though he momentarily forgot he's supposed to hate me. I just grin.

"You're really going to be an issue, aren't you?" he asks.

"You really think you can keep all men away from her until she's a spinster with a full head of gray hair?" I volley.

"Not our goal," he grumbles. "We simply don't want her getting her heart smashed to pieces this young and never being able to try again."

I stiffen for a second, mostly because he sounds sincere.

"Careful, Base Masters," Maverick says a little quieter, his tone serious but thoughtful as Britt smiles over in our direction, her eyes on me. "She doesn't even realize how much she likes you yet," he adds before walking away.

Britt makes her way toward me, and I tug her to me. If Maverick gets in my head, then the Sterlings automatically win.

"You're still here," she says as though she's surprised.

"They can't figure out what to do about me," I tell her, toying with the ends of her hair.

"Were you going to stay longer?" she asks somewhat abruptly. "Because I was going to ride with you if you're going back to the house. I need to work on my paper some."

"I have zero reasons to hang around if you're leaving," I tell her, causing her smile to grow, even as she looks away.

My arm goes around her shoulders as I start guiding us out. As we near the gate, I hear Ruby shouting something like she's cheering.

"He. Could. Go. All. The..." Her words trail off when I pause in front of the gate, looking over my shoulder at her as she holds a suspended fist in the air, her mouth parted like she's waiting to finish the chant.

Everyone is legit staring at us.

Shaking my head, I turn back, guiding Britt out, and hear Ruby finish with, "Way!" Then a round of feminine cheers follow.

Just as we get to the car, Britt pauses, her eyes widening like she's just recalled something.

Wordlessly, she turns and jogs back through the gate, and I wait, considering she didn't exactly explain what she's doing. She returns with a grin and a stack of cash that she's neatly sorting as she moves toward me.

"What's that?" I ask, only because I'm still confused.

Her bright green eyes meet mine as her grin spreads. "I won the bet. I think they finally understood you weren't my date."

I just smile to myself, shaking my head. Fucking rich people.

Chapter 22

BRITT

"Sticks is not his real name, right?" Base shakes his head in answer to my question. "Is it because he plays the drums then?" I ask, carrying on our conversation about the band as Base lies down on the opposite end of the couch from me.

He's lying mostly on the couch, but his feet are on the ground. He laughs, grinning as he idly starts massaging my ankle. "He instantly hates anyone who asks him that question."

Ankles are not notably erogenous zones, so why does that simple touch have me working to form more words?

"It's an obvious deduction, given the fact he is a drummer, and numerous drummers are reported to have the same nickname," I point out.

"Oh, that nickname is definitely because he's the drummer. But it's so obvious that he hates anyone who he feels is asking a rhetorical question and awaiting an answer. That's just how Sticks is."

"Oh," I say, trying to fully understand that.

"What question do you hate the most?" Base asks me suddenly, eyes coming up to meet mine as his massaging hands move up to my calf.

He's yet to discover I'm not wearing anything but lacy underwear under this long T-shirt. Harley told me to stop wearing pants at home if I really wanted him.

Usually, I shy away from physical contact, for the most part. I thought if anything was an issue during my quest to remove maidenhood that would be it. But Base touches me a lot. And I like him touching me.

"What do you mean?" I ask, clearing my throat as I try to focus.

"For instance, I hate it when someone asks me if my name is Base because I play bass."

"You play electric guitar, not bass, and the two forms of the words are homophones spelled differently," I state, confused.

His grin spreads. "That's why I hate the question."

After thinking about it a second, I finally come up with an answer. "I dislike it when people expect a simple answer as to why certain social interactions are more difficult for me than they should be."

His lips twitch as he continues massaging my calves, his eyes on his hands as he does so. I'm exceptionally happy I've kept my legs shaved.

"It's not as much of an issue now as it used to be," I go on, relaxing as I let his fingers do magic, finding his touch far more enticing than usual.

Maybe that's why he makes me panic. I like his touch *too* much.

"Adults are better at hiding how terrible they are than ruthless kids," he surmises, causing me to smile even as my eyes drift shut.

"That's what Maverick says. It's also because I try harder."

"To fit in," he says as though he's disappointed.

I say nothing. He seems unable to comprehend the *why* to this unending disagreement, and he's entitled to his opinion. He just likes to try and make me agree with him as well.

"What are you thinking?" he asks.

"I've never understood why people can't just disagree dispassionately, understanding where the other person stands on a matter. They want people to think the same way they do, yet rave for people to 'think for themselves' in the very next breath, simply because they disagree. None of us have to agree about anything, yet we can still exist in harmony."

His hands pause on my leg, and I shake my head in refusal to his silent request, feeling thoroughly trained at this point to open my eyes. I never gave much thought to psychology when they stood firm on the matter of "conditioning" a mind to perform specific reactions unconsciously.

Until I started sensing when I was supposed to look up for his camera without being asked. In a very unreasonably short amount of time, I should add.

I bet I'd be susceptible to hypnosis too.

"I'm not succumbing to your need to photograph my eyes, because I don't want you to stop massaging," I tell him.

A soft rumble of laughter has me tempted to open my eyes, but before I can fall prey to temptation's snare, his hands start doing those really incredibly movements again, resurrecting my momentarily disrupted relaxation.

"Yet you want to *fit in.* Doesn't that make you a hypocrite?" he asks.

"No," I state confidently.

"Why?" he asks, sounding overly amused.

Or…constipated.

One day, I will figure that out.

Bella has it written down as *number one* of my life goals. I don't find it quite that pertinent.

"If I explain myself, then it'll sound like I'm trying to convince you I'm right. And it's not important to me for you to see it my way."

"You only argue if it's important?"

"I dispute incorrect facts, but I don't usually argue a point, mostly because I'm usually confused about the topic and am on the wrong path of conversation. But I only try to make someone understand me when I want them to see it my way. Or when they're genuinely interested in seeing things my way. Not just looking for a thread to tug so they can unravel my stance and impose their own views on me as though it's the only option."

Again, his hands pause, and I heave out a breath, fortifying my belief in conditioning.

"Just one," I hear him saying as he shifts, my legs falling to the couch. "And I swear I'll finish your massage."

Why am I smiling?

My face hurts from the wide smile that won't go away as I feel him sliding up my body. Adjusting my legs wider for no logical reason, I let him settle in between my thighs before I blow out a breath of mock frustration and open my eyes.

The camera is predictably hovering over my face, and I catch a glimpse of white teeth peeking through his smile before the flash goes off. The second I stop blinking, another flash restarts the action.

"I said one," I remind him, holding my hand out in front of me when I worry he's going to do it again.

He laughs under his breath as his body presses down on mine while he leans over, making me acutely aware of how intimately we're positioned…and the fact he's definitely aroused. Because I can feel it. Against me. And there's no panic. Yet.

It's more of a physical reaction and not necessarily a conscious one. I'm sure.

Actually, I'm not really sure of anything when it comes to Base Masters. Like if he's this touchy with everyone.

He drops his camera to the table, then rights himself over me again, smirking as his gaze rakes over my face.

I have no idea where my eyes should be, so I just stare at his, as his thumb traces over my bottom lip.

My gaze mirrors his, now riveted to his bottom lip and the hoop he's wearing again.

"You don't have class on Fridays, right?"

"I have two classes, but I've already gotten too far ahead on the material, and both professors have asked that in the future I only come to class on testing days," I tell him.

"Why did they ask that?" he muses.

"I don't know. Though, it wouldn't be the first time it's happened."

I'm rambling, because the panic is starting just a little. How is his touch as comforting as it is nerve-wracking?

He resumes his grin, still tracing his thumb over my lower lip, his gaze riveted to my mouth.

"Then come with me this weekend," he says, flicking his gaze up to meet mine. "We'll be leaving Thursday night—"

"Karaoke is Thursday night," I quickly remind him.

His grin grows. "After karaoke," he assures me. "We're going to drive forever on Thursday night. Friday we'll finish the drive after we make a pit stop in our town. The gig is Sunday night—not a prime spot, but the venue is solid. And there's a party Saturday night where there will be a lot of small, but still worth-while, contacts we could make."

He studies me like he's waiting for me to answer, and preparing to argue in case I tell him no.

I answer, "Yes," before I can stop myself. It'll save us the argument where he'll easily talk me into it.

"Good," he tells me with a grin.

"I can reschedule karaoke for next week," I go on, clearing my throat as I actively try not to arch up into him. "Rain will be okay with that."

"Only if that's what you want. It's not a big deal to hit karaoke first."

"It's fine," I assure him on a shakier tone, since it's getting harder and harder not to focus on the very intimate pressure he's putting on my vagina.

A dull ache has started to grow more and more noticeable.

In my vagina.

Also, to take my mind off said pressure, before I do something to embarrass myself again, I'm idly recalling an article on erotic writing that Rain was reading over. It said it made readers cringe when they read the word *vagina*. There were a number of options listed under the clinical word.

"Is pussy, snatch, love-cave, lady parts, or cunt more or less acceptable than the use of vagina in your opinion?"

At his raised eyebrows and seemingly confused expression, I add, "Which word or wording do you personally prefer? Because Rain assures me there is not a universally agreed upon word for the most talked about piece of female anatomy."

He scrubs a hand over his mouth, and it looks as though he's attempting to stifle a grin.

"I won't even ask how your mind got from our conversation to there in less than three seconds," he tells me before he pushes off me.

A cold wash floods over my body in the absence of his heat that my body had gotten too accustomed to. His eyes dip down to my chest, and holds there.

Since I was also instructed by the girls not to wear a bra—as long as I wanted him—my very painfully hard nipples are on display, pressing against the fabric.

His eyes settle on mine again, and without warning, he comes down on top of me, his lips finding mine. I can't believe the no-bra thing actually worked!

The metal of that hoop barely *tinks* against my teeth, before he slants his head and starts kissing me from a different angle, kissing me deeper, as his hips grind against me.

"You're like a fucking drug," he murmurs against my lips, his hand sliding up my side. "And I'm really not a motherfucking saint," he adds, as his lips start dragging down my neck.

My breath hitches, and my eyes open as I try to force my body to show no signs of resistance. My shirt starts to slide up, his fingers dragging across my skin as it makes the fabric climb over my ribs.

Just as his fingers brush the underside of my breast, I shiver and tense at the same time. His hands still, and I mentally chastise every stupid bodily reaction I have to him.

I feel his smile against my neck as he presses a kiss there, leaving his fingers just under the bottom swell of my breast, teasing me with a touch I barely got and that he now keeps out of reach.

"How many bases have you…touched?" he asks, confusing me.

"Just you."

His entire body stiffens. Then, as if I just told a joke of hilarious proportions, laughter erupts from him. He has to turn his head away as his body shakes with the violent force of it.

I'm not even sure what is so funny, and still I'm tempted to laugh just because of how infectious the sound is.

He groans, shaking his head as though he's trying to stop laughing. "Fucking hell, Britt," he says like he's amused, still laughing lightly as his eyes come back to mine, a smile lingering on his lips. "I was asking how far you've been with a guy, and bases are—"

"Oh," I say, suddenly getting it as my eyes widen. "*Oh.* I actually don't know the bases. I know of their intended purpose, but I've heard numerous versions of what second and third base really are. First and *home* were fairly simple, until someone referred to what I thought of as home as a 'homerun,' which is an entirely different—"

He shuts me up when his lips come down on mine, kissing my thoughts silent, making me once again forget what I was even saying. He's the only one to ever be able to kiss me stupid.

Another term I've come to finally appreciate after years of wondering how a kiss could render one stupid.

My fingers tangle in his hair, drawing him closer. But he pulls back just when I convince myself to be a little aggressive.

"Why aren't you wearing pants?" he asks on a breath that sounds like utter frustration, as his hand slides up and down my side in soft grazes.

I suppose he's now noticed the lacy underwear.

"Because Harley suggested I not wear pants in the house if I wanted to seduce you."

His lips drag over mine, and his grip on my side grows a little tighter as he presses into me more.

"You can be scared and still be ready," I go on, leaving it 'on the table' as Tria suggested, without putting myself out there for rejection again, even though I'm very close to simply asking again.

He exhales harshly, his grip loosening on my side, as his lips trail up my cheek in soft, feather-light kisses.

When he reaches my ear, he murmurs, "I never stopped to think maybe you hadn't even worked up to that." He kisses a spot just under my ear. "First base is kissing, something you definitely feel acquainted with."

Cognitive functions start failing. I half expect alarm bells to start wailing through the house to warn me of low oxygen levels when he drags the collar of my T-shirt down, stretching it out as his lips press to the small valley between my breasts.

That's all he does before kissing his way back up my neck. "Second base is a little touching, maybe some heavy petting," he tells me.

Picturing the way Sean pets Bananas ices some of the haze, since I don't want to be patted like a dog or cat.

But then his hand slides down my hip, fingers skating across the top of my underwear, before he cups my vagina, giving me more of that incredible pressure.

He bites down on my shoulder, his hand running over the underwear. "So fucking wet," he murmurs so quietly I almost miss it.

I have no idea what to do because I don't want to mess anything up right now. So I just nod like I agree.

"It's the body's natural reaction to arousal," I state shakily, as his hand slides over, his fingertips now toying with the edges of the lace around my pubic bone.

Really expecting those alarms to wail loudly any minute now, because I'm fairly certain I'm holding my breath.

"Third base is oral," he tells me, biting down on my earlobe, then gently soothing the burn by barely teasing me with a graze of his tongue.

"Home is—"

Someone loudly bangs on the door, and I jerk, which causes Base to react. And for some unnatural reason, I squeal. Loudly. Embarrassingly.

Base gives me a comical look, staring down at me.

"Britt!" Dane calls, sounding worried. "You okay?"

"Oh shit," Base hisses, even as he laughs under his breath.

I have no clue why I panic, or why I don't tell Dane to wait a minute, or why my heart beats far too fast, or why I attempt to fling myself out from under him, but I do know our legs get tangled, making it impossible to fling myself away, and my head bangs with his when I jerk upright.

Pain explodes through the top of my head on impact, as my vision dims for a brief, cold-sweating second.

"Damn it, I'm sorry," Base says, cupping my cheeks as his eyes widen when I make a pained sound.

How hard is his head that he doesn't even act like it hurt?!

"Britt!" Dane calls louder.

"Are you okay?" Base asks seriously, hands still cupping my cheeks as I try to blink the bright spots away, though I swear he's trying not to laugh.

The door pad starts beeping, like Dane is using his code.

Panic renewed for no logical reason, I dive off the couch, but our bodies are still tangled, so Base is forced to fly off the couch with me.

Somehow he lands under me, and I land on him…with my knee slamming into his—

"*My balls*," he heaves on a groan, immediately cupping himself as he curls into the fetal position, with me still awkwardly on him, though my knee is now removed.

Just as the door flies open, I realize my shirt is shoved above my hips, my underwear is halfway down, and the brief reflection of myself granted by the mirror next to the door makes me worry how this whole scene could be perceived.

My hair is…everywhere. My lips are red and swollen, and there are a lot of red marks up and down my neck.

Also, my eyes don't look the greatest, and there's a massive welt on my forehead.

And Base is still on the ground, curled in agony, as Dane stares at the entire scene, his eyes widening as he turns an alarming shade of red.

"Please tell me you're constipated," I say to my brother, hoping he's not angry enough to change colors.

Base starts to laugh, but it ends in a pained groan and a few uttered curses.

"I'm not constipated!" Dane shouts.

"Britt, explain why this place looks like a crime scene before he kills me," Base says through those same pained sounds of strain as he rocks up to his knees.

As he seems to dry heave, I quickly tell Dane, "We had just finished up with third base being oral and started on home when you—"

"Really not fucking helping," Base says, holding his hand up as Dane stalks toward us with what I can easily deduce as a murderous expression.

"Verbal explanations about the bases!" Base shouts, causing Dane to barely halt.

Hurriedly yanking my underwear back to where they should be, I stand quickly, realizing this is where I'm supposed to get in between them. Rain always warned me this day would come.

I hold my hands up, stretching them out in front of me, even though he's still about a foot from reach.

Dane just gives me an incredulous look. "Why the hell is your forehead swelling up?"

A Klingon forehead prosthetic joke rests just out of reach, since I'm never very good at delivering jokes.

"You banged on my door and I panicked when you called my name. Following that in quick succession was a head-to-head collision, some tangled body parts, an awkward fall, and a tragic landing."

Dane just stares at me for a second, then his eyes dip to where part of my shirt is hanging inside my panties.

"Why the hell aren't you wearing any pants?" Dane snaps.

"Fuck," Base groans, still on his hands and knees and rocking as though he's nauseous or dizzy.

"Because Harley told me not to wear any if I wanted Base to—"

"Please stop talking until I'm not at a debilitated disadvantage," Base cuts in, causing me to swallow the rest of that sentence.

Dane looks...

"What's that expression?" I ask Dane, waiting on him to answer me as his eyes rapidly flick from me to Base several times.

"Horrified," he bites out, turning and moving toward the door as he runs a hand through his hair and starts texting someone.

"Are we done talking?" I ask, assuming the crisis is solved since he's moved on to talking to someone else.

"No. I'm just telling Dale why he needs to kill Harley this time," he says through gritted teeth.

"You always tell your daughter not to be a tattletale, and those three parenting books in your living room all say it's good parenting to lead by example," I reasonably point out.

Base snorts out a laugh, then groans, then curses his balls as though they have ears.

Dane just gives me another look. Possibly indignation.

I turn around to see Base with his forehead resting on the backs of his hands as he takes even breaths. To him, I say, "They don't really kill the women. From what I've been told, they mostly rant a little incoherently, the women mock their ranting, and that's about all."

Base shakes his head, laughing and groaning and laughing again.

"I don't even know how to deal with this right now," Dane growls, bringing my attention back to him. "I was just coming by to make sure the painters got the back side of the house better."

"They haven't returned," I tell him, relaxing now that the subject has changed.

"That's not currently the thing on my mind!" Dane tells me very angrily, stabbing a finger into the air for no real obvious reason.

"Then why bring it up?" I ask, confused.

He pinches the bridge of his nose, as Base finally lumbers to his feet, not standing completely straight.

"We can talk about this when it doesn't feel like my balls are still trying to work their way north," Base tells him. "And alone. You can say whatever then. Don't do this with her in the room."

I look at Base and question his intelligence for the first time. Clearly I need to be in the room if my brother is turning angry colors. He hasn't turned angry colors very often, but when he did, those guys left in tears.

Dane looks over at me, then back at Base, then curses again.

Really, all the cursing is growing redundant since no one is explaining why they're angrily saying crude words.

Dane just turns and stalks out, then walks back in, eyes on me. "Please answer the next time I'm at the door. Just say you're busy if you're busy."

"I tried. My cognitive functions haven't been functioning properly around him," I tell him honestly, gesturing toward Base.

His eyes seem to soften a little, but they turn back into a hard glare when he looks at Base again. Then he stalks back out without another word.

Base hobbles over to the couch, groaning as he slowly lowers himself down. I go to grab a sack of frozen vegetables from the freezer. I've seen all the guys do this at some point.

As I offer it to him, he takes it from my hand, lips twisting in the beginnings of a smile for no logical reason I can discern.

"That definitely ended differently than I expected," he mumbles as he closes his eyes and puts the peas on his lap.

"That would have been statistically improbable to have foreseen," I tell him, patting his leg in case he feels guilty for lacking that foresight.

I sit down on the other end of the couch, and put my legs up as I cut on the movie we paused a really long time ago.

"You swore to massage my legs more later, but you should probably wait until a night when your testicles aren't swelling with fluid," I tell him as I turn the movie up.

He coughs out a laugh, not groaning this time, as his hand gently pats my foot. "Thanks."

"I try to be considerate," I tell him, even as the TV starts to capture my attention.

My brother's presence quite literally destroyed any arousal or the potential of it for the night.

When I feel the weight of Base's gaze on me, I turn my head, finding him studying me with what I believe is a pensive set to his jaw.

"What?" I prompt.

"You never said what bases you've touched."

This time, I understand his meaning. "First and I think second. Though second was more rough groping than erotic *petting*. It wasn't at all comfortable."

He scrubs a hand over his face, muttering something I don't hear.

"You never said what word you prefer to hear when a woman references her vagina," I tell him.

Another groan is all I get.

Halfway through the movie, he says, "Hey, your calendar says something about you giving a lecture tomorrow."

He's very invasive by *normal* standards when he reads my calendar. Fortunately, I don't mind.

"It always happens the first of every month for the past two months. This will be the third," I tell him absently.

Even the giant blue woman on screen has figured out how to tempt the opposite sex. At this point, I find movies to be mocking me, making it seem far easier than it is.

"Will everyone be there? The Sterlings, I mean?" he asks.

"No. Just a few girls take turns helping me with props and such. The guys say it's not their thing."

He grunts something, then moves closer, putting his arm around the back of the couch, his side pressing slightly against mine.

Arousal remains thoroughly destroyed for tonight with just my brother's unexpected presence.

I had no idea that could even happen.

"Would it be cool if me and the guys came?" he asks.

I snap my head to him, studying his eyes to see if I can tell if he's serious or not.

"Sure," I answer, hoping he doesn't burst out laughing and tell me I'm an idiot for assuming he'd really go to something like that.

I've had at least three possible date candidates do that.

They stopped being date candidates directly after.

Instead, he grins at me, tugging a lock of my hair. "Then let me know what time."

Chapter 23

BASE

"Are we really the first ones here?" Taylor groans as I take a seat in the front row of the empty room.

About ten chairs are in a row with a narrow table in front of it, and there are at least twelve rows of chairs and narrow tables in this semi-spacious convention room inside the clinic.

"I wanted to make sure we got up front," I tell them, smirking when Sticks flips me off and plops down beside me.

"Fucking suck up," Randy says, grinning as he goes to sit down beside Sticks.

Taylor takes a seat by him, and I glance around, trying to catch clues as to what this speech is going to be—

"So what's this all about anyway?" Sticks asks me.

"I asked her to come with us this weekend, and I thought it would be good to show some support of her interests. Hell, the Sterlings apparently told her they had better things to do, but worded it like it 'wasn't their thing.'"

"And this is how you're going to be better than a Sterling. You're competing with family for no reason, you know?" Sticks asks me.

"I'm not competing. I just think it's shitty they constantly support everyone else in their circle, but can't show up for something like this," I point out. "Besides, I want her more comfortable around you dicks before we leave. This will help with that."

Sticks mutters something.

"Don't make me point out all the shit I've done for you assholes," I tell them as about five or six people walk in, stacks and stacks of donut boxes being carried and deposited onto a table.

Salem and Tria walk in, then pause when they see us. Salem blinks as she starts to grin, then goes over to start directing the donut people.

Tria approaches us, a confused expression on her face. "You guys are here for Britt?" she muses.

"Yeah. Though don't tell us what she's lecturing about," Taylor says, his words dripping sarcasm. "Base likes to be surprised. But we're leaning toward it being about breast cancer awareness, since this clinic was built by Sterlings and dedicated to Rain."

Tria's grin spreads a little wider. "I'm happy to hear you like surprises. Rain actually does most of the breast cancer awareness speeches. She usually comes to help with Britt's things, but today she had to fly to Denver."

The donuts start getting put onto plates, and weirdly it looks like they have Fruit Roll-ups as well that they're assembling on the table.

"We get free donuts?" Randy asks, no longer sounding as though he hates this.

"Yes," Tria tells him, her lips twitching. "But you can't eat them until after the demonstration."

"Demonstration?" Taylor asks, sounding as confused as I feel as Tria gets called away.

Salem goes to the back, messing with a projector, and loud chatter behind us has me turning around as waves and waves of…young girls start to walk in. Most range between ages thirteen and maybe sixteen, with a few a little older, not counting the mothers or grandmothers who are escorting the very young ones.

"Base…" Sticks draws my name out, a hint of trepidation in his tone as more giggling little girls flood in, filling up the seats all around us.

A lot of mothers cast us looks that make me want to go shower because I feel like *I've* done something terribly offensive just by being here.

"What the hell kind of lecture is this?" Taylor hisses.

"We need to get out of here. We're legit getting pointed at," Sticks mutters under his breath, turning back around and ducking his head as his neck flushes.

"Hell no," Randy says—fucking loudly. "Two words: Free. Donuts."

"Let's go. I'll tell Britt—"

Before I can finish that, Britt is walking onto the small, raised platform in front of us, grinning at me like she can't believe I'm actually here. But it's the gratitude in her eyes that has my ass staying planted in my seat.

"Fuck. We're never going anywhere now," Stick whimpers, looking from me to her as I grin at her.

Someone takes a seat beside me, and I look over to see an elderly woman's face nearly directly in front of mine the second I turn my head.

She gives me an incredulous look, snorts a sound, and faces Britt as she puts her arm around the seat of a young girl who is presumably her granddaughter.

I rest my elbows on the table in front of us as the seats continue to fill up, and donuts start getting dispensed in a row, on a long, rectangular, clear, plastic plate.

"Don't eat them yet," Taylor tells Randy, slapping the back of his head so that the donut piece he just tore off between his teeth flies out of his mouth.

People start passing out pads of paper and ink pens next, putting them in front of all of us. I glance over the donut variety, wondering what it has to do with anything.

There's one with pink icing and sprinkles, one that has chocolate glaze, one that is plain glazed, and one that looks like blueberry.

The projector turns on, listing Britt's name and the clinic's name like a header for the upcoming slideshow. Britt doesn't bother quieting the room or introducing herself before she dives in.

"We're going to start with the basics," she says, as an image pops up on screen with the lecture's intent…

Oh shit.

THE MISUNDERSTANDING OF THE HYMEN, is written in all caps.

Randy chokes on a piece of donut, at the same time Britt says, "It's surprising to know how few women actually understand the hymen."

Sticks slinks down in his seat, eyes wide as his cheeks turn red.

We're in a roomful of girls who are *young*. And we're listening about hymens with these *young* girls.

We're going to hell, and it's all my fault.

"There are four types of hymens, and determining which one you have could directly affect your first sexual experience."

We're listening about first sexual experiences with really little girls. Oh, fuck me. We're going to get arrested or some shit.

"Kill me now," Taylor whispers just loud enough for me to hear him.

"The reason it's important to know, is because the hymen is the center of a lot of easily solved controversy. Some girls say it was the most pain they've ever felt."

A few girls whimper somewhere in the room. I just want to rewind time and not ask Britt if I can come to this thing.

Salem looks like she's working to keep a straight face when she glances over at our four pale ones.

Tria doesn't look at us at all, because it seems like she's struggling to remain seriously attentive, and knows she'll lose it if she looks in our direction.

Britt is fucking stoic.

And very passionately speaking about…hymens. To a lot of little girls. We're the only dudes in here, and everyone is noticing that more and more.

"Some girls claim to have felt no pain at all," Britt goes on. "Age always helps to deal with that. The hymen naturally erodes, stretches, and thins with age, physical activity, and a healthy menstrual cycle."

"I hate you," Sticks whispers to me. "I'm quitting the band."

I ignore him, because I'm busy trying to figure out how to get out of here when this thing is over with the fewest amount of people seeing my face.

Sticks has one hand up, like he's shielding half his face, when Britt adds, "You don't actually 'break' the hymen. It just stretches. That pain or the drops of blood is often from a tear. Some women don't bleed at all after the first time they have sex, because they've whittled their hymens down so that they comfortably stretch without tearing."

Taylor passes me a note like this is high school, and I unfold it.

My balls just left my body and ran out of here. Can I go chase them?

I scribble down a response and pass it back.

Only if you want everyone seeing your face when you stand up. I'm positive the room is packed.

He groans when he reads it, and Britt glances in our direction. "Any questions?" she asks Taylor, smiling cheerfully.

Taylor looks ready to die when she singles him out, and he shakes his head rapidly.

"One question," Randy says, holding up his hand like this is class.

"He's out of the band for real now," Sticks hisses when we feel the burn of everyone's eyes on us.

"When can we eat the donuts?" Randy asks, even though three of his donuts have bites out of them now.

"After we're done with the demonstration," Britt answers, her eyes flicking to a diagram of a…vagina…as it pops up on the screen.

I definitely don't like the word "vagina," but clinical terminology is best, given the fact that diagram is ruining the female anatomy for me right now.

Britt takes some sort of pointer tool, and holds it up to a very "open" display of the vagina.

"Nude shots and donuts. Best. Day. Ever," Randy says, drawing too much attention to us.

"It's a drawing, you idiot," Taylor snaps.

"This is the part you boys probably came to take notes about," the old lady beside me stage whispers as she nudges my arm with her elbow.

I look over as she gestures toward the diagram. "Someone finally drew you numbskulls a map," she adds.

Looking at the diagram, I start to say something to the lady, though I forget what when Britt deadpans, "This is the clitoris." Britt then taps the end of her little stick on the section of the diagram in question, as though it needs to be pointed out.

My head snaps back to the old woman as she winks at me, and I jerk my gaze away from her, glancing down our table to see when Randy starts actually writing shit down.

"I really thought that thing was farther south," Randy says as he scribbles away, once again speaking way too loudly. "That explains so much."

A few, "*Oh, that's why they're here,*" comments reach my ears, and Sticks, Taylor, and I all slink down farther in our seats.

"I thought I couldn't be embarrassed," Sticks growls.

"Same here," I bite out, ready to rip Randy's head off.

"This is the urethra," Britt goes on, pointing to another section of the diagram.

"*That* I don't need to know," Randy says, pen poised and ready to write, should Britt give him anymore necessary information.

Another note slides in front of me from Taylor.

I hate you.

I scribble back, *I hate me too,* and pass it to him.

"Then you have the inner labia," Britt goes on, pointing at another section.

"Do *not* ask what the inner labia is," Sticks hisses at Randy when he starts to raise his hand. "Or I will kill you in front of too many witnesses."

Randy slowly lowers his hand, frowning over at us.

"Then you have the vaginal opening, and as long as you're a virgin, you will have a hymen of some variety blocking, mostly blocking, or partially blocking full admittance to foreign objects."

Little baggies of those Fruit Roll-ups get dropped off at our table, but they're not the actual Fruit Roll-ups. At all. Like not even a little.

I get a little queasy when I start realizing the purpose of the donuts.

"The gelatin-like candy is malleable and designed to demonstrate the different types of hymens. Without tearing them, carefully pull away the excess, then place one type of gelatin hymen under every donut, carefully lining it up."

Another image pops on screen, and I really want to die. In four different ways. One way for each of the hymens I'm about to have to replicate with a fruit candy and a donut in a roomful of mostly new-teen girls.

How did this happen?!

Sucking it up, Sticks and I begin constructing the hymens—something I never thought I'd be doing in my lifetime.

"While there are a number of ways a hymen can appear before sex, given the wear-and-tear hypotheses where some hymens can look like a honeycomb, there are four accepted labels for hymens, according to my research."

Randy is looking from the diagram to the donut, perfecting his shit like he needs to ace this test. Taylor is muttering to himself, probably constructing four ways to kill me—one for each hymen donut.

Sticks tears his second hymen, shoves it at me, and takes my untorn one to replace it. I just glare at him.

Britt better not inspect these, or I will kill him for that.

As of right now, I feel like I owe him a little. The least I can do is give him one of my hymens.

Britt grins, glancing around, as everyone finishes.

Then she moves to the diagram of all four vaginas with different hymens.

Another note slides in front of me from Taylor.

Thanks to you, I'll never hook up with a virgin now. Thanks a lot. I've been traumatized.

I crumble the paper and tuck it into my pocket, when the old lady beside me snorts indignantly, because that old bat has started reading the notes we're passing.

"No offense, but I get why the Sterling guys say this isn't their thing," Sticks whispers to me angrily. "They don't want to look like perverts in a room full of virgins, most of whom still need a legal guardian in attendance to even hear this lecture."

"The solid hymen that completely blocks the vaginal opening is the imperforate hymen," Britt tells us, her eyes flicking warmly to me.

I force a smile, and, since I don't want her knowing how uncomfortable I really am, for some reason, I wink at her. Then realize that was probably not the best time to wink.

"I don't have one of those, remember?" she tells me directly, as though she thinks that wink meant I was somehow insinuating her type of hymen.

Everyone looks over at me. I can feel it without turning around to see it.

"Really hate you," Sticks mutters, practically disappearing under the table when he slinks down even farther.

Britt goes on like it's no big deal. "The imperforate is actually not notably common, but it's more common than most people realize. And in most cases, needs to be surgically taken care of early on to avoid painful discomfort."

Randy scribbles more shit down for reasons I can't fathom.

"The septate hymen has two openings with a band of tissue in the center. Though, the openings are rarely ever equal in size," Britt goes on. "This type of hymen is still not considered common, but some stats show that one in every one thousand women have them, and very few women actually know their type of hymen. So I'd say it's more common than most of us realize."

Britt points at this mentioned hymen on her diagram, and I glance down at my septate donut, trying not to make eye contact with her again so I don't do something stupid that makes her think I'm once again assuming her type of hymen.

"Penetration is a novel feeling that can cause the stretching to be painful, and everyone will have different experiences, mostly because none of our hymens are exactly the same."

I risk a glance up as she points at the next one.

"Microperforate hymen is up next, though, you will find various names for all of these on the internet. I find these all to be the most scientifically valid. This particular hymen is known for the pinhole entrance that prevents it from being an imperforate hymen. These sometimes need more stretching before sexual penetration is considered."

Britt pulls up her stick and points to the final one. Thank fuck.

"The crescent moon-like shape of this one is the most common hymen, dubbing it the 'normal' hymen because of its commonality. It has more elasticity and can be stretched easier before sexual penetration to ensure the least amount of pain." She glances at me. "This is actually my hymen."

I hold up an *okay* sign with my hand, and start wondering how many people in here might recognize me.

She looks back around the class. "It's best to learn your type of hymen. Knowing your body is a good thing. It's *your* body. Being aware of all of its significant secrets that will directly impact your life may change a lot of your experiences just because you know what to expect. Not to mention, it's your right as a female to understand the complexities of the female body. Fear of the unknown is doubled when you don't even know your own body."

The End, flashes across the projector screen, and people start clapping. Randy actually stands, starting a standing ovation, while I stay slumped in my seat and clap.

After the applause ends, Randy starts devouring his hymen donuts, while Sticks and Taylor shove theirs away. "Two of my favorite snack foods have been ruined for eternity," Taylor grumbles.

Britt goes to shake hands, while three out of four of us try to hide our faces as the room disperses.

"What are you doing?" I ask Sticks when he posts a picture from our trip to Mexico two years ago on the band's website.

"Giving us an airtight alibi in case someone noticed us," he mutters.

We leave Randy behind as he starts eating our hymen donuts.

"Yo, you tore your septate hymen," Randy calls to my back, and the three of us walk faster, now pretending we don't know him.

A woman stops, her thirteen-ish daughter next to her, and she frowns as she studies us.

"You look familiar," she says, pointing at the three of us.

"Well, I don't know who we remind you of, but I can promise we're not The Fallen," Taylor says, causing Sticks and I both to groan. "Heard those guys were in Mexico," Taylor adds, obvious as fuck.

Her brow furrows. "I doubt The Fallen need quick anatomy tutorials designed for young girls," the woman says. "You remind me of someone else, but I can't figure out who..."

I breathe out a sigh of relief, just as Randy says, "Nurse, I need a ten blade! I'm going for the imperforate hymen donuts now."

"Let's get the hell out of here," Sticks groans, turning toward the back door and practically sprinting out.

I glance at Britt, gesture toward the back door, and actually sprint out as well when I see two cops walk in.

Holy fucking hell.

As soon as we get outside, Taylor says, "Well, you love a good surprise. Consider us even for absolutely fucking everything we've ever asked you to do."

We stand silently for a moment, allowing ourselves to be a little horrified, then suddenly Taylor bursts out laughing. Sticks and I steadily join in, laughing increasingly louder as we lose control.

Randy bursts through the doors, several boxes of donuts in hand.

"Dude, Britt's awesome. She gave us all the leftover hymen donuts we wanted."

The laughter quickly dispels and turns into groans again.

"This day will never be forgotten," Taylor deadpans.

Chapter 24

BASE

Britt's trying to kill me. With her body. Half naked all the time.

I'm really thankful to be on the road today, because I won't be tempted to throw her over the couch and forget to take things slow. Because she'll be wearing clothes. Or at least that was the goal. Until she walked out of her room looking like she does right now.

Since her brother's appearance, we haven't gotten *that* close again. But I've decided to let things roll. She knows I'm leaving in three months. She knows my priorities.

She's a fucking adult who can make her own decisions without my opinions or anyone else's.

I'm sick of fucking pretending I can be a saint. Especially since I can't keep my damn hands off her. Even standing close requires me touching her in some way.

Now she's bent over *my* couch in *my* house with the tightest pants I've ever seen as she digs out her crossword puzzle book from her purse. Apparently she thinks this trip will be as boring as the last trip.

My hand slides around her waist, tugging her toward the door, as the guys finish loading up the last of the equipment in the trailer.

"We'll be sleeping in the van tonight," Taylor tells her as she steps out.

"Already informed her," I say as I climb in behind her, straddling the trailer that's hooked behind us in order to get in.

Taylor and Randy take the front, and Sticks joins us in the back.

Just before the doors shut, I hear, "I'm here! I'm late, but I'm here!"

Britt perks up, looking toward the doors as I put my arm around her, both of us sitting on the bench seat across from Sticks on the other.

"I thought I'd invite someone you seemed to get along with, so that you wouldn't be the only one on the outside of the inside jokes," I tell Britt, smiling when she studies me for a second.

Krysta hurtles herself inside, closing the doors behind her.

"And I'm going to redeem myself," Krysta says as she drops her bag next to ours and plops down on the seat near Sticks, but not too close.

Sticks grins as he glances over at her.

"You mean you're not going to get shit-faced wasted within an hour?" he prods.

"Har. That's exactly what I mean. I'm not going to drink *at all,*" she tells him, and then glances over at Britt and smiles. "And I owe you big time."

"I didn't do much. Ruby came," Britt informs her.

Krysta's cheeks redden a little, even as she tries to pretend she's not embarrassed. "Yes, well, you didn't owe me even that much. You could have just left me at my house or in my car."

"That would have been wrong," Britt points out, as though that's obvious. "And very terrible."

Krysta just smiles a little, relaxing in her seat as Taylor starts trying to make everyone think this is going to be an *epic* road trip.

Sticks and I groan in unison.

After we're all sick of Randy singing and manage to get the music cut down, Sticks looks over at Britt, who is sitting next to a familiar stack of donut boxes that Randy brought along.

"So why'd you start up those hymen classes at the clinic?" Sticks asks, as Krysta sputters and chokes on her water in surprise.

"People consider me to be highly intelligent, but when I started trying to gather information on my body and sex, I realized how very little information I'd been made aware of," she states simply.

"So you decided to share?" Krysta asks, recovering as she tries to join in on the conversation.

Britt shrugs. "It's just small little lectures. They sprinkle the day with them and different speakers, but keep them short and fun."

It sort of goes quiet after that…like no one knows how to follow that up or what conversation will make sense now. I have no idea why I'm fucking nervous right now and making this weird.

I give Sticks *the* eye, prompting him to step up and kick conversation back up.

"So what kind of parents did you get in foster care?" he asks Britt suddenly, and I narrow my eyes on him.

However, he just looks at her, waiting on her to answer.

She doesn't even tense before answering, "A variety."

"I had a variety too," he says with a shrug. "I kept getting yanked back by my grandmother, because she was trying to keep me out of the system, but I lost three good homes before I landed in a check-casher's place for the rest of my time."

She doesn't really say anything much.

He really could have gone any other direction with the conversation than delving right for the hard stuff. Sheesh. You'd think we don't know how to socialize either.

"It's mostly a blur," Britt states noncommittally.

"What about your parents?" he asks when she doesn't readily volunteer the information.

I make a throat-slicing gesture, and he clears his throat and looks away.

"I have limited information about them."

He frowns. "You couldn't find them or anyone who knew them?" he asks, rolling with it.

"I'm not ready to know, and I feel like I should be certain I can prepare for the worst before tackling that," she says like she's thought about this a lot.

"I went crazy—a little bit literally—trying to find my father. I thought life would be better if I found him, because I just *knew* that he didn't know I existed. And you didn't even wonder about yours?" Krysta asks her like she's genuinely curious.

"I'm curious; I'm just not ready to know, because I know it's not going to be a good story. It could be decades before I'm ready. I'm in no hurry because it's not affecting my life," she says with zero emotion.

I could kill Sticks for making the topic so heavy, and for leaving Britt shifting uncomfortably.

"So, can we get a preview of the new song Sticks said you guys have been rehearsing?" Krysta asks, finally shifting the topic to something we can actually communicate.

Taylor snorts. "He doesn't let anyone get a preview. *We* barely get a preview before we're expected to play it—and kill it—the first time on stage."

"I've been trying to read the music," Britt says suddenly, causing me to grin.

"You can read music?" I ask, surprised.

"I have the notes memorized, but unless you can actually play, reading music is not as simple as memorizing notes. And my playing abilities are definitely lacking."

"You're self-teaching yourself music?" Krysta asks, leaning forward.

"Attempting to. I was curious about what all the notes scribbled on the walls actually are."

"You don't even play the songs for *her*?" Krysta asks me, as though I've committed some sort of cardinal sin.

I shift in my seat. Considering Britt's the *only* person I've seen in a club who didn't hear us at all *while* we were playing, I'm clearly not in any sort of hurry to play these songs—that I fucking love—in front of her.

"Britt's not impressed with our playing. She tunes us out," Sticks says, smirking over at me.

Britt's head snaps toward me. "That's why?"

Fortunately, Taylor is stopping for gas, so I don't have to answer that aloud. Kissing the top of her head, I hop out, thankful to be stretching my legs already.

Sticks catches up to me, and I immediately ask, "What the hell was that back there?"

He groans as he runs a hand through his hair. "You said to make her feel more comfortable. I went for the obvious bonding mechanism…kindred spirits and all that. It was all the standard questions most people like us exchange. It's usually more casual than that, man."

I glance back at Britt as she smiles and talks to Krysta, though the smile is an easy one and not too forced.

He scratches his head, trying not to laugh, before saying, "We used to be better at this."

Chapter 25

BRITT

"So what's the deal with you two?" Krysta asks quietly as the guys laugh and start turning the back of the van into sleeping quarters for all of us. "And why can't we get a hotel room instead of parking in a camp ground?" she goes on, whispering that part even quieter.

I've already started a fire, and now I'm slowly building it up. It's almost like the concept of comfort food. Camping, that is.

"I'm not really sure what is going on with Base and I," I tell her honestly. "They don't like to spend money on hotel rooms when they're trying not to live above their means and have other expenses they find more important."

"I could pay for a hotel room," she argues. "And are you okay with no label?"

Carrying on two conversations at once, I answer, "Camping is more efficient. I don't want a label. I'm not ready for that."

Leaning back against one of the logs I've rolled over, I take a seat beside her.

"But you think you're ready for sex?" she muses.

Women always bond over sex. I grin, since I assume she's making an attempt to do that by bringing this conversation up.

"Yes. I also think he's finally warmed to the idea of being my first."

She studies me with an indecipherable expression. "Okay then."

"What're you two girls talking about?" Randy asks in a mock feminine voice as he walks toward us.

"Nothing," Krysta says, at the same time I answer, "Sex."

His smile grows, and Krysta snorts out a laugh. "I forgot how honest you are," she tells me.

Randy shrugs before saying, "Well, buckle up. You're about to see something done by no man before—"

"Just because you're the only one in our group stupid enough to do this on the regular, doesn't mean no one else isn't just as stupid," Base quips as he comes to drop beside me, stretching his legs out in front of him on the ground as his arm goes around my shoulders. "Nice fire, by the way," he adds, grinning over at me.

"I camped a lot when I finally figured out the proper way to run away," I explain, causing his grip to tighten.

Before I can examine his reaction, Randy says, "*Brave* enough. Not stupid."

I'm curious about the details of this argument, since it's one I've heard a variety of scenarios about on numerous occasions. Bravery versus stupidity, that is.

Krysta's eyes flick to Base's hand as he starts toying with some small pieces of my hair, and she gives me a smile before returning her attention to the others.

I relax against him, feeling comforted by the outdoors around us.

Randy starts tearing into a pack of fireworks, intriguing me, since there's something brave he's supposed to be attempting.

"Shooting fireworks is brave?" Krysta asks him.

"No," Randy snorts. "Shooting fireworks is for pussies."

I glance down at my *pussy*, then up at him. Clearly that's the term he prefers to use, but I have no idea what it has to do with fireworks.

"Shooting fireworks is in no way affiliated with a vagina," I decide to point out, causing Sticks to snort and turn around as Randy gives me a look...

"Are you by chance constipated?" I ask him.

"No…just confused," he replies in a slow, drawn out way.

Base's body shakes with silent laughter, and he buries his face against my neck like he's hiding. But…that is very distracting, because his lips innocently brush the column of my throat and somehow still manage to set my body on fire.

Metaphorically, of course. Yet another saying I finally understand since meeting him.

"Prepare yourselves," Randy announces, before he…drops his pants.

Krysta shrieks and looks away, and I tilt my head, wondering why he's putting his penis on display. What am I missing?

"For fuck's sake, dude, you forgot boxers again," Taylor groans, causing Base's head to snap away from my throat as he glares at Randy's flaccid penis.

"Shit," Randy says, covering his penis as he shuffles his feet and turns his bare ass on us instead.

I've learned *ass* is widely more preferred over *buttocks*.

"Are you cold?" I ask Randy, given how very small his penis seemed, causing Base to make a strangled sound as a bit of laughter slips out.

Taylor and Sticks both double over, heaving out laughter. When I deliberately attempt to make jokes, no one ever laughs. Mostly they get constipated. Or confused.

One day I'll master that.

"You are so giving me a complex, Red," Randy shouts, shaking his head as he waddles around with his pants at his ankles and starts lowering himself to the ground. "I'm a grower, not a shower."

"Don't ask," Krysta says when I open my mouth to do just that.

As he gets situated on the ground, pants still trapping his ankles together, he *hoots* into the air like someone who is very excited. Though…I'm still trying to understand what's going on.

"Please don't tell me he's about to do what I think he is," Krysta says.

"What's he about to do?" I ask, genuinely curious.

"He's definitely going to," Base tells her, drawing me even closer.

"Load me up and let's do it!" Randy shouts from the ground.

"Do what exactly?" I ask louder, wondering if my volume is the reason I continue to go unanswered.

"Paper, rock, scissors," Sticks says to Base, which makes zero sense. "Get up here."

"My hands are touching Britt, and I'm not going to go the rest of the night without touching her. So I'm out this time. I call hall pass," Base answers dismissively.

"This is utterly confusing. I'm not constipated," I point out to them, wondering if maybe they're not reading my expression right for a change.

Groaning—at Base—Sticks turns to Taylor, and the two of them, in synchronized unison, shake their fists twice. On the third shake, Taylor's hand flattens and Sticks puts out two fingers.

I've seen this before…

I've never understood why it played a part in decision making.

I also don't understand what decision they're currently making.

"Snip, snip, motherfucker," Sticks says with a broad smile as Taylor curses and stares at Randy's ass like it might bite.

"Are they going to have sex in front of us?" I finally ask. "Because I feel like this is something I should video for the girls if they're okay with public exhibition."

Base laughs. Hard. And Sticks does as well.

Krysta snickers. Taylor gives me a dry look before he rolls his eyes and catches a Roman Candle that Sticks tosses him.

My eyes dart between the Roman Candle and Randy's ass, but the math just doesn't add up. Surely they're not going to—

"I really fucking hate your traditions," Taylor says to Randy as he kneels and spreads Randy's ass cheeks with a grimace on his face.

I watch, wondering what exactly is about to happen, because I'm fairly sure he's about to have a foreign object inserted into his anus, and they are acting as though this is an annoying, yet completely normal task. I'm unnervingly alarmed by how riveted the entire situation has left me.

Krysta chokes back a laugh when Taylor quickly places the Roman Candle inside Randy's butt cheeks and—

"Too close to the exit hole!" Randy squeals, confusing me.

Taylor groans, nose wrinkling as he adjusts the firework, and Randy's ass clenches, holding the stick steady as Taylor lets go and walks over to Krysta with his hands out. She squirts hand sanitizer on his hands like she received an unspoken request.

I envy how easily she adapts to confusing situations. And envy is not something I like to experience.

"Five or ten shots?" Base asks as Sticks starts flicking a lighter near the firework.

My eyes widen with realization just as Randy answers, "Five."

The fuse sizzles when it catches fire, and Sticks jogs over to us as I watch with rapt attention.

A little *whoosh* happens just as the first ball of light bursts from the stick wedged in Randy's ass, and it explodes in the air, crackling and sparking. A grin spreads over my lips when the second one happens and Randy howls in excitement.

Base chuckles, and I ask, "What's the purpose of this?"

Another little burst of light crackles in the sky. Number three.

"We haven't figured it out yet," Base answers absently as number four shoots out and goes much higher than the other three before it.

As the last one darts out and crackles, Randy hoots loudly and relaxes his ass. The spent tube drops to the ground, though it's still between his cheeks. Just as he starts to reach back and remove it, laughing like something great has happened, a sixth shot bursts out unexpectedly.

"Shit!" Randy shrieks as the shot fires into his pants at his ankles and ricochets back, slapping into his testicles.

"Fuck!" Taylor shouts, diving just as Randy leaps up, shouting, "My balls! My balls!"

Randy has his ass clenched again as he slaps at his *balls*, which are smoking.

As Randy screams and dances with his pants still trapping his ankles, a seventh shot fires from the tube and hits the ground. It bounces and ricochets, then charts a straight path directly toward my face.

No sound leaves my lips before I'm tackled to the ground, Base coming down on top of me as number eight fires in the background. Someone shouts for him to get it out of his ass, and someone else shouts for him to sit down.

"I'm not fucking sitting!" he shouts just as number nine fires and bounces across the ground again, this time skittering into the very wet woods.

It's probably for the best that there was a heavy rainfall yesterday.

The tube finally drops from Randy's butt cheeks, and he falls onto the ground when his ankle-tangling pants finally take him down. Shot number ten fires, and the tube—no longer held stable by Randy's ass's iron grip—is launched back. It slams into Randy's balls as the tenth shot explodes against the side of the van and rains crackling little sparks on everyone before dissipating into smoke.

As Randy sobs and holds his abused groin, the rest of the camp goes quiet in the absence of randomly exploding fireworks.

"For fuck's sake, Randy!" Base shouts, lifting off me and helping me to my feet. I'm still a little dazed by the madness, if I'm being honest. "You said *five* shots!"

"It was," Randy groans from the ground.

Sticks grabs the open pack of Roman Candles, and he glares over at Randy. "It's a *five pack*, you moron," Sticks growls. "Which means five fucking candles. It clearly states there are *ten* shots each."

"*Now you tell me,*" Randy whimpers as he finally starts trying to pull his pants up.

"I think he's been punished enough," Krysta says, seeming to struggle to control her facial features as her lips smile and go straight multiple times in a row.

"Damn it! It left a fucking mark!" Taylor shouts, staring at his van in horror.

I can't *see* anything wrong with just the firelight illuminating it from a distance.

"Yeah, well, it left a mark on my fucking balls too, you insensitive prick!" Randy shouts.

Base shakes his head, looking furious at some points and looking as though he's restraining a laugh at others, while he guides me toward the back of the van.

Taylor runs a hand through his hair, cursing as he goes toward Randy, still griping at him for his inability to properly read firework instructions.

"Get changed and we'll call it a night," Base says to me, kissing the top of my head before he walks off.

I'm not particularly tired anymore, considering the fact my adrenaline is working through my veins. I could jog, and I don't even like jogging.

I have energy for sex, but nowhere to have sex and no way of successfully seducing him.

After I'm finished changing, I open the door, and Base climbs in, shutting the door behind him, grinning as he gently pushes me down to the pallets on the floor of the van.

Okay then. That was easy enough for once.

His lips find mine before I can even ask what he's doing, and then I decide I don't care what he's doing as long as he keeps doing it.

Just as my fingers tangle in his hair and he gets settled comfortably between my legs, the van doors open, and he groans against my lips.

"You can't take her virginity on the floor of the van," Taylor states in an emotionless tone as the van jostles and he's suddenly coming in beside us.

"Wasn't planning on it," Base says as though he's frustrated.

Well…now I'm confused. Hopefully, people will misinterpret it for constipation.

He moves off me, rolling to the side, and tugs me up against him as close as I can physically get without crawling on top of him. I don't smile, but it's because I'm actively trying not to smile.

"How are we all going to sleep back here?" I hear Krysta asking as she climbs in and moves toward the top.

"We've done it with more people than this," Sticks answers as he climbs in as well.

With people lying in carefully placed positions, and me mostly pressed against Base, everyone manages to get uncomfortably crammed in. I'm not sure the quality of sleep will be great, but I've slept in tighter spaces than this.

Randy is the last to climb in, hobbling and hissing out pained breaths when he struggles to crawl to a spot.

Krysta suddenly groans. "I'm lying here, trying to go to sleep while wedged between two guys I barely know—"

"Sounds like a good start to a cheesy porno," Sticks says suddenly.

A snort follows that from Base as his chest vibrates with suppressed laughter.

"Anyway, and I keep smelling burnt hair. I hate that smell," she states like it needs to be said. "Especially when I know it's burnt *ball* hair."

A whimper sounds seconds before all the guys burst out laughing.

"I bet none of you fuckers would be laughing if it was your singed ball hair that was stinking up the van," Randy grumbles.

"I'm so glad you guys took me seriously when I said I'd like to keep it classy this weekend," Base says, even though he's saying it through a laugh.

More laughter follows that, and I just grin against Base's shirt that is stretched across his chest. His arm is pillowing my head, and despite the fact I'm not all that sleepy, I drift off to ball-hair, flaming-balls, and ball-busting jokes.

Chapter 26

BASE

"So…Britt Sterling. That's one of those fancy Sterling Shore names, isn't it?" my mother asks Britt the second Britt gets seated in the kitchen.

Britt just nods, and I shoot my mother an incredulous, what-the-fuck look. Hell, I've barely just made introductions.

"I like your house," Britt states as she looks around.

"Subtle," Mom snorts with some serious attitude.

"Sorry, did you suffer a concussion or something before we got here?" I ask her, genuinely worried, as Britt opens her mouth and closes it again.

Krysta shifts beside Britt at the table, having just sat down as well. She makes a silent whistle as she looks around the room.

"Very nice," Krysta chimes in. "Decorate it yourself?"

"You say you won't get sucked into Tag's world and all the pressure that sort of goal would put on you, and you bring home two Sterlings who expect the moon. Which one are you dating? Is it the blonde? You know that's not her natural color, right?" Mom asks, pointing a deliberate finger at Krysta.

I…I…I…have no idea what is going on right now.

I glance around, wondering what fucking rabbit hole I fell down, and then I immediately go to the stove.

"What are you doing?" Mom snaps as I start wedging the unit away from the wall.

"Looking for the gas leak that's made you lose your

motherfucking mind," I call over my shoulder.

"Hey, hey, hey!" Sticks booms as he comes in. "How's things in here?"

I turn around just as Britt looks over at a gobsmacked Krysta and asks, "Increasingly uncomfortable?"

Krysta gives her a firm nod, staring at my mother like she's worried about looking away. "I'd say that sums up how things are. Yep."

Sticks looks from me to them to mom and fucking grins.

"The red isn't natural either," Mom goes on, only adding to my horror.

Sticks stops Taylor from walking in, still grinning, as Mom taps her foot and swings her gaze to Britt.

"I'm naturally red, but my natural isn't this color of red," Britt says unsurely, like she feels she needs to explain.

"There's absolutely no reason why I should have seen this coming. Have you really lost your mind?" I ask Mom again, who ignores me as Britt quickly continues.

"But my brother took me to get it changed when I first told him I wanted it, and I've just kept it up ever since," Britt adds. "I'm sorry if it offends your culture or beliefs in any way—I wasn't aware. I'll cover it if I need to," she offers so sincerely.

Mom's hard look wavers, almost like she's getting confused.

"Well, no, I was just…" Mom's voice trails off like she doesn't want to point out she was being ridiculous and scrambling to be an asshole when she's *never* an asshole. At least not when she's being sane.

Britt stares like she's waiting patiently on my mom to recover.

"Which one of you is the attention-starved rich girl turned hot mess?" Mom asks, gesturing between Britt and Krysta, only adding to the growing list of things I need to apologize for.

"That'd be me," Krysta says tightly, pointing at herself.

"Which one are you…you know?" Mom asks me as she points between Krysta and Britt.

After seeing my life pass before my eyes, I scrub a hand over my face as all three of my fucking bandmates choke back a laugh.

"Oh, that's code for sex, right?" Britt asks, then carries on quickly. "Base won't have sex with me because I still have a hymen and he thinks I'm not mentally ready to deal with losing my virginity with a lack of feelings," she states very seriously.

We walked in. I said, *Hi, Mom.* Mom hugged me, I introduced her to Britt, we moved to the kitchen, and bam. Nope, retracing my steps does not explain how this whole conversation got away from me so fast.

Mom shoots me a horrified look, like she can't believe Britt just said that to her. I've never once been embarrassed by my mother. Until today. Today, I regret stopping in, since it's clearly not as casual as I expected it to be.

Britt leans over and whispers something to Krysta, who is still a little…dumbfounded.

"I think we're past the point of what is or isn't appropriate by now, but no, not under normal circumstances," Krysta tells her, brow furrowed like she can't believe this is her day.

"Sorry," Britt says to my mother. "I haven't been in a situation where I've had to meet a potential—"

"Stop talking," Krysta cuts in, patting Britt's knee.

Britt swallows the rest of her words, and my mom exhales harshly.

"Oh, sweetie, you're a virgin? What the hell are you doing with my son?" Mom asks, doing a complete one-eighty as she moves quickly to Britt's side.

Sticks comes up and claps my shoulder. "Reason number four-hundred and seventy-three not to fuck a virgin," he says quietly. "You go from don't-you-touch-my-baby-boy to what-are-you-doing-with-that-whorish-man-child."

"No, no, no," Britt is saying, assuring my mother of something.

"He told me he's leaving in four months, since the tour has been slightly delayed. We were just discussing sex. Not a relationship. But we're friends with partial benefits now."

Mom and Krysta cast a dirty glare in my direction.

"I walked in, which usually leaves Mom really happy for the first few hours and I can get away with murder," I go on, gesturing toward the front door, my head hurting with the spit-fire madness.

Mom stands abruptly and walks over to where we've moved, and she hisses, "Are you playing games with this poor girl's head?"

"Then I hugged my mother," I go on, looking over at Taylor, who shrugs and stares up at the ceiling like he doesn't want to draw any more attention to himself than necessary.

"As a man raised by a single mother, you should be more sensitive to a woman than that," Mom goes on.

"How am I in trouble right now?" I ask, seriously needing someone to walk me through how this has all transpired.

Sticks clears his throat, doing a miserable job of schooling his grin.

"I don't know what to say to make it better. I just keep making it worse," Britt says a little helplessly from behind my crazy mother.

Mom smiles abruptly, a full, takes-over-her-entire-face smile, and laughter begins bubbling out of her more and more as she doubles over.

Britt and Krysta exchange a confused glance as my dickheaded bandmates all start laughing as well. Mom actually wipes tears out of her eyes.

"I'm sorry, Britt, Krysta," Mom says, waving a hand in their general direction. "But I couldn't help myself. Your face," she says, laughing as she points at me.

She stops laughing and quickly turns around to face Krysta.

"I'm so sorry, honey. Really. I had no idea one of you would sincerely own up to being an attention-starved, hot mess. I was just tossing out a stereotype."

Krysta looks torn between laughing and hiding under a table, but Mom turns back, staring at me as I glare at her.

"You're fucking evil," I state very honestly, gesturing at all of her.

"I'm sorry, but it's rare I meet new people I can actually embarrass you in front of."

"You can be damned sure you won't be meeting new people in the future. Enjoy your one crowning moment of victory," I dutifully inform her, still feeling the urge to apologize.

Britt just smiles like she finally gets the joke, and Krysta slowly relaxes.

"Again, sorry," Mom says to Krysta, patting her arm on her way by. "Just so you know, I'm not actually all that judgmental. Usually I'm the one being judged, so let's start fresh."

"I'm just going to go splash some cold water on my face and stuff," Krysta says before scurrying out of her chair.

"You need to apologize better than that," I tell Mom.

"That'll just make it worse. Ignore it and it'll go away."

"That's the opposite of the healthy approach to problems," I point out.

"Actually, it depends on the individual and their own perspective," Britt argues in a tone that sounds like she's in a stale debate club. "Can I just ask Krysta which she'd prefer?"

"Now it's just getting weird," Sticks says as he exits in the same direction Krysta went.

"How's the road? Sex, drugs, and rock and roll still doing it for you, kiddo?" Mom asks idly. "Make sure you get him tested before letting him pop any precious cherries."

I glance over at Britt and mouth another apology, as she just tucks her hair behind her ear and smiles over at my mother.

"We've got to get on the road soon, because we have reservations at a hotel closer to the venue," I say as I stand, stretching and gesturing for Britt to get up.

"I thought we were spending the day and night here. That was why we missed karaoke night," she points out like she's confused.

Mom cuts her eyes to me. "You're an idiot," she says before turning her attention back to the stove.

I groan as I sit back down.

Britt glances between us, and her eyes widen before she makes an understanding *O* with her lips.

"So, Britt, why are you still a virgin?" Mom asks her. "No brave men left in the world?"

I palm my face, and then, like a dick, stand and abandon Britt because I can't. I just can't sit here and listen to how embarrassing my mother is still being.

Why did I think this was going to be a good idea?

Chapter 27

BRITT

"So you really teach classes on this?" Base's Mom asks me as the guys argue about something outside.

She hands back my phone as I shake my head. "Informative seminars at the clinic. I don't have the certification to teach actual classes."

"And you're legit documenting your struggle to lose your virginity. And you have a lot of people following the scoop," Krysta goes on, brow furrowed as she reads from her own phone.

"I leave out details, but still mention the challenging world of navigation. I considered random stranger sex, but then read the statistics on the danger incurred with that. I decided against it, despite how well/complicated it worked out with some other members from my family."

"This isn't just about sex. You have an entire life plan in writing," Krysta goes on, groaning a little. "I haven't even decided on a major."

"Harley has helped me out with that," I go on as commotion stirs inside the garage next to us. The guys have been outside a while.

"Seems you have a rather large support system," Base's mother tells me.

Before I can answer, Base pokes his head in the door, narrowing his eyes at his mother.

"All good in here?"

"Anyone been irrevocably offended by my bad manners since

earlier?" she asks us.

Krysta opens her mouth like she's going to speak, but gets cut off by Base's mother.

"When you boys finish your chores, perhaps you'd like to join the adults for conversation."

Base just gives her a bored look as he backs out and shuts the door.

"I've recently given myself a new nickname, and I want you girls to be the first to try it out for me," Base's mother says as she pours us another round of tea.

When Krysta nods, I do the same.

This is a social first for me. I didn't realize people gave themselves nicknames.

"Honey Bee," she says, grinning like she's brilliant. "I'm tired of my vibrator, and I need a name that sounds sweet so I can lure in the bears."

"What about just Honey?" Krysta suggests.

"Too much like a stripper and not a hot, pre-grandma woman in her prime," she says as she adjusts her bra. "Base is all grown up, and it's finally safe for me to date again—and has been for a while. I need to quit dallying before everything finishes its gravitational rotation," she adds as she finishes some minor adjustments to ensure her breasts are sufficiently perky.

"I pick the losers, so that's why I stayed single. I realize you can marry with a kid, but why risk screwing him up twice as much?" she goes on. "I've got shit taste in men."

I don't think Base is really screwed up. Is he?

"So what is he trying to save you from, Britt Sterling?" she asks when we don't speak.

Seems random, even to me.

A little surprised, I sit back. "This is my confused expression. I'm not constipated," I tell her so that she's not stuck in that horrible paradox.

I wish she'd repay the courtesy and explain her expression.

"Base only brings home the ones he wants to save, sweetie. They tried to name their band *Bastards of the Fallen* for a reason. I vetoed the first half because they were in eighth grade. So what's your story?"

"Why do people do that to you?" Krysta asks, drawing both our attention as she focuses on me. "They do it to me too."

"I'm asking her story because she's with my son. But people genuinely want to know about the rich. The popular. The pretty. They want your dark secrets so they can feel like you're no better than them; you just got luckier."

"That's true for me," I decide to say, causing Krysta to huff out a sound. "I was lucky my brother searched for siblings. He checked to make sure I didn't have any more out there either."

Honey Bee looks over at Krysta, who seems a little...annoyed? At least I think annoyed is right.

In a somewhat defensive tone, Krysta starts, "But why does she have to—"

"She doesn't have to tell me anything. Masters men are devilishly gorgeous, and they have really big hearts. Especially when they're young. A girl can be blinded by that sort of natural charm that they don't even really mean to use. But those hearts of theirs are big enough for more than one woman at a time, until that heart collapses from trying to spend too much of itself all at once."

She glances down at her tea, smiling tightly.

"But my son isn't like the rest of them," she goes on, eyes meeting mine again. "He goes out of his way to be the opposite of the womanizing stereotype. He's focused on the music, so when a girl snags his attention, it's because she needs saving. However, he has one hell of a hero complex. I'm not judging you or anything; everyone needs saving from time to time."

I'm not really sure what to say to that. I feel like I should defend Tag, but he did used to be a womanizer. However, now he's a man with two children and a wife he still adores.

"I've already been saved. I don't need to be saved again," I finally decide to say when it seems like she's waiting on me to respond.

Honey Bee leans up like she's about to say something, but the front door opens, and the guys start pouring in.

"Your fence is fixed, along with the mailbox," Taylor tells her.

"Gutters are cleaned, and the yard is mowed," Base adds as he steps in.

I've never understood the fascination with sweaty men. Until now. I now have something to share on the next girl's night when conversation predictably takes this turn again.

Base runs a hand through his damp hair, and I somehow tune out the rest of the words going on around me as I simply stare. He smiles over at Honey Bee as she says something back, but my eyes are on him, and his naked upper body.

Tattoos—I never understood the fascination with those either, until Base Masters.

It's like he pulls all the clichés together in a unique way and makes me understand why it all works at once.

His eyes finally land on mine, and it feels like I've been waiting for that, almost like I needed that acknowledgment. I'm smiling before I can stop myself, and his grin immediately mimics mine.

Until Randy steps between us and mocks a gag.

I blink like I've been stuck in a trance, and notice everyone is looking between us. Honey Bee just blinks at me a few slow times before she exhales a long, loud sigh and stands while shaking her head.

She whispers something to Base that makes him roll his eyes, but his smile stays in place as his gaze meets mine again.

"The girls can share the only guest room, and the guys will all stay in Base's room. I won't be hearing any hanky panky going on under my roof tonight," Honey Bee calls as she leaves.

Chapter 28

BRITT

This weekend, between Randy causing us all to suffer through the sense of smell in the van with burnt ball hair and his lactose intolerance, a *lot* of band arguing, and some tunnel vision for Base that left him almost absent while fully present today, has been leading up to this moment.

Base grins from the stage, and a small gathering near the front—much smaller than the one that gathers at Silk—swoon as he talks into the microphone.

When his fingers strum the first chord and his eyes stare directly into mine, I get a telling tingle that makes me wonder if I have the potential to be a groupie.

The hypothesis is cleared up when he sings the very first verse of some very dirty song strung with metaphorical lyrics that don't actually make a lot of sense. It doesn't matter if it doesn't make sense, because he really can sing. And play. And stare at you until you question if combustible panties really are as impossible as they're supposed to be.

Everything on me moves to the music, except for my eyes. Because my eyes stay fixed to him like they're permanently glued to his soul.

Each raw note and natural charisma in his altogether presence is too powerful not to feel. How have I never known this about him?

"Ruby wants to know if you're..." The rest of Krysta's words are seemingly drowned out when Base hits a chorus that just takes so much emotion from him, his face playing out the song like a an easily read canvas even to me.

It's amazing.

"What?" I ask absently, never looking away.

"Never mind. I already answered her a big fat yes," Krysta says, taking a random picture of my face.

The flash makes me blink several times, but it's only a mild hindrance until Base's eyes look away and focus on the growing crowd around us that is packing full of girls.

It's the first time I've noticed how they're all sort of groupies like me. Krysta is busy texting on her phone as I clear my throat, backing away when one group of girls starts forcing their way between us and the stage.

Then a group of guys try to start dancing with us, and it's all so crowded that I end up losing sight of Krysta as random hands go to my hips.

"Hey!" someone shouts against my ear before pulling me really hard against them.

A little panic rises up in my throat when I see a lot of shoulders and chests, but can't catch sight of any faces under the crazy, strobing lights.

I'm struggling, doing all I can to break away from the grabby hands, and end up falling forward as I quickly scramble between feet to escape.

It isn't until I'm behind the crowd that my breathing starts slowing down as the music thuds like a deep echo in my ears, my pulse throbbing louder as the fear inches down.

Krysta's face is suddenly in front of mine as she kneels, worry on her expression as she starts pulling me back up to my shaky legs. It all happens so fast, but feels like it takes forever, as more people trample by, almost toppling onto us.

Pain shoots up my arm, and bodies start closing in.

"Get out of the fucking way or get stepped on!" some guy shouts at us, as the building gets more and more crowded. "The main event is about to come on stage after these guys finish the last of their short set," he adds like he's ushering us to move as he shoves a few people away to give us room.

Krysta curses as I freeze, just staring at the throngs of people who are coming in by the hordes. Surely there's a fire-safety limit that's lower than this.

We almost lose each other again, but Krysta clings to my hand, getting knocked around by rushing bodies until she crashes into me.

"Everyone is trying to hurry and get a good spot. It's going to turn into a fucking mosh pit," Krysta says, wincing as she steers us out of it.

My hands are still shaking, and my left hand is throbbing. It takes me a second to realize that my hand actually hurts really, *really* bad.

"Krysta, I think someone stomped my hand when I was crawling," I call over the music.

"Someone got my ribs," she says through a grimace as we manage to squeeze out a side door.

We both make a surprised, terrified sound when we get rushed by a flurry of people waiting in line around the building, breaking for the door we really shouldn't have used.

We barely manage to get out of the rush after being bobbed around, and she makes a frustrated sound as I spot an uber pick-up area. My hand hurts so badly now that tears are springing to my eyes when I make a poor judgment call to reach for my phone with it.

"I think I need a hospital," I tell Krysta, who is nodding like she agrees as she limps beside me.

"Me too," she says just before she drops to the ground, her hand gripping her side.

Someone actually steps over her instead of offering to help, and I drop to the ground on my knees beside her, that panic quickly returning because I don't know what to do.

"Shit, I need a minute," she says through strain. "Don't leave."

"I-I'm not," I stutter, swallowing thickly.

My vision is boxing in, growing smaller and smaller, as my breaths come quicker and quicker, growing shallower with each one.

Everyone is everywhere, and too many are too close, and so many are so loud. The music is still so loud. All of it is too loud, and I can't tune any one thing out as it all presses down on me, trying to come all at once.

Base is still singing, because I can hear him, and he'll never hear his phone. And—

My thoughts cut off as my remaining vision lands on my brother just as he pushes away from his car, eyes widening as he just stares at me as if shocked.

I look around, wondering if my panicked mind has somehow tricked me into thinking this is really happening, since that makes more sense than Dane actually being here.

He hurries toward us, looking very much real, since people dart out of *his* way to keep from getting trampled as they fight over who was in line first.

He cuts through them all like a knife and doesn't even bother asking what happened as he lifts Krysta. She whimpers in pain, and points out her ribs. I…I can't really concentrate enough to hear her.

My hands start shaking as though the panic has doubled, and he gives me a tight expression as I force myself back to my feet, working through it.

"I wasn't stalking. I promise," he assures me as he gestures for me to follow him, his jaw ticking as he keeps any anger out of his tone. "I just worried, since this place is known for horrible crowd control, and they have two big bands coming up later. Talk to me, Britt. What do you think?"

"You were right to worry. And it's more uncaring than violent," I tell him, even as my voice shakes just a little, but I focus on *this* one conversation, just like I'm supposed to. "It happens so passively and so quickly that you don't realize it's happening."

"I imagine," he says, keeping his voice neutral as my nerves begin to calm. Safe. I feel safe. "I've been in rough crowds before. It escalates quickly."

My vision slowly starts expanding as I sit down in the passenger seat of his car, cradling my injured hand to my chest.

"I think I got stepped on," I say as he puts her down in the back. "Her ribs are hurt. Don't be mad at Base. He was playing. He couldn't see. There's a lot of important people he gets to meet tonight, and the lights—"

"I won't say a word," he says tightly, cutting off my spitfire rambling and giving me a more forced smile when I look over at him.

"Promise?"

He just nods.

"He just isn't as cautious as I am," Dane tells me as he drives quickly through the traffic. "I'll deal with this very peacefully, if you promise that next time you'll skip a club I warn you about."

I nod, definitely deciding that's a smart decision I should have made.

Dane reaches over, clutching my shoulder, and I exhale shakily again.

"You're in my car. You're safe," he says very quietly.

"I know," I tell him as I shut my eyes, feeling my muscles begin to relax. "I know."

"I'm so glad you're her brother," Krysta groans from the back seat. "Imagine that. Britt Sterling's first bad life decision is the one time I'm with her. Ruby is going to kill me."

"Ruby isn't going to kill you," Dane assures her before looking over at me as Krysta starts muttering something about being cursed.

Dane wastes no time grabbing a wheelchair for Krysta, and I go in, letting him takeover as he signs us in and starts doing the paperwork for both of us.

I sit down beside him as Krysta stays in the wheelchair.

"Britt, believe it or not, I've been behaving and giving you your space to be a grown up," Dane says to me as he continues to fill out my paperwork for me.

I should be filling out that paperwork, but right now, I'm content to cradle my hand.

"There's a *but* coming," Krysta stage whispers before grimacing.

"There's no *but.* I'm just wondering if this is really the sort of relationship you need. He's going to travel a lot, and he's about to take off for a tour, and there's likely going to be a contract in his future. You said nothing serious, but the guy is living in your house, and now you're taking off on weekend trips and visiting his mom on the way. I'm worried there are unintentional mixed signals that are confusing you," Dane goes on.

Krysta just sort of eyes him before looking over at me.

"He has a point."

I start to speak and stop, unable to formulate any sort of logical argument.

Dane's eyes look away from mine as though he doesn't want to pressure me for an answer, and I slink down in my seat.

I can't really form a debate when he lays it out so clearly.

Chapter 29

BRITT

"What the hell happened to your hand?" is a very startling question to hear when you think you're alone in the copying room.

I whirl around to find Base's stare on my cast, lips parted like he's not finished asking that question.

"I fell and it was stepped on by mistake," I tell him dismissively as I try to hide it a little behind me.

I'm not entirely sure about the lie Dane told him; I'm just glad he agreed not to tell anyone the truth. Even I know everyone will misplace blame, and it seems like a lot of trouble for my own personal decision.

"Krysta cool?" Sticks asks as he pokes his head in. "She's not answering any calls."

"Krysta decided she wasn't much of a road-trip groupie, and she's happily deep-sea fishing with the local rowing team to see if that's her new kind of man," Ruby says as she pushes into the room. "Don't take it personally."

Sticks's smile falls a little, and I almost want to tell him that's a lie. But Ruby's the one lying, and that feels like a betrayal to her. I really don't understand people, but since my brother is lying to spare Base, per my request, I have no right to judge.

Things really can get complicated fast.

"I see the party is in the copy room," Harley says as she needles her way through, eyes my cast quickly, and moves along.

"Who stepped on your hand?" Base pries, trying to move closer. "And when? Is that why you really left? Because I find it hard to believe you left because you got your period, and your brother just happened to be close by. I thought maybe he'd just shown up and snatched you because he's way too overbearing like that. Hard to tell, since you haven't answered your phone."

Dane is a terrible liar. Why would he use my period in his lie? He can't even handle me mentioning my menstrual cycle. He physically cringes every time I have to bring it up.

Base finally shakes his head when I stutter, and he closes his eyes almost as though he's mad, while scrubbing a hand over his face. I've never been good at lying.

"I didn't want you to miss your important stuff. Crowd control isn't managed well there. It's a minor fracture," I ramble on.

Sticks looks horrified. Base isn't even looking at me.

"Dane was there because he was worried it might get ugly with so much going on in one night," I finally confess on a very nervous breath.

Base just keeps his head turned, as Harley exhales harshly.

"It wasn't anyone's fault. Let's not make it a bigger deal than it has to be," Harley says, even though I overheard her using her *fierce* tone when she called the club first thing this morning when she saw my cast.

"You said you'd be ready twenty minutes ago. Can we please get out of here?" Ruby asks Harley.

"So that's why the cold shoulder the past two days?" Base asks me, cutting between them as they both dart a glance at me on their way through the door.

"I sent texts," I tell him as I start walking out.

"Very limited words on the texts. Something you were instructed to do?" he asks as he follows me.

"No. I've just been thinking, and I assumed we'd talk face to face eventually."

"Eventually is here. Why didn't you tell me you got hurt?" he asks as he lifts my cast in his hand.

"That's not what I wanted to talk about," I say as I turn to face him.

His eyebrows go up, and I exhale heavily as I stop in front of him.

"I think it's best if you and I stay friends," I tell him, causing a lot of surprise to form in his eyes. "You're leaving in four months, and you won't have sex with me because you don't think I'm emotionally capable of losing my virginity without feelings. But the truth is, I don't want those feelings. I'm too young to risk falling in love. You and I have very different life courses, life experiences, social circles, and life plans."

His expressions shut down completely as he backs against the railing.

"It could have been fun, but it was already getting complicated because we know too many of the same people. I've looked over all the lists I've made, and we aren't a good statistic for a probable future."

He gives me a slow nod, pocketing his hands as he clears his throat and looks down.

"Let me get this straight, you're done with me because I'm trying to show you respect as a woman," he says like he's pointing this out.

"I really don't want to be done with you at all. I want to be friends—like I think we are. I just don't want to risk falling in love, and it feels like that's what you're unintentionally trying to make me do. I'd think respecting me as a woman would be to respect my ability to decide what I want at this point in my life. I'm sorry."

He doesn't say anything. He merely nods sort of absently.

I don't know if I'm supposed to stay or go, so I decide to walk away.

"That whole speech sounds coached, Britt," he says just as I reach my office door. "Who typed it up and had you memorize it?"

I almost don't speak, since he doesn't usually listen. But I take a fortifying breath, and 'look away from those panty-melting eyes that make smart girls stupid,' like Rain said to do when I have something I really need to say.

Staring at the receptionist, who turns away like she's uncomfortable, I say, "I'm not intending to be offensive when I point out how hypocritical that is. People around me may voice how they feel, but you're the only one trying to tell me what I need that I almost listened to. I have a plan, and for whatever reason, you felt as though you—a guy who barely knows me—had the right to tell me how my first time should be. I don't have to do this your way, and you're by no means obligated to do it my way."

I keep my tone neutral, trying not to antagonize him or make him too defensive.

My eyes collide with his, and I realize it's a mistake, because I want to take all the words back. It's easier to tell others to stand firm than to tell myself. It took me two days to prepare all those words.

"I think, given our different views, it's better to keep things just friends. I do love hearing you sing, though. I didn't want to tell you that in a text."

I shut up before I start rambling even more disassembled things that can possibly contradict all the things I just said, as I turn and push through the door.

My phone chimes with a text from Harley that has a winky face beside her *like a boss* message that makes no sense.

I don't look back, because I feel horrible and I don't want to feel worse. I don't think we broke up. I mean, we've been living together, and had some intense moments, but I don't think that means we're in a relationship that constitutes the need for a break up.

I dwell over that the entire car ride home, and I ignore Krysta's call because I think I did just break up with him. Which makes me an idiot, because we weren't dating.

We *are* already just friends, so I don't see why I had to bring us down to that level—

Someone knocking at the door is a welcome distraction from my inner tangents as I go to open it. There's just a second to register

Base's intense stare trained on me, because he's kissing me in the next second.

Well, now I'm even more confused about what I just did.

I hear the door shutting as one of his arms winds around my waist and pulls me closer, and his other hand goes to my hair as he backs me against a wall.

He breaks the kiss, and I take a couple of really desperate breaths, wondering when my hands dug into his shirt like my body made the decision to keep this situation in play.

"You're right," he says quietly against my lips, nipping my bottom one. "Let's do this your way."

His mouth comes back down on mine, my his hands slide up his chest until they're tangling in his hair. He actually lifts me from the ground. My legs go around his waist on instinct, and he kisses me harder as he carries me to my bedroom.

My back hits the bed, and he comes down on top of me, grinding against me just hard enough to create that perfect friction. He makes a sound in his throat that does inexplicable things to my body that make zero anatomical sense.

We only break the kiss long enough for him to tug his shirt over his head, and I quickly do the same with mine before the spell can break—yet another metaphor I'm now more understanding of.

"Tell me to slow down if you need me to," he says as he breaks the kiss and slows things way down, taking his time as he kisses his way down my neck.

My body goes so still that I almost worry I've frozen again. He doesn't stop this time as he continues kissing his way down, sending rows of chills up me in crescendos of scattered waves that leave the slightest shudder in their wake.

"Where's your head at right now?" he asks as he kisses his way down my stomach, his fingers toying with the button on my pants.

"Bad poetry," I confess.

He snorts against my waist, his shoulders suddenly shaking. I practiced dirty talk; I just didn't know when that was supposed to start.

Apparently, it needs to be immediate, because him laughing is not the *sexy* Bella told me to bring when the time came.

"Sorry," I say awkwardly as he just sort of rests his weight on me, only causing his body to shake a little harder. "It was bad poetry for good thoughts, but I'm not a poet and…I'm a virgin for a reason; I'm not magically good at this."

He leans up, mouth sealing over mine, possibly to stop it from running incessantly and making it all worse. The mood comes back with effortless ease, as he continues to kiss me into a stupor.

With one-handed expertise, he unhooks my bra. I'm not sure why I grin. I'm not sure when I started grinning.

I can feel his grin growing to mimic mine. I'm going to make this weird again if I don't resist the stupid urge to speak the second his lips break from mine.

This time, as he kisses his way down my throat, he peels my bra down with his descent. I'm positive my eyes try to swap places when they cross hard enough to *feel* them tug. It happens the second his mouth connects with my nipple. I don't know or care which one. All my nerves fire on one united circuit as his hand slips down, working my pants down as his mouth…his mouth…

I can't even properly praise his mouth because I'm so bad at poetry.

"Still thinking of bad poetry?" he asks, lips teasing me a little as he pulls back to remove my pants.

I keep my eyes closed as my jaw moves like it's trying to form words without my voice. I finally catch up. "I-I just cycled back to it."

I feel his grin against my skin this time as he starts kissing his way down. Even a virgin knows where he's going with this, and my entire body squirms in anticipation as he slowly starts tugging my underwear down.

I go ahead and put my hand with the cast out to the side so I don't accidentally forget about it and give him an unintentional concussion while he's trying to give me an orgasm.

I'm actively thinking of ways not to screw this up.

It's the lowest his lips have ever gone as he drags them down the crease of my thigh, gradually tugging my underwear down so subtly that I barely notice they're gone until he pulls them free.

All my attention is on his mouth as he drags it closer, kissing across my stomach…as I remain frozen, though I feel his hair very firmly woven between the fingers of my non-cast hand again.

"Where's your head at now?" he asks, the warmth of his breath fanning a very sensitive spot that brings awareness crashing down on me.

Gibberish. I have no idea what I say, because it's gibberish, but he comes willingly when I pull him closer, my body acting before my mind can overthink. I want his mouth right there forever, because it feels incredible the second he really shows me what third base is like.

He makes that inexplicably sexy noise again that sets off a chain of embarrassing reactions, and the more I try to stay quiet, the more noise I make.

I'm only vaguely aware of it, because now I know why Raya said I'd enjoy the tongue piercing. I think he intentionally wore it tonight, because I never see it otherwise.

His hands grip my thighs when I barely arch off the bed, my body coiled tight just before I have what may be my favorite ever orgasm.

Everything hits all at once, and it hits so hard that I immediately become oversensitive and very aware of the fact this is very, *very* intimate.

He drags his mouth away, kissing up my hip, as I breathe like I've just finished a marathon, my eyes on the ceiling as my cheeks burn for no real reason at all.

Don't make it weird. That becomes my inner mantra.

But…that's a first for me—the oral. It's hard not to make it weird because I don't know what's normal after this point.

My body is still shuddering as he kisses a path up my stomach, and my hands move up his back, over his shoulders, and to his chest as he starts kissing my neck.

"I'll use one of your condoms since you've worked so hard on preparation," he says against my neck, and I nod rapidly, my eyes going to the ceiling again.

"And lube. I have an excess of lube too," I tell him.

He grins again before pushing off me, and…I quickly pull the blanket around me because it's surprisingly uncomfortable being naked when the other person is not.

But Base is less modest, because he shoves his jeans and boxers down in unison, and I just stare. At his butt. I've never seen a butt in this context before—a sexual situation being the relevant context.

The muscles in his butt flex as he steps over to my condom and lube drawers, pulling out selections of each. My heartbeat is in my ears as he starts opening the condom wrapper, turning his body almost deliberately to show me what he's doing.

It's the first time I've ever seen a penis off a screen or a condom being put on an actual penis instead of a banana.

Every warning I've been given pops into my head.

"If it's the size of a baby's arm, run. You're not ready for that," Harley told me recently.

Base takes his time, and I continue to gawk. It's not the size of Isa's arm—which seems entirely inappropriate to use as a scale—so I don't have to run.

"If it's a small penis, just enjoy the easy ride for your first time. Your vagina has a blank slate," Bella said on April fourth of last year when the topic came up.

I definitely don't think his is small, and I'm questioning everything about my body. I don't think she helped at all, because my confidence is quickly waning now.

My surveying is brought to an abrupt halt when the condom-covered penis starts moving toward me.

A hand at my chest shoves me back down on the bed, and my eyes finally detach from the perfectly sized penis as he pulls the covers back and starts kissing me again.

My legs spread as he works his hips between them, and my body stays rigid as he starts kissing his way down my neck again. I magically forget what's going on because he's really good at that.

...Until he starts working his way inside me, the blunt head of that perfectly sized penis now seeming much bigger as his lips fuse back to mine.

My body rocks on instinct, because it feels so good as he starts slipping in, stretching me in all the right ways as he slides in and—

His hips thrust quickly, and he shoves all the way inside me without warning, causing my breath to hitch in surprise. There's a small pinch of pain, much less than expected, but it is...uncomfortable.

"Everything I read said it was better not to let you get tense before doing that," he says against my cheek, lips moving up to my ear. "And to wait until you're ready before continuing."

The discomfort starts to ebb quickly as an odd sense of heat floods my body, and I turn so that our lips brush.

He gently cups my cheek, his thumb gently moving across my lips as those really pretty eyes stare into mine. It feels too intimate, but at the same time, it would be terrible to look away.

"You read tutorials on taking someone's virginity?"

At his small grin, I kiss him hard, feeling the heat roll around my body as I get really turned on. I know that wasn't supposed to be dirty talk—I've been graphically educated on that subject matter. But it's possibly the most erotic thing he's ever said to me.

He groans into my mouth, and his body moves, pulling back and pushing forward again in a way that has my legs spreading wider as the heat only continues to build.

It's a slight tinge of pain mixed with a desperate sort of need.

It feels as though I'm being consumed in physically impossible ways, urgently clinging to keep him as close as possible. He moves slow, but very deliberately, and I have no choice but to break the kiss to pant for air.

His thrusts get just a little more aggressive, and his body keeps the perfect pressure and friction right where I need it with each downward stroke.

Each time I'm forced to climb higher on the bed, he comes with me. His eyes lock on mine seconds before I'm forced to squeeze them shut, because another, less-powerful-but-still-very-perfect orgasm crashes through me.

My entire body becomes limp as my arms lazily wind around his neck, still wanting him as close as possible as his thrusts grow more insistent.

"Shit," he says on a rasp just before his hips still, while I float back down to my body, everything on me tingling.

It's so quiet throughout the entire house, that all I can hear is our breaths as we both try to catch them.

His lips move along my shoulder as he slides a hand up my thigh. I could lay like this for hours. Just him inside me and—

He abruptly pulls out, and I feel an odd sense of abandonment as he stands and glances over his shoulder, smirking at me.

"You sure you want this emotionless? If so, this is the part where I should leave."

My mouth opens and closes a few times. Finally, my words come out.

"But all your stuff is in the other bedroom."

"I can get rid of it," he assures me.

I blink a few times, not really sure what to say. I'm not done having sex.

"I'm not sore, and after sex for the first time, you're supposed to be sore," I say as I try to reenact one of the sexy poses Harley told me to use.

His eyebrows go up, as he remains distractingly naked, his very perfect butt still on display. But I'm more concerned about the expression on his face.

"That was supposed to be dirty talk, but you look a little…insulted?" I guess, still gauging his expression.

His lips curve with the beginnings of a grin that he wipes away with one hand.

I can't believe I'm going to quote Maverick, since everyone has told me to never do that. I think back to some of the things he said to girls that he claimed worked—when he didn't think I was listening.

But there was one line that stands out that also sounds reasonably hygienic and leaves little room for misinterpretation.

"I'm going to take a shower so we can do it all over again, if you're interested," I say, watching as his gaze slowly rakes over my sheet-covered body.

His eyebrow quirks, as a slow smile spreads over his lips.

"I'll meet you in the shower," Base says, lips still curved. "If you're interested," he adds like he's mimicking my line as he goes toward my bathroom.

I try to stand, but the sheet tangles around my feet, and I fall so slowly out of bed that I have to walk forward on my hands just to get my feet untangled.

"I can shower with you, but I don't think I'm advanced enough yet for shower sex," I say before I wrap up in the very twisted sheet the best I can and hurry toward the bathroom.

I really don't think he should be laughing at a time like this, but since his laugh is doing all the right things to my body, I decide it's a null point.

"And I may need help wrapping my cast if we're in any sort of hurry," I add, not even taking the time to process I'm no longer a virgin.

My identity has finally changed.

I weirdly do feel a little different. A grin only spreads wider as Base pulls out a plastic bag and immediately starts wrapping my cast, kissing his way down my neck as he does so.

I don't want it completely emotionless. I like this.

Chapter 30

BASE

Britt brushes out her wet hair as I groan at the sex playlist on her phone.

"These are not sexy songs," I tell her as she gives me recovery time.

Gives *me* recovery time.

"They all talk about sex," she argues as she moves across the room in nothing but my shirt. "And we still haven't used anything from my sex tote."

I'm lying on the bed, completely exhausted, and she's finished her second shower of the day, preparing for round three.

"Sex tote?" I ask with a growing smile as I tug her back down on the bed with me.

Her cheeks go a little red, something that has happened a lot over the past few hours, and she clears her throat as she stares at my chest.

"It has scented candles, candy underwear, and other things like that. I wanted to be prepared."

She gives a firm nod before looking up at my eyes so sincerely, and I drop my head back as I hold in the laughter.

"Candy underwear?" I ask around the laugh that just can't be contained.

"It seemed like an interesting way to lead into oral," she states matter-of-factly.

My laugh turns into a groan, and though my dick should be down for the count, the blood begins rushing south just with the thought of playing with her sex tote.

"Still not sore?" I ask as I kiss her shoulder, wondering if I'm that good or if I'm going to be ridiculed for being incapable of leaving a virgin sore and sated.

"Not really," she says quietly as I start kissing a line down her neck.

Let's Get It On starts playing, and I laugh into the crook of her neck, just because I find it adorably cheesy that she has this on her *sex playlist.*

"This song? Really, Britt?"

Her eyes turn big and very confused as I drop back to the bed, shaking the whole bed with the rest of my choked laughter.

"What? This song is on some popular movies where the sex is new and important," she says very seriously.

I pull her to me, and ignore the music as she straddles me, her lips seeking mine with more confidence as she melts against me. My hand slides through the long, soft strands of her damp hair as I sit up, cradling her face as I kiss her back.

"You shouldn't have pulled the new music from the set we did. Essentially, they said they can't play us there again, because we just aren't the type of sound they're looking for. We've always got Silk, though. Don't fuck that up by breaking Dane's only sister's heart," Sticks says on a frustrated sound over speaker phone.

"You broke my hymen. Not my heart," Britt says conversationally as she brings in two bottles of water and drops down on her bed beside me.

"For fuck's sake, man. Seriously?" Sticks groans.

"I regret putting you on speaker. I told you that you were on speaker," I point out as Britt curls up next to me, drinking her water.

"When are we practicing?" he asks like he's exasperated with me.

"I'll be by after we finish up something Britt has to do for Maverick, and I'm dropping her by campus for her to take some smart girl tests for supreme-being stuff."

She just gives me a dubious look before returning to what she's doing.

"We haven't practiced any of the newer songs you want to showcase at Silk. It's time to be less secretive, man. We're all getting anxious, and it just isn't working out our way with the old tracks."

Britt shifts off the bed again, going to pull on her shoes as I just watch her.

I finally stand and slip on my shirt, following Britt out the door. Then I steer her to my truck instead of her flashy, ridiculously clean, expensive car that makes me feel like I can't shower enough to be worthy of sitting in it.

She climbs into the passenger seat without protest, and I walk around to my door as I hang up on Sticks.

"I'll drop you off at the campus on my way to rehearsal," I tell her as I start driving us toward Maverick's. "Randy will turn rehearsal into a party, and then I'll come pick you up and we can go back to your place."

"Then maybe you can coach me on how to return oral?" she asks just as I take a long swig of the water she brought for me.

Horrible timing.

The water sprays on the windshield, and I curse as a passing horn blares when I weave on the road. Britt squeaks out a sound as she clings to the door, and I get us right once again as I shake my head and groan.

I've created a monster. I've had more sex in two days than I have in a year.

Not that I'm complaining.

"Really, Britt?" I ask incredulously.

"It seems unfair how much you do that for me, and I'm trying to be honest. You said to be honest," she immediately points out.

"Your honesty is leaving me with a hard-on before we get to Maverick's house. We can't have sex in Maverick's house."

"Why not? He has lots of sex in it. I doubt he'd mind," she states in her logical, I-don't-see-why-that's-a-problem tone.

I can't keep talking about sex, because my eyes keep moving to her very bare legs in her very short shorts. Not to mention, the T-shirt she's wearing hangs off one shoulder, and even her shoulders seem unnaturally sexy today.

I stopped thinking about sex this much after puberty wore me, my socks, and my hand out.

"So what is it you have to do at Maverick's house?" I ask, clearing my throat as I loosen my collar.

"The favor's for Sean. Not Maverick. And we're going to Ian's house, actually."

"The kid squire?" I ask, finding this conversation to be much easier on me, even though her answer just raises more questions.

"He's moved up to being my blacksmith now. Level five," she deadpans.

Things get quiet in the cab of my truck really quick, and she only speaks when instructing me on which way to turn.

I didn't realize how much we talked about her virginity…until I took it and we didn't have it to talk about anymore. I'm treading water because I have no idea what exactly we're doing.

She backpedaled on *emotionless* real quick.

We pull up at Ian's house…which is even bigger than Tag's house, something I believed impossible until this moment. Britt hops out like this is the normal to her.

"Ian's Maverick's dad, right?" I ask absently.

"Yes," she states distractedly.

Doesn't this guy have servants to do his errands?

"I'll sit here so we don't accidentally end up having sex in Maverick's father's giant house. I've already had one angry Sterling burst in on me," I call out the window.

She nods like that's acceptable.

I watch as she moves to his keypad and starts unlocking his door. Then I watch as she bends over to pick up her phone after she drops it. Those damn shorts show the bottom curve of her ass, and I decide that whoever this Sterling is can kiss my ass.

We can be fast and leave no trace behind.

It isn't until after I finish locking the doors on my truck that I glance around, taking inventory of the really expensive vehicles parked in all the other driveways. I look back and snort at myself for locking my doors.

Shaking my head at myself and feeling really out of place, I jog inside and…stop.

When I bump into a wall, my elbow hits a switch, and a massive wall across from me starts moving over the fireplace to reveal an obnoxiously sized TV.

Un…real.

A low whistle escapes me as I move through the house. I bet just one piece of furniture in here costs more than any number I've ever had in my bank account.

I'm not even sure where the hell Britt is, but just as I open my mouth to call for her, my eyes fall on a bathroom around the next turn I take.

"Holy shit," I say under my breath as I glance around at the floor-to-ceiling marble or some shit.

How many showerheads does one person need? And do I even want to know why Ian Sterling built a shower stall big enough to hold ten people?

I back out, shaking my head at the ridiculousness that is life as a Sterling. This is probably just one of his houses.

"Britt?" I call, already apparently on the wrong section of house, since this is not the way I came.

"I'm in the kitchen," she says loudly.

Where the hell is her voice coming from? How am I supposed to find the kitchen?

I startle when I see a man at the end of the hallway, hands behind him as he stares stoically at me. *Not creepy at all.*

"Britt, is this place haunted by dead dudes in fancy suits, or will I stumble into a bat cave if I pull a secret lever?" I yell.

The apparition/butler in question gives me a dry look.

"I've never read anything substantiated on paranormal activity that wasn't highly controversial, so I'm undecided on if I believe in the possibility of a death dimension with windows, or isolated breaches, to parallel planes," she answers back.

"I believe Ms. Sterling is informing you that there are no such things as ghosts, Mr. Masters," the dude dressed way more expensively than me says with thick condescension.

"And Batman's name is Bruce. Not Ian," Britt says very seriously through an intercom that carries throughout the house.

So that's why I couldn't follow her voice.

Mr. Suit holds out his arm. "Should I escort you to *Master* Sean's room, or were you still debating whether or not to use the lou's shower?"

"I'm guessing you get paid too much to feed a cat," I say under my breath as he walks in front of me.

"Certainly not, but the *darling* feline is Sean's responsibility, and he arranged to have Ms. Sterling ensure the cat's well-being."

"So someone calls Britt over here to do it because she's even less important than you," I surmise, snorting to myself at the shit-tastic way the rich really do things.

"Yes. Certainly. She's their servant too," the dick says in a serious tone before pushing open a door and walking away.

I glance inside, finding possibly the largest kid's room I've ever seen in my life. Then I realize I'm just standing in the motherfucking closet when I see another door open to an enormous bathroom that connects to a monstrous bedroom.

That little dick's a prick because he has a closet bigger than the house I grew up in.

I thought Britt's room was large, but a twelve-year-old's room make all her stuff look modest.

I only thought I wasn't bothered by all the money until this minute. To top it all off, they have Britt running around dealing with shit below a douchebag butler's salary—

A rattling in a huge set of cabinets scares the shit out of me, cutting off my inner rant as I give it a wary glare.

It rattles again, and I start to get worried that small psychopath-in-training has the cat locked in there. I yank open the door when it rattles again, and see something…*horrifying* lunge at my face as a feral battle cry explodes from its vicious jaws.

I slam the doors shut and hold them, a sound escaping me that I'll be embarrassed about later…when my heart isn't pounding in my throat.

"What?" Britt shouts as she jumps inside, hand over her heart.

"Someone fed Gizmo after midnight," I tell her in a panic as the doors beside me rattle and I try holding them too, stretching myself across the front.

"What?" she asks, confused.

"There's a fucking fed-after-midnight gremlin trapped in here!"

The doors in front of my knees start rattling, and I adjust again, wondering why there has to be so many damn cabinets and how the bastard is moving between them.

"I haven't read anything that substantiated the existence of gremlins either," Britt says slowly. "I find it improbable there'd be something like that in Banana's playhouse."

"Banana's what?" I ask just as I hear something hiss above me.

A chill spreads down my spine as I slowly cut my gaze up toward the hairless, vicious creature there. The growing growl turns into a malicious rattle in its chest just before it spits out another hiss and makes a terrifying, warning noise, poised in the pounce position.

"Britt, run!" I shout as it lunges.

I dart out the door, and Britt shuts it behind me.

"She hates most people, but she's just indifferent to me. I'll be out in a minute," she says from inside like it's no big deal, as I lie in the hall floor, unaware that I've even fucking fallen until I feel a stabbing pain in my ankle that starts helping me piece the puzzle together.

"I think I just suffered an adrenaline black-out," I say toward the door as I wince and push up to a sitting position.

The butler steps over my legs, smirking like a smug son of a bitch, as he walks back down the hallway to lurk some more.

A possessed cat with a playhouse inside a giant closet in a house that needs intercoms for better communication, since yelling is probably undignified.

Fucking. Rich. People.

Britt walks out just as I manage to get to my feet, and she shuts the door behind her.

"Sorry. I should have warned you," she says with a slight grimace. "She's a very selective sort of cat."

"Is it a rich people thing to shave cats?" I ask her, watching as her brow furrows.

"No," she decides to say as she walks away, not elaborating.

"Why do you have to feed her?" I ask as I follow.

"Because she's indifferent to me," she answers like that explains everything.

The creepy butler follows us to the door as Britt opens it, and he watches as we leave, exchanging dry, parting pleasantries with Britt like it's a rehearsed line he can't even muster up enthusiasm for.

She's just as dry and dead in tone with him.

"My brother's having this big fundraiser event in two months that I'm partially helping with. I know there's a rule about not asking for a date too far in advance, but I didn't know how far ahead you had bookings for the band. I was hoping you could be there if nothing is scheduled yet," she says like she's been working her way up to that.

I exhale heavily, scrubbing a hand over my face as I open the passenger side door of my truck for her.

I shut the door behind her, feeling her eyes on me as I hurry around to my side and climb in behind the wheel.

"Is the dress code black-tie?" I ask as I drive away from the intimidating house. "You haven't ever seen me at any of the *events* Tag hosts, because black-tie things aren't really in my comfort zone," I confess, feeling a little like a dick.

"To be clear, you're uncomfortable with the dress code and not the fact that I asked two months in advance?"

At my nod, she seems to relax. "Okay then."

We pull up on the west side of campus, and I tug her to me to press my lips to hers before she gets out. She grins against the kiss, so I deepen the kiss until she finally breaks it, her smile quickly reforming.

"I'll pick you up later," I tell her as she gets out.

"Okay then," she says with the same smile as she walks away, and I watch for a minute before driving toward my house, still a little annoyed with the fact she's feeding a fucking cat in a house capable of paying someone to handle that. Like her time is less valuable.

Randy meets me at the door, rolling his eyes as I get out and start up the steps.

"You're going to have to get Britt to call Krysta and find out why she's mad at Sticks before we're all driven insane," he says like I've missed a house meeting or two and he's catching me up.

"She's pissed about the fact she and Britt were stepped all over at a club that's apparently known for people rushing the stage like that," I answer as my jaw grinds, not wanting to think about how much worse that could have been.

"I thought she was into Taylor, but apparently she was picking up whatever Sticks was laying down, and—"

"Stop talking, Randy," I tell him as I head inside, finding Taylor and Sticks already playing around.

Sticks looks up and narrows his eyes.

"No, I've not talked to Krysta, and Britt hasn't mentioned talking to her either. I think it's time to cut bait," I say as I sit down.

"I wasn't gonna ask. Why would any of the Sterlings concern themselves with Krysta—the one they don't even claim as their own?"

Rolling my eyes, I lift my guitar from the stand.

"Britt was feeding someone's cat today because it was beneath a fancy butler's paygrade, and they say it's because the cat is indifferent to her. Trust me when I say Britt isn't like the rest of them."

"Silk is our best gig. Neither of you get to fuck it up because you don't like people who have money," Taylor says, running his fingers along the keyboard. "Because we *need* to keep getting paid for playing music, or we're just a bunch of pathetic losers who've been wasting our college years."

"No one's fucking anything up," Sticks grumbles. "I just hate the fucking way they treat her."

"She told you they treated her bad, or you're assuming this because the girl is a fucking wreck?" Taylor asks him on a groan.

"She doesn't have to tell me. It's fucking obvious. She's never in the gossip columns as anything but the black sheep."

"I remember when we sat around talking about how hot the

girls chasing us look—the way men do," Randy deadpans, earning a glare from all three of us. "Now we just sit around talking about gossip columns and girl drama—*like a bunch of fucking girls*. At this rate, we're chattering more than we're rehearsing. It's bad when I'm pointing it out."

Taylor's glare fades, and he shrugs a shoulder at me.

"He has a point."

I grab my bag and toss it to him. "Get out the new sheet music. It's finally ready."

"That's more like it," Randy says as he jogs over to find his.

Chapter 31

BRITT

"You put my napkin in my lap like I'm your child. Just admit you're eating your words and turning into an all-the-time mom," Allie is saying to Bella as I sit down at the brunch table.

Bella glares at her, as Tria and Rain just look on.

"Why couldn't we have been these kinds of sisters?" Tria asks Rain, gesturing at Allie and Bella's confusing staring contest.

"Because we both hated other women until we grew up," Rain deadpans, her smile mimicking Allie's when Bella finally blinks.

"It was one napkin," Bella says like she's ignoring everyone else.

"And you asked if I'd buckled up as you checked to pull out into traffic."

"I'm a safe driver," Bella informs her.

"And you buttered my toast yesterday morning when I stopped by."

"Isa can't eat toast yet, so that's not even part of my mom arsenal," Bella says in a tone that borders on exasperation.

"How long has this been going on?" Harley asks as she takes a seat beside me.

My phone vibrates with a text, and I start smiling the second I see Base's name flash across the screen.

BASE: Sorry we rehearsed so late last night. We finally got it right though, and I'm all yours tonight.

BRITT: Will you finally teach me oral? Or should I call it a blowjob? Which word do you prefer?

"She's smiling at her phone. Why is she smiling at her phone?" Rain asks.

Before I can answer, Harley starts choking as she leans over my phone, eyes wide.

"She's sexting," Harley hisses.

"No, I'm not," I say, looking up and finding all the wide eyes on me. "I was just asking if Base would teach me oral tonight."

Ash's hand palms her face, as Bella sputters her water.

"*Whaaaaaaat*?" Rain chokes out like it's a really long sentence crammed into one word.

"I'm referring to the act of giving *him* oral. I don't need to learn the mechanics of how he does it to me."

It's really quiet when my phone vibrates with a new text, which makes the phone sound a lot louder than it is.

BASE: No word preference, but thanks for making it awkward to sit in a roomful of my bandmates.

ME: You didn't answer the first question.

"What'd he say?" Brin asks as she leans over the table.

Again, a table full of eyes are on me.

"Begging a guy to teach you how to give a blowjob *is* sexting," Harley assures me.

"Really?" I ask very seriously.

"Really," they all answer.

I quickly text him back.

ME: I just discovered this is sexting. That's inappropriate to do in group settings, so I'll just see you tonight.

He immediately texts back with a thumb's up emoji.

"Why would you do that? Now he knows that we all know you're begging to give him a blowjob. That's too much power to give a man," Harley groans, scrubbing her hand over her face.

"I thought Base was out of the picture like three weeks ago," Bella says like she's confused.

"She's young. Don't expect her to be that strong yet," Tria says.

"Actually, three weeks ago, he took my virginity," I explain just before the waiter shows up.

"Are we ready to order?" he asks.

"No," they all say in unison before I can order my omelet.

We only have five more minutes before they won't make the omelet, so I quickly order my omelet before he leaves.

As soon as he's gone, Harley grabs my hand.

"Why are you just now telling us?" she demands.

"Because I haven't been back to the office, and I thought I'd tell you at our once-a-month brunch, since I finally had girl talk to share. I get a lot of the sexually charged metaphors now."

Ash whispers something and covers her face again, shaking her head. It sounds like she's praying for Base to not die, but I can't be certain, because Bella starts talking.

"Were you safe?" Bella asks.

"Sounds like an immediate mom question," Allie immediately retorts while I nod in answer to Bella.

"It sounds like I've worked in a hospital for my entire adult life," Bella fires back.

"So not about you two right now," Brin cuts in. "How was it?"

I try to think of how to summarize it without ambiguous

wording.

"I wish I was good at poetry," I start.

"Oh, the girl thinks it was poetic," Harley says as her eyes shut and she fans herself.

"Oh my damn. You're blushing. You never blush," Ruby says like it's an accusation as she points her finger at me.

At least that explains why spontaneous heat started blooming on my cheeks.

"It was much better than I thought possible, and I don't have a horror story to share," I elaborate.

"Much better than she thought possible," Tria says like she's swooning.

"Why have you waited three weeks to tell us this?" Harley asks while giving my shoulder a little shake.

"It's highly addictive, and we've spent a lot of time improving my technique," I tell her in my defense.

Rain slaps a hand on the table.

Tria drops her glass.

Harley knocks over her water.

Ash somehow manages to fall out of her chair.

Bella and Allie exchange wide eyes.

Brin and Ruby exchange high-fives.

In short, the entire table reacts more to that than the announcement of the dissolution of my hymen issue.

Just when I think I'm starting to predict them…

"I'd say it's always the ones you least suspect, but she's been obsessed with sex for a while, so I'm gonna say we should have seen this coming," Tria finally says as she apologizes to the man coming to clean up the glass.

"I'm fine," Ash says as she sticks a hand up and starts climbing back into her seat. "Thanks for asking."

I must have missed someone asking her how she is.

"You've spent the better part of three weeks having sex with Base Masters?" Bella asks, clearing her throat. "Like *a lot*?"

I'm not sure why I'm smiling, but I do know I can't stop. I settle for a nod, since I'm worried about how I can talk and smile like this.

Also, I have no logical explanation as to why talking about this is really making me miss him. I just saw him before I left. He hadn't been in bed very long because his rehearsal took longer than expected.

"And he's still essentially living with you?" Allie asks, not sounding as enthused anymore.

"Yes, but we're not in a relationship. I'm not ready to risk falling in love, and he doesn't want a relationship while he's in the middle of trying to build his career."

"I forget how young she is," Harley says as she sits back, looking a little deflated. "I *was* so excited."

"She's young. Let her enjoy making some of the fun mistakes. It's not like she's jeopardizing anything," Ruby says, though I have no idea what conversation they're having.

"Yes, but she's also naïve, so she doesn't even realize how bad this can hurt," Rain says to Ruby, who groans.

"You know he's going to be gone on a rock tour for a year, right?" Bella asks.

"Yes," I say slowly, confused by the change in the atmosphere.

My omelet gets dropped off at the table, but they send the man away before he can take their orders.

"Which is why it's safe to use this as a first boyfriend-ish experience, even though we're not in a relationship. I can figure out the dos and don'ts without the fear of illogical attachment, because there's a healthy expiration date."

"Boyfriend-*ish*?" Harley echoes.

"*Healthy* expiration date?" Ash asks with that wrinkle on her forehead that makes the constipation-versus-confused battle begin.

I open and close my mouth, appreciating the fish-in-the-glass-bowl metaphor at this moment.

"You've all already burst everyone else's bubbles. Let her live in hers just a little bit longer," Brin says on a sigh.

"Musicians can be intense. Passionate. Unhealthy addictions," Bella starts saying. "And you're very young—"

She stops talking.

"I really do sound like an all-the-time mom," she says as she gives a wide-eyed, panicked look to Allie.

Allie pats her shoulder like she's comforting her.

"Be careful," Ash says just as Rain opens her mouth. "Just be careful that you don't *both* get in over your heads. Base doesn't usually get this sidetracked by anyone, so that says something."

I want to ask about the *something* it says, when Brin slices her hand through the air.

"Don't take it from her today. Britt's way more emotionally mature than all of us combined, and Base has life goals he isn't ready to risk. They've got this. It's not our place," she says like she's scolding the entire table.

I finish off my omelet, finding it odd I wish they'd hurry up and order so we can all go. Usually I like it when we stick around longer at brunch. Today, however, I'd like to get back in time to see the end of his rehearsal.

"Fine. I'll just say that you need to make sure you two stay on the same page. Things can spiral out of control in tricky situations like these," Rain says in a soft voice.

"What tricky sorts of situations?" I ask, genuinely confused about what conversation I'm missing.

"The super hot rocker guy with panty-melting eyes, a voice that can leave you in a puddle, *poetically* took your virginity, is really intense, and is essentially living in your bedroom with you," Bella tells me like she's explaining something crucial. "He's your only relative introduction to the real dating world. *That's* the tricky situation."

I don't really know what they're talking about, but I nod absently like I do, because through the wide windows in front of our table, I see Base's truck pulling around to the parking lot.

"I'll be right back," I tell them.

My cheeks both burn and hurt, so I can only assume I'm blushing and smiling. Why is my stomach fluttering? I see him all the time.

"I feel so sorry for the next guy," I hear Ruby saying on a sigh as I start walking toward the doors.

"Is she really going to go call him?" Rain groans.

It's the last thing I hear as I walk out, and quickly move around the side of the building. As soon as I turn the corner, I catch sight of Base's smile before his hands are on me and his lips crash to mine.

I'm careful when putting my cast around his neck. I've hit him in the head twice in the past three weeks because he sometimes short circuits my brain and I don't think.

His fingers dig into my sides like he can't pull me close enough, and I lean into the kiss more, until he's groaning into my mouth.

He breaks the kiss, leaning back on his truck and smiling again as his eyebrows bounce.

"I was just going to wait on you to finish. The rehearsal ended quickly after you started *sexting* me, because I was pointless," he says as he starts kissing his way down my neck.

The flurry of irrational reactions seems to double daily.

"I finished my omelet, so we can go as soon as I pay," I tell him very distractedly.

I feel his smile against my throat as his hands slide into my back pockets.

"Did you drive?" he asks, kissing my neck again.

"No. I walked."

"Britt? Britt, where did you—"

Rain's voice cuts out, and I turn around just as she stumbles to a halt, gaping at us.

"Oh," she says as she shuffles back a few steps. "I'll cover your tab."

With that, she turns and heads back around the corner, and Base turns my face back to his so he can start kissing me again.

I'm not sure how long we stand in the parking lot, but we have to finally break for air. He straightens as his hands slide away from my waist.

"You still haven't answered my question," I decide to say while he's walking me toward his passenger side. "About the oral."

"It's hard to make promises like that, Britt. Once my hands are on you, all I want to do is get—"

He stops talking, and I turn to see him staring over his shoulder as he opens the door for me, brow furrowing. It's mildly disconcerting when I see…*everyone* staring at us, sans Rain and Ash.

Brin curses and yanks her head back around the corner, as Ruby falls forward, eyes wide like she's been caught. The rest scatter like roaches under a light, and Ruby gives a small, uncomfortable wave.

"This is…exactly as ridiculous as it looks," she states with a firm nod before briskly walking away.

"Ever feel like that goldfish in the bowl around them?" Base asks.

I smile too hard about that question, mostly because we had a similar thought on the same day; we don't have a whole lot in common, so the little things become big wins.

"Actually, I was just thinking that earlier."

His grin grows again too, because he thinks of the little things as big wins as well. *Or* he's smiling because I am. One of the two. I think.

"I'd rather take you out in public to eat instead of ordering takeout tonight," he says as his lips brush over mine, and he tucks my hair behind my ear. "Which means we can't go to bed as soon as we get back, or we'll never get out of it."

As if he's trying to torture me with anticipation, he starts kissing me again, making it hard to say no to bed and yes to dinner. I frankly never thought I'd be capable of such a dilemma.

"Can we attempt dinner tomorrow instead of tonight?" I suggest when his lips break from mine again.

"Deal," he says on a grin as he resumes the kiss.

I have no idea why people want to make dating so complicated when it can be as amazingly simple as this.

Chapter 32

BASE

"No, the set tomorrow will be completely new, aside from our best covers we do," Sticks is saying to the girl in his lap as he gives her a lazy grin.

My attention flicks back to the door as I lazily strum the strings on my guitar, waiting on Britt to get here.

A body drops to the chair next to me, and I look over at a smiling blonde.

"You're the lead singer of the band, right?" she asks.

I just nod,

"I thought about playing it cool and waiting for you to notice me, but clearly you're the type of guy who prefers to be noticed while you play *aloof* and mysterious," she quips. "My name's Lina."

I glance back to the parking area behind the pool, waiting for the right headlights.

"Sorry, Lina. I'm not being aloof nor mysterious, and I'm not trying to be noticed," I tell her dismissively.

"Oh. So girlfriend or something?" she asks, not sounding overly upset by the rejection.

I pause. It's oddly the first time someone has presented that question to me over these last several weeks.

"Unofficially, yes," I say instead of trying to explain the increasingly complicated situation that is Britt Sterling.

It's not like I haven't dated over the years, but it was always easy to keep the relationships easy, simple, casual and temporary.

But I have to figure out a way to get over the year-long-tour hurdle without losing Britt.

I'm not okay at all with the expiration date anymore. I'm not sure if I ever was.

"I'm good at this. Let me guess, since this is Sterling Shore, she's a model, has a lot of Instagram followers for her daily selfie, and her goal is to save the planet by running and car-pooling. How close am I?" Lina asks as she lifts her beer to her lips.

Taylor snorts as he sits down.

"She does have a lot of followers," Randy says with a shrug from the end of the table.

"She is at a photoshoot right now," Sticks adds, causing me to roll my eyes.

"Knew it," Lina says as she lazily clinks her beer bottle to mine the second I lift it.

"She's off-the-charts hot if he's this uninterested in all other women," the girl across from us says. "Now I want to see her. I'm too curious."

I have no idea where Randy even found these girls, but they're oddly not as vicious or volatile as the usual ones he brings around.

"She'll be here soon and you can look your fill," I tell them absently, checking the time on my phone.

"If she's that hot, it's possible I'll hate her just for that," the girl in Sticks says very seriously. "Some girls are just too—"

Headlights shine over us, and I stand as a lazy grin spreads over my face.

"Oh, she's going to be really hot. Look at him light up like a kid at Christmas."

I don't even know which one of them says that, because Britt comes walking up the steps to the deck, and my grin only grows when I see her.

Her hair is in tightly braided pigtails, and she apparently needed elf ears for the shoot. She's still half painted with the makeup, but some of it has rubbed off. She's wearing a T-shirt with the game logo on it, along with a pair of crazy monster shorts.

"Sorry. My locker got soaked by an ill-capped bottle of water, and I had to settle for the downstairs store for new clothes so I didn't have to go home first."

I'm officially addicted, and I don't want or need help.

"Sorry it took so long," she says just as I lift her from the ground.

She grins as her legs wrap around my waist, and she kisses me as I carry her toward the table.

"And he's officially lost to us for the rest of the night," Sticks says from somewhere behind me.

I flip him off as I sit down, keeping Britt in my lap, even though she adjusts so that she's not straddling me.

It takes a second to realize that all the women are just staring at her like they're confused, and…it starts to feel like they're insulting her with their confusion.

Just as I begin to feel defensive, one girl points at her. "I feel like I know you from somewhere. Do you always have pointy ears or is this just some weird sci-fi chick fetish thing?" Lina asks like it's not an insulting question.

Britt shakes her head. "We've never met."

Britt's eyes flick back to mine, and she gives my guitar a look. "I'm never going to actually hear you play your new songs, am I?"

I smirk, eyes back on her. "I forgot I had a final fitting for my dress that I'm wearing to Dane's charity event," she states randomly. "It put me even farther behind tonight."

"You go to so many charity events that you don't even know the name of the one you're getting a *final-fitting* sort of dress for?" Taylor asks like his mind is slightly blown.

I have no idea how he's arrived at that conclusion.

"Rich people," Randy snorts while shaking his head. "They feel guilty for being so obscenely wealthy that they have to toss some good will out into the world. They don't need to know where it goes," he adds.

"I don't want to engage in conflict. They have a firm opinion of wealth and the people who reach for it," I hear her saying to one of the girls. "Can one of you help me?"

Why is she asking them for help?

"She has an eidetic memory. Of course she knows which one she's going to," I cut in. "We know you're not actually like the rest of them," I say as I run my hand up her back.

"She really does look familiar," one of the other girls says.

"Base, your girlfriend is starting to sound more popular than we are. This is beginning to be a problem," Randy groans as his head drops to his arm.

Lina's eyes widen before she says, "Dane's charity event? As in Dane Sterling? Is that what all the 'rich people' talk is about?"

"Oh, you're Britt Sterling, aren't you? You're actually hard to recognize out of all the make-up and with the new…pointy ears," another girl announces.

Britt doesn't get to speak, because the girl sitting on Sticks leans over and starts talking to her first.

"Oh damn. Did you really lose your virginity? I missed last week's blog," she tells Britt.

"Did you really just ask her a super personal question like that before she even knows your name?" Lina asks the other girl in a little horror.

I'm not really sure what happens next. It goes from there to all of them making introductions, and then they talk about the fact Britt hasn't *blogged* about *our* sex life, as though it's supposed to be a public thing instead of a private one.

"*Find confident girls*, they said," Randy mutters under his breath. "That way they don't fight for attention and our shit stops breaking. I'd rather replace the broken shit."

Taylor wipes away the smile, clearing his throat a few times as all the women ignore Randy.

"I asked her to leave my name out of it," I cut in, my hand smoothing up Britt's back again as I narrow my eyes at the women. "I don't want someone trying to capitalize on her name and setting us up to sign with them just to use her reach."

They barely acknowledge me before they shift the conversation again. Britt leans back on me, getting comfortable, since these girls seem to be sort of…genuinely interested in Britt and her future Sterling empire.

"Having Harley personally take you under her wing has to be intimidating, but also really exciting. You're so lucky," one girl says like she just has to know what Harley is like. "She's sort of my hero."

"She's not lucky. She's skilled," I point out.

"And also incredibly lucky that Harley was looking for interns to groom," Britt tells me very firmly like she's sending me to school. "I went there thinking I was good enough, and got lucky she saw a future in me."

I just grin at her, not commenting on how her mind has also attracted plenty of other companies who'd love to head-hunt her. I see the mail load that comes in, and hear the calls she turns down.

I keep my mouth shut because I don't think Harley is taking advantage. She's legit grooming her. And to Britt, she's already family.

"This is why I don't mess with serious college chicks. I have a type. I should stick to it," Randy whimpers.

The girls talk for forty-five fucking minutes about the hardcore gaming world Britt is involved in—and it all sounds like gibberish to me.

On and on. And on. And on.

An hour later, the guys and I have moved to a different section of the patio just because we're being ignored. My lips twitch when Britt grins over at me, her eyes falling on the guitar in my hands as I gently play.

"Take your girl and have sex with her so that we can at least have a chance at working our charm," Taylor says as he eyes the ass of one girl who bends over.

"Some of them don't like women being objectified in game context. Do you really think staring at her ass is going to get you anywhere?" Sticks asks him pointedly.

"I think I like a challenge." After saying that, Taylor stands abruptly. "Let's do shots and sing a little karaoke. Music's apparently our most appreciated feature."

He gets a few smiles, but Britt just seems confused. My lips twitch as she purses hers.

"I think I prefer women who like me and don't make me feel dumber than I already feel," Randy grumbles. "Nothing wrong with my kind of girl."

"Absolutely not," Taylor agrees as I remain distracted.

"You only say that because Bee would slap you for saying anything else," Randy tells us.

"That's not why I'm saying that," Taylor groans when the girl he's been eyeing doesn't even glance his way. "I prefer being chased."

I flip through the song list, already knowing which one I'm going to choose.

"It's cheesy as fucking hell, but I can't pass up this opportunity," I say as I grab the microphone and select a song on my phone.

As soon as I start singing, I get a chorus of groans, as I rock every single word of the parody song *Talk Nerdy to Me.*

Britt smiles like I've done something right, as I sing directly to her. Her eyes are bright but also glossed over with that dazed, sexy, entranced look. I really should let her sit in on rehearsal. I'd kill it every time if I did.

Just because I'm already sliding head first in the cheese, I even run the tip of my finger over the tip of her pointed ear on the part about the elf ears not needing explaining.

Her grin immediately doubles.

I drop to my knees, dancing a little toward her, my smile only growing when her hands seem to unconsciously move up my chest. The girl with secretive sad eyes lights on fire, and I forget that I'm even singing as my lips collide with hers.

There's a loud pop and scratch against the background music when I drop the mic—literally—and lift her from the table. Her legs immediately tighten around my waist, and I kiss her harder as I carry her inside.

"Ladies and gentleman, they made it almost through the second verse. A new world record. Let's give them some applause," Randy says over the microphone, causing me to groan and Britt to smile against my lips.

She's still under the impression we're not far from amicably parting ways and going our own separate paths in life. I'm trying to figure out how I'm going to break up this perfect moment in time to bring forth the reality that we're possibly all wrong, and yet perfect for each other. We have very fucking little in common, but it just doesn't seem to matter at all.

Her fingers tangle in my hair, and I stumble over a threshold somewhere close to my room before bumping into a wall.

"Need me to drive?" Taylor calls from behind me.

"Fuck off," I tell him, my lips still half fused to Britt's as we finally fumble our way into my bedroom.

Her steady laugh grows as I lower her to the bed.

"What have I told you about laughing when we're about to have sex?" I ask her when she pulls back and turns her head, working hard to keep a straight face.

She turns on her side, and I slide into bed next to her, pulling her to me by her waist.

"That it's inconvenient for your penis," she says very seriously, then starts laughing again. "Sorry," she says, her face not straightening, despite her clearest best efforts.

"How much did you drink?" I ask, eyebrow arching as she

hiccups and giggles again.

"Just one." Giggle. Giggle. Straight face. Giggle.

I drop my head to her chest, because I'll start fucking laughing too if I keep watching her attempt to force a neutral expression. Her body shaking with silent laughter isn't much better.

"Now you could teach me oral," she suggests like she's had a stroke of genius that eclipses her paused giggle-fit.

I snort out laughter, then groan as I drop back on the bed, scrubbing a hand over my face.

"You're going to go on tour before you have time to show me oral if you keep procrastinating," she goes on, shoving at my chest as she rolls over and drapes her body over mine with so much ease.

My finger runs down her side as the humor slips away.

"Please," she says so motherfucking sincerely.

"You're literally begging to suck my dick right now," I point out, wondering if she knows just how bad this would fuck with any man's damn head.

She nods like it's not a big deal.

"I'm going to hell for this one day. I just know it," I mutter to myself. "Now that I've written a full album, tell me the true story behind those sad eyes, and I'll teach you oral," I tell her.

I'll last five seconds of coaching her on how to suck me off. Sure be gloriously humiliating for me.

"I've been assured that sad stories can put a damper on sexual exploits," she deadpans.

"I'll risk it," I say softly as I twirl a lock of hair around my finger.

"Everyone expects some really big, terribly tragic story. But it's really the most common story there is. Mine's only different because it ended good for a change," she says on a breath as she drops back.

"You can give me the Britt Sterling special and make it as nonchalant as you need to, even if you need to list it," I murmur as I kiss her jaw.

"I was never physically abused. Not all the kids were mean to me. I was just neglected or ignored. I was as miserable as every other problematic child in the system. I couldn't properly communicate the things I needed to. Conflict was impossible for me. I had to be really calm and work really hard to talk in no more than three-people-at-a-time settings. Then I got a job as a waitress, and got great tips because people thought I was mentally challenged and doing the best I could. It felt like a lot longer than it actually was."

I cringe, then suck in a deep breath when she arches an eyebrow at me.

"I'm not sad about it. I often play down how lonely and *hard* it was just to exist, because people expect me to be sad about it when they know the full depths of all I felt. I'm not often overwhelmed by emotion anymore, but it does happen on occasion, despite the robot memes people make of me."

I smooth my hand up her back. "People can be dicks."

"I know," she says with another shrug. "I understand their impression though, and I'm not offended by them."

Her eyes move up my body until they meet mine.

"But the pictures of sad eyes with practiced smiles? Those are when I have moments where I feel bad for being one of the few to get a happy ending. I feel sad for the ones who don't have a brother like I do. And I wish I could do more."

My mind goes over the countless stories and songs that played out in my head.

"I never guessed right," I murmur quietly, more to myself than to her.

It seems like it should be a little obvious, but I wrote a lot of songs about the damaged and broken. Not the healed and burdened.

"I communicate better almost daily," she goes on, dragging me out of my thoughts as I brush her hair to the side.

A loud banging at my door is followed by a few laughs. "Hey, we're going to play the set for Ralphy. He's out here if you want to play with us. If not, he's going to fill your spot," Taylor calls through the door.

"Let him fill my spot," I call out. "And tell me what he thinks about the new sound."

I turn back, finding Britt absently tracing circles over my shirt, her fingertip running the barely-there outline of my abs.

Her eyes flick to mine, and she just stares. "I told you the story," she says quietly.

Sitting up, I reach back and pull my shirt over my head, and she does the same with a shy smile on her lips. Her light skin has just a dash of freckles here and there, and my eyes rake over them before landing on the very sexy bra.

She loaded up on sexy lingerie during her virginal days and we spent a day with her letting me pick out my favorites. That was a fun day.

As I push down my jeans and boxers, she just watches, eyes half lidded as she stares very deliberately.

Scrubbing a hand over my face again, I say, "Take it in your hand, and then move at your own pace from there. I'll walk you through it."

The second her hand touches me, and she wets her lips with the tip of her tongue, I realize this is going to be a quick tutorial no matter how hard I try.

When her lips hover just centimeters over my dick for long, palpable minutes of silence, it actually jumps in her hand and startles her. I didn't make it do that. It's possessed around her.

"Just let me know when you're ready," I say as I clear my throat, while she resumes staring at it. "And no teeth. Please."

Her hand is just firm enough, but I hiss out a breath when she squeezes a little harder.

"Sorry," she says, loosening her grip again as she finally leans over and wraps her lips around the head of my cock with zero warning.

I hiss out another breath, this one of surprise, but she either doesn't hear it or doesn't care as she sucks me in a little deeper.

"No teeth," I remind her on a worried breath when I feel a graze.

After a few more trial-and-error movements, I finally work her into a steady rhythm with some really damn good fundamentals. It's going to be fun helping her *'improve her technique'* on this.

Maddening woman.

She takes me deeper and deeper, and it's fumbled and somewhat awkward, and fucking perfect—

"Britt, now's the time to back away if you don't want to finish it."

She doesn't stop, and it doesn't take but another second before pleasure spikes up my spine and spreads. My legs stiffen, and I cough out a sound as my hand finally shoves into her hair on reflex. I don't do anything but rest it there until she abruptly pulls back and takes off running to the bathroom.

My brow furrows as she slams the door, and my hand stays suspended in the air where her head was.

"Britt? You okay?" I ask, starting to worry when I hear the sink come on and water splashing.

When I hear the gargling, I bristle.

"Britt?" I call again, leaning down to grab my boxers.

"Sorry," she says, though the word is a little muffled as she opens the door, brushing her teeth.

I arch an eyebrow, lips twitching as her cheeks and neck burn a bright red.

She runs back in and spits out the toothpaste before returning.

"I'm decidedly not advanced enough to be a swallower, even without a gag reflex," she tells me with an apologetic grimace.

Because there's no way I can speak with a straight face, I just hold up an *okay* symbol with my hand, as she jogs back in to brush her teeth some more.

Dropping back on the bed, I pull the pillow over my face to muffle the bits of laughter that sneak out as my body shakes lightly on the bed.

Fucking girl.

My laughter turns into a bit of a groan. Sooner or later I'm going to have to tell her I'm in love with her.

Chapter 33

BRITT

"…third dressing room from the back in that boutique, the eastern bathroom on the third floor of the mall with the pink flower wall paper, and the pier," I say, finishing up the list that has taken me five full minutes to deliver.

Everyone blinks at me, including Corbin, who walked in mid-way through the list.

"Do I want to know what all these random places have in common?" Maverick asks from behind me.

Oh, I didn't even notice him.

"I don't," Corbin says with a firm, certain nod before walking away with his drink in his hand, abandoning us to our corner as the night dwindles on.

The important fund-raising part is finished. Now it's just the dancing and business talk surrounding us as we sit in a corner like we do at the end of any long event.

The guys keep leaving when they bring up Base.

"It's all the public places I've had sex," I tell Maverick, who closes his eyes and shakes his head, palming his face by the end.

"I walked right into it, because now I see how that should have been obvious," he says behind his hand.

Salem grins as though she enjoys his misery as he walks away, flipping her off as he goes like he knows she's smiling.

I've irrationally missed Base a lot tonight. It's just one night. But my mind sees other couples doing small things like that, and the ease and familiarity of their exchanges is what makes me miss him.

"That's a long list for a short period of time," Bella says on a low whistle. "Impressive. You're still being safe, though, right?"

Allie gives her a look I can't decipher, and Bella ignores her in a way that seems intentional.

"Of course," I tell her.

"And you're still breaking up when he goes on tour?" Ash asks like she's trying to understand.

"We'll stay in touch and be friends, I'm sure. We get along great, so there's no reason not to be friends," I go on, even though my foot taps a little nervously.

"You have a toothbrush in his bathroom, and he has one in yours, but you're still not in a relationship?" Ruby asks me as she studies my face.

"I never pictured her as one to be in denial," Tria says on a sigh.

"We're in a relationship," I tell her. "All interactions with people on a continual basis put you in some sort of relationship with them. But it's not the type of relationship you're referring to."

They stare at me. They keep doing this a lot. I know they think I'm being deliberately obtuse about something.

"A relationship requires work, maintenance, and active communication on the small problems that usually have the potential to escalate into larger, more damaging troubles if not addressed and dealt with," I explain.

They all sort of bristle in their seats, clearing their throats and darting their eyes around.

"We don't do that work. We enjoy the fun stuff like getting to know each other…and a lot of sex. It works so easily because we don't deal with any issues."

"Issues like squeezing the toothpaste in the middle? Or are we talking about deal-breaking issues?" Rain asks.

I don't know what deals there are to break. We're approaching our expiration date, and I really wish time would just slow down so I could enjoy it longer.

"Issues such as a black-tie event not being *his thing?"* Ash guesses when I don't immediately respond.

"Issues such as him not being able to step outside his comfort zone," I gently amend. "I like dressing up and going places in a variety of ways."

She gives me a slow nod, lips tightening.

"And then there's the inability to accept help because he always wants to be the hero and thinks he has something to prove instead of listening to any professional advice from people already in the industry. He pushes back against people when they try to give him advice or help, to be more accurate. And that stems to his personal life as well. It's hard to address things because he's defensive."

Ash sits back, shoulders slumping. I realize belatedly that it sounds like I'm sitting here talking badly about him, because they're all showing concern.

I was just answering the question, and now I feel like I've done something really wrong. I don't want to do anything really wrong with Base.

My palms start stinging, and I look down to see my fingernails have started digging into them.

"Did I just sound like I was being critical?" I ask them, worried now.

"No. No. We know you didn't mean to be," Allie tells me dismissively.

"You're really breaking up when he goes on tour, aren't you?" Ash asks like it's the first time she's asked that question instead of the thirteenth.

"Of course we are. He has a lot of things to accomplish before he feels whole, and his path is completely different from mine. But I think we'll always be friends because this has been…mostly perfect. We don't have to ruin it by addressing issues."

"You're sure he's on the exact same page?" Brin asks me like this is crucial information.

"He has plenty of things he wants to address with me that he hints at but holds back as well. He also seems uncomfortable around money, and this is all part of my life too." I gesture to some of the extravagance surrounding us. "It's daunting and takes a lot of adjusting and effort. However, tonight proves he doesn't intend to put forth unnecessary effort. It's practical. It also means he's not deviated from the original agreement."

A small smile graces my lips, because in fifteen minutes he'll at least get to see my pretty black dress that only goes across one shoulder and has a split up the side to the middle of my thigh. Understated sexy is what Rain called it.

Tria drops to a chair, no longer smirking. I'm not sure why they all look so sad. I'm now thirteen minutes from meeting him outside, and time is still counting down.

Slowly.

So. So. Slowly.

"Huh. I guess we were all the idiots then," Harley finally says after being unusually quiet on the subject tonight.

My phone chimes with a text, and I glance down to see it's from Base. He's been quiet all day, and between helping with the event and getting what Rain calls the 'princess treatment' that makes all the hard work feel a little more fun, I haven't been able to see him.

BASE: Running late. I'll see you in twenty.

The illogical amount of disappointment I feel from the minuscule delay is a testament to how much I want to cling to these last few weeks before he's gone.

He's already later than the original time we discussed by a full hour.

His tone is impossible to tell through text, so I don't know if something is wrong or if he just lost track of time.

Ash sucks in a breath when she reads something on her phone, and she curses as she pinches the bridge of her nose.

Rain asks me about the toothbrushes again and if our bathrooms look the same with products and stuff. Why the fascination with the random bathroom factoids?

Ash leans up, putting her phone away, and talks over Rain. "So, theoretically, if something happened to his tour, would you consider working on these unaddressed issues and give a relationship a real try?" she asks.

I pause, frowning at the very serious worry/dread on her face. Not sure which. Neither seems good.

"Did something happen to his tour?" Harley asks her, aiding me in explaining the shift in atmosphere.

Ash puts down her phone, smiling tightly at me. "A label pulled strings to have their spot given to a new band they're promoting, and the guys have been trying all day to—"

I don't hear what else she says, because I'm lifting my phone and calling Base as I stand and start walking through the throngs of people.

He won't take this well.

"Hey, sorry I'm running behind, but I'm not too far from—"

"You're definitely losing your spot on the tour?" I ask him as I needle my way through the doors to where I can hear him better, my heels clicking as I take the sidewalk around the building toward the sea of cars in the parking lot.

He exhales harshly. "I really don't want to talk about that right now. It's…definite, though. I also probably burned some really important bridges today that will send my already laughable career careening off the side of a cliff, but fuck it at this point. It was Vince Jaggons who put one of his newer artists in our spot. Stupid, arrogant, self-righteous son of a bitch. Things got heated, because his pompous errand boy stepped all over us like we were dirt. You can't be honest, hard-working, and get ahead in—"

He stops, exhales harshly again, and makes a frustrated sound.

"No tour," he sums up.

"I'm so sorry," I say genuinely, disappointment settling on my chest like I feel it for him.

He gets quiet for a minute, and I shuffle around people as they start exiting.

"The only silver lining is that you and I can do this thing for real now, Britt," he says so casually.

My spine straightens as I hear the words, and a clock seems to start counting down in the back of my mind.

"Did you hear me?" he asks a little impatiently.

"I-I-yeah. I heard," I stammer out, unsure what to say just yet as I try to quickly work my words into the right phrasing in my mind first.

"So? Are we doing this for real? No more expiration date?" he prompts.

The rain starts to drizzle twenty-three minutes earlier than the forecast predicted, and I step under a pavilion as it starts to build.

"Britt? You there?" he asks as the rain starts coming down harder and harder.

"I-I-I don't know. I need time to think about how to communicate our problems together before we jump into a life decision of that magnitude, and—"

"Communicate what problems?" he asks, his voice coming from right behind me.

Turning around, I pull my phone away from my ear slowly, finding Base staring down at me. His hair and clothes are a little wet, and he breathes heavily. His eyes are intently on me, waiting expectantly, as I open and close my mouth.

"I-I struggle with being put on the spot," I remind him, but he steps in closer, tucking a stray lock of hair behind my ear.

"What fucking problems, Britt? We never argue. Hell, we don't even get agitated around each other. Everything is too fucking perfect to say we have problems," he assures me in that smooth voice that usually makes me really stupid.

But right now my mind is firing in panic mode, and I don't speak as he gently caresses my cheek, as cars drive around the loop we're standing in the middle of, sheltered from the now-pelting rain as it loudly crashes onto the pavilion covering.

"Is it Dane? I know he has issues with you dating, but he doesn't have an actual say in your life," he goes on, which only makes my brow furrow more.

"No. It's not Dane. Dane has nothing to do with us. I need time to write this all down so I can properly communicate it after going over it with a few other sets of eyes, and—"

"What the fuck are you talking about, Britt?" he asks in what appears to be genuine confusion.

"I think I want to do this, even though it's irrational, but—"

"You *think* you want to do this?" he asks, taking a step back as he makes a scoffing noise.

"See? I'm communicating this wrong. I need time to think so that I don't say the wrong things to express myself in a non-attacking nature. You're too defensive and certain of yourself."

He runs a hand through his hair, shaking his head. "What do you *feel,* Britt? Stop overthinking it and just answer yes or no. Do you want to be with me?"

"I do. I just need to ensure the unhealthy problems are addressed before we come to that agreement," I go on, reaching for the right words.

"What unhealthy problems? Things like how you have to go to the Sterlings to ask them if what you say is fucking okay? You can think for your-fucking-self," he says, then exhales like he's trying to calm himself down as his jaw tics. "You don't need them to analyze the shit you say. *What problems*?"

"You can't just completely change the terms of a decision of this magnitude and expect an immediate answer with no preparation. Conflict is an area I'm not skilled in, and I handle situations with inappropriate finesse, especially to those who don't listen well."

"*I* don't listen well?" he asks on a bitter laugh. "If you want to say I'm not worth your time, Britt, just say it. Don't make up bullshit excuses that—"

"When I say stop, you push," I interrupt, pointing out exactly what he's doing. "You want my life story after I told you I just want to be who I am today instead of being seen for the sad girl I was. I gave it to you—"

"In small pieces, Britt. You don't expose anything. You keep everything locked away. *There's* a fucking problem. I do listen. You just don't talk."

The rain comes down harder, forcing me to raise my voice as thunder crackles overhead and lights flash all around us as cars continue to weave around our loop.

The panic tries to rise in my chest, but I work to push it down with every single mental tool at my relevant disposal.

"It's all an unimportant blur that I don't want to dig around in just to appease your desire to see how broken I once was, Base. I existed. That's it. I moved on in a healthy way that you don't approve of, because you still want to save me. Just like you did when you showed up with a picture where I had 'sad' eyes."

He laughs bitterly again, shaking his head.

"I can't believe this. You are seriously trying to make it look like I've been a shit guy to you these past few months, when—"

"No," I say quickly, some of that panic bubbling out as inconvenient tears prick my eyes. "I'm just not expressing myself right if that's what you think I'm saying."

"You box yourself inside this emotionless void where conflict can't touch you if you don't let it. *That's* why you're not good with conflict, Britt. You're sabotaging this just because you're fucking scared."

"I *am* scared," I tell him honestly, my voice cracking a little. "Just give me a second to write all this down and—"

"Just email me whatever the Sterlings tell you to say to cushion the blow to my defensive ego," he says as he backs away, his expression so cold.

"Base, that's not—"

"There's not really any sense in getting into farther conflict about it, Britt," he states flatly as he backs up more, putting his hands in his pocket as he steps out into the rain, letting it pour onto him. "It's doomed from the beginning if we need third parties involved just to start a damn relationship. It shouldn't be this hard. I need to be the one you talk to about *us.*"

My lips part, but I don't even know what to say in counter to that. When I just stay silent, he glances away.

It shouldn't be this hard.

"I'll have Sticks swing by and grab my things. It was almost great, Britt. I hope you at least got all you wanted out of it." His tone is disbelieving, cold and nothing at all like him.

That panic settles on my chest, and I just freeze, not speaking, afraid of only making it worse as more tears sting my eyes. He gives me a disappointed, sad look before he turns and sprints off into the rain, and I just stare as my clutch tumbles to the ground.

I open my mouth, but no argument comes to the tip of my tongue while he disappears into the folds of the downpour.

Absently, I lean down, pick up my clutch, and start walking in the opposite direction toward the building. Toward the chatter. Toward the lights.

Everything's neither here nor there, just sort of existing around me. My right heel sinks into the ground, so I pull my foot out of it and abandon the shoe where it's stuck. The left heel forces me to repeat the process when it sticks as well.

"Ms. Sterling, are you okay?" a man asks as he runs toward me.

I guess I've made it back. Is he holding an umbrella over my head as he walks me the five remaining feet to the covered entrance? That seems irrelevant by this point. Surely I'm already soaked.

I give him an absent nod of gratitude as I head inside. People part for me, slowly turning to stare as I head toward the laughing crowd in the back. Did Maverick tell a joke?

It's the end of the night, so this is the part where the couples get really sweet toward each other. I usually leave by now.

Maverick's eyes widen on me in what appears to be surprise. It shouldn't be surprising. I've been here all night.

Everyone else turns to look at me, and it goes silent as the happy expressions turn into the same look Maverick has. It becomes increasingly evident they're expectantly waiting for me to speak.

"Base drives me places most of the time so that we can spend more time together," I tell them, gesturing behind me as I stare at the champagne on the table. "I don't think he's taking me home tonight," I add as everyone remains silent.

The water drips from my hair, and my pretty dress is indeed drenched all the way through. I'm starting to feel the wet chill now.

"I'll dry myself as well as possible before sitting in anyone's vehicle," I add as a single tear rolls down my cheek, my gaze falling down to my bare, wet feet that have shards of broken grass blades on them.

"Fuck's sake, Britt. I'll take you home. What'd he fucking do?" Dane asks me with a worried tone as Rain moves out of his lap.

Dane stands, moving toward me, but I take a step back and halt his advance.

"I said all the wrong things, and I couldn't make it better," I manage to say in a clam manner.

My attention wanders to the slice of chocolate cake on the table that I never ate because I was saving it for Base. The cake is always the best part. I was going to share it with him.

"I already knew I wasn't ready for a functioning, normal relationship, so I couldn't give him what he was asking for. I was emotionally prepared for this to end; it's just earlier than expected," I add, still staring at the cake.

It's the best chocolate cake in Sterling Shore, and it always gets completely gone so fast at these things. He really would have liked it.

Dane exhales heavily as he drops back to a seat.

"I'll take you home," Harley says, drawing my attention to her as she gives me what is decidedly a pitying look.

"It's not his fault. He wasn't unreasonable. I'd appreciate it if no one said anything to him about this," I decide to say, just to ensure no one mistakes this as hard feelings. "I'm just not to the point in my life where I'm capable of even starting a real relationship. I still need help communicating, and that's an understandable issue for him that simply can't be rectified so abruptly."

Harley comes toward me, but I drop my clutch to the table.

"Can I have the rest of this?" I ask, picking up the champagne bottle.

"There's not much left," Kode tells me as I swirl the fourth of a bottle. "Let me see if they have more in the—"

"I don't need more than that. More would be a really unhealthy life choice," I state blandly as I grab my slice of cake as well.

It shouldn't go to waste.

Kode sits back down, and they all stay still and quiet, staring at me the way they do Bananas when she's cornered and likely to do something really insane.

I'm not going to do anything insane.

Harley picks up my wet clutch, tucking it under her arm.

Turning, I carry the cake and champagne toward the doors again.

Harley wordlessly follows me out, and her car is valeted to us before she even has to draw her ticket.

I have no idea who opens the door for me as I sit down, but I grimace when I remember I'm soaked through.

"I forgot to towel off. I'm sor—"

"It's fine," Harley says softly as she reaches over and pats my hand. "Really, completely, and truly fine, Britt."

I nod, grateful she's so flippant with her vehicle's care, as she starts driving us away.

A shaky breath comes out of me as another tear follows the same warm path as the last.

"You went into this assuming that by the end, you'd remain friends, because you built a friendship," Harley says in a quiet voice as I take a sip of the champagne. "The build-up and the sex was fun, but it's the friendship that made you walk around with perma-grin, Britt. I know you well enough to know that much."

I just nod, not disagreeing.

"Did he leave the door open for friendship?" she asks me.

His words instantly replay in my head, and the weight on my chest gets heavier.

"He's sending Sticks to come collect his things from my house. That would imply he's actively going to avoid running into me. I don't think we're going to be..." I let the words trail off when my voice goes rasp and another tear falls.

"Then you didn't emotionally prepare yourself for this, because he wasn't supposed to just walk away. It's okay to cry, Britt," she goes on as the first choked sob escapes me, and my shoulders start to shake as the weight on my chest presses down harder.

I drop the cake in my lap and quickly press the back of my hand to my mouth to muffle the next choked sob. But then they start hitting one right after another, until I can't even muffle them anymore as the tears start pouring down as steadily as the unrelenting rain outside.

I feel the car pulling off the road and slowing as I double over and cover my face with both hands, the champagne tumbling to the floor and rolling as it spills what's left.

Harley's arms come around me, pulling me to her, and I move so that my face is against her shoulder as I cry. We idle on the side of the road as the pain in my chest intensifies, constricting until it's physically agonizing to breathe.

"It's not supposed to h-hurt this much," I say, my words

slightly muffled.

She hugs me tighter. "The human element always fucks up the plans in your head, Britt." She pats my back gently as the console digs into my hip. "You're just as human as the rest of us."

That seems to make it okay to cry harder, because that's what I do. I shake my head, forcing deep breaths in between sobs, as I try to calm myself.

A streetlight illuminates the interior just enough for me to see the cake I've smeared all over her leather and carpeting.

"I'm so sorry," I say around a hiccupped sob as I wipe the tears out of my eyes.

"I have an excellent car detailer. Don't worry about a little cake and champagne."

I finish drying my eyes, and I take a deeper, less shaky breath as things start stacking back into place in my mind.

"I should pack his things and have them sent over. It'll be better that way. It's healthier to move on as soon as possible instead of dwelling on disappointing breaks," I tell her, quoting my psychologist.

"It's okay to dwell for a night or two," Harley tells me softly. "You don't have to—"

"It's going to take longer than tonight to move on," I interrupt, understanding her line of conversation and where it leads next as I slowly get ahold of my emotions.

"The human element is messy," she goes on.

"Krysta owes me a favor. I'll just have her drop it off for me," I carry on, as Harley makes a small breath of frustration.

But she puts the car in gear and pulls back into traffic as I take steadier and steadier breaths, staring absently at the taillights in front of us.

"Don't shut the door completely after one fight. I've learned people can fuck up and still be in love. Love's what makes them stupid in the first place," she presses.

"Even though we get along great when ignoring our differences, it still doesn't make us any less different, and working through the resulting issues of that will leave me in an unhealthy state of constant compromise because his expectations—however reasonable—are too high for me to reach at this point in my life. We were always going to end," I say to her, though it's mostly just me reminding myself.

"It was fun while it lasted," I add on a quieter note, finally understanding that expression as well. "But it was always going to end," I say again as the tears slowly stop leaking at last.

With shaky hands, I pull out my phone.

"Don't call him yet, Britt. Let it breathe a few days," Harley says as I lift my phone to my ear.

"Britt?" Bo asks. "I just heard. Are you okay?"

That spares me from having to explain things.

"I'm fine. It's fine. It was inevitable," I tell her as the last of the emotion leaves my voice.

I see Harley shoot a frown in my direction.

"What do you need from me? Pizza? Sad movies? I've got it all. Or is this just a temporary pause moment that's being blown out of proportion?"

I thought I was spared…

"It's an impasse. I'm not ready for a relationship. I'm not calling about that. I was wondering if I could use the favor you owe me."

"Of course."

Harley shoots me an indecipherable look I barely take note of as we pull up in front of my house and she turns off the car.

"I want to schedule a meeting with your father."

Harley groans, and I hear Bo make an uncomfortable noise as well.

"Don't lash out at his career, Britt. Telling my dad to never sign him is a little cruel. I know your emotions are probably—"

"I want to help his career. Not hurt it," I tell her, really confused about why she thinks I'd do something like that.

Harley now looks confused.

"He won't let Tag call in any favors," Bo tells me like she's warning me. "This is also a bad idea."

"It'll probably piss him off more," Harley says, essentially echoing Bo.

I put the phone on speaker so they can hear each other and not have to say similar things unless they find it pertinent.

"We're no longer sexual partners or friends, so it doesn't really matter if he's mad at me."

"Horrible idea," Harley tells me.

"I agree with her, Britt."

"It doesn't really matter at this point," I explain to them as I step out while the rain has slacked and go to unlock my door.

Harley follows me in, and Bo finally makes a sound that resembles one of defeat.

"I'll call him. As the daughter of a stubborn, oblivious, somewhat selfish *artist* with a really big heart, can I give you some advice?"

"Please," I tell her as I start pulling out packing boxes and handing some off to Harley.

"If you're actually trying to help his career, take me with you to see my father and let me guide the conversation. He's a complicated man, and you're about as good with conflict as I am."

"There's a reason he hasn't signed him yet, isn't there?"

"Knowing Dad, there's a long list of reasons. He's a very critical man of others, but he doesn't realize it. I'll guide the conversation, and then you do what you do best."

"Recite factoids on relevant topics?" I guess. It's my one crowd pleaser with our group and helps keep tensions down when they try to rise.

Bo makes a small sound of amusement. "No. You just be you. He's in town for another week, but I'll make sure he meets us tomorrow for lunch. I'll text you the place."

"Thanks," I say quietly.

"I'm glad you called," she tells me softly before hanging up.

Harley has finished making some boxes and she gives me a pointed look.

"Meddling is never good," she assures me.

"We're not together, so there's nothing at risk," I remind her as I head to the bathroom to pack up all his things.

I snatch several things, tossing them all into the box. As I grab up his toothbrush, I stop. I'm not sure why the tears spring to my eyes or why the pain starts in my chest again, or why my hand starts to shake the blurrier my vision gets.

It's just a toothbrush.

It's an irrational, completely unhygienic, and disturbingly unhealthy reaction, but I grab a zipper baggie and put his toothbrush in it before stashing it under the sink. I'll throw it away later.

Chapter 34

BASE

I stare at the wall as the ball bounces back to me, and I catch it before throwing it again.

"I know. I know. We didn't expect this tour to fall through though, and—"

Sticks stops talking, likely because Dane is telling him he's glad I'm finally away from his sister and I'm never stepping foot in his club again.

"They're not going to draw the same crowd we do. You only booked them because we were supposed to be gone, and now—"

Sticks stops talking again, eyes fluttering shut as his jaw tics.

"Yeah. I get it. Thanks anyway," he says as he hangs up and slaps the wall with a curse.

"I told you Dane wouldn't hire us back," I say before throwing the ball much harder.

It bounces back too fast for me to catch it, and I run a hand through my hair before dropping back on the couch. I don't even glance back to see where the ball went.

"He's going to squeeze us in when and where he can," Sticks grinds out. "Despite the fact you dumped his sister on a night when—"

There's a loud banging at the door, and Sticks jogs over to swing it open. Boxes shove through, and I spot a flash of Krysta's short hair before she drops them to the ground and gives me an unimpressed look.

"Hey, nice to fucking see you too. Won't you come in?" Sticks asks dryly from behind her.

"Don't mind if I do," she says with a fuck-off smile before she looks over at me. "I'm not carrying in all your boxes by myself. A little help?"

My brow furrows as she turns and walks back outside, and Sticks shoots me a quizzical look as I push up from the couch.

"What are you talking about?" I ask as I step outside to see her car wide open with the doors wide as well.

Taylor weirdly has Harley's car in our driveway, and he's cleaning furiously, wiping sweat off his brow.

"You're seriously pissed at me because the club had bad crowd control? Will you just fucking talk to me?" Sticks asks Krysta.

She ignores him as she goes to her car again and pulls out another box.

"Where's that shit I used to get that grease out of your floor?" Taylor asks me, as Stick snatches the box out of Krysta's hands.

She gives him a dry look before grabbing another.

"I don't know. Why the hell have you got Harley's car here?" I ask him instead as Sticks demands Krysta say something in her defense for putting him on block.

"Cake and champagne, man. It's a mushy, smeared nightmare, but Harley pays accordingly for her ride to look nice."

"Rich people," Randy snorts as he goes to grab some of my boxes like all this is just a normal morning. "I bet Harley and Dale got nasty with that cake and champagne."

"Seriously, dude?" I ask, willing him to shut the hell up.

He shrugs a shoulder. "What? I heard they're kinky."

"Why did Britt send you over here with my damn boxes?" I ask Krysta, who breaks the staring contest with Sticks to look over at me.

"For the same reason you intended to send him," she says,

hiking her thumb at Sticks. "She's avoiding you."

She grabs out another box, stacking it onto the one she had, and starts carrying it toward the house again.

I snort derisively, shaking my head.

"Why have you been avoiding me?" Sticks calls to her back.

She drops my boxes on the porch and turns to cut her gaze at all of us.

"I don't blame any of you for not considering crowd control as being an issue. It seriously doesn't sound like a threatening situation. I get it."

She starts walking back to the car, pulling on her sunglasses as she goes.

"But I realized something while you all sang and I was being trampled, and that's that I was with a bunch of people I barely knew. I was worried no one at all would care enough to look for me or even realize I was missing, and crawled my way to Britt, because I *knew* someone would come for her. She makes damn good life decisions and shows gratitude to people when they're thoughtful and caring."

She tosses out another one of my boxes into the yard.

"I, however, am a fucking flighty mess that just gets forgotten, and it's my own damn fault. Despite what you think, the Sterlings aren't assholes for not including me; I'm the asshole for never showing up. Britt isn't some little shiny trophy they wave around and program; she's a girl boss in charge of her own life."

She tosses another box a little harder.

"She's fucked up and deals with her shit the best she can, which is more than I can say for *any* of you. When you fuck a girl and ask for another's number the very next day, you're not entitled to a call back. You're entitled to being fucking ignored," she says, apparently no longer yelling at me as she cuts her gaze toward Sticks.

His rigid stance relaxes just a little, and his lips thin like he's finally catching on.

"That was just a random girl, and I asked for her number so she wouldn't realize I was blowing her off by walking away in the middle of her pick-up routine," he says like he finds Krysta cute for being jealous. "Girls can be overly dramatic when rejection is involved."

She rolls her eyes and tosses out another box.

"Doesn't even matter. No offense, but the bad boy rocker type who pockets a girl's numbers to prevent the hassle of turning her down is no longer my type. I want the type of guy who drives for hours to be there because he's worried about things like crowd control and he cares so much he acts a little crazy," she says to him, and then looks around at all of us again.

She tosses out my last box, and starts shutting all her doors.

"More importantly, I want to be the kind of girl who deserves a guy like that, so I'm concentrating on fixing my mess instead of expecting someone to swoop in and fix it for me."

She gets in, cranks her car, and rolls down her driver's side window.

"Have fun being so much better than everyone," she adds before spinning out in reverse and driving off in what must be a brand new Mercedes.

"I never realized she could be such a bitch," Randy says as he stares after her, then whistles as he looks down at all the boxes haphazardly lying around the small patch of yard we have.

"Fuck this," I say before going to my truck and driving toward Britt's.

The drive over is a blur of me processing Krysta's crazy ass rant.

Britt's walking out when I pull up, and her eyes widen in subtle surprise before she directs her focus toward her car and starts walking faster than she was.

I hop out of my truck and block her path just before she reaches the door.

When she releases a long breath and swings her gaze up at me, there's just deadness in her eyes. Like I'm already taking up too much of her time.

"Did I forget something or not pack it to your satisfaction?" she asks with a chillier tone than she's ever used with me.

It's not cold or cruel; it's just a pleasant, fake tone used for strangers. Even when she just knew me by reputation she didn't treat me like a stranger. I've taken that for granted until this moment.

"I have no idea how you packed it. I don't deserve this shit, Britt. I asked you to fucking date me, and you needed a side-panel with the Sterlings before committing to an answer. I'm not the bad guy," I remind her very seriously.

"I'm not assigning blame, and I'm sorry if it seems that way. Only four boxes have fragile items," she says as she tries to reach around me to open her door.

I step into her arm, and she jerks back like she's been burned before clearing her throat and staring directly at the ground.

"So just like that? I still don't know why you're doing this, and you're really going to keep acting like I'm the asshole for wanting to be with you. That's all I did, Britt."

She nods. "I know that's what you think. It's one of our many consequential differences. We see things from vastly different perspectives."

A humorless laugh comes out of me, because I seriously can't believe she's acting like this.

"Is it really that fucking terrible to consider an actual relationship with me, Britt?" I ask her seriously, feeling sick at my stomach for even being made to feel like I'm somehow less than—

"No," she says evenly.

Her eyes come up to meet mine.

"Then what's really the fucking problem?!" I ask loud enough to cause her to wince and step back.

She exhales, and I can see she's about to deliver some practiced fucking line.

"You celebrate how differently my mind works when you find it quirky and unimposing," she says very calmly, which…isn't what I was expecting. "Harley is grooming me to be her partner, because she sees the potential and admits I'm going to make her a lot more money. *One day*. But I'm not ready yet, so I'm paying my dues and working my way up. We'll be excellent partners, eventually—"

"Why the fuck are you talking about Harley right now?" I interrupt, for once finding myself unamused with a Britt Sterling tangent.

Her lips tighten, and she takes what appears to be a fortifying breath before continuing.

"I'm still working on my issues that you claim need no work. You tell me to embrace my weirdness, yet you expect me to be normal when it's inconvenient to you for me to be anything else," she says so seriously that I take a few steps to the side.

"Britt, that's not at all what I was saying. I just think you rely too much on the Sterlings and that entire group to tell you what to do."

She nods like she understands that. "Maybe I do. Or maybe I don't rely on their advice enough. Regardless, I still reserve the right to stay inside *my* comfort zone sometimes too. You won't even put on a suit for a fundraising event that I helped coordinate, yet expect me to change things I'm incapable of changing. Attending to conflict takes preparation. Like I've now had. You're too impassioned and strong-minded for me to contend with in an ill-prepared argument during an emotionally charged moment."

"Again, you make me sound like a dick, Britt. I've never been anything but good to you. What makes you think I won't work shit out? I just need you to talk to me about *us* instead of talking to everyone else first. It's not so much to ask."

"Statistically speaking, if there's this large of a communication barrier between us so early on, the probability of us having any sort of healthy relationship is substantially low. I think, under the circumstances, this should be our last exchange so that things don't escalate. It can only get worse from here."

She jerks open her door and climbs inside. She's the pinnacle of hot and cold.

"I'm sorry I wasn't ready for a relationship yet. But it was almost great. You were right about that," she says as she shuts the door and starts pulling out, never glancing at me again.

I watch her car until she takes the turn at the end of the road, and slowly walk back to my truck. Holy fucking hell.

Now I don't even know if I'm right or wrong, and I knew one thousand percent that I was right until this second.

I slap a hand to the door, staring down for a second as I shake my head.

My phone rings, and I answer as I climb inside.

"What?" I grind out, not even glancing to see who's calling.

"Hello to you too," Tag states dryly.

I groan as I crank my truck that makes a few ominous noises before it'll go into gear. If my damn engine explodes today, I wouldn't even be surprised.

"Really bad time, man," I say tightly as I finally get backed out of the driveway.

"I just got off the phone with your pathetic excuse for a manager, who called me to beg me to call Vince Jaggons before the band broke up."

"Tray hasn't been our manager for over a year," I state dismissively.

"How bad did you piss off everyone you shouldn't be pissing off?" he asks.

I punch the steering wheel at the stoplight and pull the phone away from my face as I take a few calming breaths.

"That bad, huh?" I hear him ask.

Lifting the phone back to my ear, I turn onto the next road before answering.

I can't bring myself to tell him that we made ourselves look like hot-tempered kids.

"I said some shit they probably didn't like very much, and was eventually escorted out by security. They may or may not be pressing charges for the glass door Sticks broke on his way out."

"Fuck's sake," Tag says under his breath.

He doesn't even know it was Vince Jaggons who took our spot. Well, not personally, but still…it feels personal.

"Since Dane can't give us our spot at Silk back, we're probably going to have to start over somewhere else with a new set of players. There's not much left here for us now," I state a little bitterly.

"Don't be extreme, Base. I can make some calls for you. Money makes bad memories go away really quickly for most of these guys, and—"

"I don't want you paying my way into a spot I earned, Tag. I appreciate the offer and all, but that's not how we're doing this, or we'll never feel like we earned it."

I hear the groan he tries to suppress, like he just can't understand why in the world I'd want to work for something he could *freely* give me.

"You get what you pay for, Tag. They'll pay it back in spades, and I'll—"

"Lose your soul and shit. I know the song and dance. Call me before you run off to find a new spot to start all over."

As soon as his call ends, Randy's ringing in. I press ignore and keep driving, clearing my head as much as possible before I pull up at my house.

My mom's car is in the driveway when I warily put on the brake, and my eyebrows hit my hairline as I push open the door. Mom's laughter inside the house confirms that this is really happening at the worst possible time.

Clearing my throat, I plaster on a smile and step inside. Her laughter dies the second she sees me, and pity wells up in her expression.

"Sorry, sweetie. I just heard about Britt. I know you were falling hard for—"

"I *really* don't want to talk about it right now," I cut in.

"But I do, so we should," she argues, causing me to quirk my eyebrow. "What? Did I raise you to think it's okay to tell people when they can and can't talk about things?"

The lightbulb goes on quickly.

"I see what you're doing," I tell her, pointing a finger as I back toward the door. Sticks makes an uncomfortable wiggle off the couch before stiffly walking out like he's trying to avoid getting in trouble too. "This is a little different than that situation. Which one of you dicks told her?"

"Not me," Sticks says as he shuts the door to his room.

Randy and Taylor both shake their heads before Taylor awkwardly exits like he can't get out fast enough.

Randy just grins as he pops a piece of candy into his mouth.

"How's it different?" Mom asks me.

"For one, it's actually none of your business," I remind her in the most respectful fucking tone I can muster, and she gives me the I'm-about-to-ground-your-ass-for-a-year look. "Tag called you, didn't he?"

"No. His wife did, because she's a damn fine woman who's worried about you. And I don't blame her for being worried after what I heard you idiots did after losing your spot on the—"

I don't hear what else she says, because I walk out and slam the door. I'm too pissed to talk to my mother right now, and I can't risk saying the wrong shit.

"You don't even see your hypocrisy, Base. It's growing by the day, because you just *think* you're being—"

I shut out her voice again as I start my loud truck. Ash called my fucking mother? This day needs to stop being this day.

I haul ass to Tag's house, and I don't even waste time shutting the door to my truck when I park. Without even thinking about it, jab the doorbell over and over. My fists clench and unclench, and I try to keep my temper in check, even as my jaw tics and my foot taps.

Ash is the one to open the door, and her eyes widen in surprise when she sees me.

"Base, what's—"

"You called my fucking mother because I broke up with Britt? You have *no* right," I tell her incredulously. "Do you see what you're all fucking doing to her?" I ask a little louder.

Her lips thin and she steps forward, causing me to step back as she shuts the door behind her and pulls out her phone. I'm almost worried she's calling the cops just because I'm pissed.

She holds up her phone, and my face slowly falls as I see a video of us inside that fashion place's office where we met with that stupid douche last night.

"My friend Bo owns that place," she goes on, fast forwarding the video to where I really lost my temper and acted like a pathetic kid throwing a tantrum, raking office shit off some woman's desk who doesn't even bat an eye in the video.

"She's not scared because she's seen Vince have a tantrum or two, in case you're wondering. I noticed you didn't seem to care if you scared her or not. You never even glanced at her," she carries on as my jaw tightens more.

"Three hours of intense arguing and him belittling us every single second of it was—"

"Something he was entitled to do, because he's paid his dues and deals with a man like Vince Jaggons day in and day out. You're nobody to him. Just like this woman here is nobody to you."

She fast forwards again, and it stops at the front desk when security is wrangling me out the door. Then you see Sticks kick the damn glass, sending huge cracks all over it before he kicks it again and again.

I bristle, looking away as I slowly nod, getting the point.

"You're only not in handcuffs because Bo knows you're not usually violent guys. She knows you wouldn't hurt any of her staff, just as her staff also fortunately knew. She's lived her life around passionate, intense, temperamental artists, and compared to some of the tantrums she's seen, this was just sad and laughable to her. You can pay me back for the damages whenever you can," she continues.

I clear my throat as I take another step back, and another.

"Yeah," I say a little quieter. "Sorry."

"I thought Honey Bee could help out. Yes, I brought up the split-decision breakup with Britt, since you went to see her directly after this…while you were still so worked up and defensive and ready to take it out on anyone close by. Not Britt, but possibly her family—the ones you actively avoid and publicly talk shit about. Those good people who never say anything negative about you and ignore what they hear, passing it off as possible bullshit. Bullshit rolls right off them, because they deal with it day in and day out from plenty of other people already. They've taught Britt the tools of dealing with the same bullshit, in case you're wondering. Dane started the 'favor' system to teach her how to ask for help, for fuck's sake, Base. She needs a minute sometimes, because she's different."

She tilts her head, eyes glistening just barely. I want to put my head in the sand right now. Literally.

I swallow thickly, not speaking.

"They're not even upset at you for not showing up on an important night like last night—a night when her Sterling name went on a massive check that's guaranteed to give so many graduating foster children a new goal. A new scholarship program specifically designed for them, Base. This is something dear to her, because she doesn't feel like she's the only one who deserves to be saved."

My eyes flutter shut, and I hold back my own groan.

"You didn't even ask what event it was, did you?" she asks, already knowing the answer. "Otherwise, you wouldn't have told her that black-tie events just *aren't your thing.*"

When I shove both my hands in my pockets, just staring at nothing in particular, she releases a tired breath.

"You didn't say anything to Tag, I'm guessing, based on the conversation I had with him."

"Of course not. He'd feel responsible and take all the blame, because that's the amazing guy he is. I called your mom because I know you're actually a good guy, Base. Just as you said, I have no right to act like I know you well enough to say anything to you."

I snort, even though it's a weak attempt at being petulant at this point.

"Let me guess. You look at me and see Tag, and you want me to live up to his potential," I say tightly, rolling my eyes.

Never pegged her for the meddling saint type.

"Absolutely not. Tag's heart is twice the size of yours, and he worked damn hard to keep it guarded because it breaks twice as hard too," she states a little sourly as she arches a condescending eyebrow at me. "He broke his own shit when he was pissed. Not someone else's," she adds with a small smile.

She takes a step toward me, putting her phone away.

"I don't look at you and see Tag. I look at you and I see *me*. And I'm trying to get out in front of the dominoes before they fall all the way down, because that's when you start hurting the people around you just because you're working *so hard* to defend your actions. You reassure yourself that you're awesome, because you're really insecure and trying to make it sound as though you're as confident as the world expects you to be. Otherwise you're weak and pathetic. I know this song and dance. It's not a crime to be young and naïve. It makes you normal. And it's typical to think you're right. About *everything* in life. It'll take years before you realize how stupid you really are. I don't want you to burn people who don't deserve to be burned, because I know you'll spend a long time regretting it."

She puts her hand on my shoulder, patting it once.

"Sorry I called your mom on you like you're all a bunch of kids or something. To be fair, I panicked when I saw that video."

She turns and walks back toward the door, hesitating when her hand is hovering over the doorknob.

She starts to turn around…and stops…and starts again.

"If you're struggling with whether or not you can say something, you may as well just go ahead at this point, Ash," I tell her quietly.

She groans a little as she turns around.

"She saved you a piece of cake," she says like that's supposed to make sense. "She was going to make sure you tried something from her event and liked it. She's not a doormat for the Sterlings. She's not a doormat for you. She's not a doormat at all. Personally, I think you're being a little too prideful. Careful. They warn you about the fall. They don't tell you that you don't see it coming."

She walks in after that. I stare at the door as it shuts, not having a response ready for once.

I scrub a hand over my face and then bite down on my fist as I hold back the yell on the tip of my tongue, my chest rising and falling rapidly as I keep myself in check.

My eyes burn as I yank my truck door open, hearing my phone chime with an alert.

It's been a while since the gossip columns have even mentioned Britt, since we've kept things as low key as possible.

I'm almost scared to look, but I finally click the button and voila. There's the proof I need to see just how wrong I was.

She was steadfast and stoic today, absent of all emotion.

But in this fifteen second clip, she's standing under the large pavilion just in front of the building. Her hair is completely soaked, along with her dress, and she's barefoot. She's just staring down at a piece of fucking chocolate cake and a bottle of champagne.

Champagne and cake—like what was smeared all over the interior of Harley's car.

I barely glimpse Harley coming into the frame as her car comes into the final seconds, and then the clip starts over.

The sick feeling in my stomach forces me to bend over, and my head bumps the steering wheel as I try to think of what the fuck to do.

There is only a single line captioning the clip: ***It looks like our girl is single again.***

Randy tries calling again, likely because my mother is still there, but I ignore it and start driving like hell away from Tag's home and toward Britt's office.

That's when I flip on the radio, and my eyes go directly to it, because I hear it playing one of our newest songs, but that's not us singing and playing it.

A horn blares, and my eyes come up in time to see I'm on the wrong side of the road, and I narrowly jerk the wheel in time to miss the black car by inches.

My heart is still pounding the base of my throat, and my hands are shaking, as I straighten my truck out on the road.

"Worst fucking day of my life," I mutter as I juggle my phone and answer Randy's call.

"Thank fuck," he says like he's panicking. "They're playing—"

"Ralphy singing our fucking song on the radio. I know. Deal with it. I'm in the middle of something right now."

I hang up on him and try calling Britt, but it goes straight to voicemail. I don't even bother finding a parking spot as I pull up right in front of her office building.

Harley is walking out the doors just as I hop out of my truck, and she groans as she pinches the bridge of her nose.

"She's not here, Base," she tells me. "She's at the airport."

"Text me the information," I say as I hurry back to my truck."

"Base, don't—"

I slam the door and drive like hell to the airport. I'm really fucking thankful that Harley follows through with texting me the information, and at every stoplight, I pull up my phone and work on finding the cheapest ticket I can—until the entire session times out.

Then I call Randy.

He answers in a panicky tone. "Sticks is on the phone with the radio station, but they're saying it's our word against his. Man, have you got *any* proof—"

"I need you buy me a plane ticket and send it to my email. The cheapest one you can. And I need it in like five minutes or less," I tell him as I whirl into a parking spot.

"I'm assuming this is about Britt, and she's more important than the song right now. Got it," he says through a groan. "It's bad when I'm freaking out worse about this shit than you are. It's starting to scare me," he gripes.

"Stop talking to me and order the—"

"Already did and sent. You're welcome. Now I have to intercept Sticks and Taylor before they get us banned from the radio. This isn't me, Base. This is what you—"

I hang up again, quickly pulling up my email, as I run toward security…

I stop when I see the line wrapping around, and I curse as I take my spot, wondering how quickly airport security would pounce and probe me like a suspected terrorist if I started shoving my way to the front of the long fucking line.

Everyone is casting me wary glances, and I smile tightly.

"They're about to start boarding," I say in deflection, still worrying about that probing thing.

Not only is it fucking terrifying, it'll also probably take a really long time to finish, and Britt will probably be gone.

A text from Harley has my immediate attention.

HARLEY: They'll stall her for another ten minutes, but then they have to take off to keep the airport schedule.

My phone rings, and I answer when I see it's Randy.

"Did you stop her? Was it just like the movies? Are you on your way home to solve this crisis now?" The questions come at a spitfire pace.

"I'm still in the damn security line, so no, Randy, it's not like the fucking movies," I tell him as I get closer.

"Dammit," he says. "Someone get the door and give me the phone. Neither of you—"

I hang up, and finally start making my way through security, not being one damn bit impatient or rude, avoiding the probe.

Then I sprint hardcore like every fucking cliché movie involving an airport that there ever was.

I almost trip over my feet when I see her in a nearly bare section, tucking her hair behind her ear as she types something onto her phone.

As if she feels me staring at her, her eyes lift and widen, and my feet start moving on their own, propelling me toward her.

"I'm sorry," I tell her as I grab her at the waist and crush my lips to hers.

She kisses me back, her fingers tangling in my hair as she makes some pained noise. She pulls me closer and leans into me, before she abruptly pushes back. I can genuinely feel the fallout of her whiplash emotions.

I'm forced to break the kiss as she shakes her head, lips thinning.

"No," she says, pushing her hand to my chest.

"I realize I'm messing shit up right now, Britt. But I don't want to fuck this up—*us*. You're literally all that fucking matters," I tell her seriously as I step into her.

Her fingers squeeze against my chest, but I feel her resolve wavering, so I keep talking.

"I'm sorry I snapped. I'm sorry I took shit out on you. *We* can talk this out. It's not a big deal—"

"I don't want to do this right now," she says quietly.

"How long are you going to be gone?" I ask, my jaw ticking.

"I volunteered to help Harley scout some venues so she wouldn't have to be gone for three weeks," she answers, like she's summing up all the questions I could follow up with using as few words as possible.

"Then we really need to do this now, Britt," I say as she just continues to keep that distance. "If you *want* to do this, I'm all in. I'll get a real job. I'll put on a fucking tie when you want. All the issues you have, I'll fix them right now."

She gives me an exhausted look as tears brim her eyes, and her hold gets looser as I step closer, meeting less and less resistance. My hand slides up her back, easing into her hair, as she leans her head back to keep her eyes locked onto mine.

"Let's do this for real," I say as I lean down, brushing my lips to hers. "Let's do this your way."

She turns her head abruptly before angrily biting out, *"No."*

There's silence for a minute as she remains rigid against me, and my mouth opens and closes a few times as I release her and step back.

"Ms. Sterling, we're ready for you now," someone says to her as my hands fall to my sides.

She quickly turns and walks away, following him, and never once turns around as she goes.

I run a hand through my hair as I turn around and numbly stumble my way through the airport, finding it a hell of a lot easier to leave than enter.

Just as I drop to a bench near the exit, I see my truck going by, being pulled by a tow truck.

A painful, humorless laugh bubbles out of me, and my jaw wavers as I lift my phone, clearing my throat as my eyes start to burn.

Randy doesn't answer.

Sticks doesn't answer.

Taylor doesn't answer.

My own mother doesn't answer.

I almost throw my phone, but stop myself just in time, exhaling as I lean over and dial the next number on the list.

"I hope you're not calling to say you're moving cities," Tag says by way of answering.

"Actually," I say, letting my eyes flutter shut as it all presses down on me, "I was hoping you could give me a ride."

I hear keys jingling immediately, and it makes me feel even worse about how quick he is to help.

"Just tell me where to go."

Chapter 35

BASE

The silent car ride ends as Tag pulls up to the curb, and I stare at the house instead of looking at him.

"Thanks," I tell him, feeling pathetic at this point.

"I wasn't doing anything productive, so don't worry about it," he tells me.

I look over, catching a glimpse of Ash's name on the screen, as he smiles and texts something.

Feeling like I should probably say more, but having no fucking idea what to say, I just push open the door and get out.

He drives off as I head inside, only to be cornered by Randy as he grabs the front of my shirt and looks around. He then jerks the door open and looks around, still holding onto the front of my shirt.

"What the fuck?" I ask him, just wanting to get to my fucking room so I can collapse in peace.

He glares at me. "No Britt means a really pissy Base Masters. Put. That. Shit. On. Pause," he says, annunciating each word as my brow furrows.

Sticks stumbles into the room, his eyes widening, and Taylor comes in right behind him.

I hear my mother's faint laughter from somewhere down the hall, coupled with a masculine one right behind it.

"Put it on pause," Randy says in his critical tone *again*, pointing a finger in my face.

Then he shoves me forward, and Sticks practically drags me

down the hall. I stumble back when I spot Vince motherfucking Jaggons having tea with my damn mother like there's a Sunday brunch going on in our living room.

Vince looks up, eyes catching my wide ones, and smirks like he's been waiting for the look on my face. I haven't disappointed, it seems.

"Ah, so the fourth is here. I'll let you boys catch him up while I finish up my tea with Honey Bee," he says before waving us off, eyes laughing at me before he turns back to my mother.

Mom's grin stays fixed on her face as she carries on talking to him like they're old friends.

Sticks starts dragging me away, while my mind tries to catch up to what the hell is going on right now.

I'm pulled into the practice room, and Taylor locks the door behind him, sealing the four of us in.

"What the hell?" I finally ask, dropping to a chair because I'm too fucking exhausted to keep standing at this point.

"We don't know why he's here," Taylor tells me, wringing his hands. "Maybe because one of you idiots had to shatter that door, and his freaking daughter owns that building."

I scrub my face with both hands, trying to focus on this instead of Britt, because I need to be alone for that.

Randy gestures toward the door. "We tried asking him, but Taylor can't seem to speak in the presence of rock royalty, Sticks can't stop gushing for five seconds, and I'm an unrepentant fan boy. No one's even mad anymore that he stole the spot for some unknown, shitty band his label represents. It's a hot, pathetic mess."

Sticks holds up his hands when I shoot a look at him.

"I'm trying to think why we ever thought we deserved an audience with him last night, but I'm struggling now. It all seems petty now that he's actually here, and you're going to have to do the talking," Sticks says like he's dumbfounded.

Taylor opens the door, peering around the corner like he's trying to hear Vince's voice.

"Let's just hear what he has to say before we say anything at all," I mutter, not an ounce of fight left in me, because I don't even know why I'm fighting.

We file into the room just as Vince lowers his empty cup to the table. Mom's eyes are sparkling like he's been charming the hell out of her.

Vince crosses his legs as we take a seat in front of him, and he lounges on the couch like he couldn't be more comfortable.

"Honey Bee is far more charming than the lot of you spoiled, entitled little brats," he says, making this day as imperfect as it can possibly be, because in this moment, I find myself agreeing with him.

Mom nods like she completely agrees as well.

"I feel eight," Randy stage whispers to me.

"Honey Bee, could you give me a moment to speak with the boys?" Vince asks her like this is a mom-and-pop routine, and Mom stands like she's gloating as she prisses her way out.

Sticks slumps down next to me, and we all just sort of stare at him.

"I know you think you know how this *business* is ran, because you've told the entire west coast as much," he continues, voice dripping with sarcasm.

Sticks slinks down farther on the couch, and so do I.

"The problem is, you say the words, yet can't understand at the end of the day this *is* a *business.* If you don't do business, you're just a singer. Nothing wrong with that, but you keep saying you're trying to break into the *business.*"

He leans back, propping both arms up on the back of the couch as he studies us one by one.

"I've never felt more intimidated in all my life," Randy whispers again.

"The problem is you're a half-chiseled diamond who declares you're polished and ready when you're simply not. You're certainly talented enough to be on everyone's radar, but we, *the businessmen*, know the type."

He clicks his tongue, and directs his sole attention on me.

"Self-righteous, arrogant, preachy, know-it-alls who think they're the most original thing rock-and-roll has ever seen," he adds, lips twitching in a smile.

"The attitude is setting you back, because you have to be humbled. Let's face it, it'd take someone like *me* to humble you enough to make you realize just how very differently things work when you're on the other side. You learn artists, see their limitations, and know which ones will slowly kill their futures away…"

He smirks as he pointedly looks at us.

"It's an industry full of nauseating clichés."

Randy starts fanning himself with his shirt and breaking out into red patches.

"You don't take special interest in someone unless you really want to put in the work. And to put in the work, you need a personal attachment and reason to do so."

He glances over all four of us again.

"Either people don't know or care about my daughters, or they don't think *I* care about them. The truth is, I care about them very much. I rarely ever tell them *no* when they really want something," he continues on, rambling at this point, since this doesn't seem relevant.

"Congratulations," he says as he claps his hands together. "You got my daughter's vote. This is a one-time offer, and don't get too excited. I'm not throwing you out for instant stardom, but we're going to slap together a quick foundation to build on," he goes on.

Randy gets up and runs out of the room, screaming like the kid on Home Alone, and Vince just smirks like he expected that to happen.

"I don't particularly like you, so don't make this more difficult than it has to be. I don't answer to you; you answer to me. I don't work for you; you work for me," Vince adds as though it's an inconvenience to keep talking about this.

"Why would your daughter do us any favors?" Sticks asks in a quiet voice.

"Oh, she didn't do it for you. She has a friend she cares about named Britt, who happens to think you just need the right mentor to advise you. I don't tell my girls *no* very often when they really want something. It's rare they need me at all. Hence the reason you're a very *lucky* group of individuals."

I say nothing, just rubbing my hands together, trying to figure out one simple reason Britt would do this.

"You *don't* earn your way into a chance like this," he continues. "It simply just doesn't happen. Either you become an internet sensation—*by luck*—or you luck your way into another spot, or you get lucky enough to have the right family member or friend in the correct, pivotal position at the right moment in time. It takes both hard work *and* luck to hit the rest of the rungs on the ladder just right."

My eyes come up to meet his as he leans forward, propping his elbows on his knees.

"To get what you want, you have to meet me halfway; otherwise, I'll stop caring," he goes on. "I'll find someone else who will be worth my own personal attention. I can't build your career on my own, and even if I could, I wouldn't."

Randy comes barging back in, breathing in and out of a brown paper bag, still breaking out into hives.

"I like him. He gets how *lucky* you all are," Vince goes on, hiking a thumb toward Randy, while stomping on the shambles of our pride.

To be fair, we wrecked our pride when we acted like fools.

"I'm sorry about your daughter's door," Sticks says in the lamest possible way he can.

"If that's all the damage you do once you're on my dime, then you'll be a damn cheap date," Vince chirps, pulling up a pair of reading glasses and putting them on.

"I'm old school, so all this gets put on paper and on digital. This is just a small piece of the paperwork to come, but you need to pack your shit and be ready to ride out tomorrow. This is just to get things rolling so you can go on the mediocre section of the payroll," he continues.

"Britt asked you to mentor us?" I cut in, my eyes meeting his again.

"Yes. And as your mentor, I'm trying to tell you what you'll need to do to start building your career. My platform only gets you so far. You need to start building your own to stack on top of mine, and you'll be gone for three months to jumpstart things."

"This…this is who we're opening for?" Sticks asks as his mouth opens and closes a few times. "W-why?"

"Because they complement your sound, but they're too flashy for you to steal the show from. It's a good way to build some good ties with them, and to learn from them, and to prepare for the next headliner you'll tour with and open for. It's not the ground floor, and it's still a long way from the top, but it's a damn good spot to have," Vince says like this is tedious to him.

Randy's breathing gets a little disconcerting just before he collapses to the ground like a fainting goat.

"Up his practice time. He's not on the same level as the rest of you," Vince points out, barely batting an eye at him.

I'm sure he's seen many grown men faint before. *He's a legend.* Great, now I'm a fucking fab boy too.

"Why would Britt tell you to mentor us?" I ask him.

He plucks a flower from the vase my mother must have assembled when she brought out tea, and he hands it to me. Even though I'm confused as hell, I take it.

"Lesson number one: I will never involve myself in your personal relationships. I'll give you a fucking flower to pull petals from and ask questions such as *'Does she love me? Does she not?'* if you ask for relationship advice."

He gives me a dry look, and I drop the flower back to table, getting the point. I already feel stupid, and now I feel like he thinks I was asking for relationship advice.

Defeated, I drop back, content to shut up and just listen. It gets quiet for a few seconds.

"I need your head right for this," Vince tells me as he stares at me very deliberately and rolls his eyes. "Britt Sterling is shadowing a powerful businesswoman because she wants to one day be a powerful businesswoman," he states flatly, like he's throwing me this one bone.

He gestures between us.

"It's only natural that she'd suggest the same for you, because she's already moved beyond the basic fundamentals of how to conduct smart business," he concludes before gesturing at the blanks we need to sign or initial after we finish reading. "And she's also smart enough to know that what you're currently shooting for is a one-in-a-million opportunity that also requires a hell of a lot of unpredictable luck to go along with your talent."

I nod slowly, letting that settle in, remembering hearing her talk about how *lucky* she was that Harley came to Sterling Shore just as she was looking into internships.

Sticks takes over asking questions about what venues we're going to, and all the important shit I need to be paying attention to.

My mind stays mostly on Britt. How she panicked.

She started trying to tell me what the issues were, and couldn't get it worded the way she wanted. She was trying to fix *my* problems instead of engaging in the conflict, doing all she could to deflect, and I talked over her.

"If I'm not even her friend, then it wouldn't matter if I was pissed or not," I say more to myself than anyone else.

Either no one hears it or no one cares, and I scrub a hand over my face, forcing myself to focus as I grab the pen and start signing.

"You really should read shit before signing it," Vince gripes.

I start to argue, but instead, I lift the damn paper and begin reading it word for word.

"Well, maybe this won't be quite so unbearable," Vince chirps like he's amused.

"We have one problem," Sticks says as I continue reading. "Someone jacked one of our new songs, and now I don't think we can use it. It's one of our—"

"Oh, I know. We're going to use that to start laying your foundation. Hence the reason we're starting now," Vince interrupts. "I wanted to make you sweat it out a little longer, but opportunity is knocking."

My eyes come up as my brow furrows, while he just grins.

Mom comes back in with some more tea, and Vince shoots her a charming expression.

"I was just about to ask if you'd made more."

She fucking giggles as she pours him a cup, and he gestures for her to join us. She sits down with a foot of space between them, so I drop my eyes back to the paper.

"I'm not going to be your damn manager, so I'll get you one I personally trust to *manage* you. You do your part not to make their life a living hell," Vince adds as I resume reading.

"This is the part where you boys say *'yes, sir,'*" Mom chimes in.

"Yes, sir," we state in unison.

"Yes, *sssir,"* Randy says from the ground, groaning as he rouses from his faint.

"Well, then. So much easier than expected. I think it's the effect of your presence, Honey Bee. Maybe you should join them on the road," Vince carries on as I flip the page and continue.

"Artists are fun and exciting on the highs, but I'd rather not be around for the lows," Mom says on a long sigh, eyes going to mine. "I try too hard to fix them."

"Do you want a hammer to finish driving in the nail? It's been a really rough day," I tell her.

Her expression changes when she studies me, and she clears her throat as she busies herself with the tea again.

"Studio time will happen on the road. Fortunately for you, my own Sterling Shore based studio will be finished by the time you return, and we can capitalize on this scandal. In fact, we'll fan the flames to spread the smoke as far and wide as we can," he goes on.

"Scandal?" Mom asks, sounding a little wary.

I finish reading and finally start signing again.

"Ralphy is the nephew of a rock legend. Said rock legend was accused, more than once, of stealing songs—one of which was one of my own when I was just starting out. It's just the sort of buzz we need, because these boys make those look like amateurs. And that legend is a drunken has-been, whereas I am a very powerful businessman," he explains, eyes solely on my mother as she turns into a bit of a puddle. "I know how to deal with this now."

She nods like she has all the trust in the world, and he turns his attention back to us.

"This *scandal* will be what the public will think drew me to you—not Britt Sterling. Meanwhile, I get to vicariously seize a victory once stolen from me. You'll have to owe Britt and my daughter in private, because it's too easy to fade quickly in the sea of clichés with something people will confuse with a *sell-out* start," Vince says as Sticks plucks the pen from my hand. "You need to punch your way into this world to really stand out," he adds. "This happens to create the perfect *punch.*"

It's obvious none of us have it in us to turn down a mentorship from *the* Vince Jaggons. I don't have enough pride left to even fucking bother counting the ways this makes me a hypocrite.

"How did you get us a spot so quickly on this tour?" Sticks asks as Randy scrambles to sign.

Vince stands, shrugging a shoulder. "I took the spot from someone else," he answers with a pointed look.

Taylor just remains silent as he gawks at Vince, signing on the proverbial dotted-line. Vince, the diabolical man before us, has officially schooled us in our own living room.

"Choir boys have a problem with that sort of thing, which is why they sing different music," he adds with a smirk. "Congratulations. Now that you're part of the *business*, I'll let you in on a little secret."

He levels me with a look.

"The music is always yours, no matter if you're the only one who likes it. The faith in your music doesn't need to waver just because it doesn't sell. You have to really fucking love it to push through the rough times and stay relevant. The only time this business truly steals your soul…is when you forget that it's a fucking business."

With that, a random man comes running in out of no-damn-where, and signs the blanks for a notary, before picking it all up and running out.

"See you boys tomorrow. We have a lot of work to do. I need to make a few calls to ensure they don't play their new most requested song in Sterling Shore, because it belongs to *my* artists. Make sure you look pretty when you leave, since I plan to stage a paparazzi mob. Your faces will be your best assets for a while," he adds before turning and walking out, his leather pants creaking as he goes.

The room goes completely silent until Sticks releases a long breath and drops back.

"That just happened, right? I mean, things like that don't happen, but that still happened," Sticks says like he's uncertain and needs someone else to agree with him.

I sit all the way back, staring at the tea cup the rock legend left behind.

"I don't even know what the last half of that meant, but that may be the single most amazing moment of my entire life," Randy says as he just stares at the door.

Mom fans herself as she grins. "Now *that's* a man. I may have formed a different opinion about artists if I'd met him in my wilder days," she overshares.

"Sitting right here," I remind her.

She nods. "I know. I'd have been perfect for him back then. Artists are free spirits. He said that's why he and his daughters' mother didn't work out—two free spirits. I could have learned to be his anchor," she goes on.

I lift my head, studying her as she glances back over at me, giving me a tight smile.

"I'd say let's celebrate with champagne, but you look like you're hurting too much for that right now. This is happening, Base. Differently than planned, but it's happening all the same," she goes on. "It's okay to celebrate."

I clear my throat and nod before I stand.

"Actually, I think I'm going to put some words to some music," I tell her as I walk out.

"I'm going to go fucking practice until my fingers start to hurt," Randy says as he scrambles by me, practically knocking me out of the way.

"Yeah, I'll skip the champagne for now, Ms. Bee, but I'll take you up on it another time," Sticks calls as I hear the familiar clanking of drumsticks.

I head into my room, hearing Taylor suddenly burst out a loud, *"Whoooooooooooooo!"*

I lift my guitar, eyes flicking to the mirror, before I hit the first note.

Sticks pokes his head inside the door before stepping in, and he leans against it as he twirls a drumstick between his fingers.

"What?" I ask, tuning the strings.

"We spent our whole lives trying to get to this step, and spent five minutes changing the entire course of our lives because your girl called in a favor. I'd like to hate myself for it, but it feels too fucking stupid to walk away from something this rare," he says.

I nod, completely getting it. "Suck it up. No one would pass it up, and they'd be lying if they said they would. If it pans out, we've achieved the goal, and we'll sure as fuck earn it."

He makes a snort, his lips kicking up in a grin on one side.

"You said we'd make new goals when we made it through this one—to keep us from feeling like we've hit our peak. This one was supposed to take a lot longer, even after we got our foot in the door."

I nod slowly.

"What's the new goal?"

"Three months," I answer without hesitation.

"Three months what?" he asks.

I glance up. "We do whatever in the hell Vince fucking Jaggons himself tells us to do for three months. We'll see where that gets us, while we just focus on making the music right," I answer.

His grin steadily grows.

"After that?" he asks.

"You have three months to figure that out. Because that's when I get selfish and go for the girl," I tell him as I scoot back on the bed. "I have three months to figure out a way how to be the guy who fucking deserves the girl who gets back at him by hand-delivering his fucking dream in a way he couldn't possibly refuse. She walked away at the airport because she was already in the process of fixing me."

I have to clear my throat again, and he clanks his drumsticks together on accident.

"Good luck with that. You're Britt Sterling's first love and now her first heartbreak," he reminds me, sounding a little annoyed with me. "Wards of the state usually have strong abandonment issues."

"I'll take all the luck I can get, but I do have a plan," I assure him as I start toying with a new melody that's playing in my head.

"You're not going to break into her house and take pictures of her sleeping, are you? I doubt she'd find it cute anymore," he cautions.

I glare over at him.

"I'm not an idiot."

"That's debatable," he's quick to point out.

I don't even argue with that.

Chapter 36

3 months later…

BRITT

"I still don't see why you had to cut holes in the boobs of the Girl Boss shirt," Harley is stating in a tone can only be labeled as exasperation, while Bo helps me lay out the leather strips.

"She's teaching me to pattern, and I'm breaking it down into pieces so that it's easier to recreate on my own. It's how I learn things," I remind her. "And it's one of my least favorite shirts."

"*I* bought you that shirt," Harley reminds me.

Bo coughs over a laugh. Why do people think that disguises the laughter?

Harley shoots her a look before returning her attention to me.

"I know you bought it for me exactly one year and fourteen days ago. I still had a hymen back then. I'm a woman now. And I've never been anyone's boss."

"Shocking, considering you're sporting elf ears like it's a life choice and wearing a shirt with holes for boobs. Nice bra, though," Bora—Bo's twin—says from the corner as she idly flips through her phone. "There really is a market for this real-life game clothing design. Nerds pay good money for authentic—"

"Our plate is too full to add a new line right now," Bo interrupts.

Harley groans. "It's supposed to be an empowering message, Britt. It's not literal," she says as Bora and Bo argue about adopting a new line.

"I think a more appropriate title for me would be Woman Boss In Training," I add.

Harley opens her mouth, but Bora walks by, her eyes back on her phone, as she says, "I'm going to go see if that's trademarked, and if not, I'm stealing it."

Bo rolls her eyes, and Harley shakes her head as I wiggle out of my shorts, preparing to try on the skirt I've deconstructed.

"They're in here," Bora says as she swings open the door, her eyes wide and her smile huge as she does so. "I found something pretty," she adds as…my stomach jumps up to my throat.

Base Masters.

Base…Masters.

He steps through the doorway in a pair of faded, worn jeans and a black T-shirt with some sports logo on it. My mind can't even process enough to absorb all the details, because it's Base Masters.

Why is he here? Is he here for me?

I get a little dizzy.

His dark hair is a little shorter, but his smile is just as cocky as I remember it. However, his smile is trained on Bo instead of me.

"Hey, I was wondering if I could talk to you for a minute," he says as I completely freeze in place, irrationally hoping against all odds he does not notice me.

"Of course," Bo says like she's confused, darting a worried look over at me.

I wish I could have asked her not to do that. Her gaze causes his to follow, and his smile slowly spreads when his eyes land on me. He completely turns his body, and I sense there's a deliberateness to the way he lets his gaze drop and really take in the rather inconvenient way I'm exposed.

"Hey, Britt," he says so casually.

It's hard to pretend that the last time we saw each other I wasn't walking away in tears as I ran away for three weeks to grieve a healthy amount of time in private, while simultaneously being helpful to Harley.

"Hi." It's the only word that will leave my lips, and it's as flat as I can keep it.

He glances from me to the strips of leather and back to me.

"Learning to make your own costumes by hand?" he guesses too easily, given the severe lack of details he has.

I nod, locking my knees into place when it feels like they're trying to fail me.

"So this is what you do when you're not locked in a room with me during every unoccupied moment," he adds, throwing a surprising shift in the conversation.

"Among other things," I say without really thinking about it. "C-congratulations on the tour. I heard it did well."

He nods slowly. "We'll talk about that later. I can see you're busy right now."

Talk about it later? *No. No.* I can't talk about anything at all later with him. It's clear, given my natural response and the inane fluttering in my stomach, that he's still going to be a very large issue for me.

"No need," I assure him. "I kept up. I follow your pages, and Vince's too. And where I can, I even have my notifications set to alert me about when you post—"

Harley makes a slicing motion over her throat that is a clear signal for me to stop talking.

I swallow the rest of my words.

His grin just grows. "Are you free for dinner tonight?"

"Nope," I say without hesitation. "I have a date."

He nods, still smiling.

"Okay then. I'll just see you when I see you."

He's back? He's not supposed to be back. They're…they're…they're supposed to go to where Vince lives, and I can't even think of where that is because my brain hurts so much right now.

"Bye, Britt," he tells me, and I just hold a hand up, standing awkwardly in place as he backs out.

Bo follows him, shrugging at me when I cast what I can only assume must be a panicked look at her.

The door shuts behind her, and I realize I've been holding my breath when I release the harsh one that's been trapped. It's painful when I suck in fresh air.

"Ah, hell," Harley says on a sigh as she looks over at me.

"If someone who looks like *that* is passed over because you have a date, can I at least see a picture of this guy you're going out with? I'll regrow my hymen if that's what it takes to be you right now," Bora states dryly.

"That's a physical impossibility, and I no longer have a hymen in the sense that you're referring," I tell her as I shakily lift my phone, pulling up the student website and finding Maxwell's picture to show her.

Bora's face falls when she examines it. "He must be hung like horse."

Harley just shakes her head and covers her face.

"It's a first date, so I wouldn't know. I'm currently moving into the phase of my life where it'd be healthy to form a sexual relationship with a partner who can also be a friend outside of my comfort zone."

"This guy isn't far from moving on to post grad work, Britt. He's right inside your comfort zone," Harley interrupts.

I don't say anything as I quickly start pulling on clothes that cover me, my cognitive functions slowly recovering.

"Oh, so the pretty guy with the bad boy grin left you with some serious heartbreak. Got it. Been there," Bora says as though the universe makes sense again before she walks out.

"He was supposed to be mad at me," I remind Harley very quietly.

"Yeah, you were such a bitch," she agrees with a dry tone.

The door opens, and Bo walks back in with a small grin on her face.

"What was that about?" Harley asks her.

"He was just apologizing to my staff for his outburst before he left for their tour," she says. "And the rest of them were waiting out there to apologize to me as well. Then they all thanked me. I guess the tour was good for them."

"Their social media following has steadily increased, and has had a lot of big jumps after the performances. And all the buzz generated about their start is still drawing attention. I've been assured it's a good upswing for them," I state idly as I busy my shaky hands.

When I look back up, they're both staring at me.

"You realize you're not over him," Bo says after a moment.

"I'm aware. I adopted the out-of-sight, out-of-mind philosophy, since it seemed to be the most effective tool," I tell her as I drop to a chair.

"How's that working out?" Harley asks.

"Not so well, since I just had to see him," I tell her, wondering why that isn't obvious.

She just blinks a few times before swinging her gaze to Bo.

"I'm sure he's only here for a limited amount of time. I need to know how to braid the leather tighter," I say as I start working on a set.

Bo comes to help me, as Harley leans in closer, the way she does when she tries to talk about Base. I think she believes talking about him quieter makes it less painful to do.

"They've started playing one of his new songs a lot, and it's sort of about a guy who really loved a girl."

I nod. "I know. I've heard it. But when he writes, he never writes honestly. He tells the story of what may have been. Never what actually was," I explain distractedly as I catalogue Bo's hand movements.

"Dad has a custom studio in Sterling Shore. It's possible they'll record their full album here," Bo says like she's poking more metaphorical holes in my once-effective coping mechanism.

"He showed no outward jealousy about my date for tonight, and followed up with no questions, so one can reason he's moved on and just wanted to find closure on a friendlier note," I tell them both when they continue to stare at me.

"But what if—"

I interrupt Harley's hypothetical what-if, because she always has one when she's trying to make me see her point. Today is not a day to compromise.

"If he wants more, I'll refer to the relationship chart that will remind me how impossible it is for us to work out," I remind her.

"Relationship chart?" Bo asks in confusion.

"The chart that demonstrates the fact there's no healthy way for the two of them to have a relationship, even though people can't be broken into categories. We have emotions that trump issues. The human element and all," Harley says pointedly at me.

"I need to urinate."

I stand abruptly and go to the bathroom, shut the door, and…slowly slide down the wall until I'm sitting in the floor, my eyes closing as one silly tear rolls down my cheek.

Out of sight. Out of mind.

It's worked fine. Sterling Shore isn't little. We went a long time without running into each other, despite the many people we had in common. It's reasonable to believe we won't unintentionally cross paths again.

"Britt, come on. I'll drop you off after I hit the kinky store," Harley says after she knocks on the door.

I wipe away the tear, check the mirror, and take a breath before I walk out.

My memory starts working against me as it pieces together

every frame of just how good and happy Base looked.

Harley, fortunately, doesn't mention Base again as she talks about everything else on the drive to the adult novelty store she frequents.

I focus on the store and not on the image of Base that is frozen inside my mind.

I follow her in, but I veer to the right when I spot an odd contraption made of leather. I study it for only a moment when I hear familiar laughter.

Spotting Maverick and Corbin at the register, likely making a dirty joke about their purchases, I walk toward them.

Then I back up and stare at the *very* large, thick, suction-cup dildo designed for sticking to floors or walls. The diagram shows a woman doing the splits to use it.

I pick it up and carry it with me, catching them just before they reach the door.

Corbin startles when he sees me, and Maverick's eyes widen. I keep my expressions neutral as I cradle the large phallus in my arms.

"Fuck's sake, Britt. *Why*? Just why would you be buying that?" Maverick asks me, screwing his eyes shut.

"I've grown addicted to the sensations provided by a man's—"

"Don't," Corbin interrupts, shaking his head. "Please don't finish that sentence."

"It's natural. In fact, most women find they have a very active libido after losing their virginity," I continue. "It's nothing to be—"

They both turn and walk out, and I turn around, feeling a small grin tug at my lips as I go to put the suction-cup phallus back in its bin.

As I turn the corner of the aisle, though, I slam into someone, and my eyes widen when I realize it's Randy. His eyes widen too. With no warning or preamble, he lifts me from the ground, hugging me.

"Thank you. Thank you. Thank you. Thank you," he says as he squeezes me tightly.

"I don't like being thanked this severely," I decide to tell him, feeling incredibly uncomfortable and wanting down now. "Just owe me a favor if you feel you must."

I'm stiff in his arms, and I reel back quickly when he puts me down. I end up falling back against a hard body as the phallus drops to the ground, and an overly familiar arm wraps around my waist to steady me.

"Seems like you're everywhere I am today," Base says very close to my ear from behind me, the heat of his breath fanning my skin.

Well…this is definitely not out of sight or out of mind. At all.

"Here, you dropped this," Randy says with a very large grin as he picks up the downed phallus.

"Seems ambitious for someone who's still relatively new to sex," Base muses.

"That was actually for Corbin and Maverick," I explain, only causing Randy's brow to scrunch.

I don't think he's constipated.

I feel Base grin next to my ear, because his lips brush my skin, sending a chill skittering up my spine. I quickly wriggle free of him, and take the suction-cup dildo from Randy, before placing it in the bin.

"We stopped in to kill time before we meet up with Tag," Randy tells me.

I nod like that makes sense, even though I don't understand the relative link between the two.

I turn to see Base propped up, hands in his pockets, and eyes on me with all that intensity I was starting to wonder if I over-exaggerated. I didn't over-exaggerate it; I under-exaggerated it.

I see one bag after another being placed on the counter as they finish bringing out Harley's large order.

"I should go," I say as I turn in the other direction and walk down the backside of the aisle to avoid more accidental collisions with Base.

"Bye, Britt," Base says, sounding way too amused.

I don't know how to react to him right now, and it's statistically unreasonable to think there will be any other unscheduled run-ins.

I back up again when I see a much more reasonably sized phallus with a lot of very interesting motorized functions. I pull it off the tab and take it with me to the register, never looking back, because it's really hard to keep my working philosophy *working* when he's in sight.

Chapter 37

BRITT

"Then I interned for a guy who was almost Bill Gates," Maxwell tells me as I lift my phone. "Though I'm sure you've never heard of him if you didn't keep up with the early publications during the great…"

I'm not sure what he says next, because I keep tuning him out in small intervals. I already know this won't work, because when he touched my arm to guide me in, I got sick at my stomach.

I'm not really sure what it is that caused that reaction. He's attractive, clean, and his teeth are perfectly straight. But bile rose to my throat when he kissed my hand, cementing the damning, revolting chemistry.

Both of these are not promising reactions to have toward a potential sexual partner, so the search will have to continue once I extract myself.

His IQ is two points higher than my own, but he makes me feel like I'm twice the idiot. He works harder to be misunderstood as opposed to working harder to simplify things. I've actually had to look up two of the words he used in a context I'd never heard them used.

A yawn escapes me as I subtly glance to my lap and text Harley.

ME: Are you bored when I talk?

HARLEY: On occasion I feel a little stupid, but never bored. Is he boring?

Before I can text her back, I spot Vince Jaggons walking in. Right behind him is Randy, then Taylor, then Sticks…and lastly…Base Masters.

This shouldn't be possible.

I'm afraid there would be some very misleading confusion if I got under the table to hide right now.

The band moves to a table five down from us, and I push my uneaten cake aside, glancing at the back exit.

Unfortunately, just as I turn back around, Base's eyes collide with mine as though compelled to do so. He only looks surprised for a second as a slow smile spreads over his lips, and his gaze flicks to Maxwell.

Neither man has ever shown signs of jealousy, so there shouldn't be any conflict.

Base's smile turns into a smug look before he returns his attention to his table.

"I read that it's customary to have some passionate dirty talk before sex," Maxwell says, drawing my gaze back to him.

I say nothing, because I'm not an expert on the subject matter.

"That's harder than it may seem," I caution him.

He shakes his head. "Nonsense. It's very simple." He keeps his eyes on mine as he says, "When I have you under me, you're going to see stars," he says in a pleasant tone.

I tap my fingers. "I'm confused. Are you going to get me under you and punch me?" I ask very seriously.

He gives me a bland look. "I think you're misreading the context, since, as I stated, this is dirty talk."

"Some people get aroused from physical violence, so there's more room than you're considering allowance for in terms of miscommunication."

He pauses, running a hand over his mouth, then nods.

"I'm not aroused by violence," I decide to point out.

"Duly noted. Nor am I," he tells me.

Silence stems after that like he's trying to think of a new line to use with the appropriate dirtiness that leaves no room for miscommunication. I warned him it was harder than it seems.

His phone goes off, and he directs his attention to it. My stomach is queasy just trying to discuss the possibility of dirty talk to him, so I'm glad he's unable to come up with another line.

"Sorry, Britt. I lost track of time, and my mother is already here to pick me up. We'll have to discuss the terms of losing my virginity on our next date," Maxwell states.

Every minute seemed unbearably long and drawn out to me, so I'm not entirely sure how he managed to lose track of time.

"There's not going to be a second date, Maxwell," I tell him as our bill is dropped off at the table.

Maxwell nods. "Very well. Nice meeting you, Britt Sterling. I'll inform my mother this was not an ideal match. To be honest, you're a little dull for me," he adds as he stands and walks out.

"I'll get the bill," I say under my breath as I reach into my purse.

This hasn't been my favorite day of the week.

A body slides into the seat across from me, and I glance up, unsurprised to find Base lounging in the chair as he leans back in Maxwell's abandoned seat.

"I guess we're technically at a dinner table tonight after all. I was going to invite you out with all of us," Base tells me, gesturing toward the table full of the band.

Sticks lifts his chin, giving me a wave. Taylor starts to stand and come over here, but Sticks pulls him back down. Randy starts kissing the back of his hand, for whatever reason. Vince's eyes are on the menu, not even aware anything is going on.

"It looks like a band outing. I'm glad things are going well," I tell Base as the waiter swings back by to take my tab.

When my eyes land on the ones across the table again, it actually hurts. I've seen him too much for one day.

He just stares at me, a small smirk on his lips.

"The tour went better than Vince expected, which actually pisses him off, because he thought he had us all figured out. Now he sort of likes us…almost," he proceeds to tell me, his smirk still fixed on his face.

I nod. "I suspected as much," I tell him, looking around for Alex, my waiter.

"Last I saw you, you were on your way to scout locations for some of Harley's games to come to life. Find anything?" he asks, leaning up.

"I narrowed the selection down to three that met all her specifications and ensured the pictures weren't overselling the properties," I amend. "And it won't be a relevant achievement for two years because Harley plans two years ahead for events of that scale."

I glance around again, seeing Alex caught up at another table he also has to tend to.

I really want out of here.

"I sent you some backstage passes you never redeemed," he tells me.

"I know," I answer, looking back down at my lap to where my hands are privately shaking.

Those never made any sense to me. Why send them? He was supposed to be angry at me and then learn to be happy about everything else.

He pulls out his wallet, confusing me, and retrieves a folded piece of paper.

"Before I left, I asked someone for a favor," he tells me as he unfolds the paper. "I knew you'd break down all our issues for someone, and they finally sent me the chart you apparently constructed to prove how wrong we were for each other."

I eye the table, knowing I definitely can't crawl under it now. That would be humiliating even for me.

"Harley?" I guess.

"No. Tag," he tells me as he lays down a version of the chart in his handwriting. "He read it off to me when I was in New Jersey. Apparently you have it showcased on your creative board in your living room."

I'm not sure why I'm feeling a sense of horror to know he's in possession of that knowledge. I should feel relieved that he's taken measures to finally understand why this ended at a stalemate.

"It seems harsher when things are listed out of context. I apologize. You weren't supposed to ever see that," I tell him, sincerely wishing Alex would return with my card so I can go.

He scans the chart, lips twitching. "You're just as harsh on yourself, Britt."

That's not true. That chart was just to make other people stop asking the *what-if* questions so redundantly, but I can't tell him that.

"The thing about you is that you're honest, and the biggest problem is that you can't be honest with me because I have subpar listening skills and grow immediately defensive when faced with even minor critique and/or criticism," he goes on, pointing at the section of chart that does indeed list that as a severe issue.

Oye, I really do want to hide.

"In the severe column, one of your problems is that you can't quickly adjust to new scenarios and need time calculating new odds before committing to a large decision when it's not an obvious good life choice."

I say nothing, just tapping my foot.

Relief fills me when the leather folder is returned to the table. "Thank you for dining with us, Ms. Sterling," Alex says before hurrying off to another table while I quickly fill in and sign the appropriate spots.

"I was a shit life choice to make three months ago. I get the hesitation now, and you were right," he tells me as I put my card up. "You saw me spiraling, and instead of becoming my crutch, you decided to be my anchor."

My eyes come back up, landing on his as he studies my face with an impassive expression.

"I thought I was teaching you to walk, while you were busy learning to fly," he goes on, eyes serious.

"I should go," I tell him as I close my purse at last. "I'm happy that you're happy, Base."

"I know you are," he says quietly as I stand, his eyes staying on me as I do.

"Good luck with the next phase of your life," I add, remaining as calm as possible as I start to head toward the door.

His hand gently snatches my wrist on my way by, and I swallow down the sound that tries to escape. His touch elicits that dormant heat he always ignites. Why? Just why?

I don't fight or move—remaining still as his thumb smooths up the inside of my wrist. My head turns so I can look down at him as he stares at my hand.

"The chart points out the most obvious difference between us at the very top. I think with my heart; you think with your head."

I nod in agreement, since he seems okay with that assessment.

He doesn't look at me to see the nod, but he must catch it in his peripheral as he brings his other hand over to toy with my fingers.

Innocent touch has never existed with him. Each touch, no matter how innocuous it would be with anyone else, elicits too many illogical and improbable sensations.

His gaze swings up to meet mine, and I sway toward him as if I have no control.

"The past three months have taught me to think more with my head. It's your turn to meet me in the middle when you're ready," he says, still holding onto me.

An irrational bereft feeling chills my bones when I wriggle free of his grip, and he lets me go easily enough, though his eyes stay on mine.

"I unknowingly did that already," I tell him with a false mildness to my tone.

Steeling my knees, I add, "It's not you who's the problem, Base. I'm still not able to handle conflict, and any serious romantic entanglement demands the ability to resolve conflict in order to remain healthy. I'm simply not ready for that, and it'd be unwise to end up in the same place all over again, despite the best intentions, when we've already learned what we needed to from our parting. I think it's best to focus on moving forward in our own separate paths now."

I walk away before he can formulate any sort of argument, because he's much better at this than I am.

"Says the girl who just handled impromptu conflict," he calls out.

I pause, turning to look back at him, ignoring the curious eyes on me.

"Harley fills my head with the what-ifs. I was actually prepared for this particular conflict," I say before walking out the door.

I quickly hand my ticket to the valet, and I make the mistake of glancing back, my subconscious working my reflexes before I can actively stop them.

Base is staring directly at me, and a small smile turns up one corner of his lips…as though he knows I didn't mean to look back.

I jerk my head back toward the front when my car is quickly brought around, and I actively work on not looking at him again as I get in and start driving home.

His new song comes on the radio to torment me farther, and I hear the lyrics I know by heart.

I was the boy who didn't understand the talk, too busy overlooking the reasons why. I was foolishly teaching her to walk, while she was learning to fly.

He essentially quoted that to me, which makes this song feel too real, or it makes his words feel cheap and generic. Either way, it's not healthy to dwell, so I shut off the radio and drive home in silence, trapped with the lingering sensations only he leaves behind with his touch.

It's a blur of motion until I'm pushing through my front door and heading directly to my bathroom to do my unhealthy thing of seeing his toothbrush under the counter. It's still in the sealed bag, so it's not too unsanitary.

I sit down in the floor and just look at it, unsure why I keep doing this to myself.

Taking a deep breath, I pull the baggie out, stand up, and toss it into the trashcan. Then I pull it out and toss it back under the sink, because I'm not quite ready to part with it.

"Tomorrow will be easier," I tell myself as I let my eyes shut.

Chapter 38

BRITT

Three days with no Base sightings should be good news. Except…everyone is talking about how different he is. Apparently he's turned into a bit of a social butterfly since returning, instead of a hermit artist who doesn't really find the rest of the world all that appealing.

Fortunately, tonight is a black-tie event hosted by Wren's mother. Base rarely ever gets mentioned at these things.

Two large, round tables are reserved for us as we leave the silent auction room and head into the banquet room.

I don't make enough money yet to competitively bid on anything here, but I still enjoy the learning experience.

My mind blanks when I come to an abrupt halt, spotting what has to be an illusion, because even that probability is higher than Base Masters actually wearing a tuxedo. Concussions can cause hallucinations, but I don't remember receiving blunt-force trauma to my head.

Loss of memory is a symptom as well. I could be experiencing a concussion and not remember to look for the symptoms.

He's talking to Tag, and Tag is smiling as he claps his cousin's shoulder. I turn very sharply and go to find our table, because now I know what he's doing. He's using my relationship chart against me, and he's probably very aware of the fact he looks good doing it.

He's supposed to sulk in corners in places like this and talk about how much he hates it. Not shake hands with people as Tag introduces him—

I slam very hard into a body, and hands go to my shoulders to quickly steady me.

"Ah, Ms. Sterling," Vince Jaggons says as he pulls back and looks me over.

He's wearing a bowtie on top of a T-shirt with just a blazer. The odds are that he's also wearing leather pants.

"Sorry," I blurt out, eyes widening. "I didn't see you."

"That's because you were looking behind you while walking forward. Usually we walk toward the things that ensnare our attention so thoroughly," he tells me with lips twisting in a grin.

I nod in agreement, and then look down at my shoes. Huh. No leather pants after all. I'm not sure what that fabric would be called, to be honest.

"You sent me with a group of boys, and so far they're shaping into possible men. Good eye. If you want to switch industries, make sure I'm your first call," he adds, bringing my attention back up.

"Are you seriously pitching to *my* prodigy?" Harley says as she walks up.

"Of course. I'm a businessman too. Her mind isn't limited to just some games," he tells her on a scoff.

Harley shakes her head. "I called dibs. She's mine. I'm not giving her up either."

I'm not sure why I smile, but I do. Vince nudges me on his way by. "When you no longer feel challenged, give me a call. It's rare to find a keen appreciation for artistry existing in a mind already so brilliant."

My smile only grows, because he's actually really good at being nice.

"She's in the middle of developing her first game, and it's challenging enough," Harley says as she grabs my hand and starts dragging me away.

I hear Vince laughing from behind me, and I let Harley guide me to our table.

"Your father was working his charm on Britt so he could steal her from me," Harley tattles to Bo the second we sit down.

"But Britt isn't really into music like that," Bo says like she's confused.

I tune them out as they carry on, and I let my eyes wander back to Base.

Vince is with him now, and they're talking to someone who is probably really important to the music industry. I assume that's why they're here.

Exhaling a little easier, no longer feeling like this is directly related to me, I drink from my water glass as the dishes start being delivered to tables.

I lose sight of Base as our table fills up, noticeably lacking Ash and Tag. Presumably, they must be sitting with Base, wherever he is.

My eyes scan the vast room of their own accord as everyone eats, and I absently eat my own food as each course is served.

"What's the cake going to be like tonight?" I ask.

"Finally, *she speaks*!" Maverick says, arching an eyebrow at me.

"You have been quiet," Rain points out, eyes darting in a direction behind me before coming back down.

Ah, so he's behind me and has probably noticed me looking around for him. It'll appear as though I'm sending mixed signals.

I worked so hard on losing my virginity that I never considered I'd need preparation for what happened if things ended with emotional attachments I swore not to form.

"And she's done talking because you pressed," Salem says as she elbows Maverick.

I glance down and start idly folding my cloth napkin like it's paper origami.

"Cakes are coming out, Britt," Bella says from the other table.

Harley and Dale get up to go dance, and I spot the dessert trays that are starting on the opposite end of the room. They'll be out of the chocolate before they reach us. No one ever orders enough chocolate at these things.

"Oh, shit," Maverick says under his breath.

I don't get a chance to look over or ask him what's wrong, because a small plate of chocolate cake comes down on the table in front of me as Base slides into Harley's seat with his own slice.

Sitting straighter in my chair, I cast a worried look at Base as he smirks and hands me my unused fork.

"I remember you saying they never order enough, so you always get it early," he tells me as I take the fork from his hand.

"Thank you," I state on autopilot.

"So you came to your first black-tie affair to stalk Britt?" Kode asks him dryly, as his arm goes around Tria's chair.

Tria rolls her eyes and elbows him in the side. He doesn't flinch. In fact, he looks positively lethal.

They all stare at Base, which forces my eyes to drop to the cake, because I can feel the conflict brewing and I don't want to be part of it.

"The cake is actually the best part," I remind everyone.

"Nah. That'd just be creepy," Base says like he's answering Kode. "Tag asked me to come, since I was in town, so I did."

"How convenient," Maverick drawls.

I bristle in my chair. They don't usually do this with me so close.

"I decided on a more reasonably sized phallus. One that needed surprisingly large batteries," I tell Corbin and Maverick.

Bella chokes on her drink, and Ethan buries his face in her neck as his body shakes.

"Dance with me," Corbin tells Ruby as he glares at me a little.

Ruby nods, working to keep a straight face as she stands and goes with him.

Dane walks off like he just can't sit here any longer.

Maverick and Kode act like they're about to say something else, when I say, "I think we should dance. Watch my cake."

I stand abruptly, and Base just grins as he waggles his eyebrows at Maverick and slowly stands.

His fingers lace through mine without warning, and he leans over. "Fair warning, I'm really bad at this," he tells me. "It's outside my comfort zone."

"I know what you're doing," I tell him as his arm slides around my back, pulling us much closer than is considered appropriate for a waltz.

One of my hands goes to his, and my other comes up to his shoulder, barely touching him.

"What am I doing?" he asks.

"Even I know that's a cheap version of a coy grin," I point out as his lips just turn up more. "You're attempting to render all points of conflict irrelevant, but that's impossible."

He shakes his head. "Nope. I'm just growing the fuck up, Britt. That's all I'm doing."

It's so hard to ignore how good it feels to have him pulling me closer and closer until we're essentially just swaying on the dance floor.

He drops my hand, curling his other arm around my waist, and both my hands slide to rest on his chest as I stare at him.

"You held back because we were supposed to be temporary," he says as he starts moving me backwards.

"I held back because I knew I wasn't really fucking good enough," he goes on.

"That's not what—"

"Careful. That's starting conflict by arguing with me, Britt," he chides, smirking as I blow out a breath.

"You avoid conflict because it makes it really hard to keep the emotions out of things, and you get too emotional to conduct yourself in a comfortable way when conflict gets intense."

"I know," I inform him, wondering why he's telling me things I've already determined about myself long ago.

"Which is why we're having this conversation bit by bit until we finish it. We'll just talk as much as you're comfortable with until you trust me enough to try this thing for real," he adds.

I freeze against him, and he smirks.

"I was both right and wrong, Britt. You were also right *and* wrong. At the end of the day, you're eventually going to realize you're fucking terrified of this because you can't shut the emotions out with me, even when conflict isn't involved. I don't let you."

I start to push away, but he keeps his arms around me.

"I don't coddle you, because I know you're capable of a hell of a lot more than you seem to think you are; you just keep holding back," he goes on so casually. "It's what you loved and hated about me, if you're being honest. And it's why you wanted to stay friends."

"We're not friends," I remind him.

"Sure we are," he goes on, lips tugging up in the grin again.

He leans down, lips brushing mine just enough to send my body into a flurry of wild reactions. "You'll eventually realize you're just being stubborn, and if I'm lucky, you'll come to me. In the meantime, I hear there's an opening for a friend with benefits."

My head reels back, and I…just gape at him.

"We can't do that."

"We already did that," he reasonably points out. "*Technically*, it's all we did, and we did that part very well, so why couldn't we do it again? Unless you're admitting that you have unresolved feelings for me you're too scared to face and that's really what's holding you back."

He lets go when I push at him this time, but he snags my hand before I can walk away. "I love you, Britt," he says like it's the most casual, effortless thing in the entire world to say.

The harp player misses a chord before stopping abruptly, and I feel a lot of eyes on us. I can't seem to tear mine away from his to look around the room, though.

"I moved myself into your house when I liked your eyes. Now I love you. Do you really think I'm just going to throw in the towel while you're fighting me because you're scared? I'm a little more stubborn than you, Britt. In a battle of wills, I'll win."

I want to point out how very irrational that entire statement sounds, but I turn and walk away instead, because I know what he's trying to do.

I can see it in the devilish way he grins when he tries to purposely antagonize me.

Just as I get outside, I hear someone jogging to catch up with me.

"Britt!" Base calls.

Taking a fortifying breath, I turn around to—

I have no idea what I was about to do, because my mind goes blank when his lips crash to mine. I stagger a little, and then I react without thinking. My hands go to his hair, pulling at him to come so much closer, as he kisses me into that stupor I remember all too well.

He groans into my mouth as he pushes me against the wall, kissing me harder as he slides his hand down my back and pulls me to him.

My mind keeps telling me to push him away, yet I keep surrendering and silently begging for something else to intervene on my behalf when I can't stop myself.

He's the one to break the kiss. I should feel relieved instead of slightly devastated. I hear our heavy breaths as my eyes flutter open to find him already staring at me. He softly pushes a piece of hair out of my face, eyes still holding mine in that way that always made me wonder what he was thinking.

"I'll see you tomorrow, Britt," he murmurs before his lips brush mine again.

He turns to go before I can tell him I won't be in town

tomorrow, but I decide it's probably better to keep my mouth shut because it was just kissing him. I don't entirely trust it to say the right things.

I try to move, but I feel rooted to my spot, yet another unrealistic saying that now makes perfect sense. Every time I feel that simple connection with everyone else—a genuine sense of understanding—it usually seems to stem from him.

He makes me *feel* too much.

My eyes brim with tears as I exhale harshly.

A glass of champagne is suddenly being handed to me, and I look over, seeing Rain as she leans against the wall next to me.

I take the champagne, but I don't drink it. Drinking impairs judgment, and I need all the clarity I can find in this moment.

"You and I are drastically different. I'm not even going to pretend to know how this feels for you right now," Rain tells me. "I see your struggle, though. You've probably never truly wanted anything more than everything Base Masters seems to want to serve on a silver platter." At my shaky breath, she pats my hand. "Don't panic. Just tell me what's going on. I'm sure this is scary territory for you."

I nod a little too hard, and it knocks a tear free.

I clear my throat and shake my head when I try to talk, but know I'll just blubber. She doesn't say anything for a minute, even though I hear her try to start a sentence two times.

"Speaking from personal experience," she says on the third attempt, "first loves can be intense. Even when you're not ready for them. But someone very, *very* brilliant says all relationship problems can usually be rectified with simple, concise communication skills," she finally says before patting my arm and walking away.

That Britt was as naïve as everyone dutifully tried to inform her she was.

All those endless streams of advice, and not one person accurately described how vulnerable the truth really leaves you when you realize how easily someone can simply just walk away now. In this life. Where the proverbial bubble shrouded me until it burst.

Things make more sense when you experience them for yourself. Then you realize why people try so hard to warn you.

Chapter 39

BASE

"No," I say in disbelief as I pick up what was once my expensive leather tunic. "*No, no, no, no,*" I add on a groan when I see the fucking leggings have been shredded too.

There's a bulldog puppy scratching itself right across from me, and I pull back a wet hand, gagging at the drool I didn't even notice all over my damn ruined outfit.

"Randy!" I shout.

No one else would be this fucking stupid.

"What's u—*oh, whoa.*" His eyes go wide as he stumbles into my room, and he holds his hands up. "You said I could get a puppy when we were surrounded by rock legends. That day has come."

I look at him like he's lost his damn mind, just before I sneeze. "Damn it, Randy," I say as I sneeze again, cursing as I shove by him and go to the bathroom.

"That was supposed to be fucking impossible, and I said that like five years ago. I'm allergic to animal hair," I shout as I sneeze again and again while washing my hands.

"But we were surrounded by rock legends," he calls through the door. "Just last night."

"He ate my fucking squire shit, so now what the hell am I supposed to do? I have to be there in four hours, and it's a fucking three hour drive."

"I have needle and thread!" Taylor calls.

"Do you fucking know how to use it?" I ask him.

"I can sew a fucking button back on like a champ. But that's all I got," he yells back.

Covering my nose and mouth with my shirt, I walk back toward my room, looking at the leather chew toy that fucking dog turned it into.

"Fuck. I can't wear that. Any holes or tears have to be mended before arrival, and that would take even a master several hours to fix. I don't even know if it is fixable."

"Then obviously I can't help you out," Taylor says.

"Oh! I know where we can go. I saw an elf costume, and it's basically the same thing," Randy says as he runs and grabs his keys before sprinting out the front door.

"It'd better not be a Christmas elf," I shout.

"There are more elves than Christmas elves?" Taylor asks as he comes around the corner.

I run a hand through my hair, drinking the coffee as I step over the mess of cords lying all over our living room on my way to the table where I left the rulebook. I sit down to do one quick re-read on some of the trickier things about this particular cosplay session.

I barely finish reading the last two pages when three sneezes hit me so hard and fast that I drop the book and…the dog barks right next to me.

"Taylor!"

He runs in and snatches up the puppy, laughing under his breath as he goes to shut it up in Randy's room.

"I said, *'I'm going for a run, Taylor. No one goes in my room.'* I come back, and a dog has eaten the outfit I spent a lot of money on so that I didn't have to look like an idiot. Now Randy is off to buy me a fucking elf costume."

The dick actually struggles to keep a straight face.

"This isn't funny. It's an invitation-only sort of event designed mostly for the hardcore loyal fans, or the future prospects Harley likes to wow before she recruits them. It's a big deal that she did this favor for me, especially since it could piss Britt off."

"Britt doesn't get pissed," he says like he knows her so well.

"Well, Harley does, and I'm going to embarrass the shit out of her, and she's going to kick me out."

"I'm sure it won't be that bad. Randy's going to try to make this right," he says, not sounding one bit convincing.

He even chokes back some laughter and turns away when he can't stop himself.

"This is why bands break up. The bandmates are all giant dicks," I point out, only causing his laughter to double as he leans over the counter.

"What's so funny?" Sticks asks as he walks out.

Taylor is too busy laughing to answer, but Randy comes busting back in with a bag in his hand.

"The fucking dirty store? You bought my 'serious' replacement outfit from the motherfucking dirty store?" I ask the dick I'm going to murder.

Taylor's laughter reaches hysterics, and he makes a donkey braying noise.

"It's the only place that sells shit like that around here that I know of," Randy says as he pulls out the…sexy elf costume.

Sexy. Elf. Costume.

"It's for women," Sticks says, his grin slowly growing as I silently wish I could rewind this day and skip my run.

"They don't make them for dudes. I checked," Randy says as though that changes everything, and Taylor's laughter turns into an outright riot.

I snag the bag out of his hand, out of time and options, and curse as I go to Taylor's room—*because…no dog hair*—to change, but pause.

"Randy, this is a fucking skirt. Not leggings," I groan.

"It's the only elf costume they had."

"You keep saying that like it solves all my problems!" I say while consciously making an effort not to shove his head in the toilet at this point.

The door swings open, and I see Taylor in the floor, heaving for air as he turns a shade of purple. Just as he sucks in a long breath, he bursts out laughing all over again.

Sticks stumbles into the messy room, laughing as well, as he goes to the closet and pulls out Taylor's girl box that is full of things left behind by overnight guests who wear his boxers out.

"What color do you need?"

"Any color of brown is in the dress code."

"Got nude ones here that look about your size," he says as he starts laughing a little harder, pulling the leggings from the box.

"I'm going to go try to win back a girl, who you pointed out has abandonment issues, after I gave her a really stupid ultimatum. And now I'm going to have to do it wearing a sexy elf costume and some random chick's leggings. How is any of this fucking funny?" I ask him very damn seriously.

I hear the ridiculousness, and I know why they're laughing. It's still not fucking funny right now. Not to me.

The relentless dog has apparently gotten free, because I spot it barking up and down the hall as I rip open the bag and start pulling on the tight, stupid, motherfucking top that stops two inches above my navel.

This is a nightmare. A real, present, and horrifying nightmare.

Sticks chokes back a laugh and turns around, putting his back to me as I mutter curses and work on tying the damn laces.

"This will be remembered as the day I started hating all of you," I tell him as I shuffle out of my jeans and start pulling on the leggings. "Please tell me these have been washed," I add…and then replay the stupidity of that hopeful statement.

"I want to pretend they've been washed, because I need the win at this point," I go on as all three of them laugh all throughout the house.

Taylor's laughter hits the high notes, right along with Randy's, as Sticks drops to Taylor's bed, covering his face with his arm as his laughter shakes his damn body.

"Get my fucking boots, Randy, you dick," I call out. "I can't go in my room because it has dog hair all over it by this point."

There's some stumbling heard through the endless laughter before Randy comes through with my boots that I rip out of his hand. His eyes widen on me when he finally sees the proof about how terrible he's made my life this day.

He doubles over, because yes, I look the most ridiculous I've ever looked in all my life.

"Do you need the hat?" Randy asks through a laugh as I stare incredulously at my reflection.

I look like a crossdressing Peter Pan.

Angrily, I start pulling on the first boot. "I was supposed to wind down with a run, shower, and put on my nicely made outfit that I spent a month's worth of bill money on."

I stab my foot into the other boot, and start doing the complicated buckles on both.

"I got the fucking run. I got the fucking shower. Now I'm wearing women's clothing because you got a fucking dog!"

This is pointless. The more I yell at them, the harder they laugh.

I yank Randy's keys out of his hand as I pass, because his new car has excellent gas mileage, and I'm sure as fuck not stopping for gas.

I grab my duffel bags, sneezing as that dog comes barking through the house. Ignoring my itchy eyes, I go back and quickly take a picture of the ruined outfit the dog is now growling at as he tries to drag it out of the room.

Then I leave the madhouse full of dicks with another sneeze.

"You're on the list, but you don't meet dress code," the prick with a clipboard says as he eyes my clothing with a look of disdain. "Are you sure you signed up for the right thing?"

"I'm positive. Just find the queen, and she'll let me in. Please," I tell him, uttering words I never thought I'd say outside a fairytale book.

He stares at me for a second before he laughs a little, then starts laughing harder. "Are you some sort of prank on the queen? A…stripper?" he asks through his chuckles.

Pulling up my phone, I quickly text Harley, realizing getting in is harder than just handing over an invitation and being on a list when you're dressed like a slutty-elf-*male*-stripper in women's clothing.

"Just find the queen," I say again.

"Me? Find the queen? You really don't belong here, because you don't know how these things even work," he tells me as his laughter tapers off. "Be gone, pedestrian. We don't need—"

"Base!" Harley shouts from across the way as she quickly rides toward us on an actual, real horse, wearing some outfit that makes her look like a Grecian goddess.

Thank. Fuck.

The dude beside me quickly drops to a knee, eyes widening as he stares at the ground.

"All hail the queen!" he shouts.

Harley's eyes widen in slight horror as she approaches, and I run a hand through my hair as her lips thin.

"I told you to take this seriously," she snaps as her horse comes to a stop right in front of me, leaving me staring way up at her.

"A dog ate my costume," I inform her as I quickly flip through the pictures on my phone.

She glares at me. "At least try to come up with a better excuse than—"

Her words cut out as I hold my phone up, and she snatches it out of my hand to get a better look, as her horse side-steps toward me a little.

"*Wow.* A dog really ate your costume," she says like she's impressed by this.

Her gaze flicks back to me, and her lips start twitching as she glances over my outfit with a more amused look now.

"Is that the slutty elf top from the kinky store?" she asks like she hopes I'm going to answer *yes*. "And where in the world did you find those…very tight leggings?"

"It's been a *reeeeaaaaallllly* rough day, Harley, and now I have a full three days to get through dressed like this."

I gesture at my clothes, and she just grins harder.

"Right. Well, I happened to bring one of Dale's old outfits just in case you screwed this up. It'll be a little big, but—"

"Being a little big is better than it being a lot *little.*"

She nods like she sort of agrees, eyes flicking over my bare middle as she works twice as hard not to laugh.

"Keep up. We have orientation to do in ten minutes, so you'll need to change quickly."

I don't even say anything, because that horse takes off the second she gives it the go ahead like it has just been waiting to get moving again. I sprint behind it, drawing numerous gazes as we head across an open field surrounded by woods.

I barely glimpse the elaborate things set up all around that make this place look ready for battle. Harley rides down a trail, and I struggle to keep up, because the horse is clearly faster and in way better shape than I am. My bags are also weighing me down.

We're spit out at a campground, and I stumble over my own feet as Harley rides on. I'm too busy taking in the new scenery.

"Whoa," I say as I marvel at how just insanely elaborate this all really is.

Harley stops in front of one ornate, massive canopy tent that is surrounded by numerous other tents—all of them looking regal and made out of beige or white material.

"Was I also supposed to bring a special sort of tent too?" I ask as dread creeps up my spine.

"We actually assign tents. This is mine, but you can use it to change. The spare clothes are on the table next to the stack of five—"

"They need you, my queen," a man, who seemingly appears from nowhere, says as he breathes heavily, doubling over and putting his hands on his knees as he tries to catch his breath.

"Hurry," Harley tells me as she gestures to the big one and then rides back off.

I quickly dart in, and stumble over my own feet as I glance around at the inside. The tent looks silk on the underside, and more silk is hanging down like dividers.

Large, unique, quilted pillows have been designed to look like mattresses, sometimes stacked on top of each other—ranging in size from twin to king, and scattered all around colorful rugs that are layered to cover the tent's base.

Between the décor and other things, it really does look like a royal tent.

Snapping out of my trance, I hurriedly change into the leggings I once mocked Dale for wearing, and the tunic that was made for broader shoulders than mine. It takes a second to get the boots buckled again, since they're just as elaborate as everything else I was told to wear.

Then I hurry outside and back down the trail to where everyone is now congregating. I was expecting a lot less people.

At least a hundred or more people are huddled together, clearing a path for Harley as she makes a grand entrance, slowly trotting her horse toward the center.

"Welcome to Azraya!" she shouts.

Everyone makes some random noise in unison like they've rehearsed it. I stand in sort of a stupor, propping up against a shed that hosts a lot of unique wooden weaponry designed to look metal.

"Most of you are here because you've put in the time, effort, and sacrifice to earn your way here. These three days have been something you've looked forward to, and I hope it's everything you want it to be. Some of you are here because you want to find the virtual world you belong in," she says, looking over at a group of what is likely prospective future hires.

Her eyes flick to a very familiar man near the front—Dale Sterling—as his lips twitch under her steady appraisal.

"And some of you are here just because I like you."

A few rounds of laughter ring out, and Dale winks at her as he crosses his arms over his chest. The fucker is wearing chainmail and non-legging bottoms. He's a level-sixteen queen's guard? Seriously? He had to cheat to get that far.

Harley's face turns more serious as someone hands her some really ornate white staff thingy. I don't know what it is. Level-two squires don't get to see the queen in the game, and there's a *lot* of information to absorb.

She lifts the staff, and everyone makes that unified noise again.

"Between game rounds, we'll have some out-of-character fun. During game rounds, you're required to stay in character or you'll be sent to the tent grounds to keep from stealing the magic from anyone else," she says as my eyes begin scanning the crowd for the girl I'm wearing leggings to impress.

Again, another statement I never thought I'd utter.

"Squires have been assigned to princes or princesses based on careful compatibility screenings, since we have very few true level-twos here," she goes on, that part directed toward me, even though she never looks this way.

"In one hour, we'll convene for our first round. The details of your first mission will be delivered by your assigned scribes. Take note: if you are among the few here who can't speak Azrayan, you will be considered mute for the game rounds, so don't break character."

I feel like that's directly pointed at me and possibly Dale, since he bristles and gives her a narrowed glare as she grins.

"Use this hour wisely to plan and strategize with your teams. Your princes and princesses will be waiting for you beyond the tented land," she goes on. "And may the light serve your cause!"

"*Hovehlah!*" they all shout in unison while pumping two fists in the air.

I've heard that word on the game. I can't remember what the hell it means though, and the helpful subtitles aren't a thing in real life.

With just a little nudge, her horse takes off, and Harley rides off toward the tent grounds again.

Everyone starts running, and I just stare, finding myself at the back of the pack before long. Despite all the crazed commotion, I stand still. Apparently, in a bustling crowd like this, you stand out if you stand still.

Dale Sterling's eyes collide with mine when I look over again, finding him standing still as well, and he levels me with a glare.

I'm finally going to get hit by a Sterling. Fuck my day.

"Nice tights," he calls as he starts walking off.

"They're leggings," I remind him as I jog to catch up.

"What the fuck are you doing here?" he asks like he's too tired to deal with me right now.

"I figured that much would be obvious," I point out, smirking when he makes a frustrated sound.

"This is serious to Britt. She's spent months working on her numerous outfits. You're more of a novice to this than even I am."

"I spent twenty-eight hours making it to level-two because that game is too fucking smart for me," I say as we continue walking down the trail, the only two lagging behind.

"They have an actual language. Harley hired a team of world-class linguists to create the Azrayan language. Half the time, you're going to be mute. This is a pointless waste of your time, and an unnecessary distraction to Britt, who already has a horde of groupies around her tent."

I pause, idly wondering if I'll be assigned to her tent or not. I will owe Harley for life if so. But then his words start to register.

"Wait, what? What do you mean groupies?"

"You're stalking Azrayan royalty. You have your groupies. She has hers. Actually, she has a lot more than you; hers are just scattered across the world," he continues. "The vast majority of her social media following is game related. Not Sterling Shore related," he adds as we start weaving our way through the tents. "Harley started helping her cultivate a following the day she hired her, and Britt holds the coveted record for quickest, non-programmer ascent in the game."

A small smile graces my lips when I finally spot Britt just for a split second, seeing her red hair in intricate braids that show off her very realistic pointed ears.

A body steps in front of the little bit of her face I could see, blocking her from me.

Just as I start to head there, Dale grabs my arm very firmly at my elbow, and I turn, looking at his cold, steely eyes.

"Careful. Be very careful. I don't think you realize the damage you did."

I…don't know what to say to that. All it does is annoy me that he's still holding me back from finding Britt.

I clear my throat, glancing down.

"Yeah. I'm being careful. I'm easing off when she needs me to, but if I don't push her, she'll stop looking back completely. It's what she does. I can't let her do that to me."

"Thirty minute warning," Harley calls.

Dale doesn't release me, and I don't move.

He drops my arm and gestures around us.

"You're about to see what a broken heart does to someone like Britt. Please remember when flashing your camera in her face to get some 'genuine emotion' that you're the reason behind the sad eyes and practiced smile this time," he tells me, definitely taking a jab.

I deserve it. I really have talked a lot of stupid shit about them.

"I've had some time to reflect," I assure him tightly.

He releases me completely.

"Is this where you tell me I'm not good enough for her?" I ask him. "Because I'm still working on that."

He snorts derisively.

"I don't get to make that call. She already reasoned how *right* you were with your demands, and hated herself for not—"

"I know I fucked up, but I'd rather not talk about it right now. Another time?"

He cracks his neck to the side before giving me a slightly annoyed look.

"You're the first person she's allowed herself to care about who has walked away from her since the day she came to live with Dane. Remember that too."

"Form a proper assembly!" Harley calls in warning, as I stare at Dale for a minute. "Form a proper assembly!"

"My relationship with her has to be different from yours—for obvious reasons—and I know where I fucked up. I should have just pushed and backed off. Then pushed and backed off again. You get the picture. But challenging Britt on any level is a win for me. I've spent three months putting a lot of thought into this."

I step toward him, feeling slightly more confident again.

His lips thin as he glares at me. It'd suck to be punched by him when I'm wearing his clothes.

"I really wanted to hit you today," he says like he's annoyed with me.

I pat him on the shoulder. "I know," I tell him before turning and walking away.

It's been a shit time of getting here, but it all immediately feels worth it when I work my way closer, finding a gap to squeeze through to the front as Britt finishes up whatever she's saying.

"What if they come in from the right?" a dude with a larger-than-necessary smile asks, drawing her attention to him before she can even notice me.

I notice Dale going in the opposite direction, and I finally glance around to see something…happening behind me. Dark tents are dropping down on top of the lighter ones, and men are scurrying around to make the change.

Wait…this isn't the same tent section I was in earlier. Where did those black skull torches come from?

Why is there ominous drumming going on?

Everyone else starts looking around as well, and excited chatter starts flitting through the air. I turn back around in time to Britt walking away in an outfit similar to the one I saw her in that day in the park.

Shit.

I make a move to follow her, but she disappears into a tent that immediately gets blocked by two dudes in chainmail. Before I can attempt to figure out what's going on, fireworks burst into the air, and a screen that wasn't hanging just above the tents before suddenly lights up.

A collective breath is inhaled by almost everyone around me as I look around, trying to figure out what magic show is about to go down.

Loud, suspense-thumping music begins a slow build as the game I barely understand starts running a trailer on the screen. The words in the game's language, so I don't understand a single one.

I catch a glimpse of digital avatars before the glare of the moon interrupts it again.

"It's happening. It's really happening. Oh, my sister is going to hate me even worse than she already does," a girl says from close to me as she sways, eyes on the screen.

I have no idea what's going on, because that glare is terrible, and cutting off half the screen from my angle. What I can see makes no sense. It's all swirling dark magic and a convulsing avatar's mummy-wrapped body.

I'm not as advanced of a player as all the rest of them. Obviously. Have to start somewhere.

I swear, some people even squeal like they can't believe their dreams are coming true, and it's driving me insane with the suspense.

"What's happening?" I finally break down and ask the chick who is dancing in place.

"Azraya is about to have two queens, and it'll be a whole new branch of the game," she says as she sways again. "The pure Valkyrie princess has been poisoned and consumed in darkness by the forbidden elven tree thought to have been lost with the eradication of Valhalla."

It's literally like learning an entire new world, and I have no idea what she just said even in English. This video is all in that language, which just makes me feel all the dumber.

"Everyone wondered how Harley would be able to rebrand herself with a partner, and she's so creative that we knew it'd be epic. This is everything," she says like she's swooning.

I blink a few times when spotlights suddenly blare down from above us, and the entire camp erupts into cheers on both sides of the trees, like there's a separate section.

A speaker pops above us before a man's voice comes over it. My phone starts buzzing like it's possessed. I regret signing up for so many alerts related to Britt, because I can practically feel the battery draining as it continues to vibrate in my hand.

Apparently there's an English version of that trailer that just went live as well.

"The camp you're in now is the camp for whose queen you'll loyally serve for the entirety of this rare retreat," the soothing, unknown male voice says. "The flags will be raised in times of war, and lowered when it's time to break character."

The voice continues to ramble on about rules and such, while I try to catch up to what's going on. I pull on the black garb someone shoves at me like I'm being babied. Everyone starts grabbing weaponry that has been lined up, but my eyes trail to the girl who has changed and is walking out of the tent.

She's wearing a black dress meant to bring men to their knees and heavy black eye makeup that really should not be so hot.

The second her gaze lands on mine, she freezes and her eyes widen. I can visibly see her fighting with herself not to dive back in her tent.

Just what the actual hell is going on around here?

"What are you doing here?" she asks in a surprised tone as she blinks rapidly to see if I'll magically go away.

Her dress looks almost exactly like Harley's, and it's really fucking sexy next to her red hair that's still intricately braided along the sides and woven into some big curls in the back.

I open and close my mouth a few times, eyes dipping to the warrior-queen slits that ride up her thighs. I know it's meant for practical combat purposes—though there will be no actual physical altercations and it's all for show—but...*fuck me.*

My eyes rake up and down her a few more times, trying to remember what the hell I was going to say, as she comes closer so she can talk quieter...presumably.

"This is a really serious event for Harley," she says as she glances around. "And I have a lot to do."

"I'm your squire," I tell her idly as I reach out to feel one of her soft curls, my thumb brushing her neck. "At least I think I am."

She doesn't try to pull away, so I step closer.

"I'll tell you how many hours it took me to get almost to level two whenever you need a laugh," I add.

She almost smiles, but manages to stop herself.

"I'm going to be the guy giving you your paintball arrows that are so fucking cool—"

"Harley's idea," she interrupts. "The arrows, I mean. She does them at a lot of her…"

Her words trail off, and she just stares at me for a second like she's lost her train of thought when my thumb rubs up the side of her neck, gently stroking there. Subtly pulling her closer, my gaze stays on hers.

"I kept your toothbrush," she says very randomly, catching me so off guard that I just…don't know what to say.

"I didn't do anything unsanitary with it," she feels the need to add.

I feel my smile spreading before I can stop myself, as she shakes her head and carries on.

"I kept it because you had another one and would just presume I threw that one out. It was the only thing of yours left behind in the house, and I kept it."

"I never moved yours. It's still sitting in the holder on the sink," I tell her as I step closer again.

"That's unsanitary," she immediately fires back. "I put yours in a sealed bag."

My grin only grows, but she abruptly pulls back, clearing her throat as she starts backing away.

"I have to go," she says as she turns and starts walking quickly toward the area where everyone is gathering.

I spot Harley walking toward me very quickly, and I dart another glance around.

"Do you see what this is?" she asks as she comes to stand beside me.

"Yeah," I tell her, watching Britt as she moves toward a solid black horse off to the side. "I wrote a few sad songs in the same amount of time she created a gothic branch of the universe and became the dark queen."

She nods like she's impressed that I've caught on.

"It's genius in so many business directions I can't list them all. It's the perfect way to rebrand us. It's going to make us a lot of money and generate some really good buzz. The players will decide which queen is winning at all times, so that reduces our involvement and frees up so much of our time."

She sighs like she regrets she has to add the *but* I hear coming.

"*But* it's breaking my heart, and it's also really hard to keep up with her current pace. She's speeding toward a burn-out because she's avoiding her pain by throwing herself into work. She needs a life, and you didn't hurt her on purpose. That's why I gave you the invitation."

She gives me a supportive clap on the back.

"Fix it, please. The sooner, the better," she adds before walking away.

"Hey, what am I supposed to do for Britt? I thought I was her squire," I call as I chase after her.

"Sorry. I lied. Even though we let the big secret leak, we kept up the charade that Britt would still be a princess. I'm known for flair. You're going to be with Prince Norven. Not that it really matters."

I don't even get a chance to ask questions, because she hauls herself up on her horse, and rides away like it's perfectly fucking normal.

I'm still working on adjusting to how hardcore rich people roll.

At the end of the day, this is just fun for her, and she uses business as an excuse to play like a boss.

It's like hearing Vince explain why having a stripper pole installed was a practical business expense.

I'd probably enjoy it, if I had any idea what the hell is going on right now and who this 'prince' I'm now assigned to like cattle is.

"Goggles on!" someone shouts.

I have no idea what the next words are, because they're in that language. The crowd, who is apparently way more abridged on what's going on than I am, erupts into a frenzy just as I'm pelted in the leg with a paintball arrow.

It hurts a lot less than being hit with a paintball gun.

It's not a kill shot, but I still have to run with a limp. I make it five steps before I'm hit with an arrow to the chest and have to drop.

At least I know the rules to this part of all this, but…now I have to hope no one steps on my 'corpse.' I just thought the costume was my biggest setback of the day.

Chapter 40

BRITT

"It's not as much fun being back here as it is being out in all the action, is it?" Harley asks me as the primeval battle rages on well outside of our hidden tent in the woods.

"It's fun not knowing who's winning, though," I tell her as I anxiously tap my foot, wondering if Base is already gone.

This is so far outside of his comfort zone. He really shouldn't be here right now. He's going to ask a lot of uncomfortable questions. I could see it in his eyes.

"You say not to meddle," I very reasonably point out to her. "You always tell everyone not to meddle."

"I'm only a hypocrite because I haven't had any sleep for three months, and I love you, but you have to deal with this at some point. You're too smart; people won't let you play dumb," she says as her eyes flutter shut.

She snaps them open again, and then takes a sip of coffee as she yawns and puts it back down. "I like to sneak in and play sometimes at some of the smaller ones. They usually don't recognize me, since my avatar is the only pictures I use for profiles and no one really cares what I look like, most of the time."

Her head lulls to the side as she falls asleep mid-ramble, because we have put in a lot of hours to get this done quickly. I was tired too…until Base Masters showed up as a squire.

Now I'm wide awake despite the inconvenient fact that it really is boring on this side of the tent, and I didn't bring anything to keep my attention.

I practically jump off the chair when I hear the wail of the final horn, and Harley yelps like she's been startled awake as I push through the tent's entrance.

I make it almost out of the woods when I see Base walking right toward me, goggles hanging from his hand as he breathes heavily.

He's covered in kill shots, and he's wearing a string with no less than ten revival cards around his neck.

His eyes meet mine, and I'm almost positive I see relief cross his features as he straightens and gestures toward himself.

"You died a lot," I point out in confusion. "It's hard to die that much. Very few of us are good shots in real life."

"I had a sniper on me for the first few hits. I would have died more, but a lot of them glanced off me without enough strength to break the bulb. To be honest, halfway through, I was so confused that I just started trying to die. But people kept thinking I was being selfless and heroic, so they kept reviving me," he says like he's quickly recapping.

I follow his gaze when he glances over to a group of four men and three women who are all staring at him with very big grins. Rain calls the five-finger-wiggle-wave a flirty wave. All seven seem to give him that wave at once.

He gives a no-finger-wiggle-wave back before giving me that look he uses when he's too tired to try to explain.

"I couldn't talk, because Harley said she'd kick me out if I broke her rules. So I also came off as the strong, silent type. It's…a long story," he says to confirm my assessment.

"The wars only last for thirty minutes at a time," I say, because I'm still really confused.

That's *a lot* of times to die.

"Yeah, did you know there are emergency inhaler stations set up around the edges? And there are label makers for anyone who hasn't already labeled their inhalers," he says like that's somehow relevant to this conversation.

I don't even get to respond before he's firing off the next question. "So what happens now? I no longer trust the itinerary I got, because this is all different than I thought it would be."

The spot lights all cut out at once, and he looks around as more torches light up in unison around the tables being set up.

"Rich people," he says on a snort under his breath, smirking as he looks back at me. "I'm not saying that to be mean, either."

"Now we eat," I say as I start walking, unsure what else to really say.

I didn't prepare myself for him to be here. There wasn't even a fraction of a chance he'd be here.

Harley…*the meddler.*

He pulls the string of revival cards over his head, and he nudges me as he moves to my side.

"I sat down and told you about the tour and shit. You could have at least mentioned all this," he says as he follows me to a table.

"It's hard to talk about things that need so much background explanation it detracts from the original point you were trying to reference," I tell him, absently, as people keep swinging their attention in our direction. "It's usually not worth the effort."

Harley warned me there'd be more attention on me once it went live. I thought I was ready for it.

My eyes move back to Base to find him so close our lips could touch. I pull back just barely, and his hand comes up to my waist, simply resting there.

Fortunately, Harley starts a toast, and the food starts being served directly after, interrupting the moment as the tables start filling up quickly.

This is a really big problem for me, because he's refusing to stay out of my sight.

Chapter 41

BRITT

Harley and I have been in various group discussions, and as the last person walks out of the circle, Harley collapses in her chair with theatrical, overt exhaustion.

"You're not good for my health, Britt. Go to your tent," she orders as Dale starts walking toward us, causing her smile to slowly grow.

"Was that literal?" I ask her.

"Yes. Both parts are literal in this moment." Just as I stand, she adds, "I didn't assign Base a tent. Care to handle that for me? He's probably tired too."

Dale glares in her direction. Her smile only grows as her eyes remain on me.

I just give one nod and walk away, feeling my pulse thump in every pulse point in my body as I go. Meddling. More meddling.

Inconceivable. How was I supposed to plan for her meddling when she hates meddling?

I spot him with a group, sitting on the ground with his laptop in his lap, as they all take turns coaching him.

"See? That fucking goblin thing comes up out of the ground no matter which direction I go, and it kills me every time," I hear him saying as my lips turn up in a small grin.

The girl with short, spiky hair starts to explain how to get around, when all gazes swing up to me. Base's grin slowly spreads as he closes the lid on his laptop.

"I'm supposed to assign you a tent," I tell him.

"It's fine if he stays in ours," the spiky haired girl says as she gestures to her and another girl.

My spine goes really stiff as I cast a panicked look between both pretty girls, and find myself decidedly not okay with that at all.

"Thanks for the offer, but I've got it sorted," Base tells her before he smirks at me.

He gives them all quick fist-bumps before standing, putting his stuff in one of his bags, and he picks up another to add to the load. He's in his regular clothes now, which is possibly one reason for my distraction.

I don't know what to do, so I just turn to start walking toward my tent, trying to ignore the sickly feeling in my stomach as I idly wonder what tent he's staying in and with whom.

His arm drops around my shoulders when he catches up, and I continue to walk as though this is a perfectly natural exchange.

"They've officially fucked with my head by praising you so much that I'm worried I'm in groupie territory now," he tells me like he's serious but joking.

That tone always confuses me because I don't know if he's serious, joking, or joking seriously.

"I miss you being my groupie," he goes on as my heart starts pounding.

He told me he loved me. He shouldn't have told me that. It's trying to mess with the logical plans my head had a lot harder now that I'm forced to see him so soon.

"Which tent are you staying in?" I ask him as the vast majority of people elect to stay up.

They're busy playing and not paying us much attention, absorbed by the demo of the new universe we'll be launching.

"I'm staying in your tent, of course," he answers casually, forcing me to keep walking when I try to stop, his trademark grin spreading when I stumble. "The excitement around here is contagious."

I'm too stuck on the first part of his comment to formulate a response to the second half. I certainly don't want him staying in anyone else's tent though…

He steers me through some more tents, and the closer we get to mine, the faster my heart starts to beat.

"I spent all that time telling you the ins and outs of my world, dragging you into it from the day I moved in and started invading your privacy, and you pretended to have no creative influence or aspirations," he says just as we reach my tent.

His arm falls away from me as he pulls back the entrance flap.

"I just had an idea. Harley turned it into a vision. Then together we made it happen," I quickly explain, most of my attention focused on the fact we're about to be all alone for the first time since he told me he loved me…and kissed me…and…left.

"Sounds like you're already stepping into your partner role earlier than projected," he says as he steps in behind me and puts his bags off to the side.

I shrug, not really sure why we're discussing business alone in the tent. It's like he's purposely not addressing the confusing situation.

I'm stalling while I think of any other solution, but I really don't feel comfortable with letting him out of my sight. Girls actually invited him to their tent right in front of me because I have no right to say otherwise.

"I think you keep a lot of things quiet, because you try to make people forget how smart you are," he goes on.

I have no idea what he's talking about right now. I feel stupid. Not smart. Not smart at all.

I have one large pillow mattress, but it's not really big enough for the two of us unless we're sleeping very close. That's a terrible idea.

"We should have separate sleeping areas," I tell him with a firm nod.

He just glances over at me, eyebrow arched as he keeps a

respectable amount of smile on his lips.

"Why's that?" he asks like he doesn't already know.

"For one, we've absolved our physical and romantic relationship, so it's not considered appropriate," I tell him as I stare at the pillow mattress, feeling warmer than I should as I step back. "And also, we're a primary example of the controversial phenomenon that can only be described as animal magnetism."

I look back over to see his smile growing as he tilts his head, eyes scanning me in that deliberate way of his that always does something inexplicable to me.

I take another step back, moving toward the tent's entrance.

"Are you saying you won't be able to keep your hands off me if we sleep in the same bed?" he asks with some amusement.

I nod again, because there's simply no avoiding this conversation. I've worked on preparing it on the nights when I couldn't sleep, because my mind wouldn't rest until I did.

"I know you could correct every tedious thing you perceive to be relevant on that relationship chart you were never meant to see," I tell him on a calm breath as I pinch the bridge of my nose, cringing at how horrible I currently feel for that. "You don't have to prove it. You're figuratively limitless."

When I look back at him, he's already staring at me like he's genuinely surprised.

"You keep acting like you've done something wrong. Everyone does. I don't know why, and the more I talk, the worse it just seems to get. Everyone is meddling, which makes the philosophy I've adopted to deal with this breakup a very taxing imposition, since you're suddenly everywhere."

"Are you asking me to leave you alone?" he asks as he slowly lowers himself to a chair, just staring at me a little blankly. "Do you really want to cut me out that bad, Britt?"

I start to open my mouth, but he keeps talking before I can speak.

"I was worked up, and yeah, it was stupid to throw an

ultimatum at you, especially since I was just taking it out on you. I get it. I'm sorry. I can't apologize enough," he goes on. "But I'm not going to walk away every time we argue, and you should know that. I thought I'd give you time to think, process, and hopefully prove I'm more patient than I seemed that night. I'm—"

"Can I please finish?" I ask on a shaky breath.

He clicks his tongue as he sits back and crosses his arms over his chest.

"See? You're still trying to make this about you. I never once said you did anything wrong. The relationship chart was unaddressed issues to make everyone stop asking why I was giving up so easily, because no one would listen to my practical answer."

He frowns as he just stares at me, his head tilting. "You're not ready for a relationship?" he asks like he's confused. "That was the practical, bullshit answer?"

"Conflict is just one of my many issues. I also panic when I get really scared," I tell him on another shaky exhale.

"Most people do, Britt. Don't patronize me by listing your imperfections with your 'it's not you, it's me' speech," he says on a groan as he scrubs his hand over his face. "It's fine. I get it."

I start feeling frustrated when I shake my head, tears starting to brim, but the panic stays down, because I've rehearsed multiple ways of explaining this correctly for once.

"No. You clearly don't get it. You did *nothing* wrong to me," I tell him as calmly as I can as I back up again, keeping more and more space between us so that I stay calm.

"You asked a reasonable question, and you deserved to have a prompt response to it," I tell him. "In hindsight, you were just making your new intentions clear, and I made it entirely too complicated at a really vulnerable moment in your life. You had every right to get angry when I didn't have the answer you deserved at the ready. I made that night about me, and it should have been about you."

His brow knits together again as he sits up, elbows moving to his knees.

"However, I'm incapable of making a decision that big on the spot. It's not as easy for me as it is for you to adapt, progress, and realize things so abruptly. Hindsight helps me with clarity and processing. I'm sorry for that," I tell him as honestly as I can.

He scrubs his face again with both hands and makes some sound, but I press on.

"It's me, Base. It's just me," I go on as he sits quietly. "I can't do what I can't do, and it's not that easy for me to take a leap of faith until I've thoroughly calculated the distance I'm leaping to the best of my ability."

I wipe away the one tear that falls, stepping back so far that I run out of room to move without leaving the tent.

"You have such extreme emotions. In one bad day where I simply piled onto your problems, you were ready to throw it all away. Honey Bee assured me you would have bounced back and been back on target within a few days. Now it's clear I made it worse by trying to fix it, because it's starting to feel like you think you owe me something."

He exhales heavily as he studies me.

"That's not at all why I'm here right now, Britt. And that's sure as hell not when I realized I loved you. I should have told you immediately instead of holding back, so that we could avoid this little misunderstanding."

I mentally flip to a new explanation, because I'm still apparently guiding this entire conversation wrong.

"You're intense with every single emotion," I go on, trying to ignore the growing pang in my own chest. "It's my favorite thing about you. You have this fascinatingly quick way of processing emotion, and it's so intense that you act on it in ways I never can. I weigh down your highs, and the first time you had a low, I just pushed you down harder because I *need* more time than most people to process emotions. This isn't about you being all wrong for me. This is about me being a very unhealthy life decision for you."

His brow starts to furrow again as he reaches back and randomly pulls out his wallet, opening it up.

"Here's what really happened. Please hear me out on this," I say when he starts to act distracted.

When I have most of his attention, I go on.

"Bo convinced Vince to mentor you and to start it in a way that kept your integrity intact. That way you wouldn't be able to turn it down. The only person you'd feel resentment toward would be me, and it would cause you to avoid me, and I could move on with the solace that I didn't completely mess it all up for you. You don't owe me anything, Base. After I calmed down that first night, I realized quickly that I was the one who owed you."

He blinks at me a couple of times before weirdly tossing a condom to the bedding. Is he cleaning out his wallet right now? Really?

"That's almost diabolical," he finally says as his face stays expressionless.

I don't know how to respond to that.

He slowly stands, wallet still open as he just stares at me.

"It's very messy. All of it. Things just keep escalating beyond my control, leaving me no choice but to explain it so thoroughly that you're left with no choice but to understand. Especially since Harley is unrepentantly meddling," I tell him. "I feel the urge to apologize for that."

"Yeah. Sure," he states like he's not really listening, nodding absently.

"There's no need in rectifying the relationship chart issues. I'm sorry you ever saw that. *You've done nothing wrong.* We just simply reached an impasse because I can't do what I can't do, even when you deserve it. Do you finally understand, or have I just made it worse?" I ask him, trying to find his eyes, but he just stares at the floor for a second.

His wallet claps the ground and startles me, and I struggle for the next words when he tugs his shirt over his head.

I try really hard to focus on my words instead of his body. He's always doing things at odd times, so it's not all that surprising that he's apparently decided to change for bed now.

"I've been so relieved that the tour went good for you. I'm glad you're happy. Maybe one day—"

"So when you said you're not ready for a relationship, you actually meant you're not able to meet *my* expectations," he states very calmly as he starts undoing his jeans.

"That wording and tone makes it sound like you're still the one who thinks he's in the wrong. Don't do that," I tell him with a frown. "Do I need to start all over?"

He drops his jeans and steps out of them, eyes seeming to stare at nothing in particular as he runs his hand over his jaw. It's the look he gets when he's lost in thought.

"No. I think I finally get what you're saying," he states in as an indecipherable look crosses his features and he seems to roll his eyes at himself, the way Dane does when he forgets his phone, keys, or wallet.

Does he know his wallet is on the ground?

I try not to look at his body. It's *very* distracting in this moment. I should have sent an email with all the listed arguments and counterpoints to his arguments and counterpoints.

I only have so much fortitude left in me.

"But, to sum it all up, despite the fancy phrasing, all of this is because you think *you* are not good enough for *me,*" he goes on, still seeming distant and slightly confused.

I don't know why he has to insist on that particular phrasing.

"Like you said…it shouldn't be so hard to do something as simple as start a relationship. I overcomplicate things because I need more time to process, and I'm still *too much* work," I add. "I have to let people hear what they want to hear because I can't engage in the conflict necessary to make myself heard unless I have *a lot* of preparation."

I can't help but wonder if he intentionally decided on his underwear choice because he wanted me to see he's wearing the boxer-briefs I bought him.

He puts his hands on his hips, his head falling back as his eyes flutter shut.

"People never react the way I prepare for them to act, and I'm not stopping until you understand me. I have several different arguments prepared. Do you understand that you don't owe me anything, or do you still think this is your fault?" I ask, hoping the end of this conversation prompts him to finish changing his clothes.

His head comes down, brow wrinkling again in what appears to be confusion, before he once again scrubs a hand over his mouth.

His eyes rake over me as he takes one step closer.

Then another.

And another.

"I need space for this conversation. It'll feel too much like—"

I'm not even really sure what else I planned to say. The second his hand suddenly moves, cupping the back of my head, and his lips come down on mine, I stupidly kiss him back.

I really thought he was finally understanding me.

There's such a weak realization when you feel your strength evaporate so easily because of the inexplicable power one person holds over you.

My hands slide up the back of his neck, kissing him harder, when I'm supposed to be keeping space. His other hand slides down my back, as he starts walking me somewhere. My eyes are shut, so I don't know. I'm pausing my brain on purpose.

It's not until he starts lowering me to the mattress that I summon the strength to break the kiss.

His head drops, and he groans into my neck, as I pant for air, becoming very aware of the fact he's settled between my legs.

"I think I need to start over, because I've miscommunicated crucial information somehow," I decide aloud as he starts kissing his way down my neck.

I press into him, mostly because I've really missed him and he's making this conversation very hard to have. I never knew I could be emotionally starved for someone's touch after having it in such abundance…until this moment.

Just kissing him, feeling him hold me like he used to, is such a very unexpected reckoning to face. The weight tries to lift off my chest at the hope of reconciliation.

This is the real why people never make the logical decisions they look back and see so clearly.

They're powerless.

His hand slides up my bare leg as I become twice as aware of how indecent this dress can be when lying down.

"I heard you perfectly well, Britt. But we think very differently, and I *strongly* disagree with most everything you just said. I guess we'll just have to agree to disagree," he says before his lips lazily brush back up my neck and he starts dragging my underwear down very slowly.

"I'll do better at listening in the future so we can avoid these *miscommunications*," he says, once again making this his fault, even as his lips curve in a wry grin.

My underwear stops at my knees, because he stops pulling them off when I put my hands on either side of his face and force him to look at me.

"Britt, I don't want you to be fucking perfect," he says before I can try to start over, his lips curving like he's amused by this.

"You're oversimplifying," I say very seriously.

He pulls my underwear down my legs the rest of the way, his eyes never leaving mine as he lifts enough to get them off one foot. Then the other.

My eyes stay locked on his as his gaze grows more intense. He settles himself between my legs again so subtly that I don't even try to stop him.

"I shouldn't have ever made you think you had to try so hard with me, Britt. You're practical and honest. You should have just been able to say what you needed to say, and I should have heard it. We would have gotten here a lot sooner. *You're* overcomplicating it," he volleys.

I've drastically overestimated my ability to reason with him.

"Let's say we meet in the middle and call these last three months a chance to focus on ourselves and our careers while you processed your emotions. Now we can move on to the next phase," he says, now just being absurd with his oversimplification.

"What next phase?" I ask, because I need some direction on where he's misunderstanding me.

"Now it's time to do this for real," he adds, leaning down to brush his lips over mine again.

I can't tell if he's stubborn, determined, or obtuse right now.

"Do you need to go ask a Sterling if they think you're good enough for me? Because I'll wait right here while you do that, if that's what you need right now," he goes on with a straight face.

"Anything said out of context sounds silly when used in that tone. You're not taking me seriously."

He reaches up, pulling one of my hands off his cheek, and kisses the palm of it.

"I already told you I love you, Britt. Who's not taking whom seriously?" He darts a look at me. "Did I use *whom* right in a sentence?"

When he grins, I sink down on the mattress, letting my head fall back as he resumes kissing the side of my hand.

"You admitted to stalking my social media these past three months, want nothing but good fucking things for me, and became a dark queen while coping." I feel his smile growing against my hand, and I open my eyes as he meets my gaze and adds, "I'm gonna say it's safe to guess you love me too, and for the record, I've come to a great number of epiphanies these last three months."

I feel a tear escape the far corner of my eye and roll down the side of my face.

"Statistically, the odds of this getting better instead of worse are highly discouraging, and you should look at the compilation of information I've gathered on the subject," I tell him as a last ditch effort, my will not as stubborn or determined as his.

I miss him too much.

"You know you can't put people in the smallest boxes designed for them, Britt," he says as he smirks down at me. "The human element fucks with the plans in your head all the time. *Do you love me?"*

I know he doesn't suffer from the disillusion that love truly does conquer all, so I have no idea why he's pressing this.

"I cry when I try to throw your toothbrush away. The thought of experiencing intimacy with anyone else still nauseates me. Obviously, that's a forgone conclusion by this—"

He kisses me again, his body coming down on top of mine as my fingers slide up his bare back and my legs wind around his waist.

"I'm trying to be mature and practical about this," I say against his lips, even as my nails press against his skin on reflex.

"Stop trying to save me, Britt," he says between kissing me and pulling my legs wider. "I don't need to be saved."

I pause, idly wondering if I should have factored in a hero complex on my side of the statistical disadvantages in our relationship. It'll have to wait, though, because he kisses me to distraction once again.

I give up the fight, because the last resistance in me is gone, all the aching fading more and more the longer he kisses me.

His hand moves away from us, and I hear the crinkling of what can only be the condom wrapper that he threw on the bed...

I break the kiss and pull back as he rips open the package with his teeth.

"You made up your mind twenty-three minutes ago and I shared more of my rehearsed arguments during that time for no reason," I say as my mind finally pieces together the real reason he started undressing.

Pushing up to his knees, his lips tilt in a wicked little grin as he stares down at me and starts rolling the condom on, no shame or modesty. Another one of my favorite things about him.

He doesn't answer as he leans back down, his lips teasing mine as he shoves my dress up.

"My newest realized fantasy is fucking a dark queen with pointy ears and gothic eye makeup. I'm seriously turned on by this dark, evil-genius sort of angle you take when you're missing me," he adds, still oversimplifying.

"Never knew I was into that sort of thing until you stepped out of this tent earlier," he adds before his lips find mine again.

It's completely inappropriate for me to smile against his lips, but I simply can't stop it from happening.

"The dress and ears stay on," he adds as I feel him lift me just before he rolls us without warning.

I end up sitting astride him as I adjust in his lap, and he keeps kissing me as I feel the teasing glide of skin and latex against my bare skin under my dress.

He starts guiding himself inside me, and I really don't know how I made it three months without sex when he does. It's almost like setting all my nerves on fire at once, and I sit up more, using his shoulders to steady myself, lowering my body inch by inch as my eyes flutter shut.

Sweet agony—an oxymoron that now makes perfect sense.

"Where's your head at right now, Britt?" he asks as he sits up abruptly, his front pressing to mine.

His hands go to my hips, dragging me down the last centimeter or so as he ghosts his lips over mine.

"A poor oxymoron pun about an oxymoron," I absently tell him as he grins against my neck.

He shifts his hips under me as he grips my sides harder, holding me to him.

His breath hitches when I roll my hips, and I'm positive an

involuntary sound escapes me to vocalize how embarrassingly much I've missed this particular part about *us.*

He starts moving me, and my eyes flutter open to find his already concentrated on my face, lids half shut as he just rakes his gaze over me.

The intensity in his eyes is simply too much right now, which shouldn't be a possible thing.

"Where's your head at now?" he asks as he leans forward, moving my body with his in a way that feels too natural…and all I want to do is get even closer.

Our skin glides together, and I kiss him because I need him to stop talking right now. It's as if it sets off his own sense of urgency, and he deepens the kiss as he groans into my mouth. I idly notice he's missing his piercings, not that it detracts from how good he is at this.

I stop thinking altogether when he starts building the perfect rhythm, somehow controlling all of this from the bottom. I'm forced to break the kiss, because I can't focus enough to feel all the sensations and kiss him at the same time.

He rips the top of my dress down, introducing more skin-on-skin contact that pushes me over the edge.

My nails dig into his skin, and my body tenses as a shockwave of pleasure rockets through me.

A series of random sounds escape me with *too much* abandon, as my head falls to his shoulder, forgetting that he's still chasing his. I'm too busy basking in my own this time.

He shoves his face against my throat as he makes a muffled sound, his body stilling against mine as his arms close around my waist.

It's just our breaths in the otherwise silent tent for a second, our bodies still somewhat sticking together.

Still breathing heavily, I ask, "Did you bring more than one condom?"

I feel his grin spreading a few seconds before I realize we're not the only ones submitting to carnal acts in a semi-public area with minimal privacy.

He pulls his head up, smirking at me, as the sounds outside our tent get louder and louder, as well as more telling.

"I only brought one, but I'm guessing it won't be hard to find a few more," he says as he starts kissing his way down my neck again. "And people think musicians are the ravenous ones," he adds on a more mocking note.

Someone makes a very loud cry that I think also represents *sweet agony*.

My arms stay around his neck, as he continues to kiss along the side of my neck, moving up again.

"If you're this determined to disregard logic, will you be my date to Raya and Kade's wedding?" I ask him.

"Sure, if you'll go with me to New York to a thing I have to play the weekend before," he says before playfully nipping at my ear.

We should separate, and we should definitely sleep. But I want to do this too much to take a step back.

"You'll be backstage, because I have no fucking idea what sort of crowd control the scene has, but there's a badass backstage area guaranteed to make that an irrelevant issue where you're concerned."

I don't even get to respond, because he starts kissing me again, leisurely now, the way he kisses me when all he wants to do is kiss me.

"Britt, I'm coming in," Harley's voice says very abruptly.

I hear the rustling of my tent just before Base jerks me against his chest, and I dart a look over my shoulder as Harley walks in.

"I brought some more clothes for—"

Her eyes go wide, just as Dale trips in. His eyes come up, widen to a dangerous point, and he curses before turning and stumbling back out in one big rush.

"Damn it, Harley. My eyes!" he snaps.

My mouth opens and closes a few times as my brain stalls long enough for me to consider the awkwardness of the entire situation. My chest stays pressed against Base's, and my dress hangs at my waist, covering most of the essentials.

"I-I-I…my bad," she stutters before choking back a laugh and also running out.

Base drops back, laughing as I come down with him.

He brushes my hair out of my face before asking, "Where's your head at now?"

My eyes fasten onto his. "I think we should find more condoms."

Epilogue

BASE

A shudder spreads up my spine as I partially collapse to Britt's back, eyes on her in the mirror as she pants for breath, hands still clutching the edge of the bathroom sink.

I grin against her shoulder, kissing it as I pull the strap of her dress back into place and start fixing myself as she does the same, a smile on her face the entire time.

"You're adding this to the mental tally of public places right now, aren't you?" I ask as I strategically hide the condom.

She just continues to smile, not answering, before she turns and gives me a quick kiss.

"They're going to wonder why I've been gone for so long," she says as she hurries out the door.

After washing my hands, I pick up the bouquet, and I hold it out just before the door bursts open again.

"Thanks," she says as she snatches it and starts to turn again, but I grab her wrist and haul her to me.

She comes willingly, kissing me as I walk her out of the bathroom.

"I really do have to go," she murmurs against my lips, a slight groan barely escaping her throat.

I finally let her go, and she hurries down the hall as quickly as she can in her heels.

It's not until she disappears into the room that I realize I'm once again holding the damn bouquet. Stifling a laugh, I knock on the door, expecting Britt to answer immediately.

It's not her.

Bo answers the door, and her eyes immediately drop to the bouquet.

"Britt, it's impossible for you to actually forget something. What really happened to my bouquet?" I hear Raya asking in a slight panic. "Did it get ruined?"

"Found it. And it's in pristine condition," Bo says with a smirk as she opens the door wider.

Raya, standing there in one really extravagant wedding gown, takes one look at me and then darts an unimpressed look at Britt, who is smoothing her hair down in the mirror, playing it cool.

Britt's eyes meet mine in the reflection briefly, and the barest of smiles flirts with her lips.

"Be glad I still appreciate the disgustingly sweet phase," Raya says on a grumble as she turns around, her dress zipped only partially—but it doesn't look like it's going to zip anymore.

"How does Paul Colton himself mess up measurements this badly? Why am I trying to fix it instead of him?" Bo asks, somehow managing to make it across the room without me noticing.

I glance back over at Britt as she makes her way toward me.

The room is full of girls, material, fancy bridesmaid shit, and various other really pink and purple things.

They all fuss over something that Raya is freaking out about, trying to calm her down. I don't really pay it much attention because Britt is pulling me down by my tie.

"Britt, can you go get the other fabric from my office to see if it'll match up since Raya doesn't want to tell her future father-in-law he messed up?"

Britt starts to leave, but Rain squeezes by me. "I'll go get it. Britt will make too many detours," she quips as she hurries toward the back doors.

"Did you not do a final fitting or even try it on?" Bo is asking incredulously, as Raya huffs out an annoyed breath. "Are you that tired of this wedding before you even have it?"

I tune out the intense backstage drama that will be eclipsed with a show and bright, shiny photographs that will probably make it feel like this never happened.

"So you're going to Houston next?" Harley asks us. "After the reception?"

"We'll be riding in the back of Taylor's van instead of flying private," I tell her, knowing what she's about to offer. "He just had it refurbished, so it's not *as* terrible as it sounds," I add.

"Enjoy it. Before spoiled grandparents that keep delaying your wedding. Don't forget there are also the prenuptials, a stupid perfect wedding dress, extravagant venues, conmen and wealthy moguls all on the same monstrous guest list…"

Raya stops her rant, and exhales again as tears start springing to her eyes.

I just nod like all that makes perfect sense.

"I'll save you a piece of chocolate cake at the reception," I tell Britt as I back away.

She grins as she slowly shuts the door, and I turn, twirling the bouquet—

"Fuck's sake," I groan as I turn back around.

Britt opens the door before I can knock, rips the bouquet out of my hand, and shuts the door again.

Laughing under my breath, I swing by the bar, grab a bottle of whiskey, and head back to the room where the guys are.

Everyone's eyes swing to mine. It's never fun walking into a room full of Sterlings.

"How long does it take to get whiskey?" Kode asks me as he takes the bottle from my hand.

I drop to a seat near the door and shrug as he goes to start pouring shots. Kade adjusts his tie in the mirror, not looking half as stressed as poor Raya.

"You wouldn't believe the line I suffered through for that whiskey," I say with a straight face. "You're welcome."

"Proposed to Tria yet?" Kade asks Kode in deflection when Kode just stares at me like he's trying to figure out why my tie is crooked.

"No. And I don't plan to until your shit-tastic wedding monstrosity is finally over so that she can remember that not all weddings have to be this hard," Kode answers dryly.

Dane points his shot glass at me. "You propose to Britt this young, and I'll finally have a reason to hit you," he tells me seriously.

"I'm not an idiot. I know she's not there yet," I say as I take my own shot glass that Jax—Bo's dude—hands me.

"Here's to the groom who has waited for-fucking-ever to finally be married to the girl whose heart he stole…after he destroyed her house," Maverick says, lifting his shot glass.

"I didn't destroy her house; I was her knight in shiny fucking armor," Kade is quick to correct.

We all throw our shots back, just as the door cracks open and Tria pokes her head inside, a very not-good look on her face.

She pinches her fingers together. "Little problem. I could use some help."

I stand immediately, looking for any excuse to get out of this room and back to Britt.

"Everything okay with Raya?" Kade asks as he moves closer.

"Of course," Tria says as she bats her hand in a dismissive way.

I walk out with Kode and Dale, and she shuts the door like three is enough. We follow her as she walks down the hall a little ways before turning to face us very abruptly. The fact she's wringing her hands is not a good sign.

"Call every discreet person you know, who may know where Raya is."

"What are you talking about? She was just in the room with all of you," I remind her.

"What the hell were you doing in the room with the girls?" Kode asks like that's the pressing issue right now.

"She went out the bathroom window, and now we can't find her," Tria goes on as she holds up a piece of shredded fabric of some sort.

"What?" Kode and Dale hiss at the same time.

"I know. I know. She was panicking about the dress, because there are only so many ways you can make a dress bigger before it's noticeable that it's the wrong size. The next thing I know, she was in the bathroom for ten minutes, the window was up, and this was left torn at the edge," she goes on, her words coming out so fast that they almost slur together.

"Ah, shit," is the first reflexive thing that comes out of my mouth.

Tria runs off in the opposite direction, as I run a hand through my hair.

"She's never going to fucking marry me after this," Kode groans as he chases after her, pulling his phone out as he goes.

Dale claps my shoulder. "Welcome to the fucking family. Do something useful."

I hurry into the room where the girls are in a frenzy, but among the chaos, Britt is sitting calmly, one ear in her finger as she speaks to someone on the phone.

I watch as she hangs up and calls someone else, and I go to take a seat beside her as she thanks whoever it is.

I hand her my phone, and she dials a number on it, handing it back to me, and I put it to my ear just as a man answers.

"I don't suppose you've seen Raya Capperton anywhere, have you?" I ask him as Britt asks someone else a similar question.

We do this for thirty minutes…until we run out of 'discreet' numbers to call.

"Everyone else is part of the wedding, and we risk exposing a missing bride, which is what you informed me not to do," Britt tells Harley.

Harley nods absently, looking over a chart of some sort.

"So we see who doesn't show up as early as they should and hope they have a hidden bride stashed somewhere. We'll just stall the ceremony until we find her."

"We can start with Brin. She's still not here," Britt notes. "And she's not answering her phone."

"Neither is Rye," Ash says from the corner.

"In case she's not with them, I'll draw up a quick chart of her friends and family, ranking them in the columns of importance and familiarity with Raya," Britt offers as she stands and walks out without giving me any sort of direction.

I awkwardly sit for a second. No one glances at me, so I stand and chase Britt out the door.

"Tell me how to be your MVP," I say to her.

"I have no idea what we're doing, so I'm just escaping the tumultuous tension inside that room. I didn't even know why I felt the need to panic," she says as she exhales heavily just once, and turns into a private, *quiet* room.

"Why do you think she ran?" I ask as I drop to a chair.

"She and Kade have been more withdrawn from the group this past year. But she doesn't ever look at him differently. Someone should have gotten him to calm her down before it escalated. That was my repeated suggestion when she broke out into hives," she says as she sits down and starts scribbling down a chart on a piece of paper.

"It's bad luck for the groom to see the bride before the wedding," I remind her.

"Worse luck than the bride disappearing out a window?" she asks as she continues jotting down names in various columns.

I pause. "Touché."

I slide my chair up so that I can see what she's writing as I put my arm around her chair.

"The best outcome is that the wedding will be delayed. The worst is that there will be a lot to do if the wedding gets called off. Regardless, you should prepare to leave without me. I'll fly out tomorrow morning and meet you," she says distractedly.

I pull out my phone, and she flicks her gaze to me as I fire off a quick text to Randy.

"What are you doing?"

"Getting two flights to Houston for tomorrow morning. I owe them one, so I informed Randy that he gets to take his dog, since I won't be in the van with them. Taylor won't be laughing so hysterically when that damn dog tears his van up, and Sticks won't be amused when his drumsticks turn into chew toys."

I glance over to see her brow furrowed.

"I don't understand what some of that means," she says very seriously, shaking her head as she resumes her task.

"Not important," I tell her as I finish up with the tickets and shoot Taylor a text.

Putting my phone aside, I look over at the paper that is mostly full now.

"What can I do to help?" I ask, noticing Kade pulling up just outside the window.

Why is he in Dane's car?

He looks like he knows, because he runs his hands through his hair over and over before he kicks the air and starts walking.

I hope that doesn't mean she's not coming back.

Britt remains oblivious as Kade walks on.

"Just help me identify these people who are already here," she says as she hands me the paper.

"Let's go see if we can find a runaway bride," I tell her as I try to figure out how the hell I'm supposed to help her find all these people. "No one will ever say we lead boring lives," I add.

She turns just as I stand, and she pulls me down by the back of the neck. My lips bump hers, and I kiss her as I wind my arm around her waist and step into her.

"I love you," she murmurs like it's difficult and she's in a hurry to say it as casually as she can. I chase her lips as she pulls back. "Thank you."

"Don't thank me yet. We won't be flying anything close to private," I dutifully point out. "It'll still be better than the back of Taylor's van, though."

A small smile curves her lips, and considering the circumstances, I call it a win.

"I love you, too, by the way," I add as I twirl a piece of her hair around my finger. "Now let's go find the missing bride."

As I start guiding her out, I smirk.

"I'll add that to the list of things I never thought I'd say," I tell her as we head down the hall.

"Oh! After the wedding is over, can we compare lists? I think that could be fun," she says with genuine excitement. "I also have a list of places I don't want to have sex. Do you have a list like that too?"

My lips tug in a lopsided grin as I snake my arm around her shoulders and kiss the top of her head. "I love it when you talk nerdy to me, Britt."

About the Author

C.M. Owens is a *USA Today* Bestselling author of over 30 novels. She always loves a good laugh, and lives and breathes the emotions of the characters she becomes attached to. Though she came from a family of musicians, she has zero abilities with instruments, sounds like a strangled cat when she sings, and her dancing is downright embarrassing. Just ask anyone who knows her. Her creativity rests solely in the written word. Her family is grateful that she gave up her quest to become a famous singer.

You can find her on Facebook, Twitter, and Instagram.

Instagram: @cmowensauthor

Twitter: @cmowensauthor

Facebook: @CMOwensAuthor

There are two Facebook groups, the teaser group, and the book club where you can always find her hanging out with her fans and readers.

www.cmowensbooks.com

Sign up for her newsletter and get no more than one email a month with new release information and/or a list of her fave books from other authors and deals. (No spamming from her and no one else will get your email address from C.M.)

Printed in Poland
by Amazon Fulfillment
Poland Sp. z o.o., Wrocław